THE BELLE AND THE BEARD

KATE CANTERBARY

VESPER PRESS

Editing provided by Julia Ganis of Julia Edits and Erica Russikoff of Erica Edits.

Proofreading provided by Jodi Duggan.

Ebook Cover design provided by Sarah Hansen of Okay Creations.
Ebook Cover photography provided by CJC Photography.
Ebook Cover modeling provided by Jake McManus.
Paperback art and design by Qamber Designs.

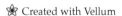 Created with Vellum

ABOUT THE BELLE AND THE BEARD

Jasper-Anne Cleary's guide to salvaging your life when you find yourself publicly humiliated, out of work, and unemployable at 35—not to mention newly single:

1. Run away. Seriously, there's no shame in disappearing. Go to that rustic old cottage your aunt left you. Look out for the colony of bats and the leaky roof. Oh, and the barrel-chested neighbor with shoulders like the broad side of a barn. Definitely look out for him.
2. Stop wallowing and stay busy. It doesn't matter whether you know how to bake or fix things around the house. Do it anyway. Dust off your southern hospitality and feed that burly, bearded neighbor some pecan pie.
3. Meet new people. Chat up the grumpy man-bear, pretend to be his girlfriend when his mother puts you two on the spot, agree to go as his date to a

big family party. Don't worry—it's only temporary.

4. Cry it out. Screwing up your life entitles you to wine, broody-moody music, and uninterrupted sobbing.

5. Get over it all by getting under someone. Count on your fake boyfriend to deliver some very real action between the sheets.

6. Move on. The disappearing act, the cottage, the faux beau—none of it can last forever.

Linden Santillan's guide to surviving the invasion when a hell in heels campaign strategist moves in next door:

1. Do not engage. There is no good reason you should chop her wood, haul her boxes, or pick her apples.

2. Do not accept gifts, especially not the homemade ones. Disconnect the doorbell, toss your phone over a bridge, hide in the basement if you must, but do not eat her pie.

3. Do not introduce her to your friends and family. They'll favor her over you and never let you forget it.

4. Do not intervene when she's crying on the back porch. Ignore every desire to fix the entire world for her. By no means should you take her into your arms and memorize her peach-sweet curves.

5. Do not take her to bed, even if it's just to get her out of your system.

6. Do not, under any circumstances, fall in love with her.

Warning: *This hot, modern take on* Beauty and the Beast *includes a meet-burglary, an immortal cat, a biohazard of a banana bread, a meddling mother, fancy toast, and a temporary fling that starts feeling a little too permanent.*

PREFACE

Into the forest I go, to lose my mind and find my soul.

~ John Muir

ONE
LINDEN

To be clear, I never *truly* believed she was breaking into the house.

Anyone would have questions if they saw a strange woman walking up to a vacant house with a crowbar and power drill in hand. I was reasonably curious about the situation.

But I didn't assume she was a burglar. I didn't assume a damn thing. I just wanted to know what was going on over there.

If there was anyone guilty of assumptions, it was my brother. Ash reveled in figuring everything out before anyone else. Big on having the right answer, he was.

"There's a person breaking into the house next door," he called from the front door in lieu of any proper greeting. "Were you aware of that?"

I didn't look up from the newspaper. It didn't hold much of my interest but the meeting I was about to have with my brother promised to hold even less. "Was I aware of an in-progress felony? No."

Ash set his laptop bag on the chair across from me at the kitchen table and gave me a slow-blinking stare that explained he didn't appreciate my response. Even if I hadn't known him for the past thirty-six years, I would've known that. My older (by twenty-nine minutes) brother was an easy read.

"I don't appreciate that response." He glared at me as he rounded the table and selected a glass from the cabinet. "Anyway, don't you think we should check it out?"

"And skip our monthly discussion of my business accounts?" I closed the newspaper, folded it in half. There was nothing going on next door. Nothing ever went on over there, not anymore. "I didn't realize your brain knew how to generate that as an option."

He elbowed the refrigerator shut as he shook a bottle of cold brew coffee. "We'd check out the crime in progress first, review your statements after. Obviously."

"Obviously." I pushed away from the table, strolled to the front window to get a better look at the alleged burglar.

The bungalow next door, the only other house at the bottom of this dead-end street tucked into a shady edge of Wompatuck State Park, looked as forgotten as it'd been for a couple of years, since Maureen "Midge" Misselbush passed away. The paint was peeling and the wood trim was surrendering to woodpeckers and rot. On the opposite side, the back door had been boarded up since a tropical storm that blew through last year left the glass shattered. The curtains were drawn and the windows gave off the dim, milky haze of abandonment. Save for the diehard hydrangea bushes and several trees now sliding into the gilt of autumn, the place was a ghost town.

Midge would've hated that. She would've been out there

on her rickety, rusty ladder, scraping away the paint and then sampling ten or twelve new colors before banging on my door to announce she was sticking with the same "good old-fashioned gray" she'd always used.

I didn't see anyone though I couldn't get a good look at the front door from this angle. The car parked half in the driveway, half in the street, coupled with the broad daylight, suggested this burglar wasn't aiming for stealth. More than likely it wasn't a burglar at all. Probably a salesperson or someone following bad directions. Maybe a mixed-up address issue. No one veered down the dogleg bend of this street otherwise.

See? No assumptions. Never did I assume.

"Since when does anyone use an old-as-stones Volvo station wagon as a getaway car?" I asked.

Ash came up beside me, iced coffee in hand. "Valid point." He jerked a shoulder up. "Still strange. Definitely looked like that person was trying to get the door open."

We stood together, staring at an empty house and a parked car, and said nothing for a minute or two.

"How long has it been? That it's been vacant?" he asked.

"About two years."

"Long time."

I nodded. Midge didn't have much family and they didn't live here in New England but it annoyed the shit out of me they hadn't bothered to visit since her death. Hell, I'd been the one to board up that back door after the storm.

"I wonder who is paying the property taxes." Ash would wonder this. That sort of thing dawned on him. It did not dawn on me. "Probably the estate. Do you know who the executor is?"

I shook my head. "Nope."

"Nothing's happening here. No breaking and entering, no robbery. I don't have time to watch the grass grow. Let's deal with your finances."

Staring out the window while waiting for nothing to happen was far preferable to any discussion of finances, ever. Even with my brother, the accountant. I knew it was a privilege to say I didn't care about money and I was fortunate the demand for arborists was reaching all-time highs but having a booming business didn't mean I wanted to talk about business. "Can you give me the quick rundown and call it a day?"

"I mean, yes, of course, I *can*. As always, I'd rather you know something about your most recent profit and loss—"

"Because you think I'll do something with that information?"

Ash ran a hand down his face. I smothered a laugh. I hated talking business but I loved the opportunity to bust my brother's balls. As the youngest of a set of triplets, it was one of the few privileges bestowed upon me. It was my birthright to rile up Ash and our sister Magnolia every chance I got, regardless of our age.

"Will you alter your day-to-day work as a result of last month's P&L? No. Your overhead is extremely low and your revenue streams are stable, which makes a fine case for keeping your focus on the tree doctoring rather than the accounting."

"I enjoy when you make my arguments for me," I said.

"Will you take last month's P&L as further evidence that you should consider Magnolia's partnership proposal which would open you up to greater—"

"Hold that thought."

My hands braced on the window frame, I leaned toward

the glass to watch a white woman walking toward the Volvo. But to say she was simply walking was a gross understatement. This was striding, each step purposeful and sharp, as if she wanted the earth to know she wasn't about to repeat herself. Energy radiated from her, far from warm but not exactly cold either, and it was clear she could stomp one of those pretty high-heeled shoes, crack open a chasm deep enough to fully digest those who got in her way, and be finished with them without getting so much as a smudge of dirt on her hands.

I couldn't tell you the color of her hair or eyes, or anything about her body, but I knew everything about her from the way she walked.

And that did something to me. Something I couldn't explain. I couldn't even begin to examine the rattling, rumbling hum it ignited inside me.

I gestured toward the woman. She wore a dress that looked like an artifact from the 1950s. "Is *that* your burglar?"

"I think so."

Jabbing a finger in her direction, I continued, "What kind of burglar is that?"

"I'll admit she appears to be an unorthodox burglar." He edged closer, his shoulder bumping mine as he shifted. "What is she carrying? Is that a tire iron?"

"No, that's a crowbar and—oh, for fuck's sake—a power drill." I took a step back, reached for the doorknob. "Let's go. Come on. Let's see what this is all about."

My brother fell in step with me as we reached the end of the driveway where a dense row of roses separated my property from Midge's. "What's the plan here?" he murmured, still clutching his iced coffee.

I cut him an impatient glance but there was no changing

my brother's hardwiring. He required a strategic plan to make a roast beef sandwich. Ignoring him, I called to the woman, "Good morning. Need some help?"

She pivoted from Midge's door, the drill in hand and the crowbar tucked under her arm. She didn't smile when she replied, "Hello there. Good morning. I'm all set, thank you."

In a silent dismissal, she turned back to the door.

Ash lifted his coffee, saying, "Should we call someone?"

"Unnecessary. We've got this." Leaving my brother behind, I stepped around the roses and crossed into Midge's yard, stopping a good distance from the door. Regardless of what was happening here, I wasn't going to be the guy who trapped a woman on a porch. Especially when that woman possessed several weapons and a thick cloud of fearlessness. "Excuse me. What are you doing?"

She shifted to face me again, her cocked hip the only visible reaction to my questioning. "I'm prying open the door as this lock is not interested in my key."

"So, you—you have a key."

She held up a chain, a single key dangling from the ring. A bedazzled charm in the shape of a peach winked from the other end of the chain. "I have a key."

There was honey in her voice, something warm and southern and completely at odds with the rest of her *unhinge the jaw, drag you into the ocean, and crush your bones and destroy you like a kraken* vibe.

"This is Midge's house," I replied. "And I'm sorry but I don't know who the hell you are so I'm gonna need some more information before I let you bust open her door."

"Before you *let* me. Mmhmm. That's fascinating."

I fisted my hands on my hips. "Is it?"

She blinked at me for a second before that expression of

authority shifted into something much more terrifying. Her eyes brightened and her lips pulled up at the sides in the faintest whisper of a smile, and the trap of her momentary amusement distracted me long enough to realize she was *gorgeous*. Hair like rich bourbon, dark eyes, full, luscious curves. She reminded me of summer—screen doors banging in the breeze, ripe strawberries, and the kind of oppressive heat that sent sweat rolling down your back.

This, too, did something to me. I couldn't explain any part of it but I knew I was bothered enough by my reaction to continue arguing with her.

"Your concern is appreciated though unnecessary. Midge is my aunt. Rather, *was* my aunt."

"Your aunt," I repeated. I didn't remember hearing anything about a niece and I'd heard a whole fucking lot of Midge's stories. "She was your *aunt*?"

"That's right. She left this house to me."

Because all I could do was repeat her words back to her, I said, "She left the…house. To you. *This* house."

"That's what I said."

"Then why didn't she talk about you? She talked about every other damn thing that came to mind," I said.

"As I'm sure you're realizing, I have no way of answering that." She shifted and my belly flipped at the way she moved. Rather than bending at the waist, she crouched down, dropping her backside in a manner that caused her dress to fall around her legs like the curtain at the end of a play. It was dignified in a modest, vintage sense that didn't align with busting a door open or haphazard parking jobs.

I didn't get it. I didn't get anything about this woman.

And all of this *really* bothered me.

"I was the one who mentioned Midge. How do I know

you're not breaking in and playing it off as being her long-lost niece?"

"Mmhmm. It seems we are well on our way to playing this little game." She set the drill and crowbar on the porch, sanded her palms together, and stood. "You mentioned Midge but you didn't mention she'd passed away. Yes, you could checkmate me there and suggest I was on the lookout for run-down homes and tried my luck with this one but then I'd have to ask you why I'd choose this polka dot of a house for my heist. It doesn't make good sense, not when there are multimillion dollar homes sitting empty down on Cape Cod and gullible doormen at every high-rise in Boston. The truth is, as it usually is, far less exciting than a whipped-up story of me as a mastermind burglar. Maureen Missel-bush left me this place though I was unaware she'd left you in charge of enforcing the perimeter. That note wasn't in her will." Holding out her hand as she descended the steps, she said, "I'm Jasper-Anne Cleary. How do you do?"

TWO
JASPER

"I'M JASPER-ANNE CLEARY. HOW DO YOU DO?"

I marched down the porch steps, eyeing this great bear of a man intent on *helping*. The last thing—I mean, the very *last* thing—I could handle today was another person complicating my plans, let alone a brute who felt welcome to tromp all over my front yard and tell me where I belonged.

All I wanted to do was get inside, plug in my toaster oven, and sleep for twenty to thirty hours. Forty if my need for sustenance didn't win out in the middle. That was it—toast, sleep, and solitude, and not a single reminder that I'd ignored this cottage since Midge died two years ago.

I stopped on the second step from the bottom because if this guy planned on arguing with me over my rightful claim to the cottage, he'd need to haul himself on over here and give my hand a proper shake first. I wasn't about to close the distance for him.

He glanced at my hand from his position on the lawn, muttered something to himself, and charged forward like he and his beard had some serious doubts as to whether women were allowed to own property.

It was a damn good thing I'd stayed on the steps. He would've towered over me otherwise and we simply could not have that when it came to holy wars between homeowners.

He gave my hand an irritable glance before swallowing it up inside his for a quick shake that was substantially less aggressive than I'd expected from him. "Linden Santillian. That's my place." Dropping my hand, he pointed to the twin cottage next door. "Like I said, I didn't know Midge had a niece."

I offered Linden the most practiced smile in my arsenal. This smile never failed me. It'd charmed crusty old politicians and bulldog-belligerent donors. It'd greased the wheels with incessant reporters, errant mistresses, and more than a few strict security details. It was going to work on this guy too. It always did. "I didn't know she had a guard dog for a neighbor."

"Excuse me but it looked like you were breaking and entering."

"It's not breaking and entering when it's your house. It's just opening a stuck door with the help of some tools."

His only response was a hard stare which I would've interpreted a million different ways if I had the energy. I really didn't.

I hit him with the smile again. It had to work this time. It was all I had left. "Thanks for checking in. It was real nice visiting with you."

I scooted back up the steps to the front door. The blasted thing stood as one last mile in the most unpleasant marathon of a week in my whole life, and much like me, it was both falling apart and standing stubbornly firm.

As I collected the crowbar from the porch floor, I heard, "Wait just one second."

"Sorry. Can't. Won't." I attacked the door again, going for the splintered wood between the lock and the jamb where there seemed to be a bit of wiggle. Just as I started to feel some give, the bar flew out of my hands. I whirled around to find Linden glowering at me. "May I ask what you think you're doing?"

"That's not the right way to do it," he said.

"Certainly not," I replied. "Not when there's an excessively helpful neighbor man here to do it for me." He gestured for me to step aside. I didn't. "You've mistaken me for someone who requires assistance. You've also mistaken me for someone who can put up with even a minute of nonsense after the week I've had. Here's what you need to understand. I don't care whether I do this wrong so long as I do it."

"The side door is boarded up."

That easy, jocular tone cut through the last of my patience. Maybe it wasn't patience or people skills or any of the other things that usually held me together like a corset of strings. Maybe it was the recognition that I couldn't get where I needed to go by mowing this man down and I'd have to go around him instead.

"I noticed that." Since I wasn't about to beg him to return my crowbar, I tried the key again. It slid into the lock easily enough and turned without too much trouble but the deadbolt caught and the door wouldn't budge. "Let's save that issue for another day, shall we? As I'm sure you would agree, we've covered a good deal of ground today."

He bobbed his head while he turned the bar over in his hands. I didn't want to care about his hands but I couldn't help but notice they were huge. With paws like that, he could rip my door clear off its hinges.

Honestly, I could live with that approach. I needed to be alone with my toast, and I didn't care how I got there at this point.

"I mention the side door because it needs to be replaced before it's operational. If you continue with this"—he tossed the bar up in the air, catching it as it flipped end over end —"you'll bust the lock and damage the frame. That will leave you with two doors you can't use and several thousand dollars in repairs." He tossed the bar again, catching it by the opposite end this time. "But you don't care if you do it the wrong way, right?"

On any other day, I would've dismantled that little analysis of his. I would've countered a circle around him and done it with so much southern-girl sweetness, he wouldn't realize he'd been bested until long after he'd left me blissfully alone. *Any other day.* I was all out of sweet and fight, and the only card up my sleeve was the belief that I had this under control. I always had it under control. Even in chaos and calamity, I always knew what I was doing. I couldn't lose that right now and I could not fall apart in front of this guy.

I'd shed enough tears over men who didn't deserve them from me.

"Old doors stick when it's muggy like this." He waved like he could gather up the late summer humidity and hand it to me. "I have the same problem. Sometimes it just needs one helluva shove."

"Mmhmm. Yes." I tapped my finger against my chin.

"Pushing did come to mind. I tried that before you rushed over here with your alarm for women using tools."

"I have no problem with women using tools. I do have a problem with anyone using them incorrectly, Jasper-Anne."

"Jasper will do, thank you," I replied. "And it is possible your definition of correct is too limited in its scope."

"That might be, but Midge would haunt my ass if I minded my own business while someone broke into her house."

"Your knee-jerk assumption about me being a burglar lacks both imagination and reasoning. Kindly stop suggesting it."

"If the crowbar fits." He shrugged. "Let me take a look at that key."

"Are you *still* under the assumption I'm some sort of criminal? Because it's getting old."

"And so is your attempt at breaking into this house. Let me see." He beckoned for the key. Since I was making no progress, I handed it over. "Sometimes they need to be polished off. Warmed up, you know? Like dollar bills in a vending machine. You have to smooth them out a few times, breathe on the corners. Or video games from those old-school consoles where you had to blow on the prongs."

He buffed the key on the hem of his heather gray t-shirt, pulling the fabric up just enough for me to catch a glance at the dark, fuzzy trail of hair running down his belly. His jeans hung low on his hips, revealing a glimpse at the hunter green waistband of his boxers. As he rubbed his shirt against the key's every edge and notch, it occurred to me Linden was as thick as a redwood and nearly as tall. His sun-kissed skin only made his deep brown hair and beard shine darker.

I'd noticed he was a big, burly guy when he'd stalked

across the yard but I hadn't put all the pieces together until right now. Hell, I'd barely noticed my surroundings in this white-knuckled sprint to get away, to disappear.

I'd left at two in the morning and driven through the night to keep a low profile, and it'd worked beautifully until the hot neighbor insisted on helping me open my door.

In truth, it was rude. It was downright disrespectful for all those brutish good looks to be wasted on this know-it-all, mansplain-my-life-to-me, uninvited knight in ripped denim. Where were the drop-dead sexy guys who didn't appear out of nowhere to announce a woman shouldn't use a crowbar to open a door? Where were the ones who asked if they could assist, and when refused, offered to simply hang out and serve as eye candy? What about the ones who didn't automatically assume I was a criminal? Why couldn't *they* be my neighbors?

Not that I had the room in my life for anyone but me and my steamship of homemade problems. There wasn't a human being alive who wanted a piece of my mess.

"All right. Give it a try."

Linden shifted, his arm extended in my direction and a fierce smile stretching his lips. His shoulders spanned the width of the door and I had to talk myself into glancing away rather than eye-fondling him.

Taking the key from him, I dropped my gaze to the lock. Broad shoulders didn't matter. Wolfish grins didn't matter. Insanely meddlesome neighbors didn't matter. Nothing mattered but the next move.

I gave the lock a few tries, twisted the knob several times, and thumped my shoulder against the door as hard as I could but nothing happened. I was ready to call this experiment off and return to my method of beating and bashing until I got my way when Linden said, "Stop eyeing the crow-bar. That's not going to help."

"Then propose an alternative solution," I replied, now fully exasperated at this man and his presence. "Otherwise, I'll take care of this on my own, thank you."

"Go another round," he said, tipping his chin up toward the door. "You work the knob, I'll add leverage on the door."

"That sounds—" I really wanted to argue with him. I wanted it so much and not even because I disagreed with him on this issue but because my frustration and anger needed a place to go right now. It was supremely unfair to unload any of it on this guy and I knew that. I knew better. "Okay. Fine. I'll try it your way this time."

He ran his hands along the panel of the door, thumping with his fist every few inches. "This is the spot," he murmured like some kind of deranged door whisperer. "Come on. Let's do this."

I hooked a glance over my shoulder at him as I closed my hand around the knob. He was right there, his body crowded up against mine. We were close enough that I could pick up the scent of coffee lingering around him. Under normal circumstances, I would've preferred some polite distance from the rude dude I'd just met but I'd been awake and wearing the same clothes for a day and a half, my life was stuffed into the back of a station wagon, and my career died in a grease fire. There were no normal circumstances and there was no other way to do it.

"I can feel the deadbolt sliding out of the lock," I said. "It's almost there."

"Hold on," he murmured.

Before I could ask what and how I was to hold on,

Linden rammed his shoulder against the panel, the door swung open, and we stumbled inside.

He recovered quickly, pushing to his feet and saying, "Like I told you, sometimes these old doors stick."

Sticky old doors and the beastly men who break them down.

"I appreciate your efforts," I replied, ignoring his outstretched hand as I gathered myself up and stood. It was the best I could do. I was in too much of a miserable snit to properly thank him for his help.

"Don't mention it." Then, leaning into the open doorway, he frowned. "Do you hear that?" He set his hands on his hips —which required me to study both—and glanced from side to side. "It sounds like—" He suddenly pushed me to the floor, one hand on the back of my head as a sudden burst of high-pitched squeaks exploded from somewhere inside the cottage. "Bats. Stay down. Stay out of their way and they'll ignore us," he said, his words warm as he spoke them against my ear.

All at once, the noise was upon us, a long-rumbling roll of thunder punctuated by squeals and slaps. All told, this exodus lasted less than a minute but every second pressed facedown on a dirty porch floor while a swarm—flock? who knew?—of startled bats passed overhead was a series of increasingly ridiculous eternities.

As for the hot neighbor who didn't know how to mind his own business, he was doing a fine job of shielding me from the bats with that girth and muscle of his. Whether he needed to cup my breast to accomplish this was debatable but he wasn't taking advantage any more than I was with my elbow cozied up between his legs.

The accidental intimacy wasn't his fault though I was

reminded once again I could've managed all of this on my own. That included the bats. Surprising? Yes. Incapacitating? Absolutely not.

"I think that's the last of them." He unhanded my breast and peeled himself off me. Not even a *thank you, ma'am* for the groping. "But let's get away from the door in case there are any stragglers."

I didn't know when this had evolved from an *I* endeavor to an *us*, though it bothered me enough to once again ignore the hand he offered to help me up.

Help was the last thing I wanted from anyone. Help was an unclosed loop and it never failed to cost me more than I could afford.

Help was off the table but I didn't mind common sense, which was why I marched down the porch, Linden following behind me. My nipples, after the pleasantly rough treatment received, were one step ahead of us.

"I'll call my bat guy. He'll be able to tell us how they got inside and where they nested," he said when we reached the driveway. Again with the *us*. "Whether they left any friends or family behind too."

There was a snicker and I blinked hard at the man beside Linden, the one I hadn't noticed until now. The one who looked strikingly similar to him but also completely different. They had to be brothers.

"Of course you have a bat guy," he said.

"Yeah, I have a bat guy," Linden replied. "Just like you probably have a tax fraud guy."

The other man consulted his watch and bobbed his head. "I have a tax fraud *lady* but I get where you're going with this." He glanced at me. "Hi. Ash Santillian."

"Hello." I shook his hand, which was nearly as large as

Linden's. They were like copycat versions of each other, one light, one dark, and varying shades of severe. "I'm Jasper-Anne Cleary and I assure you, I wasn't attempting to break into this house."

"I can see that now," Ash replied with a laugh. It was easy to joke with him. He didn't seem poised to rip a door off its hinges or a tree clear out of the earth for the simple pleasure of proving he could.

I offered Ash a pleasant smile as Linden strolled inside the cottage, phone pressed to his ear. I didn't recall inviting him to wander around but the recurring theme of this morning seemed to be Linden's general disinterest in such niceties.

"You both live next door?" I asked.

"No, no," Ash replied. "My fiancée and I live in Boston."

From somewhere beneath all of this exhaustion and stress, my social graces switched on. I was nothing if not a robot when it came to chatting people up. "Oh, what do y'all do in Boston?"

"I'm an accountant and she's in grad school for archaeology." He peered at me for a moment, his eyes narrow as he studied my face. "You've visited before, right? You look so familiar."

I grinned around a gulp of panic. "Not in a long time," I said. "I just have one of those familiar faces."

He tapped his cheek near the corner of his mouth, in the exact spot of the thumbprint birthmark on my cheek. "I swear I've seen you before. Do you happen to work in financial services?"

I couldn't cover up the birthmark without a gallon of stage-grade concealer which meant I needed to adopt a hat-and-sunglasses disguise if I wanted an ounce of anonymity.

That was a nightmare, considering my head was all wrong for hats but there was no way in hell I was coloring my hair. I'd just hide it. I'd hide everything. I was appallingly good at it. "No, not in finance," I said. "I don't believe we've met."

That much was true.

"What do you do?" he asked, still studying me with far more interest than I needed right now.

"Mmhmm. Consulting, mostly," I managed. That was *somewhat* true. "I'm taking a break to see to my aunt's estate."

This would've been a fine time for another battalion of bats to emerge. Anything to keep Ash from connecting my face to the disasters in my wake.

"Does that take you on the road a lot?"

I managed a mild "Mmhmm" as I watched Linden descend the steps. Still couldn't get over him roaming about my property. The boy just didn't require an invitation for anything.

"The bats are the least of your problems," Linden announced as he joined us.

"Such a ray of sunshine you are," Ash said.

They traded brotherly expressions for a moment and the plain authenticity of it almost drew a laugh from me. *Almost.* Laughing was for people not dead on their feet and thinking up clever disguises to avoid being recognized by anyone with cable news access or an internet connection.

"Listen," Linden started, "my guess is the bats came down the chimney. They fucked up the living room. It's a disaster in there."

I waved a hand. "It's fine. I don't need a living room right now. There are plenty of other rooms for me."

He chuckled. "You can't stay in that house."

I peered at him, my emotions and exhaustion fighting to

get the better of me, and I knew I had to politely end this conversation. *Thank you for the help. Thank you for the fondling. I should be getting on about it now.* Instead, I folded my arms over my chest and said, "Remind me again why the hell you're still here?"

THREE
LINDEN

THE LADY ASKED A DAMN GOOD QUESTION. WHAT THE HELL *WAS* I doing here? I could've called up my bat guy and left her to it. I didn't need to supervise. I didn't need to stay. I didn't have to care about any of this.

It wasn't any deep, lingering loyalty to Midge. She was a nice neighbor, always up in my business, but I didn't owe it to her to look after the niece she'd never once mentioned.

I didn't have to care. I didn't know why I did.

It annoyed the hell out of me.

"All things equal, I'd rather not have your bats looking for a new home next door," I replied. It was a weak response seeing as bats did not behave that way and nocturnal pollinators were pretty much essential for the ecosystem but it was better than grabbing this woman and shaking some sense into her the way I wanted to.

"Are you going to reach up and pluck them from the sky? Maybe you'll just shout at them until they decide it's not worth the trouble. Is that how it's going to be? Unless that's your plan, I can't see why you need to park yourself in my presence."

"Lin, maybe we should—"

I held up a hand to silence my brother. "The water heater kicked the bucket at some point and flooded the basement. Everything down there is trashed and you don't have hot water. There's a small but steady roof leak in the main bedroom." I folded my arms over my chest. "Maybe if you hadn't waited two years, the place wouldn't be in shambles."

Jasper looked me up and down, her gaze severe and her lips pressed tight into a smile that offered no warmth. Any minute now, she'd open up the ground and get rid of me for good. Part of me couldn't wait to see it happen. "Where I have or have not been over the past two years is not subject to your concern."

"What my brother is trying to say"—Ash gripped my shoulder and forced me back a step—"is this house doesn't seem safe or comfortable for you."

"That's not for him to determine."

Ash tightened his grip on my shoulder, saying, "I would suggest it wasn't as much his decision as the collective decree of the water heater, the bats, and the roof."

Jasper shifted to face the house, her hands propped on her waist. She stared for a long moment before a sigh rippled through her body, rustling her wavy, whiskey-hued hair. Turning, she said, "I've worked with worse. Thank y'all for your consideration, though I'll manage just fine."

"What?" Ash shook his head. "No. That's not—"

"Please don't give it a second thought," she interrupted.

Funny thing, she said all these nice words and she made them sound sweet as hell but she was actually slapping you back into your place. If I wasn't totally fucking annoyed about everything right now, I'd admire it.

"It's a little more rustic than it used to be but it's nothing I can't handle," she continued, giving the house another glance. "After the drive I had, the last thing I want to do is hop in the car and start another journey."

"You can stay with Linden."

I pivoted to face my brother. "She can fucking *what?*"

"Oh, come on," he replied. "You have the space."

"Care to tell me where?"

"You have a foldout sofa in your den," he said, scowling at me like I was the troublemaker here. "It would be fine until Jasper can get a plumber in and any other stray animals out."

I stared at him, my mouth open but words failing me. Of all people, Ash knew how closely I guarded the peace and quiet that came from living in a one-bedroom cottage on the edge of a forest.

"While that offer is extremely kind," Jasper started, "I really will be fine on my own. I might not look like someone who makes a practice of roughing it"—she gave a self-depre-cating laugh—"but I'm well acquainted with such things. This isn't nearly as bad as you might think it is."

She couldn't stay at Midge's house. Even if she was capable of crushing bones and opening chasms, she couldn't stay there. And this had nothing to do with any degree of chivalry, seeing as I possessed none of that. *I* wouldn't stay in there and I'd stayed in many questionable locations over the years.

"I can't imagine you boys have all day to see to my trou-bles," Jasper said. "I feel terrible for keeping you."

"Great," I said, taking a giant step backward. "I have

appointments this afternoon. My schedule is jammed. Completely jammed. I don't have a single free minute the rest of the day. But the bat guy will be here soon. He'll be able to give you a referral for a plumber. Probably a roofer too. And that should take care of everything."

She couldn't stay there. She couldn't. That was all there was to say about the situation.

"I'll just let y'all let me go," she said, that warmth flooding her words again.

"Yeah, and I have to get back to the city," Ash said. "Please consider the offer to stay next door, Jasper. He's all bark and no bite. You're welcome to the den if you want it. He keeps the back door open if you change your mind."

She couldn't do that either. Not an option. To start with, I didn't have the space. My den was a glorified pantry. This woman and all of her…well, whatever she had with her wasn't going to fit in there. But more importantly, I didn't want anyone in my space. It was *my space*, for me, and I loathed the idea of strangers hanging out in my home. I could put up with Ash—in small doses—and my mother came and went like this was an extension of my childhood house, and all of that was tolerable. I could *tolerate* it.

Inviting this maybe-burglar, probable-problem into my space was not tolerable.

"Your offer is very gracious," she said, her gaze fixed on Ash like she was making a point. "Though I swear I am quite content with Midge's version of shabby chic over here. Heavy pour on the shabby, garnish with the chic."

Because I just couldn't help myself, I asked, "Where do the bats figure into that?"

"Chic for sure," she replied easily, like she'd anticipated

that question from the start. "Spooky is always chic. It's why we love vampires."

Ash saved me from digging into that comment when he said, "Okay, I'm actually late now and—"

"—and that makes you itchy," I said.

He rolled his eyes. "Don't you have appointments? Isn't your *totally jammed day* the reason we had to meet before noon? Where are you even going today?"

"It is very jammed," I said. "I'm supposed to be down in Hyannis for a consultation, then Milton for a tree warden visit, and then a swing through Plymouth to check on two golf courses."

"By all means," Ash said, gesturing toward the street. "On your way. No one is stopping you."

"I will just as soon as"—I glanced over to resolve this issue of inviting Jasper to wander through my back door whenever she pleased—"where'd she go?"

"Inside, probably. Come on, I need to grab my bag from your kitchen."

I stared at Midge's house for a long moment while Ash crossed the yard and went in through my front door. I wasn't sure what I expected to see here or why everything that'd occurred left me feeling terminally unsettled, but it required Ash beckoning me toward his car to finally get my feet moving off Jasper's driveway.

"Hey," he called over the roof of his vintage Porsche. "I'll call you later to discuss the partnership proposal Magnolia has developed. Before you go off about your compulsive need for independence, I'll remind you the primary changes you'll see from this merger are efficiencies in operating costs and the benefit of support staff for scheduling and billing and the like."

"You do my billing."

"Yeah and it's a pain in my ass. You think translating your illegible notes into invoices is an effective use of my time?"

I shrugged. "I have a feeling you're going to tell me it's not."

He glared at me. "We're going to have a talk about this. I see a lot of opportunity in it for you."

"You mean a lot of money."

"Money won't kill you, Lin."

"Bullshit. You're billing me for this hour."

"I'll back out a tenth," he replied with a laugh. He jabbed a finger toward Midge's house. "Here's some free advice about *that*."

It was my turn to roll my eyes. "Your advice is never free."

"Listen. Take it from me. Give the strange girl a place to stay."

My brother had a bizarre story about meeting his fiancée on an airplane, immediately hiring her to work in his office, and then taking her home with him the same day. *So bizarre.* "I'd say that advice applies once in a blue moon."

"All I'm saying is, be a good neighbor. Let her crash in your den for a night or two while she gets her place sorted out. Don't be an ass about it. You never know what might happen."

"What is that supposed to mean?"

He eyed Midge's house for a second, his brows lowered. "Nothing. Just don't be an ass. Seems like she has enough to deal with right now."

"I'm not being an ass. I'm being extremely reasonable. It's ridiculous to invite a random woman to stay in my den just because you did something somewhat similar and it didn't go down in flames."

"You assumed she was a burglar," he called as he dropped into the driver's seat.

"So did you," I cried.

He pointed to his ear as the engine roared to life. Either he couldn't or didn't want to hear me. My money was on the latter. "Don't be an ass," he repeated.

"Not wanting random people in my space doesn't make me an ass," I said as he backed out of the driveway. "I don't even like having you around."

He only waved in response and drove up the street, leaving me here with all the trouble he'd chased into my life.

After scowling at the empty street, I glanced back at Midge's house only to catch sight of Jasper climbing the porch stairs, a toaster oven tucked under one arm and two grocery totes hanging from the crook of her other elbow.

The bags were crammed and cumbersome, swinging and twisting around her arm with each step. She had to hold her arm out to prevent the bags from careening into her leg but that unbalanced position made her wobble a bit.

She'd said she had this under control. That she knew what she was doing. If I sprinted across the yard to take those bags off her, she'd tell me the last thing she needed was me rushing in and telling her how to carry her stuff.

She didn't need any help from me and, like she'd said, she didn't want it either.

And I preferred it that way.

FOUR
JASPER

ONE OF MY WORST HABITS WAS MY TENDENCY TO IGNORE THINGS I didn't want to deal with. At this point, it was probably more of a personality trait than a habit. If I could navigate around something, even if it demanded more time and energy from me, I'd do it in a damn heartbeat.

I avoided my banking app when I knew I was running low on cash. If I didn't look, I wouldn't panic over money.

I pulled back from relationships that didn't work anymore. If I didn't participate, I wouldn't have to acknowledge the problems.

I unfollowed my nutty, conspiracy-theory-addled cousins on social media. If I didn't see their posts, I wouldn't have to engage with them on batshit crazy ideas.

And speaking of batshit…

I'd shoved all evidence of Midge's death in a drawer. The funeral, the estate, everything. If I didn't slip on an understated black dress and if I didn't eat ham salad sandwiches in a church basement— If I ignored calls from her attorney— If I tucked the paperwork in the back of my closet and pretended it wasn't there— If I did all of this, it didn't have to be real.

Unfortunately for me, there was nothing more real than rubber-gloving up to the elbows and scrubbing Midge's walls with diluted bleach for six hours.

Because of the batshit, both literal and figurative.

On the other side of my compulsive avoidance of unpleasant topics sat my compulsive drive to get it done. Though I was completely unemployable at the moment, one of my most attractive professional qualities was my ability to plow through *any* problem.

I didn't need to ask questions. Didn't need to call any meetings or set any agendas. I'd be well on my way to fixing it before everyone else finished debating and defining the problem.

I'd always been this way. No time to dally around when you can shake open a trash bag, snap on the gloves, and get down in the dirt. For the past decade, my style of problem-solving and my record of getting it done every damn time meant my job security was never in question. I was the irreplaceable right-hand woman.

Until five days ago.

So, I forced open another door, scrubbed another wall, filled another trash bag. I hadn't slept more than a handful of hours all week but I was good at this. If I kept going, I'd find the way through. I'd figure it out. If I kept my eyes ahead, I'd nail this situation the way I nailed everything.

It had always been this way. Always problems, issues, tragedies, disasters, dramas. One lined up behind the other. It had been this way when I was a small child spending summers with Midge while my mother worked her ass off to keep the wheels turning. There was no time to examine these things, no time to deliberate over them or file them into any context other than *the problem to solve today.*

I didn't have to look back. It wasn't as though it would change anything. What was the point? I couldn't go back in time, couldn't erase the mortifying things I'd said on a hot mic, couldn't stop the dual train wreck of my humiliation—and termination—on live cable news, couldn't prevent so-called friends from turning their backs or colleagues from blacklisting me. Couldn't prevent others from blowing up my phone with messages of support and thinly veiled requests for more gossip. Couldn't even shut up the cable news bookers determined to get me on-air again so I could dump out the whole teapot on what it was really like inside a pointless bid for the presidency.

The only way out was through.

Pay the bat guy, call a plumber, scrub the ceilings. I was going to figure this out the way I figured everything out, and I had some money saved. I could get by for a bit before things grew hairy.

I could stay here at Midge's cottage and clean up two years' worth of avoidance while the news cycle beat my gaffe-turned-scandal to a pulp. It would take a few months and a good, humble comeback story—or someone else stepping in something far worse than a few unsavory complaints about my former boss, the senator from the great state of Georgia and hopeless presidential hopeful, Tyson Timbrooks. In this sense, it was nothing more than a waiting game.

Scrub the floors. Empty rotten food from the cupboards. Plug in my toaster oven.

All I had to do was get through.

———

FALLING ASLEEP SHOULD'VE BEEN EASY. I SHOULD'VE BEEN comatose the minute my head hit the pillow but I was too tired to sleep. I hated trading in these extremes but it seemed to be my way. So hungry I lost my appetite. So stressed I was calm. So angry I came off happy.

And now, some thirty hours since the last time I'd slept, I couldn't keep my eyes shut. I'd filled eighteen trash bags and sanitized the cottage from top to bat-loving bottom. I'd hauled every sheet and towel, every tablecloth and curtain to the laundromat and made lists of everything I had to do while the spin cycle shook the machines.

I stocked up on food and supplies after getting turned around several times on my way to the grocery store. Then I got turned around on my way back. Say what you would about Washington, D.C. but at least the streets made sense.

I made Midge's home as habitable as any place with flickering lights and a shortage of hot water could claim to be, and I'd made a comfortable space for myself in the den. Midge's room was still musty from the roof leak, but more than that, I didn't feel right taking her room. The den had always been my room and I wasn't ready to change that.

After all that work and everything I'd slogged through this week, I should've been dead to the world. But I couldn't push all the way to the far edge of this extreme and let myself rest. I was a few months away from turning thirty-six and I still couldn't make responsible choices for myself. My body didn't know how to do that because I always pushed myself past the point of listening to my needs and now I had to push myself out of this point.

I called up a sleep story on my favorite relaxation app

and I reached over, fumbling blindly for the tote I'd set near the trundle bed. My sleep mask and bottle of melatonin gummies were down at the bottom and I had to empty the whole bag to reach them.

Even with that attack squad, it took an hour and the creation of three more lists (Things to Review: House Documents; Things to Review: Estate Provisions; Non-Beltway, Non-Consulting Work Possibilities) to chill out enough to feel my eyelids droop. I was almost there when I fully recognized that my so-hot-it's-rude neighbor *knew* Midge.

I'd skated right past that detail earlier in the day and I'd filed him away as nosy, mansplainy, and built like a barn. Nowhere in my comprehension of that exchange did I connect the reality of him living next door to *knowing* Midge.

That wasn't even the whole of it. He understood she was serious about coming back as a ghost and haunting anyone who'd crossed her. He'd heard about her family—and that she didn't actually have a niece. He'd lived next door long enough to *care* about her.

This hit me right in the guilts.

Midge had asked me to visit every time we'd talked and I'd promised to try, though it was never a full-bellied promise. It was always the meager *I'll see what I can do* and *I might have a long weekend coming up* and *we'll be in Boston for two hours for a fundraising dinner but I might be able to get away after*.

My crowning achievement in life was being indispensable, and indispensability didn't come with a great paid-time-off package. There was never a good time to get away. If anything, there were terrible, out of the question, work through the flu times. Politics beat like a heart and the heart wasn't known for pausing.

I hadn't visited in more than a handful of years. Hadn't even called too often. I'd missed my chance to say goodbye when her health took a sudden turn. I remembered calling from the back of a cab and leaving her a quick voicemail, and knowing I needed to give her another ring. But I let myself get swept up in work and didn't try her again. She passed a few days later.

And I wasn't terribly polite to her neighbor, the one who regarded her highly enough to confront a suspected burglar.

Dammit.

Midge would've baked him a banana bread. She believed in the restorative power of baked goods, particularly those meant to be sliced, warmed, and slathered in butter. A banana bread would smooth things over. That would make this right.

Sitting up to grab my phone from where it sat on the floor, tethered to the charger, I glanced at the window—and screamed out loud at the figure silhouetted there.

I ended up falling out of bed, landing flat on my ass, and clutching both hands to my chest as my heart thumped. "Where did you come from?" I asked the cat perched on this side of the windowsill.

Since I wasn't the only one skimping on polite greetings, the cat let out a disgruntled hiss and batted its paw against the window.

"I'm terribly sorry but I don't speak feline," I said. "You'll have to state your demands more clearly."

Unsatisfied with that request, the cat leapt down to the floor and stalked out of the room, glaring at me as it passed.

"Y'all really need that to be the last of the unexpected creatures in this house," I muttered.

FIVE
LINDEN

I GROANED INTO MY COFFEE WHEN THE DOORBELL RANG. I WAS not a morning person. I worked on trees but that didn't require me to keep farmer's hours, and thank god for that.

The beautiful thing about living alone and working for myself was that no one interfered with my slow mornings. I didn't have to put up with anyone rattling around the house or chatty coworkers. If I timed it right, there were days when I didn't have to speak to anyone until after lunch. Those were the best days.

Days when the doorbell rang before nine were not the best.

The sound of firm, eager, wouldn't-be-ignored knocking had me groaning again. I had a good idea who was waiting on the other side of the door.

Jasper hadn't taken Ash up on his offer to stay at my house and that was a relief. When I'd arrived home late last night after grabbing dinner in Plymouth, I caught sight of her inside Midge's house. The lights were on, the curtains and windows flung open, and she was standing on a stepladder in the middle of the large front window, a giant sponge in hand. She hadn't changed out of that fancy dress and her hair still hung around her shoulders in waves.

For reasons I still could not explain, seeing her there twisted and tightened the muscles between my shoulders. She'd stayed. She'd stayed and she was so unbothered by the conditions, she didn't even change out of her nice clothes.

I'd sat in my truck for longer than necessary, messing around with my phone while I stole glances next door. I didn't know why or what I wanted to see but I needed to see it before I ducked inside for the night.

Now that I thought about it, I was mostly concerned with the bats. I was a nature guy but that didn't mean I wanted bats hanging around my house. Or hers. That was my real concern. The bats.

I shuffled toward the door, half asleep and fully disinterested in another visit with Miss Cleary. Maybe it was Mrs. Cleary. Not that it mattered one way or another. It didn't matter. Why would it?

With that irritating question in mind and a matching scowl on my face, I swung open the door. As expected, Jasper was on the other side. She wasn't wearing a dress today but a bright yellow skirt with lots of little pleats. It made me think of an accordion, and I wanted to touch it. I wanted to touch it very much.

Instead, I flicked a glance up at her face—and all that honeyed hair spilling over her shoulders—and then down to the dish she carried.

"Good morning," she said, rather pointedly. As if I was supposed to say something before imagining the feel of her skirt between my fingers.

"Yeah," I grunted. "What's up?"

She stared at me for a second, a stiff grin on her face while her eyes flashed cool and hard. "Well, then. This will have to do," she said under her breath. "I never got a chance to thank you for your help yesterday."

I leaned a shoulder against the doorjamb and crossed my arms over my chest. "You had plenty of time to ask why the hell I was helping in the first place."

She gave a quick head bob in response. "Mmhmm. Okay." She held out the dish. "I made you a banana bread. To thank you."

The object on that plate looked nothing like any banana bread I'd ever seen. For starters, it seemed…wet. And yet, it also looked overcooked. Those things never, ever belonged in the same thought process as banana bread.

"You didn't have to do that."

"It was my pleasure," she said, pushing the dish in my direction again. "Yesterday was rather hectic. I wanted to thank you for everything. The door, the bats—"

"The attempted felony," I murmured.

She offered a playful expression that appeared completely forced, saying, "I can see how it came across that way at first glance. Now, I'd just *love* to hear more about your history with Midge. Why don't you invite me in?"

It was a question only in technicality. It was a direct order and this woman wasn't playing. I was half convinced she'd whip that crowbar out of her skirt and wag it at me if I didn't follow her lead.

Again, it did something to me. I was annoyed as hell and I wanted to argue with her. I also wanted to listen to her spitting that sweet, sweet fire while she forced those hollow smiles, and I wanted to close the door in her face because she made me feel far too many things at once.

"I can think of plenty of reasons why I wouldn't invite you in but…" I stepped back, gestured for her to follow.

"Such a warm, inviting host you are." She stepped inside and headed toward the kitchen, overtly eyeing the space as she went. "You opened up this wall," she said, gesturing between the kitchen and living space. "Wow. After being in Midge's house, I can really see the difference it makes."

I didn't respond.

Most of the houses on this street were built in the 1920s. The floor plans were all the same, save for a few quirks and variations. It made for a string of tidy bungalows lined up one after another.

Over time, many of those houses had been renovated or razed, new construction taking the place of old. Only my house and Midge's remained from the original string—and they were mirror images of each other.

"My word. Do you have a decorator?" Jasper asked as she turned in a circle. "This design is to die for."

I shoved my hands in my pockets. "Were you expecting ugly old recliners and some *Godfather* posters?"

She set the dish down on the countertop and studied the cabinetry. "You're assuming I made assumptions about you? That's an exciting turn of events."

"Then why do *you* assume I hired a decorator?"

She busied herself opening and closing drawers like she owned the place, which was a fine reminder this lady was a real fucking handful.

"Because it's difficult to make everything look like"—she yanked a long serrated knife from the drawer and waved it around with the same flippant attitude she had with the crowbar—"*this*. You know. Put together. Grown-up. Magazine quality."

I shifted away from Jasper and the knife-wagging, and scanned the living area with its marine blue walls. Sure, I'd had the assistance of my sister's best friends—both of whom happened to be architects—when I wanted to knock out a couple of walls and install several big banks of windows. They'd offered some pointers for making it all come together. None of this qualified as magazine quality.

Not that I minded the praise, seeing as I had put a fuckton of time into hunting down the right pieces and working on this space until it was exactly what I wanted. But this woman was buttering me up for something. That, or she routinely switched between two grossly different personalities: the sweet peach pie and the blistering hot pepper.

"I'd just love a cup of coffee." She nodded toward the mug I'd abandoned on the kitchen table.

"I bet you would," I murmured.

When I made no move to fetch that coffee for her, Jasper said, "Well, you just sit right down and I'll serve up this banana bread."

Knife still in hand, Jasper glanced between the wet bread and the upper cabinets as if she couldn't decide what to explore next.

What was with this woman and casually wielding weapons?

I pulled another glass mug from the cupboard and slid it across the counter. "Here." Then I grabbed the cold brew from the fridge. "Help yourself."

"I can see why Midge liked you." She hit me with another one of those smiles that just didn't seem connected to any real emotion, saying, "No nonsense with you. Right to the point."

I plucked the knife from her hand because I really did not

want to deal with anyone slicing off a fingertip or nicking a jugular. But doing this meant we were crowded between the kitchen table and a corner of cabinets. I could see all the golden flecks in her eyes at this range.

"Milk's in the fridge, if you want it."

She chuckled and—for no good reason—I dropped my gaze to the hollow of her throat. Beneath the jean jacket she was wearing a gauzy white shirt, making her neck the only bit of exposed skin on her. The only bit of vulnerability. Everything else was fake smiles and forced laughs and comments that slapped so hard you didn't realize it until five minutes after the fact. But that pale, flawless skin was true.

"You and Midge must've gotten on famously." She topped off her mug with a heavy splash of milk. "Such a scrappy old bird, she was."

I sliced the banana bread because what else was I supposed to do? I couldn't stare at her neck much longer and I sure as hell wasn't interested in reminiscing. Not when her skirt was translucent in the morning light and she was working damn hard at playing nice after showing me her teeth yesterday.

I dropped slices of the banana bread—which was cement on the outside and mud in the middle—on two plates and nudged one toward Jasper. I made no move toward mine.

"We hardly got a moment for proper introductions yesterday. With all that commotion," she added, twirling past me to return the coffee and milk to the refrigerator then thinking better of it and setting them both on the counter. "Tell me, what do you do? You said something about trees, I believe."

"Arborist," I grunted out.

I tried to keep my focus on the plate, even if I didn't touch it. I didn't want to stare at her or that skirt but there weren't many other options. I might've blown out a wall but this kitchen was still small and she still smelled...lovely. There was no specific fruit or flower to pin down but rather a soft, gentle scent that was...lovely. That was all I could say about it. *Lovely.*

"Forgive me," she said with another one of those self-deprecating laughs. They annoyed me enough to forget all about the lovely. "What does the work of an arborist look like? I can't recall ever meeting one before."

"Trees. It looks like trees." When she shifted to face me, her nose scrunched up and her brow wrinkled, I added, "Tending to trees and woody plants. Maintaining ecological communities. Diagnosing and treating disease. Or fungi. Removing trees when they pose a danger to people, places, or other healthy trees. Removing those species that are becoming overabundant or invasive." I shrugged. "Like I said, trees."

She bobbed her head several times and pointed toward the woods visible through the wall of windows along the back side of the house. "I gather you have plenty of work around here."

"Plenty," I echoed. I thought about telling her more, explaining the work of tree wardens in this area and the ongoing fights against devastating disease and misguided residential plantings, but I didn't carry on conversations at this hour. Hell, it was a blessing I was fully dressed.

"That's always the good kind of trouble to have on your hands." She lifted the mug to her lips, watching me as she sipped.

I was supposed to ask something about her now. That was how this worked. She expressed an interest in me and I was due to return the favor.

I could manage that just fine—I didn't mind people too much once I was awake for the day—but I didn't want to do it with Jasper. It didn't spring from any deep desire to be rude or hinge on the fact Midge had never once mentioned this lady. No, I didn't want to do this with her because she confused the absolute hell out of me.

She interrupted my morning with her plastic cheerfulness but I couldn't stop thinking about her skin.

She brought me a biohazard of a banana bread and she smelled like heaven.

She stubbornly insisted on sleeping in a teardown bat cave but made me want to wrap her skirt around my fists.

It was too damn confusing and I didn't want any of those contradictions in my life. None of it. Not even the pieces that'd kept me tossing and turning all night, half convinced I needed to march over there and drag her out of that house, half convinced I'd lost my damn marbles if I thought ripping a woman out of her bed and taking her home with me was a worthwhile idea.

I didn't want to feel like that. I didn't want to feel any of it.

I gulped down a mouthful of coffee. "You're not from around here."

"You're right about that."

Please, god, don't make me ask her another question.

As the silence stretched on, I realized I was now staring at the mark on her cheek. It was medium brown, like a pale freckle, but had the shape and size of a shelled walnut. I wanted to touch it even more than her skirt.

Somehow, I managed, "Down south?"

"Caught that, did you?" She grinned at me over the rim of her mug. It seemed like she was intentionally holding it up to her face to keep me from eyeing the mark on her cheek but she'd forgotten it was a clear glass mug. "I lose my accent whenever I'm away from home for long. It's a wonder I still have any of it."

"And where is home?"

She glanced down, her brows lowered. "I grew up in Georgia. Haven't lived there in ages though. Just visits."

She reached for the coffee, refilled hers halfway, and then held the bottle toward me in question. I pushed my mug closer. "Leave some room for milk."

Jasper nodded, sending her wavy hair swaying against the collar of her jacket as she topped me off.

"Where do you live now?"

She peeked up at me as she poured the milk and I felt it low in my belly.

What the literal fuck was wrong with me?

Once she had the milk capped, she clinked her mug against mine. "As far as where I live, well." She fixed a severe smile on her face. "I live next door."

That was when I bobbled my mug and sent coffee splashing down my shirt. That was bad enough but Jasper was there with a dish towel, patting me down. Her hands were everywhere and all I could do was stand there while we kept talking over each other.

Her hand dropped to my waist. "Let me just—"

I tried to snatch the towel from her. "It's fine and—"

"Hold still and I'll—"

"Really, you don't have to—"

She yanked the towel back. "Maybe you should change out of this—"

"That's not where—"

She reached for the roll of paper towels. "Don't move, there's a puddle—"

"You don't have to try and fix everything."

"Actually, I do."

"I'll just change. It's fine. Don't—" I took a step back, held up my hands. "Stop. Stay here. Let me handle this."

I stalked into my bedroom, whipped off my shirt, and shoved my fingers through my hair. If I stayed in here long enough, she'd eventually leave. Right?

Unless she came looking for me.

She'd definitely come looking for me.

Maybe I wanted her to come looking for me.

"What the fuck is wrong with me?" I grumbled.

"What was that?" Jasper called.

I scrubbed my hands down my face. "Nothing."

She wasn't leaving. Even when she did leave, she'd be right next door. She wasn't going anywhere.

Fuck me.

Still smelling of coffee, I pulled on a new shirt and returned to the kitchen—where I found Jasper kneeling on the floor. Her hair fell in a curtain around her face as she mopped up the coffee and all I could do was stop and stare.

It wasn't the position. It was *not.* It had nothing to do with the sight of her on her knees, head bowed, skirt fanned out like daffodil petals. It was that she was *here*, in my space and scrubbing the floors like they were a personal keepsake of hers, and I wanted her to stay equally as much as I wanted her to go. And I hated that more than being forced to speak before noon.

"All set," she said, pushing to her feet.

I stared. How could I not? She was a gorgeous pain in the ass.

I reached for my mug to keep my hands busy. It was mostly empty and I required two to three full cups of coffee to get going in the morning but there was no way I was doing the kitchen tango with Jasper again. "Thanks."

"I must thank you properly for your assistance yesterday. I had no intention of needing it but you rose to the occasion nonetheless. I'm sure Midge admired that about you."

We shared a glance over the banana bread. Neither of us made a move toward it.

"Midge had a lot of opinions about a lot of things," I said. "It seems you managed well enough over there last night."

She sighed as she tossed the paper towels in the trash. "I managed just fine. Believe me, I've worked with worse."

I didn't see how that could be true but I wasn't going to argue with her. No more than I already was. "I take it the bats have moved along?"

"Bats, yes, though a cat scared a decade off me last night," she said, a breathless laugh in her words. "Appeared out of nowhere."

Now, that—that wasn't fake. I wasn't convinced it was real but it wasn't another empty smile or canned comeback. "Little black cat with a white triangle on his chest? Looks like he's wearing a tuxedo?"

She shook her head as she lifted her mug. "It was dark. I didn't get a good look."

"If it was a black cat, it was probably Sinatra."

"Is he yours?" she asked between sips.

"No, he lives in the forest." I tipped my head toward the back windows. "Midge named him Sinatra for the tux. Apparently his eyes look a little blue in the right light too."

Since I couldn't look at her face or her neck or her skirt, I dropped my attention to the banana bread in front of me and broke off the most edible corner I could find. *Edible* was too optimistic a term. It tasted like burnt cardboard with a strange, hot-garbage-esque finish.

"Mmhmm. Does he make a habit of inviting himself indoors? Because I need to prepare myself for that."

"Not usually, no. I've only seen him in the yard. Sometimes he'll come sit on the deck. Months will go by without seeing him. Once it was almost a year."

"And you're sure it's the same cat?"

"I'm not sure about anything but Midge was convinced. She knew his markings. I think she left food for him on the back steps but then she kept getting raccoons hanging out on her porch. At least that's what she told me when I moved in here. That was the first thing she said to me. 'Don't feed the cat because he only sends his raccoon friends to eat.'"

Jasper drummed her fingers on the mug. "How old is this cat?"

"No one knows."

"No one knows?" she repeated, a twang of irritation in her voice.

There was definitely something wrong with me because I enjoyed the shit out of that. "He's been around since before I moved in five years ago. Midge mentioned seeing him on and off for years before that. She figured he liked hanging around here because this place hadn't been occupied for fifteen or twenty years so there were plenty of mice." I shifted to drop the knife into the basin of the sink. I didn't need Jasper grabbing that thing again. "Surprised you've never heard about him, seeing as you were so close with Midge. She had a ton of stories about that damn cat."

If Jasper was fazed by these comments, it didn't show. She grinned at the old barometer and tide chart stationed below the clock on the wall opposite the kitchen. "What a curious bit of history. I get a house and an occasional cat."

"You're sticking around, then. You're not just visiting. You're here to stay."

Jasper's eyes brightened. "You seem very concerned about this."

"I'm not *concerned*. I'm making conversation, just like you," I replied with a wave toward our mugs. Mine was still miserably empty. "You're the one who invited yourself over."

"Which I did to acknowledge your help yesterday."

"Which you've done." I shoved my hands into my pockets. They were safer there. They wouldn't wring her lovely neck there. "Clearly there's something else you want."

She took a step forward, propped her hands on her hips. "I'm being neighborly. You should try it."

I matched her step. "And what the fuck did you think I was doing yesterday?"

A noise rattled in her throat, something strangled and hoarse. I *loved* that noise—and I had the privilege of hearing it in its purest form now that we were standing toe to toe. "You thought you were interrupting the commission of a crime."

"You had a fucking crowbar, Jasper." I folded my arms over my chest. "What was I supposed to do? Hand you a muffin basket?"

The gold in her eyes flashed. "A muffin is always preferrable to mansplaining."

We stared at each other for a long moment. A few strands of her hair brushed against my forearm. It was nothing, but those sensations still rippled over my skin and down my spine. And *lower*.

"Yeah, so, anyway, what is this?" I asked, tipping my chin

toward the dish. "It's a lot of things but it's not banana bread."

"It certainly is," she snapped. "I mashed those bananas myself."

"And what else did you throw in with those bananas?"

"The usual things. Flour, sugar, eggs, vanilla. Stuff like that."

I gestured to the loaf's squat, dense appearance. "Some part of that went wrong."

"I don't know what went wrong," she replied. "I followed the recipe. The grocery stores are a nightmare, of course, but—"

"What do you mean, the grocery stores are a nightmare?"

"They're just impossible to find," she said, touching her fingers to her temples. "I swear, I drove in the same circle for an hour just to get to the store."

I peered at her. "Are you talking about the rotary?"

"The traffic circle," she said.

"The *rotary*."

"It's called a traffic circle. That's the name."

I shook my head. I wasn't arguing the New England dialect with a southerner this morning. "It took you an hour to exit?"

She lifted a shoulder. "Maybe not a full hour."

"But close enough?" When her only response was a blink, I continued, "And then what happened, Jasper?"

With a defiant shake of her head that was practiced only in its purity, she said, "I mean, I think I got the right ingredients. I haven't actually visited a grocery store in years. It's just so overwhelming without the list of items you usually buy right there in the app. Do I use bread flour or cake flour? I don't know. How am I supposed to know that? And all the different types of sugars, my word. How am I supposed to know the correct one for baking? Aren't most of them interchangeable? They didn't even have the brand of bread I prefer which was truly disappointing. All I can say is I really miss the stores where I used to shop."

"And where were those?"

Jasper turned a piercing glare toward me. "Mid-Atlantic."

"Right. The mid-Atlantic." I motioned for her to continue. "Then what happened? How did you commit this crime against bananas?"

"I had to bake it in the crockpot because the oven wasn't heating up but—"

"Let me stop you right there." I shook my head. "You baked it in a crockpot?"

"That's what I said."

"Crockpots aren't for baking."

"Crockpots are for everything," she replied. "Crockpots can cook anything and you're light on the imagination if you think otherwise."

I motioned to the loaf again. "That's a real nice argument but this begs to differ. You're sure about the flour? And the sugar? You're sure it wasn't spackle? I'm positive I tasted some spackle."

If my brother was here, he'd tell me I was being an ass.

He wouldn't be wrong.

She fisted her hands. "I was trying to thank you. It's a kind gesture, you know."

"Yeah, I caught that part. Just not sure if you're trying to kill me with your kindness."

Her cheeks were red now, almost comically so, and I swore I could hear her molars grinding together. I was really, *really* sick because I was enjoying the hell out of this.

"If I wanted to kill you, I wouldn't do it with kindness."

I leaned a hip against the counter. When I crossed my arms over my chest, my knuckles brushed the front of her jacket. "How would you do it, then?"

She glanced down at where the back of my hand lingered against the denim. "That shouldn't concern you."

"Why not?"

She dropped a hand on my chest, saying, "Because I've thanked you for your help and fulfilled all expectations of courtesy, and now I'll live happily knowing I've done my part. I'll also live happily if our paths never cross again. Help me out with that, would you?"

After another pat to my chest, Jasper spun away from me and marched straight out of my house, the front door banging shut behind her.

———

JASPER SPENT THE NEXT SEVEN DAYS MAKING IT IMPOSSIBLE TO ignore her.

I tried. I tried like hell, but the woman was everywhere. Pacing the yard and taking measurements of god only knew what. Leaving all the windows and curtains open, all the time, and the lights on too. Emptying the garage out onto the driveway and then, apparently, shoving it all back in there.

There was no avoiding Jasper.

Even when I tried my damnedest to pretend there wasn't a flamethrower of a woman next door, I couldn't ignore the hammering.

Hammering fucking everything. *Everything*. And I had no clue what she was pounding but she did it day and night for three days straight.

The real kicker was the curb. Without fail, every time I left in the morning or returned in the evening, Jasper was dragging something out to the curb. Trash bags—so many trash bags—boxes, wrecked furniture, rolled-up carpet, all kinds of shit.

I couldn't look away from it if I tried. I couldn't close my eyes and pray I managed to steer my truck into the driveway without incident. I had to go in with eyes wide-open and force myself to stare through Jasper.

As if that was even possible.

As if I hadn't formed a mental catalog of her dresses and high heels and the coordinating cardigans she wore as summer gave way to the crisp bite of autumn. As if I didn't growl at the sight of her, waves hanging loose over her shoulders. As if I didn't lie awake at night, wondering whether it was time to take this situation in hand.

Every time I spotted her in the yard or at the curb, there was a split second where I was finished playing by her rules. Just fucking finished.

That split second hit me as I drove down the street this afternoon and found Jasper lugging a huge, water-stained box out from the house. It was so big she disappeared behind it, leaving only her arms and legs visible.

The closer I came, the longer that second stretched. It continued on like a long thrum of hunger deep in my belly and it didn't stop when I pulled into my driveway.

I watched as she followed the comma curve of the walk-way, moving with more grace than anyone who couldn't see ahead of them had any business. She almost made it too but that box was doomed. The bottom fell out in a sodden rush, leaving a heap of wet, damp-browned papers at her feet.

She kept her hands fixed on the sides of the box as she

lowered it, her lips folded in a line that spoke of her intense displeasure. As if a box had any business failing her. Then she closed her eyes, turned her face to the sky, and let her shoulders drop. I was certain I could hear her sigh all the way over here.

Before I could stop myself, I was out of my truck and crossing into her yard.

Before I could stop myself, I was shouting, "Mind telling me what the hell you're doing?"

SIX
JASPER

I knew he was watching. I knew he saw today's disaster and filed it away with all the other disasters he'd watched from his front-row seat next door.

There was no escaping the man. Everywhere I turned, he was there. Lurking in his windows, lingering in his yard, staring from inside his truck. I couldn't breathe without a scowling audience.

It was all he could do, the scowling. As if he was forever sucking a lemon while looming in my shadows.

Then— "Mind telling me what the hell you're doing?"

I kept my eyes shut a moment longer. My dress and shoes were soggy and the box's contents smelled vaguely fungal but I needed a minute.

Just a minute to absorb the sun's warmth and pretend I wasn't covered in damp basement trash. One quick little minute to myself before going another round with the ever-present hot neighbor.

The ever-present hot neighbor who could've had me on

his kitchen table last week if he'd asked nicely. Or not so nicely.

I turned my face from the sun to stare at Linden Santillian in all his tree-doctoring glory. Plaid shirt rolled up to the elbows, jeans that fit *just right*, ball cap shadowing his hazel eyes. The cap made it difficult to tell for certain but his eyes seemed bright today, almost feral.

Where I was from, wolves were bad news. They decimated chicken coops and spooked horses. They were the reason, or so I was told, my uncle stored a handgun in the cupholder of his truck.

Yet the odd thing about wolves and all the bad news they brought along with them was they didn't exist. Not really, not after decades of hunting, not where I was from.

But this man right here, he was all wolf.

Everything about him was large and dark, like a new moon in human form.

And the most overlooked quality of wolves—and moons—was their beauty. There was no law prohibiting predators from being both beautiful and deadly. This man was both—in the best ways. He'd destroy you, he'd wreck you, he'd tear you apart and watch you bleed, and he'd smile about it.

Wolves were nothing like foxes or coyotes or mountain lions or any of the creatures known to stalk farms and rural spreads.

Wolves weren't sly or cunning, and they weren't exactly brazen either. They were bold in a simplistic sort of way. They went after what they wanted—and that was that.

When coming face-to-face with a wolf, you had to square up and stare them straight in the eye. Running scared was to feel fangs sinking into your skin.

I wasn't going to run.

I set the remains of the box down, dusted off my hands, and straightened the ribbon belt at my waist. I wasn't afraid of this wolf, even if I knew he'd go for the throat if I gave him the chance.

He blinked at me with those eyes, wordlessly repeating his question. He didn't have to do anything but stand there to command my attention and he knew it.

"Did you say something?" I asked. "I couldn't be sure. I heard some grumbly sounds but not actual words. Was that you? With the grumbly sounds? Are you making those noises?"

"You"—he shook both hands at me—"that"—and the disemboweled box—"what-what-what the bloody *hell* are you doing?"

I glanced at the mess in front of me. "Does it truly require explanation or do you simply enjoy having everything narrated for you?"

"Yeah, it requires some fucking explanation, Jasper. Why are you hauling this stuff yourself?"

"Because I can." And I was in no position to hire out for every little job.

He motioned toward the wet, fungal midden. "Obviously not."

"That was the box's malfunction, not mine," I shot back.

"You should not have been moving that box in the first place."

"Unravel that one with me, if you please. First, you're hot and bothered because I wasn't here to handle these things sooner. Then you're mad I came—and stayed. And now you have feelings because I'm taking care of the place? Do I have that right?"

His hands resting on his hips again, he turned a frown up the street. After a pause, he said, "Are there more?"

"Excuse me?"

"Are. There. More." When I didn't respond, he added, "Boxes, Jasper. Are there more boxes you need to be moved?

"Yes, however, I—"

"They're in the basement?"

I glared at him. "I'm not interested in your assistance."

"I'm not interested in watching another moldy carton disintegrate. Holler at me all you want," he said as he took off toward the house. "But that's all you're going to do."

"What business is it of yours?" I called, trailing behind him.

He thundered down the cellar stairs, each booted foot-step smacking the treads like he meant for them to splinter in his wake.

In truth, I was slightly concerned those old stairs would not take kindly to the full force of Linden Santillian. And then what would we do, trapped in this watery grave of a basement? He'd yell, I'd yell, there would be a reason for me to put my hands all over his chest yet again.

Perfect. If perfect was a hell equally as dysfunctional as the one I'd left more than a week ago.

"I would advise you to respond when I ask a question," I said.

"I didn't figure you for a lawyer."

"I'm not."

He scanned the basement. "That's the old, busted water heater."

I followed his gaze to the rusty cylinder of my night-mares. "You're correct."

"*Why* am I correct? Why hasn't it been replaced yet?"

I shook my head. "That's not your concern."

He smiled, his teeth shining at me in the dim subterranean light. "I'm being neighborly."

Oh, he was a wolf all right.

My palms heated as I crossed my arms over my chest to keep from rubbing them on my skirt. "The plumbing needs more involved work than replacing the water heater alone. Something about clay pipes. I don't know. It also seems the electrical system isn't in tip-top condition either, and requires updating before anything else can be installed."

He paced between the tank and the electrical panel with its old knob and tube wiring, silent save for his footsteps against the concrete. "And—and you're still here. You're still staying here."

Of course I was still here. I had nowhere else to go, and a small issue like the absence of hot water was hardly the worst thing I'd ever encountered. I had a free trial membership to a local gym for showers—one not located off those infernal traffic circles—and boiled water for anything else I needed while I cleaned this place up.

"That's plain to see, Linden."

"Fuck me," he muttered, flipping off his hat and running a thick hand through his hair. With that thought behind him, he turned to inspect the items I'd gathered at the base of the stairs for disposal.

As far as I could tell, Midge had made it her mission to keep every copy of *The Boston Globe* printed in the past forty years. The flood destroyed nearly all of them. I couldn't find a reason to save the others.

"This is it? This is what you're putting out on the curb?" he asked.

"Why do you think you can carry them out any more successfully than I can?"

"I don't think I can." He reached down, scooping up two of the oversized boxes off the floor. "I know I can."

He climbed the stairs easily, as if the boxes weighed nothing, leaving me gaping after him. "I've absolutely had it with men," I grumbled to the empty cellar.

I picked through the pile, finding a small box with a relatively dry bottom, and marched up to the main floor. Linden was already outside, the boxes set side by side on the grassy wedge between the street and the sidewalk.

"This is extremely unnecessary," I called to him. "I am capable of doing it myself."

"Sure you are," he replied, passing me on his return route. "This is what it looks like when everything goes to plan."

He was out of earshot, probably hefting three boxes this time, when I whispered, "If you only knew how much this isn't the plan."

He reappeared a moment later and deposited this trip's load without incident. He met my eyes as he prowled back toward the house, an accusation simmering there as if to say, *You can't do this. You can't do anything. You shouldn't even try.*

By the time he'd returned, my anger was percolating. "Why do you find it so offensive that I—what?—clean out my house? What exactly is your problem?"

Linden didn't respond.

It was like he hadn't heard me or he'd decided that listening to me wasn't worth his time.

There was nothing—not a single blessed thing—I hated more than my voice being rendered mute and worthless.

I stepped into his path. "I advised you to answer my questions."

He stared down at me. "I didn't answer because I don't have anything to say that you'd want to hear."

Stepping around me, he walked into the house. My heart was thumping against my breastbone and my stomach had taken on that shaky, shivery quality I'd worked like hell to leave back home in Georgia. My good sense had taken a back seat to my very bad sense, the one that thrived on confrontation, gambles, and games of chicken.

I followed him. I had to. I couldn't leave those comments unaddressed. I'd decided a long, long time ago I wasn't letting anyone stomp all over me anymore and this man didn't get to change my rules because he lived next door.

I barreled down the stairs and parked myself behind Linden. "I'll ask you one more time. What is your problem?"

He glanced at me over his shoulder, his eyeroll undisguised. "Are we still doing this?"

"Yeah, we're doing this. You're in my basement. You can answer a damn question."

He shifted to face me, holding out his hands and letting them drop to his sides. "I'm gonna grab these last two boxes and then I'm leaving. You happy now?"

"Not in the slightest."

He tipped his head to the side as if he needed a better look at me. "Are you really upset about this? Or have you decided this is the sort of thing you want to be upset about and you play the part real good whenever you get the chance? Because it seems like you haven't experienced a true emotion since you realized you can manipulate people with those plastic smiles and fake-sugar comments."

My heart lodged in my throat. I tried but I couldn't speak around it. Couldn't form the only defense I ever had—my words.

"Yeah. That's what I thought." He bent, wrapped his arms around the remaining cartons, and left me alone in the basement.

A minute later, I heard the front door close.

I sat down on the stairs, my elbows on my thighs and my head in my hands. Nothing was working for me this week. Nothing was going right anymore.

First it was the water heater and its assorted problems. This house needed serious work and there was no way I could finance all these projects on my own without steady employment. While I did have a few offers, most of them were of the political commentator variety, but creating a talking head persona out of my on-air scandal wasn't the path for me. I wasn't even particularly good at the mechanics of television—hence the hot-mic screwup—and the idea of it made me cold. Being penned up with the other squawking politicos and scrabbling for five uninterrupted seconds of airtime was my last resort.

I didn't get into politics because I wanted to make it seem like the sky was falling as a result of every little political maneuver. I didn't come here for entrenchment and tribalism, or purity tests.

A long, long time ago, I was an idealist. A believer. I thought change was possible and that people did this work for the purpose of serving the greater good.

A few weeks ago, I was a master campaign strategist. A weapon of political destruction. I had the personal phone numbers of everyone who was anyone and I wasn't afraid to call in favors. All that in my hot little hands.

Now…well, now I was persona non grata in a big way. I was exactly what Linden accused me of being. Everything was an engineered moment, a sound bite, a photo op. Always a political maneuver.

I had a run-down old house which I couldn't afford to repair. Not the big stuff, anyway. If it was only a matter of ripping up the shag carpets and tearing out the weird cabinets, I'd have this locked down. But I couldn't rewire a house or replace turn-of-the-century plumbing.

It was a mess but it wasn't like I could go home. No, home was nothing like Hogwarts—help wasn't granted to those who asked.

Even if I did return to Georgia, my pride and principles slashed and burned, it wouldn't make anything better. I'd get the same old bullshit as always, the same toxic stories about where I belonged, what was good for me, what I deserved, and the same trap of shame and powerlessness.

That place was like falling down a well. I could always see the light but it didn't matter because I'd already screamed myself hoarse and worn my fingers down to the bone trying to climb out.

Home wouldn't help. Even if I was allowed to stay there rent-free—doubtful—I'd be endlessly crucified for everything I'd done since leaving there almost twenty years ago.

Earning a college degree? Elitist.

Working for a progressive candidate? Baby-killing devil worshipper.

Moving to D.C., sharing a bed with a man before marriage? Harlot. I refused to repeat the word they'd use if they knew I'd also shared a bed with a woman before marriage.

Bad-mouthing that candidate's lactose intolerance on live television? Shrew.

That last one though…I wouldn't be able to fight that.

Home wasn't an option, and that was an ancient ache but it didn't trouble me. I'd solved that problem ages ago. There was no sense being sad about it now.

Selling Midge's house *was* an option. Even in this condition, the market was ripe enough to leave me with enough cash to get through a few years without a paycheck. If I played it right and made the place look a little less like a forgotten fallout shelter and more like an exciting fixer-upper opportunity, I'd walk away with enough money to reinvent myself.

All I had to do was bide my time and keep my ear on things, and I'd have my choice of campaign gigs.

That sounded fantastic but it also required me to *sell the house*. To hand it over to someone else and never return again. I wasn't sure I could do that. I wasn't sure I wanted to. It had taken me two years and a personal disaster to acknowledge Midge's death in a real way. Selling her house meant accepting it and I was nowhere near prepared for that.

Hell, I teared up every time I found another Country Crock tub filled with expired coupons or buttons or matches from restaurants she'd visited back when matches were still viable swag. I shed a tear or two when I ripped out the raspberry carpet in her bedroom, which she'd loved and treasured to no end, and again when I found a load of her navy blue nylon knee socks in the dryer, cold and waiting all this time to be paired. I cackled and cried over the boxes of All-Bran in her cupboards and the coffee can of Allen wrenches labeled *L-shape things* under the kitchen sink. And I didn't think I could stay in my skin after discovering the plastic bag filled with all the Mother's Day cards I'd sent her over the years, from the crayon-scrawled homemade ones to the drugstore *For a Special Aunt* variety as I grew up. There were Christmas and birthday cards in there too, and photos my mother must've sent from graduations and other celebrations.

I couldn't walk away from the only safe space I'd ever known, from Midge.

There was no solution to this problem for me, no amount of get-it-done to get this particular task done. I couldn't fix this, and that realization, more than the home I couldn't return to and the aunt I couldn't say goodbye to and the gut-punch email I'd ignored for nine days, knocked the air out of me.

SEVEN
LINDEN

Well, I was an asshole.

I'd known it when I stomped up those basement stairs. Known it when I cleaned up the mess from the broken box. Known it when I'd hopped in my truck and drove to the liquor store forty-five minutes away, the one that stocked the good white ale from Clown Shoes Brewery. And I knew it when I looked out my kitchen window and caught sight of Jasper sitting on her back porch, her shoulders shaking in the unmistakable shudder that accompanied sobs.

That was my fault. All my damn fault.

I didn't stop to think. I hooked my fingers around the beers and made a beeline across the backyard. I didn't know what I was going to say but I knew I couldn't watch anymore. I couldn't do it earlier today, I couldn't do it now. And maybe that meant I was all the things Jasper accused me of being. Maybe I was a terrible neighbor. But I couldn't sit back and watch her cry out here, all alone.

She sat on the edge of the porch, her legs folded in front of her and one arm banded over her waist while she kneaded her forehead with the other hand. Loud, hiccupping sobs filled the night air—and made my arrival more stealthy than I'd intended.

I had to announce myself. It was that or wait until her tears slowed enough to notice me here, standing sentry to her meltdown.

Couldn't do that either. I couldn't just *be* here, I had to *do* something.

What the literal fuck was wrong with me? For real. What the fuck.

I set the beer down on the porch's battered floor, hard enough to grab her attention. "Hey, Jasper." I snagged a folded bandana from my back pocket and held it out to her as she lifted her head. "Sorry about, you know, everything."

She plucked the bandana from me and pressed it to her face. "Oh my god. Linden, seriously, I can't right now."

"I'm not—"

"Can we do this tomorrow? Please?"

I shook my head. "I'm trying to tell you—"

"I can't fight with you tonight and I can't just sit here and take it while you yell at me either."

I sank down beside her. "Would you shut up for a minute?" She sniffled. "I brought beer."

She dropped the bandana, just enough to eye the quartet of tall cans. Her brows lifted before she resumed mopping her face. A time that bordered on painfully long passed with only the sounds of early night mingled with her sniffles and shuddered breaths between us. It was a warm evening for this point in September, the breeze mild and dry. Hoots and calls echoed from the forest.

Then, "I have wine." Jasper held up an unopened bottle. "I don't need your beer."

"When did I say I was sharing any with you? I just said I brought it."

This pulled a splashy, hiccupping laugh from Jasper. "I can live with that. If you'd brought a cheese plate and refused to share, things might be different."

"That's your end zone? A cheese plate?"

"Oh, yeah. I'd fight you for that." She patted the porch floor, its paint nothing more than a faded suggestion of color now. "No one sits on my ramshackle porch without sharing their cheese with me."

I cast a glance over the structure, its wood planks rotted in some spots, warped and jutting up from the surface at others. "Goddamn, this place is one problem child after another."

Her shoulders shook as she pressed the cloth to her eyes again but her sobs seemed to mingle with laughter this time. "It's like you're physically incapable of keeping these observations to yourself, Linden." She glanced over at me. "Like, for once, do you think you could not call out my shit? Just once?"

"I didn't mean—"

"I know what you meant. You came over here after being in your clean, sturdy house with its fancy hot water and reliable electricity, and you can't *not* stare at the deck that's five minutes from collapsing under us."

I freed one of the beers from its ring and popped it open. "Sorry about that. And what I said earlier too."

Jasper dropped the cloth to her lap and shifted to face me. "Is that why you came over? Because you thought I was —I was upset about this afternoon?"

I jerked my shoulders up in agreement as I sipped.

"I wasn't crying because of anything you said." She

reached back, grabbed the wine bottle by the neck. "I was crying because I don't have a corkscrew."

That didn't make sense. Not even a little bit of sense. No one became this upset over inaccessible wine.

I set my beer down and pushed off the porch to reach into my back pocket. "I can take care of that for you."

"Why am I not surprised to hear this?"

I pried open my Swiss Army knife and beckoned for the bottle. "You could've come next door and asked to borrow a corkscrew."

With the cork freed, Jasper held out her empty glass. "The last time I went over there, you insulted my baking."

"Your baking insulted me," I replied, filling her glass.

"See? This is why I didn't ask you. I didn't need another round of unwelcome commentary."

I returned to my spot on the porch floor while Jasper tucked into her wine. "You would've changed your mind about that if I had a cheese plate."

"Do you?"

I mentally paged through the contents of my refrigerator. There wasn't much. "No."

"Don't tease a girl like that. Can't you see I'm up to my ears in issues, Linden? Don't dangle cheese in front of me unless you have the goods."

She wasted no time putting that wine away and soon held out her glass for a refill. "There's this little market around the corner from my apartment. They sell cheese plates for one. Just a little assortment of cheeses, some apple slices and fig jam, a bit of bread and nuts. Whenever I was in town and had the night off, I'd pick up one of those. Even knowing exactly what was in it, I don't think I could perfectly recreate it. I don't know why. It just wouldn't come out the same."

"Really is your end zone," I murmured.

She replied with a quick shrug. "You don't have to stay. You've uncorked my wine and saved me from attempting to saber it with the axe I found in the garage—"

"Jesus Christ, Jasper."

"—which is an adequate apology for your little rant today."

"Please don't use that axe for—for anything. Okay?"

"I do not need your permission." She turned her gaze toward me now, her brows lifted and her eyes softer than I'd ever seen them before. Probably the wine at work. That was it. Nothing else. "This thing really is five minutes from falling apart, isn't it?"

I glanced around the weathered structure. "Yeah."

"It took me most of the week just to fix up the side steps, and since we're on the topic, why does a small house need so many entry points? The side door, the back door, the front door. It's bananas. Just one door, in and out, that's all I need." She frowned at the floor. "It would take all month to tackle this thing. My god." Her frown deepened. "I guess I have the time. There's gotta be a YouTube tutorial for it."

"Is that what you were hammering? Those little stairs on the other side?"

She nodded slowly. "Mmhmm. Since I was replacing the broken glass in the door, it seemed like the next logical task."

"How'd it go?"

"I only did it wrong three times. I think that's probably good." She cut a look in my direction. "You were listening to my banging?"

Two things were true right now. One, Jasper was a *mess*.

A *hot* mess but a mess nonetheless. I'd lived a lot of low days, and I knew breakdowns like the one I walked into weren't the result of a missing corkscrew.

And two, I didn't hate her when we were sitting here and talking like this. I didn't hate anything right now.

"Couldn't miss it if I'd tried."

"Still not sure why it bothers you so much that I'm here."

"It doesn't *bother* me," I replied quickly. It bothered me in many complicated ways, none of which I could explain to myself, let alone Jasper. "I'm…I'm concerned. This place is in bad shape. I wouldn't be comfortable staying here for long." Since I enjoyed making things worse, I couldn't stop myself from adding, "I wouldn't let my sister stay here."

Jasper took a sip, blinked at me over the rim of her glass. I could almost sense her coiling up to strike—and seeing as I was more than a little perverted when it came to this woman, my pulse quickened in anticipation.

"You have a sister."

"Yeah. Magnolia. We're triplets."

"Triplets," she repeated, nodding. "Well, that's nice."

"Something like that."

"And you decide where and how this sister spends her time?"

I almost—*almost*—said Magnolia had a husband for that now but stopped myself with a long pull of my beer. Now empty, I set it aside and reached for another. "If my sister was living in this place, I'd get my ass over here and help her fix it up. It's the right thing to do."

"Is it though? I'm sure your sister is capable of looking after herself or requesting support when she needs it. Why is it incumbent upon you to insert yourself into the situation?"

"You're missing the point."

She shook her head. "I think I'm seeing it rather clearly."

"You're seeing what you're choosing to see. Sometimes it's not that complicated. It's helping someone out, even if they have a hard time asking for that help." Before she could interject with another twisted remark, I added, "You know who always inserted herself into situations? Midge. The first year I lived here, I couldn't get her to leave me alone. I started thinking I'd made a huge mistake buying my place because I couldn't go a day without her banging on my front door over one thing or another."

Jasper wanted to continue debating me. She wanted to make her point and make it hard enough to be sure it stuck. I saw it in the way her lips parted, poised to fire back with another explainer on my overbearing behavior. It was in her eyes too, narrowed in contempt. And her hands, my god. Her hands were frozen in an *I'll explain your problems to you* gesture.

Yet she dropped those hands to her lap. "What? Why?"

"Any number of reasons. She was going to drag the weed whacker out of the shed, did I mind if she trimmed around my driveway? She had an extra jug of milk, did I need some? She thought her electricity was flickering, was mine? And whatever it was, she was mad about it. Like, the power had personally offended her by going out for a second and she wanted to recruit allies for the fight."

"That sounds like Midge."

"It took some getting used to. When I moved here, the last thing I expected was a neighbor who yelled at me when she had extra milk. It was so confusing."

"Tell me more."

"She was very concerned that I'd be hosting a lot of loud parties. She provided me with a copy of the town's noise ordinance and the fines for violations so I knew she meant business."

"That old bird loved her ordinances and bylaws, didn't she? I keep finding town council meeting agendas covered in her notes and remarks for the public comment sessions." Jasper laughed, her eyes warm and her mouth soft. The beauty of it hurt. It made me ache. "I went to a few of them with her when I was a kid. She said it was important to keep a close watch on elected officials because they lost their sense and their spines when they got elected but they grew an iron grip on the purse strings."

"She'd bang on my door at the crack of fucking dawn to give me a rundown of the meeting the night before and—"

"She didn't know how to sleep in! She didn't know how to get a minute more than her six and a half hours of sleep and there was no way in hell she'd just lie in bed for an extra hour."

I refilled Jasper's glass when she pushed it toward me. "Loved mowing the lawn at six in the morning on Saturdays. It was religion to her."

Jasper was quiet for a minute as she considered the wine. "She had such a good heart. Even when she was impossible. Even with all her nutty quirks. She'd help anyone, anytime."

Even if they said they didn't want it.

As much as I needed Jasper to face that fact, neither of us were going to be proving any points tonight. We'd stopped hurling insults and we'd managed to share each other's presence without resorting to violence. And seeing as Jasper was gut-twistingly beautiful with her blotchy cheeks, swollen eyes, and slightly buzzed smile, I'd swallow my own fist if it meant a few more minutes with her, just like this.

"I'll drink to that," I said, lifting my beer.

"To Midge's good heart," Jasper replied, leaning in to clink her glass against the can.

That was what should've happened. A light tap, wineglass to beer can, a toast sealed.

That wasn't what happened.

I angled my beer the wrong way. She came in too hard. Beer, wine, and shattered glass went everywhere.

She shrieked. "Oh my god."

"Okay, it's fine, don't move until I clear the glass."

"What did you do?"

"What did *I* do? You smashed your glass—"

"You were too close!"

"I was exactly as close as I was when I raised my beer."

"Okay so I'll address that later but now I'm bleeding. Ohhhh, wow. Oh, that's some blood."

"Oh fuck, you're bleeding." I glanced up at Jasper's face and found her pale, her eyes glazed. I pushed off the porch and reached for her, one hand on her elbow, one on the small of her back. "We're going to my place and taking care of this. Come on, this way. Don't look at it. I mean it, looking at it won't help."

"You're asking me to ignore the blood gushing out of my hand. That seems like a poorly formed choice."

"I saw the way your eyes crossed back there. Maybe you can hang with bats but something tells me blood is off-limits."

"I'm not comfortable with you being right," she replied. "It's like writing with the wrong hand."

"Sure it is, sweetheart." I led her into my house through the deck, not stopping to switch on the living room lights as we made our way into the kitchen. "Here we are."

Holding her by the waist, I lifted her to sit on the countertop. I held her injured hand over the sink and flipped on the tap, passing my fingers under the stream to test the temperature.

"What gives you the impression I want to be manhandled?"

I couldn't stop the laugh rumbling up from my chest. "Oh, there's a few things." I brought her hand to the water. "Hold still. Let me wash this out."

She obeyed this request but couldn't find it in her to stop arguing while I used both of my hands to gently lather the soap. "We've had a number of conversations where I've made it clear I am not a fan of your hard-headed"—I laughed again because *fuck*, she did not know the hard half of it—"meddlesome, antiquated attitude."

"I'm gonna stop you right there. Not because I see it differently, not because I've had legitimate reasons for everything I've done, and not because it's possible you're wrong about me."

She peered at me, a cute little crease forming between her brows. "Then why?"

"Because I've cleaned your cuts and they're mostly minor but the first aid kit is in my bathroom. I need you to tell me whether I can leave you here for a minute. I don't want you passing out in my kitchen. That would be worse than another one of your banana breads, and for both of us. The floor is hard. It will hurt. I'll have to pick you up and I'll probably have to drag your ass to a clinic."

"Is being an asshole part of the treatment?"

"Nah, that comes free for you." I wrapped a paper towel around her hand and elevated her forearm above her head. It was more about keeping the blood out of sight than any crazy amount of bleeding. "Stay just like that. Don't move. Not even to yell at me."

The bathroom was only a few steps away and it didn't take more than a minute for me to grab the kit and return to Jasper but it was long enough for me to remember how all this started. I went to her because I'd been out of line earlier. Even if it bothered the hell out of me that she had to do all this work alone. Even if there was *clearly* much more to her situation than she was sharing. Even if sparring with her filled me with perverted joy.

Fuck. Especially then.

It wasn't my business to call her out. I didn't have the right to criticize her as I had.

This, plus the fact nothing good would come from pursuing my neighbor, shifted my thinking enough to stuff away any notions of keeping our flirty, fiery banter going tonight.

Until I caught sight of Jasper bathed in the warm glow of the kitchen light, her hair tucked back behind her ears, and the skirt of her dress hiked barely above her slightly spread knees.

There was nothing specifically amazing about it but maybe that was what made it amazing. She was gorgeous and freaked out by blood and maybe a little drunk too. And she was in my kitchen, waiting for me to help her.

There was nothing else in the universe I wanted right now. Not a single thing.

"I'm impressed," I said, stalking toward her while a hot tingle spiraled through my muscles. "You followed directions. Is that a first?"

Her face brightened in a rueful smile. "It might very well be. I'm not one for coloring inside the lines."

I wrapped my fingers around her elbow and took my time skimming them up to her wrist. Her skin was unreal. So soft, so smooth. I could lose a day to the creamy expanse of her forearm.

"Stopped bleeding," I said as I peeled back the paper towel. "Some antiseptic, a couple of Band-Aids, and you'll be hammering away in no time." I blotted the cuts on her palm once more. "Maybe not first thing tomorrow morning though."

She shook her head, her gaze fixed on mine. "Not tomorrow morning."

I couldn't look away. Couldn't even breathe.

"Do you want me to do it?" Her eyes widened at my question. "The antiseptic. And the bandages. Do you want me to do this for you? So you don't have to look?"

Her lips parted on a fast breath. She nodded but then stopped herself, saying, "It's okay. I can do it."

"I know you can." I gave her wrist a squeeze that fell somewhere between comfort and restraint. I didn't know what I wanted to give her more. "There's nothing you can't do, Jas, but there's nothing wrong with letting someone else deal with the problems for a minute. Especially the gory ones."

"That sounds all well and good but it's never that easy. Never."

She ducked her head down, out of the overhead light's glow, as her eyes grew shiny. Whether it was alcohol or emotion, she didn't want me to see.

I thumbed open the antiseptic cream. "I'm not gonna prove you wrong."

"Because it's the truth," she muttered, her gaze still averted as I dabbed the cream on her palm. "People don't usually do it right. When they deal with the problems, I mean."

"I'm actually going to agree with you on this one."

She jerked her head up. "I'm not sure how to respond to that. What do we do now? We can't just…agree."

I swept a bit of extra cream off her palm and wiped my hands on the paper towel. "You know the saying. 'If you want something done right, you have to do it yourself.' You probably have it inked somewhere." I lifted her wrist, gently twisted her arm to inspect the underside. "Not here. Maybe the other one." I ran my hand down the opposite arm. "Nope. Not there either." I dropped my hand to her knee, stroked my thumb in the tender hollow there. "Come on. Where is it?"

"No tattoos. Hate to disappoint." A lazy smile stretched across her lips.

I eyed her up and down. "You're sure about that? I could check for you."

Her cheeks heated and she giggled, a sound so strange and novel that I found myself laughing too. "You could look but you won't find anything."

"And now I'm back to disagreeing with you because I would find plenty, Jasper." I tickled the back of her knee. "*Plenty.*"

I held her gaze for a heavy moment before turning my attention to the first aid kit. I had to find a bandage to protect the span of her palm while these cuts healed.

"Out of curiosity, did you find anything when you grabbed my breast? You know, last week at the front door?"

"Shit. I am sorry about that."

"Don't be. My elbow was…"

"Oh, I know where your elbow was that day. I know *all about* that elbow."

She rubbed her temple, saying, "Glad I made a good impression."

"Are you holding up all right?" I ripped open the bandage's wax paper packaging. "Not too woozy? Not going to pass out on me?"

"I was never going to pass out on you," she replied, tart as ever.

"Course not."

"I just get a little lightheaded when there's a lot of blood. I don't see much of it," she mused. "It's funny since my work tends to be something of a blood sport. Metaphorically speaking."

I smoothed the bandage into place, my thumb passing over the adhesive several times. "What is it you do when you're not replacing rotted staircases?"

"It's not interesting."

My thumb still stroking her hand, I glanced at her, my brows arched. "Who said it has to be?"

She looked down at the bandage and pushed her lips out in a pout. I wanted to bite that pout right off her.

"I'm going to have to bake you something new," she said.

Oh, fuck, no. Please no. "Why?"

She jerked her chin up, in the direction of her injured hand. "For that. For helping me. *Again.*"

Now that her hand was treated, I stepped between her legs. "Just being neighborly."

She brought her hand to my chest, pressed it to the center of my breastbone. Tilting her head back, she gazed up at me, her lips barely parted. With the light bouncing off her honey hair, she looked like magic. Like the magic that existed in certain golden-limned corners of the forest, warm and electric and infinite. Like the vulnerability and defiance of pure, unburdened nature.

And I still wanted to bite that pout.

I pushed my fingers through her hair and sealed my mouth to hers. A squeak sounded in her throat but she twisted my t-shirt around her fingers and kissed me back with the same zeal she brought to arguing about anything. I leaned in, pressing hard against the cradle of her thighs, and drew my hands down her torso. She was a dream of ripe, rich curves and the sort of softness that didn't seem possible when considered alongside the hard edges she'd sharpened to a point. I shoved both hands under her backside, boosting her up and holding her tight against me. She responded by yanking my shirt up and baring my belly, and squeezing her knees to my hips like she planned on riding me right here.

Yeah, she could crack the earth open. She could snap me in half. She could do *anything* she wanted and I'd let her. I'd fucking let her.

And right now, she wanted this.

"Jasper," I breathed, edging back just enough to meet her dreamy gaze.

Her hands still in my shirt, her knees still trapping me inside her thighs, she lifted her gaze to me and said, "Linden, I-I'm married."

EIGHT
JASPER

LINDEN BACKED AWAY FROM ME, HIS HANDS RAISED AND HIS eyes wide.

Every inch of my body screamed for his heat and closeness now that it was gone but I had to say it. His hands in my hair and the hard ridge of him against my belly turned my thoughts to applesauce—which never happened, not even the time I was loaded up on sedatives for a root canal and I'd given the oral surgeon a thorough explanation as to why he was supporting the wrong candidate in the D.C. mayoral race. I stopped going for spa days and getting massages because the technicians always commented on my steel-tight shoulders as if it was my fault I carried a lot of stress in my body.

There was never a time when I wasn't on. Even in my dreams, I had poised, on-message conversations. It was as ridiculous as it sounded but it was my reality. I never forgot myself, never blurted things out.

And yet… "You're *married?*"

There were several ways to spin this because not all

marriages were formed alike, and mine—what remained of it—met only the barest definition. But my mind had stopped working the way it always did around the time Linden plopped me on the countertop and it went fully offline when he secured that Band-Aid in place. I didn't understand how someone running water over my hand could make me feel like I was floating. And also melting. And maybe conducting electricity through my skin.

It wasn't sexual. Even when Linden's touch lingered longer than necessary, that didn't hit me as hard as the attention he put into that touch. Into *me*. I couldn't remember a time I'd felt this way. I would've known if I'd experienced this before. Would've remembered it.

And that was how I ruined a perfectly scalding kiss with a poorly timed announcement of my current marital status.

"Yes. I am."

Linden shoved his hands in his pockets, the front of his jeans still bulging with the thickness I'd savored moments ago. He gave a quick shake of his head, saying, "That's— that's not what I expected." Before I could explain or qualify the matter, he continued. "I'll walk you home."

"You don't have to do that."

"I don't," he said, shifting to pack away the first aid supplies. "But I'm going to."

Instinct told me to fight this point but I couldn't put any words together. I pushed off the counter and stepped toward the door leading to the deck.

Linden led the way out of his house, the night darkness now heavy and cool. He maintained a measured distance between us, his hands stowed in his pockets once again. We were a few steps away from my porch, the rusty old overhead lamp still giving off a faint light and our drinks still abandoned on the floor, when I said, "It's over. My marriage, I mean. He's not part of my life…anymore."

Somehow, this had no impact on Linden. He grunted out a disinterested "Uh-huh" and skirted the perimeter of the porch. "I'll deal with the broken glass."

"You've done enough. I can clean up the glass. It's my glass."

"Not with one hand, you won't. Take the night off, would you?"

I recoiled at the idea of anyone cleaning up after me but a sudden wave of drowsiness washed over me and I couldn't assemble a decent fight. Or the energy to figure out where I'd left the dustpan.

When we reached the short set of steps at the side of the porch, the ones I'd replaced three times more than necessary, Linden turned to face me. "All right, Jasper. Listen. I'm due down in Marion tomorrow morning and I'll be on the Cape most of the day. Earliest I'll be back is five, maybe six o'clock. I'll leave the back door open. Come over and use the shower, washer and dryer, whatever you need. The Wi-Fi password is on the refrigerator. Just do me a favor and come over. No banana bread necessary."

I nearly laughed at the implication of Linden inviting me into his house *only* when he wouldn't be there. No awkward bathrobe moments for anyone! "You don't have to—"

"Could we press pause on your survival mode for one minute? Believe me, I know you can do everything and you don't need anyone and help is unwelcome. I get that, Peach. Loud and fucking clear."

I fiddled with the belt at my waist. "Okay." Since I could not leave it at that, I added, "There's nothing wrong with relying on myself. Men do it all the time without anyone making an issue of it. When women do it, they need someone to ride to their rescue."

He stepped back, shaking his head as he stared into the forest. "There's a difference between relying on yourself and insisting you don't need anyone under any circumstance." He waved an irritable hand at the house. "It just means you went through a fuckton of shit alone and haven't realized it's not supposed to be that way." He shot a brief glance at me. "Lock up, okay? I'll handle the glass."

For the second time today, Linden Santillian walked away from me after bullet-pointing my problems.

It was funny, really. That used to be my job.

As I watched him dissolving into the darkness, I considered chasing after him, telling him all the ways in which he was wrong and drawing a few lines in the sand. Sharing one kiss was not an invitation to pick apart my life. He didn't know me. He didn't know anything. He saw what he wanted to see, and made his faulty interpretations based on that. He didn't know the first thing about me.

But I didn't chase after him. Didn't call out with my objections. I folded my arms over my torso and went inside. A significant part of me was still floating, melting, conducting electricity, but another part of me needed to curl up into a ball and block it all out.

Still wearing today's dress, I dropped onto my bed and pulled a quilt over me. I needed a minute before washing my face and changing into pajamas. Just a minute to settle down. A minute to stop that shaky, shivery feeling from words that had sliced down to the bone.

———

The next morning, I watched as Linden lumbered out his front door, oversized travel mug grasped in his oversized hand. I ran my thumb over the bandage on my palm, remembering the feel of those fingers on my skin.

He climbed into his truck without so much as a glance in my direction. Not that he would've seen me anyway. The folding television table and kitchen chair I'd positioned perpendicular to the front window gave me a perfect blend of sunlight and invisibility.

I paused, my pen frozen over the notebook dedicated to lists, staring as he backed out of the driveway and drove up the street. When the truck's taillights disappeared, I set the pen down and picked up my phone from the makeshift desk.

I avoided calling my mother even when my life wasn't in disarray. I had my reasons just as she had her reasons for allowing that avoidance to grow into distance.

She lived outside Seattle with a man named Martin Mayo. He was a commercial airline pilot with thirteen years on her, she was a first-class flight attendant, and they vacationed in places like Singapore and Seoul and drove matching seven-series BMWs. That was how it was with them. High cotton.

All of which was a long way of saying my mother could help me out with money if I ever asked but I wouldn't ask. Not while I could manage to sublet my Georgetown apartment and I was able to leave my retirement account untouched. I'd raid that fund before I made a request of my mother. Hell, I'd probably sell my plasma *and* harvest my eggs before I asked my mother for anything.

She'd spent enough time worrying over me and money. I didn't want her worrying now, not when she had a new car every three years and a month-long vacation on the Java coast. Not when things were finally good for her.

And that was one of the reasons I'd ignored her calls over the past few weeks and replied to her text messages with quick, vague nonsense like *I have a lot of plates spinning right now. Talk soon!* and *Service is super spotty here! I'll check back in when I know I won't immediately drop your call, okay?* and *It's all good, just making some moves.*

I couldn't keep that up much longer. Her last message had mentioned something about a fruit bouquet being refused delivery at my apartment building. She wanted to know where I was if I wasn't living in D.C. anymore and I supposed that was fair.

My phone pressed to my ear, I paced the front room while the morning sun streamed in, warm and so blindingly bright I had to shield my eyes. The call connected, ringing only twice before she answered with, "Hello? Hello, are you there? Hello?"

Through the line, I heard, "What's going on, Tawney? Who is it?"

I sighed. "Mom?"

"Jasper? Where in the world are you?"

Her pointed tone stopped me and I turned to face the window. I had to close my eyes against the sun's rays. "I'm at Midge's house, Mom."

I heard a door close and some rustling, and while it was early on the West Coast, I knew I hadn't woken her. She went to exercise classes first thing. Spinning, Zumba, Pilates. Things like that. Things that comfortably wealthy women enjoyed early in the morning.

"Will you tell me if you're all right? I've been trying to reach you."

The sun heated my face and neck. "I'm okay. I'm just taking a break from things."

There was a heavy pause where I could almost see my mother twisting her hair around her index finger. Eventually, she said, "So, you're in Massachusetts."

"I'm just taking a quick break," I said again. "I'll get back into the swing of things soon." When she didn't respond, I went on. "I wanted to leave Timbrooks, you know. I started planning my exit last winter."

That was true in the sense I'd sat on the floor of my bathroom and cried for twenty minutes before work one morning last January after waking up to a dozen rage-filled emails from a dozen different ragey people. I didn't know that wasn't a normal way to start the day. I figured everyone cried all the time. That was the definition of adulting, right?

"I know you always have a plan," she said, the uncertainty dripping from her words.

"Oh, I do. I definitely do. I'm looking at some consulting opportunities. I have a lot of interest from media outlets as well. I have a lot to choose from."

"Is that what you want?"

"Of course it is," I said quickly. I didn't recognize my voice. It sounded hollow. "Why wouldn't it be?"

"I don't know. I'm just asking."

We were silent a moment, the sun still blazing over my face. I knew my cheeks would be pink when I stepped away from this window.

Then, "I'm all right, Mom. Really. I'm just taking a break."

"And Preston?"

Please don't go blowing that storm in. "Taking a break from him too."

"You're sure you're all right?"

"I am. I'm actually really busy with projects here." I glanced at the ceiling, which needed several coats of paint. "Really busy."

"How's the house?"

"It's a little worse for the wear but I don't mind. It's amusing, you know, working on little updates, little projects. It's mostly painting, ripping up old carpeting, cleaning out the basement."

I didn't mention the bats. It didn't seem like a necessary detail. Neither did the husky woodsman next door. Didn't need to talk about him at all.

"I miss her," Mom said softly. "I wish I'd visited more. Called more. Letters and emails weren't enough."

I felt a sudden rush of tears stinging my eyes. "Me too."

"I regret it," she said. "Not spending more time with her. That's the shitty price of grief. You're always left with one regret or another and it never leaves you alone."

I didn't want to talk about regrets. "Mmhmm."

"I'm not sure I could do what you're doing," she said. "So many memories. I couldn't possibly go through her things. It's just too hard."

"I haven't started working on her room yet. Not more than pulling up the carpet because it was musty."

"It takes a lot out of you," she said. "You need to be ready for it."

My face was so hot. I knew I wouldn't burn from a few minutes in front of a window but it felt like I might. "Yeah, well, I have some calls to return today and I should probably get to that. There's a think tank looking to talk to me about some of their strategic priorities and I need to look over my notes."

"I understand," she said. "Call me, okay? Let me know if anything changes or...or you need anything."

I turned away from the window and headed into the kitchen. "All right, Mom. I will."

I wouldn't. I didn't need her or anyone else, and that wasn't about to change. Just like I wasn't about to stop thanking Linden for his generosity with some homemade goodies.

The oven was still acting fritzy so I was relying on my crockpot to cook two small pecan pies this morning. I'd never made pie dough before, not on my own, but what else was there to do after waking up at daybreak, yesterday's clothes plastered to my body and the memory of a breath-taking kiss buzzing on my lips?

I didn't have the exact ingredients required by the recipe but I knew enough about pecan pie to wing it. I'd seen it done plenty of times. After growing up on a three-hundred-year-old pecan farm, I knew a thing or two about making these pies.

Linden would like them. He looked like the kind of man who enjoyed a good slab of pie. He probably liked cheddar folded into the crust of an apple pie. The senator from Vermont always served cheddar crust apple pie—all from his home state—at special gatherings for his staff. It was legendary.

After making an unpleasant story about his daughter hazing sorority pledges go away, I always received an invite to those gatherings.

I did in my past life.

That senator forgot my name weeks ago. Even if his daughter was caught on tape making a pledge choke on a strap-on again, he wouldn't call me. No one was calling me, not even the think tank I'd mentioned to my mother. My scandal made me radioactive and I was nowhere near the half-life of my toxicity to fix anyone else's.

The pies looked ready so I pulled them out to cool. Linden would like these. He'd do it grudgingly but he'd do it.

I returned to the front window, glancing toward his driveway to confirm he hadn't circled back for some reason. A lucky chainsaw or…whatever arborists used. Finding the driveway empty, I swung my tote bag over my shoulder and hefted my laundry basket. I'd come back for the pies after I'd showered and the wash was running.

While rolling out dough, I'd decided I'd only use Linden's shower. There was a perfectly good laundromat nearby. But going to the laundromat and sitting there through the wash and dry cycles would eat into my day, and I'd decided I was very, very busy handling Midge's affairs. Too busy to sit in a hard plastic chair and scroll through emails that seemed to take a cherry pitter to my soul.

There was the hate mail. The people hopped up on contempt and condemnation because I'd joked about the senator's digestive distress. I should know better and I was a whore and they hoped I died. Some even offered to help me with the last one.

There were the late-night talk show requests. Those bookers did not stop. They wanted me to spill tea and shit-talk all of Washington, and basically turn myself into a precious little dancing monkey who didn't care if she ever got a job again.

There were the interview requests from across the print journalism spectrum. *People*, *Us Weekly*, *The Wall Street Journal*, *The Washington Post*. All the Georgia papers. They wanted an act of contrition or a tell-all, and nothing in between. And print was desperately unforgiving. Everyone thought television edited with a hatchet but that was print.

The broadcast journalists came at me hard. They promised to let me tell my story and offered to paint me as a staffer forced to work in a hostile environment, but I knew better. Those stories were only meant for individuals needing to save face after stepping in problematic mud. They didn't work on people who'd stepped in the mud, tracked it through the house, and found themselves disowned on television. Besides, the only time a woman could sit for one of those interviews was after she'd been fucked over and fired or forced out, and now had a book or documentary on the fuck-over to promote. I had neither.

Yet cable news hosts, the source of this scandal, were the worst of them. They didn't say it in their emails but it was clear they wanted me to unleash on live television again. They wanted the same unfiltered, insider info I accidentally blabbed when I should've been talking about states closing polling locations and making it harder for people to vote.

For every thirty messages I had from the media, I had one vague response from my contacts at consulting or lobbying firms, or political action committees.

If I had to guess, my inquiries were handled something like this: "Jasper-Anne Cleary? She's one helluva campaign strategist. But isn't she the one who went on TV and complained about Timbrooks? And said he had no chance of placing in the primaries? Hmm. No thanks. Whatever she's asking, we can't answer. No turncoats on this team. Send the thanks-but-no-thanks."

Radioactive was a dark place to be.

I'd run the numbers enough times to know I could

manage six months without a paycheck before dipping into that retirement account if I held my expenses to the barest minimum, never, ever got sick, and continuously sublet my D.C. apartment for a slight bit more than my rent.

Saving two dollars a week on the laundromat wasn't big money but there was no reason to sniff at small money. Same with forgoing a gym membership for showers. It wasn't like I was going to exercise there anyway. Stomp-walking in heels used to get my heart rate up. Now, I sparred with my hot, husky neighbor.

As I stepped through the door off his extremely enviable deck, my gaze immediately landed on the kitchen counter that haunted my unfulfilling dreams. Things could've gone much differently if I hadn't chosen that moment to drop that bomb.

And Linden wasn't going to let me forget that moment because he'd left a notepad propped up against a fruit bowl, *Jasper* scrawled in big, blocky letters across the top in case I had any doubts about where he wanted my attention.

"Mmhmm. This is great. Not passive-aggressive at all." I set my basket on the table and grabbed the notepad.

Jasper.
The bathroom is through the door directly behind you and the laundry is in the basement. The door is on the other side of the bedroom. Help yourself to the supplies, or anything else you need. I'll be out from ten to four tomorrow. The door will be open. Don't even think about baking another biohazard. Poisoning is not neighborly.
–L

"You'll have a new tune after you try my pies," I muttered.

Since I wanted to get in and out long before Linden arrived home, I dropped the notepad and headed toward the basement. Unlike mine, it smelled clean and dry. A metal shelving structure running the length of the far wall held tidy rows of boxes and tools. Everything was so precise and not at all fungal. I loved it, not because I harbored a deep need for organization (I did not) but because it was so vividly Linden. Everything in its spot, everything the way it should be. Order and structure and utility. Nothing fouling the system.

It was another one of the many reasons why Linden and I would never work, even on a short-term, fling basis. He craved that structure and I excelled in structure's fault lines.

Last night was a mistake. Talking on the porch and sharing memories of Midge was good but the rest of it was another strike in my poor judgment column. It was strange to keep fucking up. This wasn't how I existed. Aside from getting married to someone I didn't love the right way, I'd never made such significant mistakes—and so many of them.

What was wrong with me? Why was I wrecking my career and throwing myself at a man who was all wrong for me? Not to mention doing it while my marriage was still on the books.

It was like I *wanted* my life to implode. That was ridiculous, of course. "Completely ridiculous," I murmured as I loaded my clothes into the washer. "Completely."

I chewed on this as I climbed the stairs, carried my tote

into the bathroom, and turned on the taps. I had no reason to torpedo my life. It didn't make sense. I didn't actually want any of this to happen.

I was thirty-five and steering the direction of major campaigns. I was well-known and highly regarded in some of Washington's most powerful circles.

I had a cozy apartment in Georgetown and enough friends with summer homes up and down the eastern seaboard to have my pick of summertime destinations. What more could I ever want?

Yes, my primary purpose for those in power was inventing ways to keep them in power and extinguishing any challenge to that power. It wasn't pretty and it wasn't fun but it was the task I'd accepted.

And yes, the apartment was unspeakably expensive for its dime-sized space but that was Beltway real estate for you.

I didn't get any time for summer getaways to the shore either but that was the price I paid for being successful. The reward for hard work was more hard work, not a trip to the Hamptons.

As for friends, they were scarce these days. I'd expected more from them but that was my fault. I knew better than to expect anything from anyone. They'd always let you down.

All of this at thirty-five didn't resemble much of an achievement these days. Those years didn't add up to much when I looked back on them. I had an absentee marriage and hardly any reliable family to speak of.

There was a time when I told myself my turn would come. That everything would fall into place for me. My marriage would right itself, the work would slow down enough for me to breathe, and I'd find all the things I craved but never let myself need.

I'd find my place and my people, and then things would begin for me.

Now, with thirty-five slipping out of my grasp, I wasn't sure about my turn anymore. I was going back to square one with everything. If I had to spend five or ten years rebuilding, where did that leave me?

I knew little of hobbies, and my entire personal network was a product of my profession, and none of that seemed like a problem until now. If anything, it had been a badge of honor. *Look, I'm so deep into this, I can't recognize myself without it!*

My life was my work but I didn't have my work anymore and I didn't know what to do with myself except keep going.

Replace some stairs, bake a pie, kiss a neighbor. Just keep going —and don't think too hard about it.

Once I was bathed and dressed, my hair twisted into a low bun that would dry into loose curls, I tossed my wash into the dryer. Linden's high-end machines were a big improvement over the industrial whales at the laundromat. His entire house was a big improvement with its amazing river rock shower and the bold blue walls. I couldn't stop thinking about the precision of it all. The basement, the colors, the décor. *Precise.*

"That's why he hated my banana bread," I sang to myself on the walk across our yards. "And everything else I've brought his way."

When I returned to Linden's house with the cooled pies, I tore off his note and wrote one in response.

Linden,
Poisoning might not be neighborly but pecan pie is. Please enjoy

these treats as a small thanks for allowing me into your enormous
shower. I'd ask who designed it but you're very sensitive about
these things. Enjoy my pie.
~ Jasper

I GATHERED UP MY BASKET AND BAG, AND CROSSED THROUGH
the backyard, a grin warm on my face.

———

WHEN I STEPPED INTO LINDEN'S HOUSE THE NEXT MORNING,
there was another note waiting for me. In truth, I was
relieved to see it. Even if he hated the pies, a note meant he
had something to say to me. I liked that.

Jasper.
I'm concerned that you thought you'd baked pies. They tasted like
hot rubber. Those were nutty hockey pucks. Did you chop up real
hockey pucks and blend them with the nuts? I'm forwarding my
dentist bill to you.
Yes, my shower is big. Nothing about me is small.
I'm heading up to Swampscott tomorrow so I'll be on the road by
nine. I'm meeting up with my sister for dinner in the city so I
won't be back until later. The place is all yours.
–L

I SMILED ALL THE WAY THROUGH MY SHOWER. I DIDN'T EVEN care that he'd hated the pies. Chances were high he'd hate the cupcakes I had for him today too. The only thing on my mind was my response since I had to keep this exchange going. It was the only thing keeping *me* going.

I paced Linden's living room for ten minutes, coiling my hair into a twist and then shaking it out and starting over several times. I couldn't get it right but that was due to the fact I was busy studying the knickknacks and photos on Linden's bookshelves. And the books, of course. *Allllll* the books.

I couldn't get the twist right but I knew Linden's family was adorable, his beautiful sister was recently married, and he was a massive *Lord of the Rings* fan. *Massive* didn't even cut it.

I'd lost track of all the different editions he had of the same books. Hardcover, paperback, movie tie-in covers, specialty covers, illustrated, annotated, translated.

When I refocused on the wall beside the bookshelves, I realized the quartet of framed watercolors weren't random landscapes but scenes from the books. This guy adored *Lord of the Rings* and it was a revelation because he seemed like the type of person who made a point of not going hog wild over anything. He had interests, sure, but nothing bordering on fanaticism.

I tore off his note and grabbed the pen he'd left nearby.

Linden,
Nothing about you is small but yet you choose to live in this cozy bungalow. Are you secretly living out a Hobbit fantasy? Is this your Shire, Bilbo Baggins?

As for your commentary on my pies, I'm concerned you don't know much about baked goods. The cupcakes in your fridge will change your mind.
How's your sister?
Thanks for the water.
~J

———

Jasper.
Those were not cupcakes. They weren't cake of any kind. Are you using some kind of WWII-era cookbook where the ordinary ingredients are replaced with the things they didn't need to ration? Or is it a dietary thing? Is this stuff gluten-free? Or vegan? That frosting had the disappointing flavor of carob.
Not sure if I've mentioned this enough but you don't have to bake anything. I would appreciate fewer treats to choke down.
It should come as no surprise I enjoy putting big things in small, tight places. If I wanted a Hobbit fantasy, I would've installed a round door. Good catch though.
My sister is pregnant with twins and happily miserable about it. Apparently she misses beer, not that I remember her drinking much of it before the pregnancy.
I have residential appointments in town all day. I'll head out around nine or nine thirty at the latest, and be back around five.
—L

———

Linden,
Pregnant with twins allows her to be happily miserable. Is this your first time around as an uncle?

Is it possible you don't have a taste for sweets? Could that be it?
Because everything I bake cannot be dreadful. While you have said
the baked goods aren't strictly necessary, I am honor bound to
recognize your hospitality. You'll have to put up with the molasses
cookies I've made for you today.

Also, please don't feel obligated to give me your hours. If I don't
see your truck in the drive during the workday, I'll assume you're
out for a bit.

I am curious, however, about your thinly veiled commentary about
big things in small places. Seems like an intentional choice, no? Is
there something specific you're getting at?

~ J

————

Jasper.

Did I hear you running a saw this morning? What are you
building now?

The cookies had no sugar in them. Not a single grain. Can you tell
me if this is an alternative lifestyle thing? Are you still cooking
everything in a crockpot? Because that's not helping matters.

Is there a way for you to work out your honor without leaving
"treats" in my refrigerator every day? It's really starting to
remind me of the birds and mice Sinatra leaves at the door
whenever he's around. Thank you but please make it stop.

I'm going to keep telling you my schedule because it forces me to
figure out where I'm going before I hit the road in the morning.
You shouldn't have to keep watch. I'll be out from ten to six
tomorrow.

Last thing—you know what I'm getting at. You know you're
living rent-free in my head too. Enjoy that shower. —L

———

Linden,

Yep, that was a saw! I'm tackling the porch now. It was getting on my nerves and I needed a break from painting.

Here's the thing: you don't like the birds I murder for you—or treats, as I call them—but I'm using your shower and laundry and I need to drag something dead to your door as a show of my appreciation.

Should I chop your wood instead?

While you mull that over, enjoy some authentic homemade southern biscuits.

Also, the crockpot is not up for conversation. Please accept that it's an important part of my life.

Why do I get the impression you'd wander in the woods all day if you didn't check that schedule in the morning?

~J

———

Jasper.

Three things.

1. Don't even think about chopping wood. I've seen the way you wield a crowbar. An axe is out of the question.

2. The biscuits weren't terrible. They were burnt on the bottom and undercooked in the middle but they weren't terrible. I'm not sure if I've grown accustomed to your baking and anything edible seems like a blue-ribbon biscuit or these are somewhat good.

3. Why isn't your husband rebuilding that deck for you?

–L

———

Linden,
Because he lives in Northern Ireland with his fiancée.
~J

———

Jasper.
Why the hell is he in Northern Ireland?
–L

———

Linden,
My husband moved because his boss was appointed Special Envoy
to Northern Ireland. It's a plum gig and being asked to join a new
envoy as chief of staff is an offer you don't refuse.
I stayed because my work is here. More than that, there was no
reason for me to join him. There's nothing for me there.
~J

———

Jasper.
None of this makes sense. I'll be home around three or four today.
You can explain it to me then. Stay away from that axe.
–L

NINE
LINDEN

"You're emotionally constipated."

I pinched the bridge of my nose, my fingers pressing hard against my skin as I traced the notches and grooves of my brow. My eyes squeezed shut, I heaved out the kind of thorny, painful breath one could only gather when your mother made bananapants comments while strolling through the lanes of the local garden center.

"What…does that even mean, Mom?"

"It means you're backed up. You don't let anything out."

Maybe she was high. My mother popped cannabis gummies *all* the time. Oddly enough, it prevented her from reverting to her naturally scatterbrained ways. "That's the situation, huh?"

With a young spruce tree between us, she jabbed a finger in my direction. "Don't get smart with me, young man. And don't think you can tell me you're thirty-six so you're not a young man anymore. As long as I'm alive, I'll always be older than you and I'll never be able to breathe easy while one of my babies is unhappy."

"Believe me, Mom. I'm happy. I'm great." I peered at her, not knowing what the hell this was about. When she offered no explanation, I continued, "What brought this on? What happened to replacing your bayberry bushes? Have you been hitting the candy already? It's pretty early for recreational use, don't you think?"

Bent over a collection of five-gallon azaleas, she replied, "We can do two things at once and I'm bringing this up because I can *sense* it, Linden. I feel it in my heart and that has nothing to do with my medicinal herbs. You're holding something in and you're giving me a distinctly unsatisfied vibe." She stood, a hot pink azalea cradled in her arm. She had nowhere to put it but she'd squeeze it into her garden somewhere. "Why don't you just tell me what's going on? Is it one of your intimate friends? Or…more than one of them?"

It felt as if screws were turning on either side of my jaw, drawing everything tight and close and on the verge of snapping, but there were two reasons I allowed this conversation to continue instead of enforcing some boundaries.

First—and the thing most people found surprising about me—my mom was one of my closest friends. Not in some fucked-up way where I leaned on her to wash my clothes and cook my meals in exchange for the smallest insight into my life, but as an actual friend—or whatever it was when you and your parents were finally adults and your interactions weren't moored by the stagecraft of parenting.

Obviously, as this moment proved, the stagecraft of parenting was never completely absent.

The meddling aside, Mom and I shared some of the same interests and I enjoyed her perspective on things. She was big into gardening and my job was looking after trees. She volunteered with several conservation causes in the area and

I supported those efforts. She championed lots of small, local restaurants and bakeries and I liked to eat. It worked out for everyone when she didn't pull a lunch hour shakedown.

Second—and probably most importantly—I wanted to fast-forward this day. I wanted to get back home and get in front of Jasper before I lost my damn mind. I needed the full, unabridged story of how she came to be married and living an ocean away from her husband.

Since my mother would carry on this conversation as long as she wanted, I couldn't dodge her and expect it to get me out of here any sooner.

Even on the topic of *intimate friends*.

Ever since my mother let herself into my hotel room and encountered me in the middle of a sweaty, sticky pile of pansexual skin the morning after my sister's wedding last summer, she'd made the occasional pointed statement about my romantic life. The overarching message was one of support, but at the same time she was growing weary of my avoidance of serious relationships. She wanted me to settle down and she didn't mind needling me about it when she got the chance.

I inclined my head. "There's nothing going on. Nothing to tell."

She narrowed her eyes and pursed her lips in a grim maternal smile that invited me to go ahead and lie to her face. "Have you met someone? Is that why you're distressed today? Someone new?"

The quick answer was yes, I'd met someone, and yes, she was the source of most of my problems right now.

But I hadn't *met someone* the way my mother wanted me to meet someone. I had a painfully beautiful belle of a neighbor who shouldn't be allowed to use power tools or kitchen appliances without supervision. She was naked in my house every day which meant she was naked in my dreams every night but she was also the pain in my ass intent on poisoning me.

None of this was tracking in the direction my mother wanted and it wasn't what I wanted either. I liked chill, uninhibited people who understood I wasn't looking for anything serious.

Jasper was serious like dynamite. Every moment with her was explosive and there was a very good chance one of us would die.

For reasons that had nothing to do with self-preservation, I still liked her. I still wanted to understand her marital status and the circumstances of her arrival next door, and if given the chance, I wanted to get her under me. That was all it would take to get her out of my system.

My mother cleared her throat, arched her brows up. I rubbed my forehead again. "Is that really the conversation we need to have right now?" I crossed my arms over my chest. "We need to find a replacement for those bayberries and I have two tree warden stops to make today. Can we set this aside for another day?"

"You'll only be more backed up with emotional shit the longer you wait," she muttered.

"Is there a different metaphor you could use? Literally anything else? I'm not a fan of this one."

Very much ignoring me, she peered at a five-year-old dogwood that was much too big for her yard. "Has it ever occurred to you," she started, strolling down the aisle again, "that every time you've been presented with a path in life, you take the solitary one? Even if it means you're forging your own trail and blindly hacking your way through the woods?"

A headache was gathering behind my eyes, a dark, heavy cloud of pressure born from too little sleep and too much coffee. I squinted in response to the pain but that only diffused it into my temples, the base of my neck. The smart course of action involved leaving this greenery, drinking a ton of water, eating a meal that didn't come in a cup from Dunkin' Donuts.

Yet I stayed here, my fingers flexing and my head throbbing, my throat dry and my body strung tight from too many days spent wondering what the hell was going on with Jasper. Whether she was all right. How anyone could leave her and leave so abruptly. It seemed abrupt to me. Maybe it wasn't. Maybe…I didn't know. Maybe there was an explanation, like she was hoping he'd come back for her. "There's something wrong with that? I had no idea. No one ever mentioned it."

My mother whirled around and ducked under the branches of a lilac tree to face me. She folded her arms over her chest, her persimmon cardigan clashing with the thunderous glint in her eyes. She stared at me until I was certain that thunder was real, that it was rumbling in my ears and threatening to kick up a downpour.

"Linden, listen to me. Of all my babies, I've given you the most time to find your way. You were the last to arrive and you did so well when I stopped expecting you to follow anyone else's path."

I stared at my mother, unmoved by the millionth reminder that I pulled up the rear of the Santillian triplets on all things, born about thirty minutes behind my brother and sister and damned to a lifetime of last-place comparison.

She tapped her index finger twice as if hammering her thesis to my sternum. "You've never been in a rush like Ash or lost like Magnolia but you have been *alone*—and I don't believe that's what you truly want from your life."

"And that's why I'm—what is it, full of emotional shit? Because I'm alone? As you love to remind me, I have plenty of *friends*."

"I don't have to explain to you the difference between that kind of company"—she pinned me with the most unimpressed stare in human history—"and meaningful emotional connections."

I was very interested in offering a quip about sex being an especially meaningful connection if you did it right but I could still hear her thunder inside my head and she would totally send me to my room without supper. Even if I lived in my own home and cooked for myself.

"All right." I jerked my shoulders up with as much acquiescence as I had to offer. "You make some fine points. I will think about them. Sorry for worrying you."

"Oh, no, no, no." A brisk laugh cracked out of her as she dropped her hands to her hips. "No, Linden, you are not getting off easy with a hangdog shrug and some 'sorry, Mom.'"

"What did you have in mind?"

After flaying me with a stare, she crossed to the autumn annuals arranged on waist-high tables. She didn't need another dozen chrysanthemums to clutter the front steps but I wasn't going to be the one to take up that fight.

"Your father and I are celebrating our fortieth anniversary this year," she called over her shoulder while I trailed behind her. "We haven't finalized all the details yet but we're throwing ourselves a big party. We didn't want to wait for our fiftieth. That seems like a terrible way to tempt fate."

"Don't say shit like that." I shook my head as she gave a quick shrug and tucked a few strands of hair over her ear, as if she hadn't thrown a mortality grenade into this discussion. "Just…don't say shit like that, Mom."

"We won't be around forever. There's no reason to pretend otherwise."

"I know that. I get it. Okay? But we've covered a fuckton of messy topics today. I'm going to need you to hold the circle of life convo for another time."

My mother offered a series of grumbles, sighs, and harrumphs before returning to fully formed words, eventually saying, "We're planning a party for November or December. Probably November because we don't want to compete with holiday gatherings and your sister's due date."

"That sounds delightful." I was aiming for sincerity with that comment but also hoping like hell I didn't have to help plan the menu or hire a band.

"You won't have to do anything other than show up," she said, and that wasn't the first time my mother had more or less read my mind. "But I expect you to bring someone special. Someone you *care* about." She tossed open her hands. "Or two people. Whatever your arrangement is, as many people as you want to love, Linden. Whomever your heart chooses."

Of all the fucking things, the memory of Jasper crying on her porch chose this moment to flood my mind.

What the actual fuck was that?

Just…*fuckkkk*. No. Not that.

Jasper aside, I didn't want to experience any form of heart-choosing. I wasn't like my brother or sister. My heart didn't choose anyone because it didn't want anyone. My heart loved solitude with some fun thrown in when the mood was right. My heart craved the predictable cadence of the earth moving through seasons. My heart wanted to beat free of entanglements.

My family was enough for me. I had my siblings and the families they were creating. That was enough. It was *plenty*.

"Mom, I hear where you're coming from," I said with as much patience as I could manage. "And I appreciate it, I do. But look. It's almost October. I'm not going to meet anyone and develop this epic relationship before your anniversary party."

"Yes, you are."

That was it. Just "Yes, you are" and a firm bob of her head and a pert grin that made me stand up taller and straighten my shoulders.

"And don't think you can bring a hookup friend or someone you met that week and play it off like you're mad for each other," she added. "I will figure it out. I know these things. I am your mother and you've never successfully lied to me once. I've let you think you've successfully lied to me but I always know. You will not pull that kind of stunt at my party."

Oh, for fuck's sake.

My parents weren't the kind of people who imposed their expectations on us as kids or adults. We were always free to pursue our own interests and goals without much backseat driving. The rough side of that coin was the rare event in which they *did* levy an expectation. It was so uncommon that rising to the occasion was never in question.

But I couldn't do this for her. I couldn't. More than that, I didn't want to do it.

And Jasper Cleary had to get the fuck out of my head right now.

"Mom, really, that's extremely ambitious and—"

"And if you don't," she cut in, "I will make it my job to find someone for you. As you know, I had no problem doing that for your sister and I'll be happy to do it for you."

That wasn't an option. Nope. Hard pass. It'd been amusing to watch my mother take charge of my sister's romantic affairs but there was no way in hell I wanted first-hand experience with that kind of inquisition.

"Mom, get real. That won't be necessary."

Another crisp nod. "Because you'll make an effort at meeting someone."

"No, that's not what I mean," I said. "It won't be necessary because I'm not Magnolia and I don't need you setting me up on dating services or launching surprise blind date attacks."

"You're right. You're not Magnolia." My mother grabbed two purple mums from the table, her arms now over-loaded with plants. She wandered away but returned quickly with her goods in a wagon. "Magnolia had her own emotional shit but she wasn't busy pretending she was better off alone. You, my darling son, are full of very different shit."

"You're asking a lot," I said. "You're asking me to meet someone tomorrow, pretty much, have a ton of intense feel-ings, and bring this person to your party. That's a crazy timeline."

At this point, I couldn't get Jasper out of my head. All I could think of was the press of her lips and her hungry little hands yanking up my shirt. It wouldn't stop. I ignored it just the same.

"It seems like a lot to you because you've determined people are too risky, too much work."

That wasn't true. Not at all.

She reached for another purple mum before glancing up at me. "Prove yourself wrong for me and give me that as a gift."

"You're asking me to disappoint you," I said.

She wheeled her wagon to the cash register. I followed. "You know I'm not asking you to give anything up, right? I'm asking you to expect more. I'm asking you to care about someone and let that person care about you too. I'm asking you to try it out and see what happens. I'm asking you to invite someone into your bed when they mean something to you and not only when it's entertaining. And don't misunderstand me when I say some*one*. If you're happy with more than one person, then I'm happy. If you tell me you're settling down with the Seven Dwarfs, well, honey, I'll just have to find room for them at the supper table on Sundays. But I want you to try caring and being cared for. You haven't let yourself do it in too long."

"You said it yourself. I'm fine when I follow my own path."

She tipped her head to the side as a frown pulled at her lips. "That's just it. You're not following your path. You haven't in ages. Do you really think I can't see the way you hold everyone at a distance, even Ash and Magnolia? Do you believe I haven't noticed you drowning yourself in all the available fish in the sea these last few years? Or that it's been much more than a few years since—"

"Hell fucking no," I interrupted. "*No*. We're not talking about that. I will stand here and listen while you say these things and make these ridiculous demands but I'm not hashing *that* out with you."

After a pause, she said, "You should hash it out with someone."

I didn't say anything. I didn't really know what to say. Arguing was pointless. Defending my quiet, calm existence wouldn't get me anywhere. Being a moody bastard wouldn't help either. Carving through layers of scar tissue and fossilized memories would solve nothing.

Eventually, I managed, "I'm sorry I snapped at you just now. And that you feel you need to give me a kick in the ass—"

She reached into her purse. "Oh, stop it. Enough apologies."

"Fine." I ran a hand through my beard. "Then I'm not sorry."

"Now you're just being belligerent. I don't need that attitude from you on top of everything else." She beamed up at the cashier. "I have the azalea and three mums, and I'd also like the dogwood back there. The big one. Can you deliver that this week?"

"Why am I even here?" I mumbled.

"Because it pleases me to spend time with you."

"Even when you're driving me crazy by overplanting your yard and meddling in my personal life?"

She nodded. "Especially then. Remember what I said, young man. Find a date for my party or I'll find one for you."

———

Instead of fulfilling tree warden responsibilities in Scituate, I went straight home after leaving the garden center. It was fine. The trees would manage without me for another day or two but I would not manage if I didn't talk to Jasper *today*.

Also, I had to get that conversation with my mother out of my head, and obsessing over someone taking a job on another continent and abandoning their wife worked wonders. I didn't understand how such a thing could occur or why anyone would stay in a hollowed-out marriage.

Then again, I'd spent the last week with my brain throbbing in my jeans because Jasper was in my shower and I wasn't there with her to experience any of it, and nothing outside the criminality of that made sense to me.

She baked biscuits every day now. They weren't awful. They served as a handy distraction when I arrived home every evening and wandered through the rooms as if I'd find a forgotten pair of panties waiting for me. The biscuits helped. Nothing like carbs to keep from barging next door, throwing your neighbor over your shoulder, taking her to your bed.

Yeah, the biscuits helped with that. The exterior was dry enough to require a full glass of milk to wash them down, and there was nothing like chugging milk at the kitchen sink to cool thoughts of mouthy women mouthing off at me in bed.

Mostly.

Enough that I didn't bang on her door.

What I did in the shower was another story.

And that was the reason I needed to know why her husband lived overseas and—apparently—had a fiancée there too. Those were only two of the reasons I hated the guy.

How anyone could just up and leave their wife was a mystery to me. And how could she accept that? She came at me hissing and spitting when I carried a couple of boxes for her. How could she tolerate a husband walking out of her life and still allow him use of that title?

Maybe it was an immigration status marriage. Or a health insurance marriage. Or something that wouldn't inspire outright loathing in me for the man.

Those were the questions on my mind as I turned down the dogleg bend of my street—and spotted a pair of fire trucks outside Jasper's house, lights flashing and firefighters streaming around her property.

"*Jasper.*"

Once my heart got back to beating and I wheezed out a breath, I steered the truck to the side of the cul-de-sac, out of the way of the fire trucks.

There I was able to confirm that neither the house nor the yard was in flames, the firefighters were ambling in and out of the house without urgency, and the only concern seemed to be a charred box on the driveway.

As I exited the vehicle, I spotted Jasper sitting on the curb. She had her legs folded in front of her and her arms braced on her thighs. The red skirt she wore was wet and dirty, and her navy blue sweater wasn't in any better shape. Her head was bowed like she was praying or meditating but I doubted she did much of either. Didn't seem the type.

I dropped down beside her and stretched my legs out. "How's it going, Jas?"

She sniffled. I handed her a bandana from my back pocket and she accepted, saying, "We can't keep doing this."

"What's *this?*"

"You coming over here and handing me a hanky because I'm crying again. I have a reputation to uphold, and routinely needing a hanky or any other rescue isn't part of it.

I'll have you know I once managed twelve hours with a broken finger before leaving the office to see a doctor and there was another time when I worked a full week while I had pneumonia."

"Those are not the badges of honor you think they are, but sure, I'll stop handing out the hankies. That's one way to fix a problem that doesn't exist."

"You're very rude," she said on a sob.

I glanced away as she blotted her eyes. "Sorry."

"You can ask," she said.

"About what? I need you to be more specific."

She waved a hand at the fire truck in front of us. "About this."

"Okay." I ran my fingers through my beard as I watched several firefighters pile into the truck. "What's going on here?"

She gave a pathetic little shrug that squeezed my heart. "Oh, you know. Just a small fire in the kitchen."

"Please tell me it wasn't the crockpot."

"Nope." Another shrug and I ached. "The toaster oven."

I glanced to the driveway again and the box abandoned there. It was about the right size for a countertop oven.

"I was making some toast for lunch and—"

"What do you mean, you were making toast for lunch? That's not lunch."

She turned her tearstained face to me, her expression as fierce as ever. "Toast is a perfectly appropriate lunch."

"It's…it's just bread, Jas."

She gave me a look that said I knew nothing. Not a single thing in the whole world. "I take my toast very seriously. It's my favorite thing to eat, and fancy toast can be—"

"Fancy toast? What the fuck is fancy toast?"

She planted her hands on the grass behind her and leaned back, her face upturned to the late September sun. "Not really in the mood to go another round with you on toast today. I don't have a lot of favorite things but toast is one of them and I'm not defending it to you right now."

The second fire truck pulled away.

"Come on." I pushed to my feet and held out a hand to her. "Up you go."

She studied my hand for a beat before accepting. "Thank you."

I dragged a glance over her clothes. "Is it safe inside?"

"Yeah, it wasn't too bad. Just a small fireball in the toaster. Everything except my lunch is salvageable."

"Then go change into something else. Like those yoga pants girls like you wear."

"Yoga pants? That girls like *me* wear?"

I crossed my arms. "You know what I mean. You, my sister, my mom, my future sister-in-law, women everywhere."

"And why do I need yoga pants specifically?"

"Because I have to check on some trees and you're coming with me. Do you have normal shoes?"

"Normal shoes," she repeated under her breath. "Wow."

"You can't wear those"—I motioned toward her pretty heels—"in the woods."

She gave me a long, measured look. "So, I need the yoga pants that girls like me wear and normal shoes. Because we're going to see some trees."

I jabbed a finger toward her front door, still standing open. "Stop repeating me and get dressed. You can be outraged when we hit the road."

Jasper absently smoothed her hands down her skirt. "The

kitchen is going to be a mess. I should deal with that."

"It will be a mess later." Then, because I couldn't help it, not really, I added, "Come on now, Peach. Let's get you out of here for a bit. You need a break."

After a pause, Jasper nodded and marched into the house. I stared after her longer than necessary, longer than made any damn sense. Then I grabbed some heavy-duty gloves from the back of my truck. That burned-out oven would be better off cooling on the gravel-paved path along the opposite side of my house for now. She didn't need any more reminders.

When that was handled, I stored the gallon of stew my mother had plied me with in the fridge. That was when I spotted today's batch of biscuits—and Jasper's latest note.

Linden,
I could've explained why my husband left last week. What's changed?
~J

"Isn't that a great fucking question," I muttered to myself.

For the next five minutes, I waited in my truck, alternately screwing around on my phone and glancing next door. Rare was it that I brought anyone along with me to check trees but rare was Jasper. That was all I could say about this decision.

Soon enough, she stepped out her front door and I was smacked upside the head with my mistake. Jasper in skin-hugging yoga pants only emphasized how much those skirts and dresses of hers concealed. The loose-fitting shirt that skimmed her hips made me think about fisting the fabric and twisting it around my hand. The ponytail swishing behind her had the same effect.

I'd created this trap and now I'd fallen into it.

"Hey," Jasper said, a bit breathless as she opened the door. She settled in beside me and shot an arched eyebrow in my direction. "What?"

A grunt sounded in my throat before I managed, "Nothing."

"Oooookay."

We drove in silence for several minutes but it was comfortable silence. It was the sort of silence I favored in the morning, between the states of sleep and stepping into the woods for the first time that day.

I looked after all the trees on public land in Scituate, which was handy since I did that in Hingham and Cohasset too, and these towns shared craggy, skeleton key borders. Today my concern was an old maple in the Conservation Park. This slab of protected land sat wedged between two golf courses and two rivers, with the Massachusetts Bay as its southeastern border. It was a coastal marsh with a relatively young woodland and the town was eager to preserve the land. It was one of my favorite spots on the southeast coast.

"I think it goes without saying but I don't want there to be any surprises. I am not what anyone would call an experienced hiker." Jasper scrunched up her nose as if such a thing mortified her. "In case that was unclear."

I pulled into a spot in the empty parking lot and smiled over at her. "Yeah. I figured that out."

"I mean," she continued, "I can handle it. I'm used to running in heels and I grew up on a big spread in the country. I have a basic knowledge. I'll manage perfectly well—"

"I like how you're rattling off your bona fides while also making it clear you refuse to put up with anything but flat, dry terrain."

She pulled on the haughty, *no help needed here* face she relied on so much. "I'm preparing you for what will happen if I am forced to scale a mountainside or get whacked in the face with a branch or fall in the mud."

I gestured to the sea-level terrain. "Do you see any mountains here?"

Not interested in answering, Jasper exited the truck and took off in the wrong direction, that ponytail swinging behind her. I'd spent a lot of time thinking about her hair. Fantasizing could also be an appropriate term for this new fixation of mine. All of my previous thoughts involved her long waves loose around her shoulders, often spilling down like *The Birth of Venus* right there in my bedroom. I'd never imagined her hair tied back in a ponytail, exposing her long neck and the pale, delicate skin there.

It effectively doubled my fantasies.

I whistled to her, hooking a thumb over my shoulder when she turned. "This way. That direction is the marsh and you will fall in something cold and wet if you keep going."

Jasper fell in step with me and we started down the trail.

I waited until the parking lot fell out of view before asking, "How are you doing?"

"I'm all right," she replied automatically. "It was just a toaster oven."

"Okay, sure," I murmured. "I can roll with that but what about the part where there was a fire in your kitchen?"

"Not what I expected when I started out this morning, that's true."

I touched her elbow, pointing to the left. "This way. There's a maple I want to see that's down here."

We veered off the trail and I stepped closer to Jasper. If I was going to keep her out of mud and clear the way of errant branches, I had to stay within grabbing range.

"How does this work?" she asked. "Do you keep track of *all* these trees?"

"Yep."

"Like, every single one?"

I bobbed my head. "Yep. Every single one."

"And…you do this in other places too? Other towns and…I don't know how that's possible."

"I have maps. Diagrams." I smiled at her. The yoga pants really were a mistake. Something about her dresses had trapped my attention between her hips and breasts, and I'd skipped her legs altogether. Those pants allowed for no such oversight. She was on the short side but strong and sturdy— and I knew sturdy wasn't a word I could toss into complimentary conversation but it was an important piece of Jasper I'd missed from the start. She was sturdy as hell. Maybe it was strange but I wasn't sure there was anything more attractive. "I don't have to rely on memory, if that's what you're asking."

She pressed a palm to her forehead. "That is a very logical explanation and I can't believe that did not occur to me."

"No worries. My brother knows all these IRS forms and UCOA classifications, and it still baffles me how he can come up with that shit like it's nothing." I grazed my hand across her shoulders because I couldn't be here with her and stay fully apart. "I'm sure there's something you know from your work that baffles other people."

"There're a few." She barked out a laugh. "I can name every congressional district in every state. Where it is, what it's known for, who has been elected to the seat. Governors and senators too. All the counties in every swing state and their voter registration deadlines. Every secretary of state and when they're up for reelection."

"I take it you work in elections, then."

"Mmhmm. Something like that."

I gestured toward the woods. "I have the trees. You have that metric fuckton of information. Everyone has their thing, their bag of tricks."

"Why are you being so agreeable?" she said suddenly. "Why aren't you screaming at me about using appliances or nearly setting the whole house on fire? Why aren't you freaking out on me right now?"

I lifted my shoulders, let them drop. "Because I really need you to explain to me why your husband left you for a job overseas, and yelling about the old, wonky wiring in that house—which is not stable enough to run an oven and a night-light at the same time—isn't going to get me that information. And I gotta tell you, Jasper, I can't think about the fire for more than a second without also thinking about forbidding you from staying there alone ever again. Since I doubt you want to revisit that discussion, I'm letting you tell me about the random shit you know."

Jasper stayed silent as we traveled deeper into the woodland. I didn't mind. I didn't interpret lulls in conversation as awkward, and since I spent much of my days alone, I didn't find the quiet bothersome. Even if Jasper was stewing over my comments.

Then, "I told you. His boss was appointed Special Envoy to Northern Ireland last year."

"Yeah, you said that. You also said your work can't pick up and move there. Why did he leave if he knew you couldn't follow?"

Jasper stopped walking, scanned the stand of trees around us, and settled her hands on her hips. "Haven't you ever married your best work friend because you hooked up *one time* after moving out of your ex-girlfriend's apartment? And that one time seemed like something you'd want to do on a permanent basis? And haven't you ever realized your best work friend is the last person you should've married because living together and sharing household chores is not nearly as entertaining as texting each other at midnight to complain about congressional aides? And haven't you ever stayed in something too long because ending it would be irrevocable, even if it was inevitable?"

"I haven't," I said slowly. "But I have ended a relationship with a woman and promptly moved onto one with a man, so I get that piece."

She laughed a bit, saying, "I like people. The anatomy comes second."

"Same." I shoved my hands in my pockets. It was difficult to stand here like this, holding myself separate and distant while Jasper unpacked her baggage. This wasn't the time to reach for her, even to offer comfort. She had to empty this particular bag before I could offer anything. "And now he's engaged."

Her rueful smile pinged my chest. "Sure is. We didn't even make it two years." She dragged the toe of her running shoe over a rock. "He asked for a divorce last month. Sent the papers last week. Right before you came over and hollered about my box-hauling technique." She laughed at that. "I knew it was coming but I wasn't prepared for it then. Not on top of everything else."

I fisted my hands. I couldn't touch her the way I wanted to while she traced the perimeters of her marriage. "On top of what else?"

"Well, I came here because I got fired. That's another one of my current problems."

I blinked. "And the other problems?"

She kept her gaze trained on the forest floor. "I was terminated in an inglorious manner so the majority of my issues revolve around that."

It was the wrong reaction but I laughed out loud. "What does that mean?"

"I was fired on television."

"What do you mean? Like, a reality show?"

She pressed the heels of her palms to her eyes. "Some people like to treat American politics like it's reality TV but no, that's not what happened. I was on a cable news program to discuss voter suppression efforts across the South. I didn't get to touch on any of that because, before the segment was due to start, my mic was broadcasting on-air and I didn't know it." She dropped her hands and started walking, saying, "They caught me talking to a staffer at the day's campaign stop. I was complaining to her because my boss gorged on ice cream during a photo op."

I caught up to her with two strides. "Ice cream?"

"He's lactose intolerant and yet he can't be a responsible human being and simply take one or two licks from the obligatory cone and smile for the cameras. He has to eat the whole damn thing and then guzzle a milkshake too, and later board the tour bus and digest all that dairy while the rest of us try not to asphyxiate."

I stopped, a laugh spinning through me, and leaned against a tree for support as I doubled over. I could barely catch my breath as I howled. "You—you said that. On television."

"Mmhmm. Yes. Then I switched gears and told her how my boss likes to get his daily briefings in his briefs while chain-smoking and gulping black coffee."

"Oh, shit." I clutched my sides. It was too much.

She hummed in agreement. "And when she asked whether she ought to continue putting all her energy into running the local campaign office when it seemed like my boss might not make it past the early primary races, I told her not to waste her time, especially not for the lucrative salary of zero dollars. I said he didn't have an ice cream cone's chance in hell but it didn't really matter because the presidential bid was primarily focused on raising his progressive street cred and elevating his status as a power player in the Senate." She tossed her hands up. "I spilled the house secrets live on-air. Before I fully understood what'd happened, the host informed me that the campaign tweeted out a statement and I was no longer on staff." She glanced at me, smirking as I struggled and failed to contain my laughter. "It's kind of amazing you had no idea about any of this. I'm a meme, a punchline, a cautionary tale."

"I don't watch television." I sobered a bit. "And social media is too noisy for me so I miss all that." I closed my hand around her wrist, drawing her to a stop. "But even if I hadn't missed it, I wouldn't give a fuck."

"I see we've returned to you manhandling me."

"Can you back up a few paces and explain what you do?

You're on TV and you're briefing a chain-smoker in his underwear and there's enough dirt in your vent session to bring down a presidential candidate? Who the hell are you, Jasper-Anne Cleary?"

She gave a flippant little shrug, saying, "I'm the special advisor to Senator Tyson Timbrooks of Georgia."

"And…what does a special advisor do?"

"During campaign cycles, I drive the strategic agenda. In the off years, I fix problems. Basically, I play a really fucked-up game of chess."

"Yeah." I studied her for a moment. I never would've guessed any of this but it fit. Jasper was nothing if not unstoppable and I bet she fixed the hell out of those problems, but there was no missing the bitterness in her tone. The hardness. "Yeah, that sounds right."

"Once upon a time it did. No one in Washington wants to be within fifty feet of me right now. The campaign has blacklisted me everywhere. The only people returning my calls are reporters and TV hosts, and campaigns that want to pump me for free opposition research."

Now it all made sense. "That's why you're here. Why you're staying in Midge's cottage."

She reached down to run her fingers over a fern, again missing my eyes. "Only place left to go."

"What happens next?"

She looked up at the canopy, squinted at the dappled sunlight streaming in. "I meet with an attorney tomorrow morning to review the terms of the divorce and sign the papers so Preston can marry this new gal of his. After that, I keep fixing up the house and hope I'm freed from this exile eventually. I can't see the Beltway gang permanently banning me. That only happened to Nixon. Everyone else bounces back."

Fuck. I wanted to hug the stuffing out of her. What a fucking horrible time she was having—and I kept criticizing her baking. It was objectively terrible but she needed to catch a break somewhere. I could've faked it for someone suffering through this much personal garbage.

"Do you *want* to bounce back?"

Her head snapped up, her eyes hot. "Of course I do."

"If you say so." I gestured to the trees ahead as we walked. "How did you get this job in the first place?"

"I started working for Timbrooks in high school. My senior year U.S. government class required everyone to volunteer with a campaign, and since my family is flat-earth, dinosaurs-are-a-myth conservative, I chose the most progressive candidate in all the races."

"Nice." I chuckled. "Spite is an undervalued motivation."

"I worked on his first U.S. Senate bid that year and managed the local campaign office after graduation."

"Of course you did. Of course you went from intern to manager in—what was it? A month? Two?"

"Eight months," she replied, giving me her first true laugh of the afternoon. "But that only happened because he was a long-shot, no-name candidate and there was no support from the party."

"But he won."

"He did." I could hear the satisfaction in those two words. I could lick that pride right off her. "I worked for the senator through college. Mostly get-out-the-vote initiatives, voter registration drives, setting up small, community-based fundraisers, and organizing phone bank centers. Basic stuff like that."

"You ran a grassroots senate campaign while you were in college. That's a big deal. I lasted one summer as a bartender. That's what *I* did in college."

"It kept my family mad, so yeah, I kept doing it."

"As good a reason as any," I murmured.

"When I was finishing my last year at University of Georgia, the senator lost a bunch of his top staffers to other opportunities. It happens like that when an elected official comes in with a fresh new class of staffers. They lose a good chunk of them after three or four years because few people can handle the pace for much longer than a sprint." She pulled the sleeves of her shirt down over her fingers, closed her hands around the fabric. It was adorable. "I was hired as the deputy state director, which basically meant I kept the wheels turning in Timbrooks's office back home in Georgia. Scheduling appearances and coordinating locations, fundraisers and phone banks."

"Same things you did in college," I said.

"Yeah but you don't complain about it when you're working for an upstart underdog. You do whatever it takes to get the job done."

"When did you become the fixer of the problems?"

"When I started fixing the problems," she replied with that no bullshit, *I can kill you with my words* tone. "When the chief of staff in D.C. botched the handling of an event and I cleaned up the mess before it became a public-facing mess. I moved to D.C. that year and took over as deputy chief of staff. I've been fixing and cleaning for Timbrooks—and anyone he loans me out to—ever since. The titles have changed but it's all the same. Make the problems go away. Even better if they're gone before anyone notices them.

Invent ways to avoid problems—or pass them off to someone else. Do whatever it takes."

I stopped in front of the maple I'd come here to see. Studying the stressed-out tree was a good diversion from the stressed-out woman beside me and the cold hollowness of her words. It was that fake smile all over again. Did she even know she did it?

Perhaps the tree wasn't a distraction at all, seeing as I could only focus on Jasper and the discontent radiating out from her. "And how long have you hated your job?"

TEN
JASPER

"I do not hate my job!"

"You're positive? Because this whole time you've been talking, you made it sound like a day at the gallows."

That was inaccurate. It simply was *not* accurate.

"I always thought I'd get Timbrooks into *the gig*—whether that was a cabinet post or maybe a vice presidential pick—and then I'd peel off for something else. Something higher profile, you know, something that felt less like duct tape and bubblegum to keep the train rolling along."

"But that didn't happen. The gig didn't come along," Linden said.

I shook my head. "I figured it would after this election." Then, "I do not hate my job," I repeated.

"Uh-huh," Linden muttered as he plucked a small, leatherbound notebook from his back pocket.

He flipped through the pages while I stared at him, waiting for more than "Uh-huh."

When it didn't come, I presented my case. "I had a sweet setup with the Timbrooks campaign. I had the last word on

—on everything. The senator offloaded the majority of his priorities and projects to me. How many people can say they have the ear of a sitting senator?"

"Not many," he mused, still busy with that notebook.

"Exactly. How many people know what really goes down behind closed doors at the Capitol?"

"Just a select few."

"I was the person they called to make things happen."

"I bet you were damn good at it too." He shoved a pencil behind his ear and gazed up at the tree. "Being good at something doesn't make it good *for* you."

"And what do you know about what's good for me?" I exploded.

"Only what you've told me, Jas." He glanced at me then, his cool stare skating over every furious inch of me. "Are you upset about this because I'm wrong and that wounds your pride worse than getting fired on TV—don't get me started on that, by the way—or are you upset because it's possible I'm right?"

I stared down at my shoes. I didn't want to talk about myself anymore. The whole mess of it was depressing. Fired, divorced, displaced, and without the use of a toaster oven. I could handle those things on their own but the snowball of it made me want to crawl into a corner. A small, narrow place to slide down the wall and press my forehead to my knees where I could disappear for a moment. Where I could be very, very quiet and hear myself think without all the noise of my family, my work, this world for one minute. Sometimes it seemed like I could hear those thoughts far off in the distance but they never made sense. They couldn't make sense, not when they only came to me as pings in my heart, twists in my belly that seemed to say, *It's not supposed to be like this.*

I'd always drowned them in antacids and went on with my day.

But now, with Linden watching me and only the sound of the woods around us, I couldn't drown any of it.

"Let me just say this." He stepped closer, swung his arm around my shoulder. "People who love their jobs don't sabotage themselves in such irreversibly brutal ways."

"But the mic wasn't supposed to be—"

"Is that really the nail you want to hang this on?" He dragged a hand down my back and brought me in for a loose hug. "You don't have to answer that but what they did to you was bullshit. There's a right way to let people go, especially people who've been around from the start, and that wasn't it. I'm sorry you went through that."

I turned my face to his bicep and closed my eyes for a moment because I was not crying again. It was one thing to cry over the oven, the one that made the most perfect, even toast, but it was another to cry over termination by tweet.

It was then, with Linden all around me and that long overdue apology releasing some of the tension in my shoulders, it struck me that he was right.

Holy shit. I hated my job.

I *hated* my job.

I hated my job.

I turned that sudden, choking truth over and over in my head as Linden stroked my back. All my exasperations and frustrations, the disappointments over never being promoted to chief of staff and always lingering on the pick-me fringes as special advisor—I'd swallowed all of it down, gulp after gulp, year after year, and now I couldn't swallow any more. Not another bit.

Except it was the only job I'd ever had and it was the primary source of my identity. "I don't know how to do anything else," I whispered.

"That's not true," he said, his lips pressed against my hair. "Not true at all."

"I don't know what to do if I'm not working on a campaign."

"It will come to you."

"I don't know who I am without a candidate to manage," I said.

"You will figure it out."

I tipped my head back, away from Linden's glorious warmth. "Where is this optimism coming from? Why aren't you telling me that I wasted almost half of my life on a job I hated and I needed you, the burly neighbor man, to explain it to me like you explained bats and water heaters and sticky doors and everything else?"

"Because years are not wasted. You were alive. You lived those years. You experienced more than a job in that time."

"But—"

"No," he interrupted with a firm squeeze to my ass. We were doing that now. Ass squeezing. "Come on. Over here. Look at this old oak tree."

"The one leaning against that other tree? Isn't it going to fall over? Shouldn't you do something about that?"

"That tree has been here for three hundred years, give or take a few. It was here before most of the others in this woodland too. The settlers chopped down trees like they were getting high on sap. Deforested most of the South Shore and Cape, but that's not the point."

"Am I getting some *Lord of the Rings* wisdom here? Is that what this speech is about?"

"Be quiet and let me teach you something." Another ass squeeze since we were very much doing this now, and doing a substantial amount of it. "That tree grew up with the first colonies. It witnessed wars. It gave life to generations of other oaks in this wood and beyond." He pointed out trees at various stages of growth around us. "And for the past several years, it's been dying."

"Oh my *god*, are you comparing my career to this tree?"

"No but it's so fun to see you mad. Real mad, not that fake, forced shit where you're all eyebrows and painful smiles." He pointed to the tree in question, which seemed to be standing only because the branches of another tree gave it a sturdy spot to lean. "For years, that oak has provided a home to nesting robins and chickadees in a hollowed-out knot in the upper trunk. It's hosted lichen, moss, and two species of fungi that live only on decaying trees. Would you say this tree has wasted those years?"

"Obviously not but the next step in my career cannot be collapsing onto the forest floor and turning into mulch. I need something in upper management."

"You're going to figure it out, Jas. There's no penalty for changing directions. You're free to start over at any time."

"Do you have any idea how long it takes to start over? I've spent half my life on this. I can't just—I don't know, how do people find careers? I've been doing this since I was seventeen. This is who I am. This is my plan."

"You know how people do it? They decide to fuck the plan. Seriously. *Fuck the plan.* Walk in the woods. Reject anyone's definition of success. Abandon expectations. Listen to your heartbeat. Take no one's shit." He brought his hand to my neck, sliding it around to cup my nape. "And steal every kiss you can."

He leaned in, captured my lips, and dropped his other hand to my hip. My spine connected with the bark of a tree as I knotted my hands in his shirt, desperate to steady myself. He pushed his thigh between my legs and there was no denying the solid ridge of him behind his zipper. There was no way to miss that.

He groaned against my lips as he pressed into me. "*Jasper.*"

The thing about these leggings was they hid nothing. Absolutely nothing. When he wedged himself up against me, that erection was *right there*. And we were in the middle of a forest, in the middle of the day, in the middle of my total life collapse.

And I arched against him because I didn't want to stop.

"Say something," he ordered as he moved his lips down my jaw, my neck.

That beard of his. My god. I didn't know how it could be soft and rough at the same time. Which was why I asked, "Do you use beard oil?"

He let out a quiet chuckle on my shoulder. "Jesus Christ, Jasper."

"I'm just wondering," I said as I looped my arms around his neck.

"You're wondering about beard oil," he murmured. "I must be doing this wrong if you can think about anything."

Linden hooked my leg around his waist and raked his hand up from my knee to my backside. It was profane, really, the way he touched me. Like he was making it clear how he'd touch me if we weren't out in the open where anyone could see us. Like he wanted to be extremely profane with me and he didn't mind me knowing that.

"You do, right? You have a whole beard oil system," I said.

He glanced down at our bodies, his brows pinched. He tipped his chin toward the place where the ridge in his jeans notched against my barely covered center. "If I ever come across this husband of yours, I'm going to have some words with him."

"Could you not talk about my ex while you're"—I cleared my throat—"you know, doing that?"

"I wasn't sure you'd noticed. With your concern about beard oil and all." He rubbed his hand along the small of my back, then under my shirt and beneath the waistband of my leggings. He didn't delve any deeper. "Let's not talk about your ex at all, okay?"

I bobbed my head in agreement. "That would be—"

Linden didn't let me finish. He stole my lips and rocked his hips against me and that was it. That was the end of the discussion and the start of the most aggressive kiss I'd ever experienced. To call it a kiss was an obscene understatement. It was closer to having sex while fully clothed and I knew that didn't make sense, it didn't make any sense in the least, but that was how it went. It was sex with mouths—but also hands and bodies and scary-big erections. It was everything and I couldn't remember the last time I'd felt everything.

I wasn't sure I ever had.

No one ever grabbed me because they were just so greedy to get their hands on me. They didn't nip my tongue and tighten their fist around my hair. No one sank into me like they'd been starved for my body, like they were relieved just to touch me. They never came at me with a rush of need so intense, so unavoidably present that everything felt quiet and fuzzy and overwhelmingly real, like that moment right before waking up from a dream.

"Is this all right?" he asked, his mouth on my neck. Which meant his beard was also on my neck and the double duty made me feel hot and dizzy and wonderful.

"Mmhmm," I managed.

He bucked against me, growled into my shoulder. "Give me the words, Jas."

I was surprised to find I enjoyed those growls of his. If someone had told me Linden was a growler, I would've looked at him and said, "Yeah, that tracks" and I would've considered it highly concerning behavior. Why would any adult human *growl?* Seriously, why? There were no conditions in which growling was appropriate, let alone sexy. But this…this was something I wanted in my life. It was a predatory hum, a groan that got twisted up in desire and turned into a snarl, a primal warning of what was to come.

Those growls made me smile. They filled me with feminine triumph and I wasn't sure I'd ever experienced triumph that I could call specifically feminine. He was reacting to me, not threatening me. And I liked that.

I dragged my nails up the corded muscles of his back and shoulders. I shouldn't have been able to feel that much definition with several layers between my hands and his skin but I did. I felt it all. I dropped my head back, only slightly surprised when I connected with the bark.

"Jasper," he grunted. "Talk to me. Say it. Give me the words, baby."

"What words?"

He growled again before pulling that tree trunk of a cock away from where I needed it. "You're not ready."

"I'm—I'm *what*?"

"You're not ready," he said, my leg still looped around his waist and his erection still outlined in his jeans. "I shouldn't have pushed."

"I believe I'm the one who gets to decide whether I want to be pushed or not."

He tipped his head to the side. "How would you like to be pushed?"

"I, well, I mean, I'd, um"—I gestured between us—"that was fine."

He gave one decisive nod and said, "You're not ready."

"I'll get ready," I snapped. "I can—"

"Don't," he interrupted. "Don't force it, okay? When you can say it, when you stop distracting yourself with bullshit like beard oil—"

"I am actually curious about that."

He stared at me the way parents stared at children who were covered in chocolate sauce but swore they had no idea where it came from. For reasons that were completely unkind and unfair, he looked magnificent doing this. I was as turned on by the stern, disappointed stare as I was by the growling and kissing that bordered on sex.

"Like I said, when you can say it, then you'll be ready. I'm not going to be the guy who pushes you into anything." He glanced up when a bird squawked somewhere nearby. "Not today."

"Some other day?"

He ran a thumb over my cheek, my birthmark, my lips before leaning in and kissing me again. This wasn't like the time before but it was possible this was better. It didn't make me think about all the things I'd never felt before, rather it made me think about fucking the plan. Abandoning expectations. Rejecting anyone else's definition of success. Maybe I could do this. Maybe I could start over.

I could climb a man in the middle of a forest and not give a damn about it. Maybe I could do this too. *Maybe.*

"Some other day," Linden whispered against my cheek. "If I don't invite myself next door and steal you out of your bed in the meantime."

"I can't tell if you're serious about that."

"I spend most nights thinking about it."

"About…kidnapping me?"

"I wouldn't call it kidnapping so much as preventative retrieval," he replied. "I've told you since the start, you shouldn't stay there."

"I thought that was because you didn't like me."

"I didn't like you being in that house alone."

Still feeling some of that feminine triumph, I said, "But if I wasn't alone? If my husband was there?"

"I've already told you," he warned. "We're not talking about that guy. Understand?"

"I think so."

He eased me back onto my feet, his hands firm on my waist as he held me steady. "All right there?"

I nodded, touched my fingertips to my lips. "Yeah. I'm fine."

Ugh, why am I such a mess? Such a terribly needy mess who has to cry all over this man's shoulder then dry hump his leg?

I stared at his shirt because I couldn't meet his eyes. Somewhere between setting the kitchen on fire and wrapping my legs around his waist, I'd uncorked my personal shit and poured it all out. I couldn't believe myself. I never did this. I never talked about Preston or why our marriage had been doomed from the start. I never shared my plan for leaving Timbrooks. I never exposed myself like this and I couldn't undo it now.

I couldn't clean this up.

Every time Linden looked at me, I was certain he saw the pointless marriage and the bombed-out career. He saw the person who wanted to leave but hung on to both of those things longer than was smart or even sane. What did that look like through his eyes? And why did he have to be so nice? Why couldn't he go back to yelling about crowbars and insulting my pies? Why did he have to see so much of me—and then kiss my lights out?

His arm hooked around my waist, he steered me toward another tree. "Now, this is why we came here."

I lifted my face to take in the full height of the tree. Linden was talking about nature and things like that, making marks in his notebook and circling the tree to inspect it from different angles, but I didn't hear him. I continued staring at the sky. It was a gorgeous, cloudless day and it kept my attention away from Linden's thick thighs when he crouched down to inspect the base of the trunk.

What was I going to do about that? It was dangerous to even think about what came next with me and Linden.

No, really, it was actually dangerous. The fire had started when I wandered away from the kitchen to check if he'd arrived home yet. At that point, it was much earlier than he said he'd return but I wanted to see him and couldn't stop looking for him. And then my toaster turned into a fireball because I was daydreaming at the window.

It seemed I couldn't manage Linden and living a safe, fireball-free life at the same time. It was one or the other.

And when he came up beside me, twined his arm around

my waist, and flattened me against him, fire seemed like a fine consequence for all the barrel-chested goodness.

"Let's head back. We have about half an hour before we lose the sun."

I dropped my forehead to his chest and let my shoulders sag. "What changed?"

"What do you mean?"

"My note. The one from yesterday, what's changed?"

I kept my face stowed against him as I waited for his response. He took a good, long moment formulating it too, long enough to start me thinking that his notes, his kisses, perhaps they held no meaning. Perhaps this was a bit of fun for him, a game, and—

"I realized I was wrong. Last week. I didn't give you a chance to explain how it was and why you let me kiss you if you were married."

I shook my head but it had the effect of rubbing my face between his solid pecs. "I don't like this new, amenable side of yours. It's confusing."

"Would it help if I threw you over my shoulder right now and carried you back to the truck?"

My belly flipped. I wasn't the kind of woman anyone threw over their shoulder. No one even joked about that sort of thing with me. "You wouldn't."

"I would. I'd smack that ass while I had the chance too." He drew his hand down my spine to settle, once again, on my backside. "You were in my shower. All week. Do you know how many times I turned around? How many times I almost went home? How much I wanted to walk in there and, fuck…just watch?"

The hard shaft nudging my thigh suggested the number

was greater than zero. And that wasn't the worst thing in the world. "Why didn't you?" I asked.

"Because we'd established the rules and I wasn't about to break them until I knew you'd want me breaking them. Until you were ready for me to break them."

So precise.

"I never pay much attention to rules. I look for ways to get around them."

He smoothed his hands down my sides and back up. "That's a solid argument for me to respect them even more."

"You might be right."

I hadn't been desired—not in a non-sexually-harassing way—in a dreadfully long time. I'd stopped believing I could be desired like this.

But that was one stop too far on the self-discovery train.

I wanted it, I wanted Linden's interest and attention. And I wanted to be pressed up against trees and kissed silly, to be playfully kidnapped, to be thrown over his shoulder, to be smacked on the ass. Though I couldn't experience any of those wants until my world stopped spinning. I'd just now— this afternoon!—turned clear eyes on my life and I had to understand what I was seeing before I allowed it to get blurry again.

"We're losing the light," Linden said. "And god forbid you get your shoes muddy. We better go."

We untangled ourselves from our embrace and walked side by side back to the main trail, our hands linked. Linden pointed out birds and commented on the trees, which were young or old, healthy or declining, native or non-native. He didn't seem to mind that I was only half listening. He might've been giving this guided tour for that exact reason, considering he rarely spoke more than necessary. With every murmur and nod I offered him, another newly distilled realization sounded in my head.

You only stayed in that job because you didn't know what else to do.

You stayed because Timbrooks let you do whatever you wanted.

You stayed because you didn't want to start over, didn't want to work your way up all over again.

You stayed because you felt important there.

You stayed because you wanted to prove to your family you were better and smarter and more capable than they said you'd ever be.

You stayed because you wanted to prove it to yourself. Because you wanted to believe it.

————

WE RETURNED TO LINDEN'S HOUSE AND THERE WAS NO DEBATE as to whether I was coming inside with him.

There was stew in the fridge, he'd said by way of explanation.

We'd have stew and we wouldn't talk about any of my confessions, I'd decided. Though I didn't say it, Linden picked up that signal without a problem. From the moment we stepped inside, he chattered on about a golf course on Cape Cod he visited frequently because they insisted on planting trees that didn't belong in this region, the baseball game he recently attended with his siblings, and something about neighborhood Halloween festivities.

I leaned against the countertop while he poured the stew into a cast-iron pot to warm and went on about the baseball season and how it was running long this year. Everything he said hit me about ten seconds after he said it, as if my brain was stretched beyond the point of withstanding regular conversation. I knew it was happening because he'd stare at me expectantly in moments when I was due to react or respond but I'd only blink at him.

"What was that?" I asked. "I'm sorry. I didn't catch the last part."

"No worries," he murmured, setting several muffin-y things on a baking sheet. "I just asked if you like popovers."

I pointed at the sheet. "Those are popovers, I take it?"

"Yeah. My mom bakes them whenever she's cooking stew. She believes it to be a symbiotic relationship." He cocked his head to the side, frowned. "Are popovers not a thing in the South?"

"I can't speak for the whole of the South but they're not a thing where I'm from."

Nodding, he shoved the tray into the oven. "They won't be as stunningly bad as your cupcakes so you might not like them."

"It's a risk I'll have to take."

Linden pulled a bottle of wine from the fridge and I decided it was pure coincidence he had the same bottle I was drinking last week on hand. Lots of people drank sauvignon blanc. It was nothing. This was nothing.

"Would you like a glass?" he asked.

"Please." I wanted to cross the kitchen and stand beside him while he prepared the meal, letting our hands and hips bump as we worked together. I wanted to drop my head onto his shoulder and be content for one minute. I wanted to wrap my arms around this thick torso and bury my face in his shirt. I wanted to crawl into his lap and let him hold me. I wanted to link my arm with his, tip my head toward the bedroom, and let him lead me there. I wanted to be the person who asked for those things without talking myself out of it, without convincing myself he'd refuse me. Without believing I didn't want or need it. "So, this stew. Does your mother cook for you frequently?"

He barked a laugh into the refrigerator as he reached for a beer. "Hardly. I mean, she always has a freezer full of soups and casseroles and will send me home with twenty pounds of rice if I'm not careful."

"And somehow you ended up with half a dozen popovers and a week's worth of stew."

He rolled his eyes. "My mother was in rare form today. I took a lot more than stew."

"What does that mean?"

"Some of the shrubs in her yard died over the summer —that drought was a bitch—so I agreed to meet her at a garden center to pick out replacements. To say my mother is a kid in a candy shop when it comes to garden centers would be an insult to kids. My mother doesn't care whether a tree is too big for her land or she doesn't have room for more potted plants. She will buy it all and then she'll get back to the house and holler at me to make it work for her."

"The next time you accompany her on one of these shopping trips, I'd really love to come along. I won't say a word, I just want to watch."

"You're hilarious." He tapped his beer bottle against my wineglass. No disasters occurred this time. "But here I am, thinking I'm along to help with the shrubs, and she busts out with all this—" He stopped himself, taking a deep pull of his beer. "Well, she had a lot of little things she wanted to share with me and then she casually says she and my father are having a fortieth anniversary party because they don't want to wait in case either of them die before they hit their fiftieth."

An unpleasant wheezing noise came up from my chest. "Oh. Oh, wow. That's—"

"It's fucking nuts," he said. "And, like, do I need to think about my parents dying sometime in the next ten years? No, I really don't. That's what we have my brother for. He's the one who handles that shit. Not me."

I stared at my glass for a moment, my pointer and middle fingers on either side of the stem. There was never a time when this topic didn't hurt like hell. "But you got stew out of it, so that's not a terrible bargain. Right?"

"The stew only came my way because my dad took off on a last-minute golf trip with some of his friends yesterday. I'm told she gave him a very hard time about choosing between golf and the stew, which she'd spent all day making."

"Sounds fair," I replied. "It also sounds like you see a lot of your family."

"I do." He pulled open the oven door, bent down to peer inside. "My brother and sister both live in Boston and my parents are in New Bedford. I'm always seeing one of them."

"That must be nice." There was a note of bitterness in my tone that I hadn't intended and Linden noticed immediately.

"What about your family? Are they in Georgia?"

I shook my head because no, I didn't have any real family there but more importantly, no, we could *not* talk about this now. "Not too much. Can I get out some dishes or set the table? Tell me what to do. If you don't, I'll invent something to do."

He stared at me for a long, knowing beat before saying, "Yeah, sure. Grab some of the deep bowls up there, in that cabinet."

We sat across the battered old kitchen table from each other as we ate. The stew was really good. It was the kind of meal my mother liked to call *stick to your ribs* food. And the popovers were interesting. The hollow muffin seemed like a symbol of my present stage of life but it was tasty with butter.

Also symbolic.

We discussed my projects at Midge's house and the times I'd spotted Sinatra wandering around the yard. We discovered neither of us had seen a new movie in years and we seemed unscathed by this. There was a touchy moment when Linden asked if Cleary was my married name and I only shook my head in response. He grabbed a recent copy of the local paper and pointed out an article about the Halloween events.

Halloween was a big deal around here.

Apparently it was almost October and I needed to start caring about Halloween.

We washed the dishes together, me at the sink because I was going to crawl out of my skin if Linden refused to let me *do* something. He parked himself beside me while he dried the dishes, an eye on me as if he expected me to light the sponge on fire. Then he set the last spoon aside and came up behind me, his hands falling to my waist and his body warm against my back.

"I want to kiss you again." He dragged his lips along the back of my neck, under my ear. "But I don't think that's what you need."

I braced my palms flat on either side of the sink. "And who are you to determine what I need?"

There was a moment where he hesitated but it was gone before I could examine it. He tightened his hold on my hips and rocked against me, every hot inch firm against my backside.

"Someone who tends to be right about these things."

I didn't know whether he was trying to be amusing with that comment but I laughed just the same. "Why do you think you're right about this?"

He hummed against my neck—maybe it was a growl—and I nearly lost my balance from the rumbly waves that noise sent coursing through me. "Because I know I won't stop at kissing you."

He was *so* hard. His shaft was thick and solid, even through the layers of his jeans and my leggings, and my thoughts condensed down to the empty, needy clench between my legs. I was pinned here, between an unyielding man and a cast-iron sink, burning up, and everything was blurry when I tuned into the rolling pressure of his body. Of what it could be.

"Because I'll want more than your mouth and this is not the night for that," he added.

"That's a decision you own?" I asked as his hand traveled up my belly, settled on the underside of my breasts. "All yours?"

"Yeah. It is."

It wasn't only my thoughts gone blurry now but all of me, every eyelash, every centimeter of skin, every muscle that couldn't decide whether to clench or melt.

"For as much as I want you"—he ran his knuckles over my pebbled nipple, tearing a gusty sigh from me in the process—"tonight's not the night, Peach."

With all the severity I could muster, I asked, "And what has led you to that determination?"

He passed his knuckles over me again, catching that

nipple between the joints of his middle and index fingers when he reversed course. He clamped down—and didn't release. "Because you need your rest. It's been a long day and you've been through a lot."

"Excuse me but—"

"I'm not hearing it. The fire was enough, but everything else? Not happening. You need to get the shadows out of your eyes."

"And my divorce official?" There I was, fixer extraordinaire, negotiating with the man pinching my nipple so hard I could feel my pulse throbbing in my core.

His beard rasped the back of my neck when he nodded. "It would help."

"Preston went ahead and got *engaged*. He didn't wait," I wailed.

"One of the many reasons I hope I never come face-to-face with him," Linden replied, growly as ever.

He brought the heel of his palm to the center of my back, kneading his way up my spine until he reached the base of my neck. He pressed, gently forcing my chin to my chest while he rubbed the gathered tension.

"This seems unnecessarily paternalistic." It was possible I moaned this but I stood by my point. I didn't need his strict daddy routine.

"Maybe so." He continued working my neck and shoulders while holding my nipple hostage. "Doesn't change anything. You need sleep, Jas, and rest too."

"Those things are the same."

He dug his thumb into a knot between my shoulder blades. "They are *not*."

"Don't decide you know better. I'll agree, it's a moment of upheaval for me. But that doesn't mean I can't say yes or no.

It doesn't mean I don't want to hear your kidnapping fantasies while you back me up against a tree."

He leaned in, his beard brushing my ear. My nipple was *throbbing throbbing throbbing* and he went right on pinching as if he could do this all day, all night. "You liked that, did you?"

"Just because I liked hearing it doesn't mean I want you to do it. If you think I want you stealing me out of my bed in the middle of the night, you have a crowbar coming your way."

I felt the laugh move through him. "There goes that plan."

"Yeah, workshop that one a bit. Shine it up and come back to me with a fresh version."

"Here's what's going to happen, Jasper," he said, his voice drained of all teasing. "I'm going to offer you the fold-out bed in my den or that sofa over there in the living room because there was a *motherfucking fire* in your house today and I don't think it's a good idea for you to stay there. I've slept on both and can say, without a doubt, the sofa is much more comfortable. I'd offer you my bed but I know you'll pitch a fit over that and then set the kitchen on fire again with whatever you bake to live up to your honor code. "

"I couldn't possibly—"

"Hush. I'm not finished. Since I know you're not going to accept these offers, even if you should, I'll just invite you to come over and use the shower and anything else, anytime you want. I have a packed day tomorrow and I'll probably be out early but you don't have to wait for me to leave or get out of here before I come back."

He eased up on my nipple but that was worse. Very much worse. I was still pulsing like I was one great heartbeat and not a stitch else, and the slightly reduced pressure only made it pound harder. And that didn't even account for the ceaseless ache between my legs and the cock grinding against my ass. Just a heartbeat.

"Right. Well. I—um." I waved a hand in the general direction of my place. Included in that gesture was the cozy sectional where I could vividly imagine myself settling in for the night as well as Linden's bedroom. The one he slept in. Ohhhhh, he probably slept naked. I bet he did. "I should be on my way."

"You sure about that?" Linden asked this in that imperious way of his, as if he knew the answer, knew what I needed better than I did, knew everyfuckingthing yet he asked because he wanted me to think I had a choice in the matter. I had the option to leave and I could very well do that but then we'd both know it wasn't what I wanted. Not even a little bit.

"I am completely certain."

He peeled away from me, his heat and the pressure pinning me to the sink gone in one breath. He released my nipple in another. I nearly pitched over, my legs shaky and my midsection desperate for something to squeeze. And my nipple, well, I could barely feel that specific area of my body. I imagined it looked like a cartoon character's thumb after a good smash with a hammer—five times its normal size with a chorus line of exclamation points popping above my areola. Oh, yes, I was completely certain that it was time for me to go.

"Of course you are," he replied, something smug in his tone.

I turned around. He was already on his way to the door. "Yes, I have an appointment in the morning."

Linden dipped his chin, acknowledging my decision but

not buying a word of it. "Do you have good directions this time?"

I smoothed my hands down my sides and strapped on a resolute grin. "My directions are fine, thank you for asking."

He paused at the door while I stepped into my shoes. He intended to walk me home and I could argue if I wished but I wouldn't change his mind.

As he held the door open for me, he asked, "Where are you headed?"

Cold evening air bit at my cheeks and nose. "North, I believe."

He chuckled as he fell into step with me. "That covers a lot of territory."

I didn't know why it made me nervous to discuss my appointment with the divorce attorney but an anxious shiver stirred in my belly. "I'll be just fine."

A noise rumbled out of Linden though he didn't form any words until we climbed the front steps. "Do you want me to give you a ride?"

My throat tightened. "You said you had a busy morning lined up."

He shrugged. "Nothing I can't reschedule."

I swallowed around a thick, throbbing stone of emotion, one sure to be a product of this strange nervousness. His questions were polite and reasonable yet everything inside me prickled and worried like I was warding off some kind of attack. "No need. I'll be all right on my own."

I turned my attention to the very important work of digging the keychain from my pocket. Linden eyed me as I did this. Always eyeing me, always sizing me up. Always thinking about sinking those teeth right into my neck.

"I'm sure you will be," he said. "I can still give you a ride. So you'll be on time."

I shifted away from him, now busy with the work of unlocking the old door. "I'll be all right," I repeated. "You have a busy schedule."

"Where is this office? Do you have an address?"

I rattled off the street name, adding, "I've already checked out the directions online. Seems straightforward."

"There's nothing straightforward about the roads into Boston. In fact, we go to great pains to make sure they're as curved and convoluted as possible."

"I've noticed this."

"There will be rotaries," he continued. "You might want to plan an extra hour or two into your commute."

"Traffic circles," I murmured. "Thank you for the advice." I pushed the door open and stepped over the threshold. Turning back to face him, I grinned, saying, "Thanks for walking me back. And everything else today. Unnecessary but very kind."

He folded his arms over his broad chest and tipped his head toward the door. "Lock up, all right? I'll wait."

"Have a good night." I closed the door and leaned back against it, my cheek flat on the panel. I didn't need to glance through the peephole to know Linden was still there. True to his word, that one. I was willing to bet he'd stay until he heard the deadbolt slide into place and it wouldn't matter whether it took me two minutes or two hours. He'd wait and I didn't know why that sent another bolt of unease through my chest, into my belly.

The strangest thing was this wasn't any form of worry I'd known before. Something was happening inside me, something that danced along the edges of worry, but that wasn't it. All I knew about this sensation was I couldn't decide whether to move toward it or away from it.

I ran the pad of my finger over the cool metal as I drew out this ritual a few seconds longer. What would he do if I didn't engage the bolt? Would he turn the knob and step inside, press himself up against me while he announced he'd lock the door for me? Would I allow that? Would I let him barge in and issue orders? Would I acquiesce to those orders? Would I let myself enjoy it?

Seeing as I didn't have firm answers to any of those questions but most notably the final one, I closed two fingertips around the bolt and flipped it into place.

Through the panel, I heard, "Night, Jasper."

I sank my teeth into my lower lip. I couldn't help it. No one had ever invested so much energy into looking after me before. No one had ever walked me home, waited until I was safe inside. No one had ever offered me a hanky while I cried or required I change into yoga pants for some nature therapy. No one stood by while I fully and completely fell apart and then fed me stew for supper.

I worried my lip some more and gave myself a moment to be the object of his concern without trying to convince myself I wasn't enjoying it.

———

WHEN A KNOCK SOUNDED AT MY DOOR THE NEXT MORNING, I was one leg into a pair of slim black trousers. I hop-stumbled toward the front of the house as I wiggled into the other leg. As much as I adored my dresses and the disequilibrating power of knife-sharp femininity, there was something about a pantsuit that said, *I am in fucking charge here. Try me at your own peril.*

Even though this attorney was on my side, I felt the need to walk in with some ass-kicking armor in place. A bit breathless from struggling into those trousers, I pressed a hand to my forehead as I opened the door.

I'd expected to find a delivery person with another fruit bouquet from my mother (and Martin) on the other side. Maybe one of the salvage and reclamation companies I'd contacted about hauling away the assortment of bricks piled up in the backyard. Those puppies sold for as much as a buck a brick, which could add up to enough to replace the water heater and electrical panel.

I did not expect to find Linden. "Ready to go, Peach?"

"But—what are you doing here? What about your schedule? You said—"

"Everything can be moved," he cut in, twirling his key ring on his index finger. "I'll be in the truck when you're all set."

Without any further explanation or—or anything, he turned, hulked down the steps, and disappeared around the driveway. Still frozen in the threshold, I heard a door open, then shut, and the roar of an engine followed.

The damp morning air wafted over my bare feet and I shook myself back into action. I had to locate shoes, run a brush through my hair, and dust on enough makeup to disguise the shadows under my eyes from sitting up all night, wondering what to do with my life now. Busy with those tasks, I didn't allow myself to form assumptions or acknowledge the warmth coursing through me at Linden's appearance. He was driving me because he expected I'd get lost. That was it.

There was nothing special or significant about this gesture. *Nothing*.

After checking my hair one last time, I joined Linden in his truck. He was tapping out a message on his phone while I settled in beside him. "You really don't need to do this—"

He held up a hand. "I got it, Jasper. I know."

"Oh. Well. Thank you."

He draped his arm over the back of my seat to glance out the rear window. "No worries."

"I didn't say I was worried. I said thank you."

He cut a piercing grin in my direction as he drove up the street. "It's all good."

"But you know how I feel about people doing things for me. I'll have to fire up the crockpot."

I was aiming for some self-deprecating humor but it was clear I'd missed the mark when Linden said, "I know you won't let anyone help you. I know you see it as a liability, a weakness."

Still hoping for humor, I continued, "I'll have to whip up another batch of biscuits. Maybe a banana bread."

"Oh god, please don't. The bananas deserve a better fate than your baking."

We shared a laugh at that and fell into comfortable silence by the time we reached the interstate. Though I wasn't about to announce it to him, handing off the task of navigation was a treat. One less thing to worry about today.

I wasn't worried, not in any true sense of worried. It was more like the feeling of standing on the end of a diving board, toes curled around the edge, heart racing in your chest as if *anything* could happen when you jumped, anything at all. It could be fun and perfect but it could also hurt. It could be an embarrassing, uncoordinated splash of limbs. Even if you wanted to dive, even if you'd climbed up there because you wanted to go through with it, getting to the edge was something else altogether.

I fished my phone out of my bag and checked the notifications. Nothing new—and that came as a thin, mild relief coupled with unspeakable confusion. I needed to figure out my next steps sooner than later.

Linden reached over, covered my hand with his. "You're nervous," he said as he stilled my fingers. I wasn't sure when I'd started tapping my nails against the screen.

I nodded. "A little, yeah."

He shifted his hand to lace his fingers with mine. "About the lawyer or something else?"

"I don't know. I have a lot to figure out. The lawyer and… everything else."

"Not today you don't. One thing at a time." He turned into an office park and stopped in front of the last building. It was low and gray, and completely ordinary. "Here we are."

I stared at the shingled building and the sign announcing the practice partners, and it struck me that I'd never told Linden the specific location. He must've looked it up in advance. I didn't know how to react to that. I wanted to take it as proof he cared about me—he cared much more than he was annoyed by me—but that seemed foolish. When I boiled it all down, it didn't matter that much and it probably mattered nothing at all to him.

"Would you like me to come in with you?"

This was nothing. I meant nothing to him. He was just *very* neighborly. "Um…"

"Let me put it to you this way: Would it make you uncomfortable if I walked you inside?"

I shook my head. "No."

"Would you get stressed out if a receptionist made an offhand comment referring to me as your significant other?"

"I don't want you to deal with—"

"I asked if it would stress *you* out. Would it?"

Again, I shook my head. "No."

"Then that's what we'll do." He squeezed my hand. "Stay here. I'll come around."

I watched him kill the engine and disengage his seat belt, and I wanted to honor his request. I wanted to stay in my seat, I wanted it more than anything, but my entire body rebelled against the notion of *sitting here and waiting*. I couldn't let him help me out of a vehicle when I was perfectly capable. It was a pleasantry but it was also a doorway to leaning on him, relying on him, expecting things from him.

That was the last thing I needed, especially after—*oh god* —yesterday.

When Linden rounded the hood of the truck and found me standing there, straightening my hair in the side mirror, he blew out a breath, muttered something to himself, and gave me a slow up-and-down stare. "All right, Jasper. Let's get to it."

Linden was right about being mistaken for my significant other at the front desk, and his repeated insistence that it didn't bother him saved me from apologizing all over the situation while I waited to be called back into a meeting room.

"Why would it bother me?" he asked. "Why would I put any effort into reacting to the presumptions of a stranger?"

I wanted to provide him a thoughtful explanation as to why it was reasonable to feel some sort of way about this but all I could offer was, "I don't know. Sometimes men get weird about being misrepresented."

"*Men* get weird about being misrepresented?"

I threw my hands up. "Please don't goad me into a 'not all men' moment."

"No, that's not what I'm getting at," he replied, impatience thick in his voice. "What I mean is, if someone can't handle being logically and reasonably mistaken for a significant other in a low-stakes situation, that person is probably forcing a lot of their own insecurities onto you. So no, not all men. Just the ones too fragile to deal with the idea of significance."

I studied him for a moment, his large body wedged into the chair beside me and his gaze steady in a way that made me feel extremely unsteady, like an awkward hatbox on the top of a precarious pile. Like I could come crashing down at any minute and he'd go right on staring, waiting for me to do something better than fall to pieces before him.

"Ms. Cleary? We're ready for you." A woman with a tablet cradled in her arm smiled at me with expectant eyes. "Your partner is welcome to join us too."

He glanced over but kept his gaze on the floor. His voice lowered, he asked, "Will it make you uncomfortable if I go in there with you?"

"Seems a little intimate, considering I've only cried on your shoulder twice and gagged my personal problems all over you."

He bobbed his head as he laughed. "If it would make you feel better, you're welcome to come home with me after this and get naked. I'll also get naked. To balance things out. If you wanted, we could be naked together. That's about as intimate as it gets, Peach."

I smiled in spite of myself. "You don't need to do that."

"Maybe I want to."

"Are we talking about the naked stuff or the divorce stuff? I've lost track."

"Will it make you uncomfortable if I come in?" he repeated. "That's all I care about."

"Ms. Cleary?"

I stood, swung my bag over my shoulder. "I won't be uncomfortable."

Linden pushed to his feet and flattened his hand low on my back. "Then tell me if that changes."

I'd imagined doing this alone. Paging through the legal documents, signing my name a million times, handling it all with only myself to lean on—same as it always was. Never in my mental calculus did I see a flannel-shirted man with thighs like tree trunks doing any of it with me. It was tempting to rewrite my plans to include him but I'd learned that lesson the hardest way. Moments like these didn't add up the way I craved, they didn't lead to the permanence I wanted, and they didn't last.

I smiled up at him all the same.

He was polite enough to distract himself by studying the trees on the other side of the window while the legal assistant identified the documents waiting for me and pointed out the information I had to verify. It would only take a few minutes, she explained, unless I wanted to make changes to the agreement. That would require another round of review by the other party—Preston—and we'd have to reconvene to finalize our dissolution.

It was such an unlikely word. *Dissolution.* It made me think of ripping open a pouch of Jell-O mix and stirring it into boiling water. It was the wrong thing to think about. Divorce and Jell-O had nothing in common. This piece of me was falling apart and Jell-O only came together. It solidified. It even wiggled.

There was nothing solid in my life. Not even the house I called my home. Any day now, a good gust of wind was going to blow this little piggy's house right down. What would I do then? Where would I go?

Sign the papers, sell the bricks, sweep up the broken home. Keep moving. Don't look back.

I wouldn't need another round. There was nothing to change. Preston and I had nothing to divide up, nothing shared between us but a friendship that'd once functioned as the very best thing in our young lives. We didn't have joint bank accounts or property. I'd moved out of our apartment and into a smaller, more affordable place after he followed his boss to Northern Ireland. I didn't have a married name to erase from my driver's license and credit cards as I'd had no interest in the lengthy process of paperwork and filings to do away with my maiden name.

No, we'd dissolve this today and nothing would be different tomorrow.

The legal assistant left us alone, promising my attorney would be in shortly and offering us every variety of coffee and tea under the sun. There were also pastries and break-fast breads, if we pleased, and several brands of bottled water.

She only referred to Linden as my partner twice.

I only winced over it once.

After a pause, he asked, "You're sure you're not uncomfortable? I'll go. It's fine."

With my knees pinched together tight and a hand

clutching the lapels of my blazer, I shook my head. "I'm beginning to think you're the uncomfortable one."

"I'll survive."

Because his presence, even as he gazed out the window with his back mostly turned away from me, was more reassuring than it was awkward, I replied, "Then I can survive too."

ELEVEN
LINDEN

I couldn't explain why I took Jasper into the woods with me again.

I couldn't explain why I rearranged my plans for the day to escort her to the attorney's office either but I'd made up my mind last night.

All I knew was I couldn't drive her home after watching her sign those papers and leave her there. I couldn't let her retreat into that hard shell constructed of *I can do it myself* and contempt. It wasn't like I could go inside with her. I'd have her freshly freed ass bent over the nearest surface, those prim trousers around her knees, and my cock laying claim to her before the door closed behind us.

All that sounded outstanding but Jasper still looked like a deer in the headlights. I didn't know much about divorce or the realization your job was eating your soul, but I knew none of that was the right starting point for what I wanted with her. It wasn't tender or polite, or even considerate. I wanted to fuck her so thoroughly she forgot how to argue and then curled up beside me, sweet and sated.

Aside from the vibe being off, it didn't seem *right*. I knew Jasper could make decisions for herself but there was something wrong about making advances on a woman when she was climbing out of quicksand. Even if she said yes—and her body seemed to say yes—I didn't want it to be that way between us.

I could wait until the shadows were out of her eyes, until she slowed down long enough to catch her breath. Until she stopped running on adrenaline and crockpot biscuits. Until the forest air filled her lungs and the worst of this trouble was behind her. I could wait.

When Jasper emerged from the house in athletic gear, I motioned to a narrow split in the woods at the far edge of my property, saying, "There's a small trail. We'll start there."

She slipped her hands into the pockets of her zip-up jacket, and I was once again an idiot for putting her in such form-fitting clothing. Anything—even if it held me on the razor's edge of arousal all day—improved on the pantsuit that seemed to swallow her up and spit her out in some robotic, empty-eyed version of herself.

"This makes for a quick commute." She glanced up at the shock of orange, red, and yellow leaves on the maple branches. "I always liked this time of year. So pretty."

I slapped a hand to the trunk of the old tree. "It's good to see these maples holding on to their leaves this long. Too many of them are turning in early September and are fully bare by now."

"That's not how it should be?"

Her hair was looped in some kind of bun and her eyes seemed big and owlish, as if she'd never really stopped to look at autumn leaves and couldn't believe what she was seeing. Perhaps she hadn't stopped to look in a terribly long time.

"No. Early aging and death in leaves is a product of tree stress. Drought, disease, extreme weather—those are the big factors."

"Okay but we still like it when the leaves change colors, right? Just not at the wrong times?"

"Yes. Fall foliage is the result of chlorophyll—the compound that makes plant life green—breaking down when the summer growing season slows and the sun is positioned farther away from the earth. Less daylight and cooler air temperature signal the start of autumn which then kicks off a chemical response and, in some trees, pigments are released which drive the changes in colors."

She regarded me with an odd smile. "That was such a scientific answer."

"Were you expecting something else?"

Jasper continued down the trail without responding which was fine since it gave me time to study her without her watching while I did it.

I wanted to solve all of her problems for her. More than once, I'd picked up the phone to call the plumber who'd overhauled my system and get him working on Jasper's house as soon as possible. There was one time when I'd almost called my sister in for backup. As a landscape architect specializing in historic homes, Magnolia worked with contractors and designers accustomed to wonky old houses. She'd have the situation in hand before we hung up. I didn't care if I had to foot the bill, I just wanted this resolved.

I held back every time. It was one thing to insert myself into small, inconsequential matters such as the basement boxes, but hiring a plumber was another. There weren't enough crockpot biscuits in the world and Jasper would probably launch them at my head for interfering in such an unwelcome manner.

I couldn't take the reins and do it for her any more than I could solve her career crises. She had to do this for herself, and as much as it pained me to sit by and watch, I knew she'd freeze me out if I took a few problems off her plate.

I didn't want her to freeze me out—though I could explain that no better than I could explain the inner workings of Jasper-Anne Cleary. That was to say I had some loose ideas but I was no authority on anything save for the trees around us.

"So, what's this?" she asked, pointing at an old cedar.

"That's a White American cedar. Between a hundred and twenty to a hundred and forty years old, if I had to guess."

She turned in the opposite direction, pointing blindly. "And that?"

"Shag bark hickory." I gestured to a great tree in the clearing ahead. "Chestnut oak. The species diversity is one of my favorite things about this area."

"What about all this stuff?" She motioned toward the forest floor. "What's this?"

I crossed toward her, taking her hand in mine and leading her deeper down the trail. "Let's see what we find. We have a good amount of American holly. You can see the berries on that one. Some of the last blooms of the season are still hanging on to that hardy geranium over there. It's probably too late for any lady's slipper but we'd find them over here, on a mossy slope. They like to hang out with the fiddlehead ferns and swamp azalea, though they don't all grow at the same times."

She leaned into me as we walked, her shoulder against my bicep, our joined hands brushing her thigh. "And you know this from looking at it? You don't have to examine it more closely or anything?"

"All these trees and plants have characteristics you can pick out from a distance. I don't need to examine the holly because I know its shape and its dark, glossy leaves. Nothing else in this area is exactly like it."

"That's wild to me," she said softly. "I just…I don't know. I can't imagine knowing something so well I can name it and explain it from twenty feet away." She tipped her head to the side, resting on my shoulder. I stared at her birthmark a moment longer than necessary. It was cute. Like a splash of creamy coffee, if that could be cute. Whatever. I thought it was cute. "Not something new anyway. Not something I learned from the start."

"Who says you have to start over?"

"Um, you did. Yesterday. In a different forest that somehow looked exactly like this one. Are you sure they aren't the same? Is this a prank?"

"Different parks, I swear." I shifted to press a quick kiss to her forehead. "Just because your last job was wrong for you doesn't mean everything about it was wrong."

"You say that," she started with a laugh thick in her words, "but I was making some lists last night—"

"I told you to sleep last night, Peach."

Surprising the ever-loving shit out of me, Jasper dropped my hand to loop her arm around my waist, slide her hand under my shirt, and brush her fingers down my back. It wasn't the gesture itself. An arm around the waist was nothing, considering I came this close to dry humping her against the kitchen sink last night. Not to mention the tree yesterday afternoon. It was that *she* initiated. As far as I could remember, she'd never been the one to reach out. I'd assumed it was part of her aloof vibe.

As Jasper had mentioned once before, my assumptions were wrong.

In this case, it was good to be wrong.

"You did but I had to think," she replied.

I gathered her close, my arm tightening around her shoulder. "I'm sure you did. What did you come up with?"

She snickered. "I promise you, it's not even close to interesting."

"You were up all night instead of sleeping like you needed, so you better believe I want to hear what came from all that stressing."

A sweet grumble sounded in her throat. "I didn't come up with anything good. Just the same stuff—writing a book, consulting, think tanks. Then I made some lists of things that could be promising, like teaching government or public policy."

"I bet you'd be good at that. You know government the way I know these woods."

"Maybe. I don't know. I'd probably have to go back to school for that. Working in the Senate doesn't automatically qualify me to teach anyone unless I want to start a YouTube channel and that sounds terrible."

"What do you think about going back to school, then?"

"Not my favorite idea. Grad school is expensive. It takes a long time. There's also a load of busywork involved. Writing papers a certain way, researching things that don't matter anymore, debating odd bits of constitutional history. That's not how government works and I don't have any patience for people who think they know how it works based off their in-depth analysis of tweets and *The West Wing*. I'd end up yelling at people every day. I'd get a reputation real quick."

"You would terrify them. I'd pay to watch."

"You know, at least six men have told me I've appeared in their nightmares."

"Not that you're bragging."

She smiled up at me. "I would never."

"All right, so, teaching doesn't stay on the list. Cross that off. What else? There had to be something you liked about working for the senator. Something that got you out of bed in the morning."

"Blind panic usually got me out of bed in the morning. Like pimples, problems developed overnight. Mornings were about damage control."

"You can't say things like that to me, Jas. You just can't. It makes me want to wrap you in blankets and tuck you into my bed for a very long time. At least until I'm finished strangling that boss of yours."

At that, Jasper buried her face in my chest. "Don't be nice to me. It's confusing."

"You'll have to suffer, then." I kissed her hair again because she was right there and I couldn't have her *right there* without kissing her. I could not. "Back on topic. What did you like about your job, and for fuck's sake, don't give me another reason to swaddle you because I'll do it."

For a moment, she didn't respond, didn't move a muscle. Then, she tipped her head back, casting an unfocused gaze on the woods behind me. "I liked the purpose. Even when the actual work was tedious or nothing more than creating diversions. I felt like I was doing something that mattered. That it was bigger than me. Timbrooks has always been an imperfect candidate but he voted the right way when it mattered. That was enough for me. That justified it. I could forgive and excuse everything else when we were advancing the right issues."

"That's the piece to hold on to," I said. "Advance the right issues. Do something that matters—to you."

"As great as that sounds," she started, still watching the trees, "no one working on those issues wants anything to do with me. My bridges are burnt and all my boats too."

I tucked a few strands of hair behind her ears. "Everything looks like a dead end right now and that's why you need to give yourself a break."

"I don't have time for any breaks. I'm already several weeks into this break and I can't waste any more time with"—she flapped a hand at the hardy geraniums—"wandering in the woods and exploring the depths of my soul."

"Nothing blooms in every season," I said. "You shouldn't expect that of yourself when it doesn't occur in nature."

"That's a charming sentiment but I've been figuring out how to bloom nonstop since primary school. Not going to kick back now just because my life went to hell in a handbasket overnight."

I scooped her up, my arms cradling her backside and her spine against a tree trunk, because I didn't want to hear any more of this bullshit. "I'll find the time for you. We'll start by eliminating the baking from your day."

"Ahhhhh. There's the rude bear I've come to expect."

I watched the humor drift over her lovely face. She was beautiful in a painful sort of way, the kind that tightened your chest a bit too much. "Did you like being nightmarish?"

"What?"

"You said you'd been featured in nightmares and we had a laugh about it but I want to know if you liked that."

"I...I liked being taken seriously."

Nodding, I gave her ass a thorough squeeze, seeing as it was tremendously squeezable. Every time I laid eyes on her, I just wanted to dig my fingers in and *squeeze*. One more perversion where this woman was concerned but this was as far as I'd let it go right now. There was no fun in taking a bewildered, emotionally exhausted woman to bed, not for anyone. Especially not her. If we were going to do this, we were going to start it up the right way.

And that meant waiting until she didn't look like a breeze would blow her over.

"Sometimes," she continued, "people look at me and... they think I'm not intelligent or I can't do anything—"

"First time I saw you, I was positive you could crack open the earth to discard the bodies of those who got in your way."

"And yet you still came over and got in my way," she mused. "Put me down. I feel like a doll."

"What's the trouble in that?"

"Dolls aren't in charge. They have to wait to be taken off the shelf to play and even then, it's someone else's game."

I set her down, purposeful in running the length of her body against mine. "It's your game, Jas. There's no question about that. But you will sleep tonight. If you can't, call me. I'll bore you to sleep with stories about fungi."

She gave me a tart look. "Do you have many fungi stories?"

"Everyone has some good fungi stories but to someone who doesn't find that sort of thing intriguing, it could be the difference between sitting up and making a ton of lists and sleeping a solid eight or nine hours."

"Now I'm curious about this. What kind of fungi stories are we talking about?"

I pointed to a decaying conifer several yards away. "That's a Purplepore Bracket. It only lives on dying trees. Same with the False Turkey Tail, although we don't see that in this species of tree. And that, near the trunk of that red oak, is Bitter Oyster. It starts out small and knobby like that, but when it's fully developed it becomes bioluminescent. Since glowing mushrooms are not what anyone would expect to find and the whole thing is rather disarming on moonless nights, the glow they give off used to be known as fairy fire. There was a load of Native folklore around it but that's just how saprophytic fungi behave—unexpectedly."

"You really do have fungi stories."

"Look, mushrooms are wild. They exist in their own kingdom, neither plant nor animal even though they possess many qualities of both. And they hate being classified. Every time it seems like we have it all worked out, someone finds a new mushroom somewhere and the whole thing gets fucked up again. All we know is some of them are poisonous, some of them are edible, some of them are medicinal. Some will kill you with a single touch. Some will activate portions of your brain that rarely pop. Others are bioremediative and others might be immortal. We don't know for sure. We just don't know. It's very complex."

Jasper pressed her lips together in a flat frown. "Yeah, none of this will put me to sleep. I just have a million more questions."

Even though I knew better, I really did, I said, "I'll find a way to tire you out, Peach."

Her eyes widened. "I'm sure you will."

Because I knew better, I pointed to the Bitter Oyster again. "I can also talk about mushrooms."

With a nod, she leaned into me, her head tucked under my chin. "Okay. Let's talk about mushrooms."

TWELVE
JASPER

I woke up with the earliest light of dawn and spent a full minute blinking at the ceiling because I didn't know where I was. There was a moment where I gazed at the hand-carved beams running along the midline of the ceiling and I believed I was in Texas. There was a hotel in Houston we favored for campaign stops that had beams just like that one.

It took that full minute to realize I wasn't in Texas. I wasn't on a campaign stop, and I wasn't married anymore. Not legally, at least. I hadn't been emotionally married since before Preston left for Northern Ireland. Since...ever, really.

I was single in all the ways that counted and I felt nothing. Nothing new, nothing different. Maybe this was numbness. I didn't feel anything because I couldn't feel anything, not because I'd already felt everything associated with this part of my life ending.

My gaze shifted away from the ceiling beam and settled on the rich blue wall. I had no memory of falling asleep on Linden's big sectional sofa but the pillow under my head and the heavy blanket tucked into the cushions around me said otherwise.

The morning after my divorce was finalized and the only thing I felt was disappointment Linden hadn't carried me into his bedroom instead of letting me sleep here. I'd always wanted to be scooped up and carried to bed, even if it was very unrealistic. There was no way I'd sleep through that sort of thing and even the most petite women turned into solid blocks of dead weight while they slept. Still, it would've been nice.

But this was better. Linden would've put me to bed only to post himself on the sofa and that would've erased all the carry-to-bed fun. This was better. Even if he'd snuggled in beside me and we'd rubbed up on each other in our sleep, this was better. No awkward tango getting out of bed come morning, no awkward conversation of defining *this* and what it meant. Nothing awkward at all.

This was better. The sofa was better.

————

SOMEWHERE BETWEEN CONVINCING MYSELF THAT SLEEPING alone on the sofa was preferrable to late-night spooning and debating whether it was time to sneak out and go home, I fell back to sleep.

It turned out to be the kind of dark, dreamless sleep that left your mouth feeling gummy, your eyes sandy, and your mind unfocused, almost as if you needed the day to recover from sleeping.

"What time is it?" I murmured to myself as I sat up. My body was not convinced that being upright was worth it.

"Ten forty-five." I swiveled in the direction of that deep

voice, finding Linden seated at the kitchen table with papers spread out in front of him. "Figured you'd wake up when I started the bacon but that was eight thirty and you didn't stir."

"Oh. Wow. Sorry about that."

"You needed the rest. Don't be sorry."

I stood, folded the blanket, set it on top of the pillow. "Well. Thank you for letting me crash here."

"No worries." He flipped over a paper, tapped the end of his pen to his temple as he studied it. "You should do it more often."

I stared at him. "I should—what?"

He dropped the paper and pen. "Look, I'm not equipped for morning conversations. I can't talk at this time of day and—"

"That explains so much," I murmured. "If only you'd said something sooner."

"—you talk all the time, which is obviously a problem, but you should stay here more often. You can use the Wi-Fi and, you know, your crockpot won't short out my electrical system. It's better than spending the nights at Midge's place, especially after you've been painting. Can't be good to breathe all that in. You have to air those rooms out. And the hot water, for fuck's sake, Jas. I'm not gonna insist you do anything because god knows that will bite me in the balls but I think you should stay here. Every night. If you want. That's all."

"Not equipped to talk in the morning," I repeated. "Mmhmm."

"What was that?"

I shook my head as I retied my ponytail. "Have you eaten breakfast?"

He felt it necessary to look worried. "Please, Jasper. Don't bake anything. *Please.*"

"No baking involved." I breezed past him to grab the shoes I'd left beside the door. "Just toasting. I'm gonna run next door and grab a few ingredients—"

"I have everything you'd need."

"Probably not." I stepped into one shoe, then the other. "I like a certain bread. Oh, and my avocados should be perfectly ripe."

He shouted something as I closed the door but I didn't worry over it. We couldn't have him overdoing it on the words. Not this early in the morning.

I filled a reusable shopping bag with everything I required for fancy toast and then stopped into my room for a change of clothes. My tote bag was ready to go with my regular showering-at-Linden's gear, which made it easy.

I gave the room another glance, saying out loud, "This is enough. This is fine."

Because I couldn't move into another man's house the day after my divorce was finalized and years after it became fact. Regardless of his invite and the devastating sweetness of his gruff, grumbly way of asking. Really, I couldn't. Even if part of me wanted to.

The other part, as always, needed to shove him off. Accepting that kind of help wasn't something I could do, even if it looked tempting on the surface. Sure, it sounded great and chances were good I'd get some decent sleep if I didn't have to worry about whether the heating system would short out the electrical overnight and kill me in a ball of fire, but at what cost? I'd exchange one problem for another, a fiery death for Linden's steadfast concern for me.

Because, of course, that was completely unnecessary of him.

Very nice and warm-fuzzy inducing, and fall-off-a-cliff foreign to me but completely unnecessary. So unnecessary.

I pushed open the door from Linden's deck and hefted the shopping bag over my head. "Time for toast."

Still stationed at the table, Linden pinned me with one arched eyebrow. He didn't respond, instead staring as I set down my tote and unpacked the grocery items, that eyebrow busy climbing into his forehead.

"What are you in the mood for this morning?" I asked.

A rough laugh rasped out of him. "Ask a different question, Peach."

I had to bite my lips together because he didn't need to know how much I enjoyed those words. "I have avocado, banana, eggs, a bit of brie, and a nice lemon curd. Just tell me if you hate any of those things."

"I'd hate those things all together so please tell me that's not the direction we're going."

I put my hands on my hips. "Seriously, Lin. Why would I do that?"

"I can't explain any of your baking choices."

I grinned. "Lucky for you, fancy toast is not baking."

While Linden shifted through his papers, I introduced myself to his kitchen appliances. I needed a minute or two to contemplate his retro two-slice toaster versus the high-end range with gas burners. I didn't *need* to broil the bread but it wasn't a matter of need nearly as much as *want*. I wanted that bread broiled even if I knew the odds of charring it and setting off the smoke detectors were high. I was willing to deal with some blackened crusts. I didn't mind that, even if I rarely used the broiler back home in D.C. because it was too much trouble to babysit the bread. Who had the time to supervise bread? Not me. Definitely not me.

But now I could sit by the stove, watching and waiting. I could risk the crusts, the smoke alarms. I could do this. I could do things I'd assumed were off-limits to me. It would be amazing, it would be perfect. The best toast I'd ever made.

I dropped two thick slices of sourdough into the toaster instead.

I didn't know how Linden's oven worked. How hot it got, how fast it cooked. And I didn't want to ruin everything while he watched. I could scrape a little extra color from the toast but I couldn't serve him charcoal and pretend everything was cool. I knew what to expect from the toaster and I knew it wouldn't give Linden another reason to doubt my skills.

I'd use the broiler another time. It wasn't going anywhere. I'd get to it.

Once I had the toast prepared, I swung a glance to Linden. He was focused on the same paper, leading me to believe it was an exceptionally difficult topic or he didn't trust me with his appliances. Possibly both.

"Do you have any big knives? Something long and sharp I can cut these—"

He pushed away from the table. "I'm not giving you a long, sharp knife, Jasper. I'll do a lot of things for you but that's not one of them. Sorry but no."

I had a *huge* argument ready to go. Massive. There was a slide deck hot in my head. I had so much to say about this but then it just—poof—evaporated. There was a spot behind the argument, beyond the self-preservation, where I wanted someone to *insist*.

It was a terrifying spot to revisit because my ex-husband had insisted we were perfect for each other, my mother had insisted she was doing her best, my father insisted he loved me more than anything in the world. Even if they all believed what they'd said, they still let me down. They were still wrong. Why was I to believe Linden's insistence would turn out any differently?

"Okay. What are we cutting?" He dropped his hands to my waist and leaned in to inspect my creations. "This looks surprisingly edible."

I wiggled my shoulders. "Fancy toast is my jam."

He laughed into my hair. "That's adorable."

"Now, if you'd point me in the direction of a knife…"

Yanking open a drawer to the left, he asked, "Tell me how you want it cut."

Admittedly, the knife he retrieved could double as a samurai sword and it was possible I would've taken my finger off with that thing. "Triangles. Please."

He cut the toast and shifted beside me to rinse the knife when he was finished. "All right, then. Tell me what we have here."

My gaze fixed on the plates because I didn't trust myself to look up at Linden right now without asking whether it was possible for him to insist without breaking my heart, I said, "This is almond butter, banana, honey, and chopped walnuts. That one is avocado, soft boiled egg, and some of the hot honey sauce I found in your spice cabinet when I was looking for crushed red pepper flakes. It's fine if you hate it. I'll just—"

"That sounds amazing." He took a bite of the almond butter and banana. "Shit, that's good."

"I usually sauté the bananas to give them some

caramelization but I didn't want to use every single one of your pots and pans."

"No, babe, this is perfect." He pushed the almond butter and banana plate toward me, saying, "Take the other half before I inhale it."

"I can make more."

His fingers tucked inside the waistband of my leggings, he steered me toward the table. "What you can do is sit your ass down and eat." He set the plate in front of me, asking, "Coffee?"

"Oh. Yes. That would be great. Do you have any—" A carton of milk appeared in front of me, followed by a mug. "Thank you."

Linden pushed his papers aside and settled back into his seat, the avo-and-egg plate positioned between us. "I need you to explain one thing." He filled my mug about three quarters of the way with cold brew and topped it off with milk, just the way I liked. Which was nuts because how did he know my ratios? How? *Why?* "All those cupcakes and banana breads—you were fucking with me. Right? Because this is awesome and that was as close as you can legally come to poison."

"I was not fucking with you. Like I said, toast is my jam."

He devoured half of the avo-and-egg, then pushed that plate toward me too. "There's more I could say about this but let me simply ask, one more time, that you never bake again. Definitely not in that crockpot and not when you could make this instead."

"I think your real argument is with the crockpot."

"I think I like the way you're smiling this morning so I'm not going to say anything that might change that, even if the crockpot is one part of a larger problem."

I grinned down at my toast. I didn't feel different today but maybe that didn't matter because I *was* different. "The crockpot is not the problem. I've had it since college and it works like a charm."

Linden shook his head. "Not taking your bait, lady." Then, "What are you doing today?"

I drew my shoulders up as I chewed. "I need to get back to work on that porch. And by get back to work, I mean figure out what I'm doing."

He dusted the crumbs from his hands and frowned at his plate, as if he had some very unfortunate news to share with me. "My sister owns a landscape architecture firm. She has two designers on staff who do porches and decks all day, every day. I could give her a call."

"Professionally remodeled porches are for people with gainful employment."

He frowned. "I'll make sure you get the family discount."

I had no desire to verbalize my financial situation to Linden or anyone else but I pressed on. "As delightful as that sounds, I will have to pass. These DIY projects aren't my idea of a good time but I like doing them. I like solving these problems and learning new skills that I hope to never use again."

He continued frowning. "She'd get it done for free. If I asked."

"Do you have any idea how much toast I'd have to make you—and your sister!—if I got my porch rebuilt for zero pennies? I'd…I don't even know what I'd do. But I can't allow that."

He reached over, scooped up my legs and set them in his lap. "You'd be doing me a favor."

"How"—I blinked hard at his hand on my knee—"how is my porch a favor to you?"

He gave my shin a long stroke before saying, "She wants me to join her firm. She's expanded in the past two years and used to be able to get by with subcontracting for arborist services but she has design *and* maintenance clients now, and farming it out is becoming difficult. Expensive too."

"And you want to be wooed?"

"No, not wooed." He picked up the last quarter of the avo-and-egg toast, which I'd pushed his way. "But I don't want it to be a foregone conclusion. I'd have to shift some of my existing maintenance contracts and the tree warden appointments—"

"What is a tree warden?"

He gestured toward me with the toast. "In this state, every city and town is required to have a warden responsible for the trees on public property. It's a law dating back to the 1890s."

"So, you'd need to balance your current arborist commitments with the demands of Magnolia's business. What's in it for you?"

He downed the last of the toast and took a deep drink of his coffee. "A stake in her firm. A hefty one. We'd be partners, essentially. Plus support staff to handle billing and scheduling, which—apparently—is not my brother's job."

"I can understand how one could see that conclusion as foregone," I replied. "What's holding you back? Is it working with different people or priorities? Giving up or scaling back your existing business?"

"A bit of all that but mostly the responsibility. Right now, I can take on as many clients as I want. I can work four days a week if I feel like it. I'm not accountable to my partner or my employees if I decide I want to slow down or take a month off to travel. I'm the only person I'm responsible for and I'm not sure I want that to change. Even if she does have some really cool equipment."

"Then it's not about the money. Not for you."

He shook his head. "No. I'm fine as I am. If I partnered with Magnolia"—he shrugged, lifting both hands and letting them fall to my shins—"well, I'd have more but that wouldn't change anything. It's just money."

Spoken like someone who never found himself without enough to get by.

"Anyway"—he waved a hand at the papers—"if you want me to make a call, I'll do it. She'll have a team down here within two hours."

"If you did that, I'd have to empty out the garage or the other side of the basement, or decide what I'm going to do about Midge's things, and I don't want to do any of that. Not yet. The side door, the carpets, the walls—that stuff doesn't require any real decisions, and I have to tell you, I've made enough decisions for this month. Fixing the porch doesn't require anything like that."

Linden reached across the table and gathered up the plates, and jerked his chin in the direction of the dirty dishes I'd accumulated. "You cooked, I'll clean up." When I made no move to pull my legs from his lap, he added, "I'm catching up on paperwork this morning and then heading out for a residential appointment in Weymouth but don't let me interfere with your plans. The shower is free if you want it."

We stared at each other for a moment, my legs in his lap, his hands on my thighs, all the tension in the world between us. I might've spent the night but I'd never taken off all my clothes and bathed with him only a door away. He'd never listened as water rushed over my body and we both knew it.

"Yeah," I said on a sigh. It was a big sigh too, the kind that fell into the heaving bosom category. Me, heaving my bosom. "That's a good idea."

Except I didn't move. Not even an inch.

He ran a hand through his short beard. "Need anything?"

I gave a slight shake of my head. "I think I left my bathrobe next door but I'll manage without it."

I didn't mean to imply that I'd sashay out of the bathroom dripping wet. I wasn't suggesting I'd strip down naked here in the kitchen. But Linden's eyes went hot and wide nonetheless—and he yanked his plaid shirt over his head.

"Take this," he said, holding out the flannel to me, leaving him in a tissue-thin gray t-shirt. There was a tattoo on the inside of his bicep, a single rangy mountain with a dragon flying over its peak, and some kind of inscription ringing around them. On the other arm, the blade of a sword poked out from under his sleeve. I couldn't see the rest.

I took it, held it to my chest. "You won't miss it?"

He closed his fingers around my ankle, shifted the sole of my foot flat against his fly. He was hard—and working himself through his jeans with my foot while I clutched his shirt, and *this* was what I meant by all the tension in the world. *This* was why my bosom was heaving. This was it. Right here.

"I should get started." I pushed back in my chair though that meant I gave him a firm, unexpected press with the ball of my foot.

"Jasper," he groaned, both hands wrapped around my ankle now. "*Fuck.* Jasper."

With as much grace as I could manage, I retrieved my

legs and pushed to my feet, grinning at Linden's unmasked distress as I grabbed my tote bag. He didn't move from his seat at the table, his hands cupped over his crotch and his gaze raising a blush to my cheeks. I didn't look away until I had the door closed behind me.

————

As luck would have it, I ended up needing Linden's shirt. I'd left my robe at home plus the "until I put on my real clothes" top I usually wore. The only article of clothing worth wearing was a fresh pair of leggings, unless I wanted to give yesterday's outfit another spin—which I didn't.

So, while I twisted my hair into a knot, I stepped out of the bathroom in leggings and his shirt, which fell to my mid-thigh. "Thanks for the—"

The front door swept open and in came a tornado of a woman, moving and talking and dropping packages in a loud, colorful blur. I stood frozen while I watched this tornado blow through.

"Linden, be a good boy and get the box of preserves from my car. I didn't mean to can so much, I got carried away with the fruit. It's just so good and I have so much fun and—oh, hello dear." She stopped, grinned at me with a deep pink lipstick smile, and without taking her eyes off me, called to Linden, "You didn't tell me you were having guests today."

Her purple ankle jeans and pink pullover with a crisp white blouse underneath reminded me of a Talbots catalog, though the dark hazel eyes, just like her son's, sized me up right away. It was the middle of the workday and I was fresh from the shower, and that meant only one thing as far as mothers were concerned.

"Just the one guest, Mom." He stood up, gave me a *sorry about this* shrug. "Jasper, this is my mother, Diana, who has forgotten how to knock. Mom, this is Jasper-Anne Cleary."

I held out my hand to her. "How do you do?"

Her curious grin melted into a comically gleeful smile as she pressed both hands to her chest and squealed. She *squealed*. "Linden! You should've told me you had such a beautiful *guest!*" She shot him a wink that said she was in on the joke. "Oh my goodness, you are just gorgeous!"

Then she flung herself at me, gathering me into a crushing hug that stole my breath and seemed unnaturally strong for such a petite woman. Since I was a guest of Linden's but not a wink-wink guest, I wasn't sure how to respond, but after a beat passed, it didn't matter. I had no choice but to return her hug. "That's so kind of you."

She pulled back, holding tight to my shoulders. "Good gracious. Is that a touch of the South I'm hearing from you?"

I laughed because she asked with the most *Steel Magnolias* accent I'd ever heard, and *everyone* mimicked my accent when they met me. What was left of it.

"Oh my *god*," Linden murmured. "Mom. Stop. You're being ridiculous."

"Quiet, Linden," she replied, smoothing a hand over the arms of my shirt. Which was her son's. Which she knew. "I'm having a chat with Jasper-Anne."

"Jasper will do, thank you."

"*Jasper*," she drawled. "So lovely."

He shot me a look that seemed to say *are you good?* and I nodded. I wanted to scoff and say *of course I'm good*. I could handle far stickier situations than a pop-in from Mom.

He dipped his chin, arched his brows up. *Are you sure?*

I gave him a nod, a quick smirk. *Oh yeah. I got this.*

"I'm going to grab that box from the car," he said, pointing to Diana. "Behave yourself."

She blinked. "Whatever could you be implying?"

"That I know your tricks. Behave," he repeated.

The door closed and I was alone with Linden's mother. Wet hair, bare feet, borrowed shirt. Obviously not my ideal look for any introductory situation but I wasn't in the business of getting my ideals anymore.

"I am just so happy to meet you," Diana said, gripping both of my hands and leading me into the kitchen. "Where are you from, sweetheart?"

"Originally, Georgia," I said, allowing her to steer me into a seat. "Then Washington, D.C., and now I'm here."

She gave me a subtle up-and-down glance as she smiled but it was clear she wanted to know what I did, why I was here, and how wonderful her son was to me. "This quaint town must be quite the change of pace for you."

I was prepared to joke about the culture shock but instead answered, "I'm enjoying it."

"As you should." She patted my arm with so much maternal reassurance, I felt tears prickling behind my eyes. "Now, before my son returns and tells me to keep quiet, I just want to apologize for walking in on you. If you're anything like me, you don't meet company until after your hair is set for the day." She touched gel manicured fingers to her dark, silver-streaked bob. "Not because you aren't perfect just like this—because you are just gorgeous—but that's how I'd feel. I'd also want plenty of warning before meeting my significant other's family"—*oh, wow, she was going there*—"and I should've called ahead. I am learning this, slowly but surely, as my children keep growing up and leading their own lives. I'm sorry for popping in unannounced. I just came from my daughter's house and, because of her aversions to certain foods during this pregnancy, she didn't want to see a jar of preserves. Since my canning closet is full and the food banks won't take home-canned goods, I thought I'd stop here—"

"Jesus, Mom. Don't put her to sleep with the hand-me-down history of your jams, jellies, and preserves."

"Don't forget the marmalades!" She gave me a conspiratorial grin. "I went *to town* on the Meyer lemon marmalade this year. I hope you love it."

Since that sounded phenomenal and I did enjoy anything intended for spreading over bread, I said, "I'm sure I will. I love toast."

"She really does," Linden added as he set the box on the countertop.

"Then I've come to the right place. Oh, Jasper, you have to join us for Sunday supper this weekend. We haven't managed to get everyone together since July because Rob and Magnolia were visiting his family and then Zelda was off on her fieldwork adventures and Ash had all those audits in Arizona—"

"Mom. For real. Jas doesn't need a rundown of everyone's schedules." He turned toward us, his arms crossed over his chest. Without the benefit of his plaid shirt, he was all bulging biceps and thick forearms. "Have you thought about selling this stuff? Even if Jasper eats toast three times a day, every day—"

"I've been known to do that."

Diana hit me with another one of her sly winks.

"—we will still have enough spreadable fruit for several years."

"Where would I sell it?" she asked, tossing her hands up like it was a real mystery. "And I don't have the time for that.

I just like making my preserves and giving them to the people I love. I'm not interested in any kind of entrepreneurial adventure. Please. I have grandbabies on the way." She shook her head at him like he should've known better than to start with her. "I'm sure you'll manage. Give your clients a jar or two when you visit. They'll enjoy that. A personal touch."

He stared at her. "Not gonna happen."

"Anyway," Diana started, patting my hand again, "I am looking forward to Jasper joining us on Sunday."

For a split second, Linden looked completely stricken. He recovered before Diana glanced up at him but I saw his jaw hang open and his eyes pop, and I knew exactly what he was thinking.

"I will have to check my schedule," I said. "Now that I think of it, I might have a commitment that day."

He cut a sidelong glance in my direction. "Jasper *is* really busy."

Diana shifted in her seat, made a pointed glance at the wall clock which clearly stated it was eleven thirty in the morning and I was hanging out in her son's kitchen, and offered a pleasant grin. "I hope you can make it. I understand if you can't, given the short notice."

I figured that would be the end of it. I figured Diana would find something else to talk about and Linden would let her because this wasn't the conversation he wanted to have with her today, mainly because there wasn't a conversation to be had. I wasn't his girlfriend. I was the girl next door who showered here every day, occasionally slept over, and engaged in some very un-kitchenlike behavior in this room when the mood was right.

I didn't figure Linden would drop his hands to my shoulders and say, "We'll see what happens, Mom."

Diana rolled her eyes toward the ceiling, whispering, "He tells me we'll see. We'll see!" She pressed her hands to her chest again. "I'd love to have both of you around my table on Sunday. It's just supper. Only a few hours from your busy days. You have to eat, right? You can't spend all day on the go." She shrugged, and wow, this lady was slick. She knew a maneuver. "Linden, I know your sister is hoping to get some time to speak with you and Ash together. While you do that, Jasper can help me make sense of the menu for Magnolia's shower." She smiled at me. "I can just tell you have the best taste. You'd really be doing me a favor too."

"I know a few senators who'd do well to get you on their payroll," I said under my breath.

Linden kneaded my shoulders, his thumbs digging into the back of my neck. "Do you think you could swing it, Jas? What do you think?"

I peeked up at him as best I could while he massaged me. Did he want me to say yes? That couldn't be the case. He didn't want to bring me home to the family. When I caught his eye, he gave me a quick, jerky nod.

Okay. I was rolling with this.

I smiled at Diana again, who was busy beaming at her son. "Thank you for the invitation. It's very generous. It would be my pleasure to join you."

"Oh, my word. I cannot hardly contain my excitement," she cried.

"That's enough out of you, Scarlett O'Hara," he quipped.

"Tell me what I can bring," I said.

"No, Peach, you don't have to do anything. I'll grab a few bottles of wine."

"That's right," Diana said, gripping my hand again. Very handsy, this one. "When you come to my Sunday supper, you're coming home. All I need is your smiling face, sweetheart."

There was no way in hell I could live with that but I said, "Thank you."

"And you'll have to come to the party too," she continued. "It's going to be such a fabulous time."

From behind me, I heard Linden's ragged exhale. Then, "Mom."

"What?" She worked hard at looking very innocent as she stared at him.

"You know what," he replied.

"I haven't a clue." She turned her attention back to me, saying, "We're having a little get-together—"

"Two hundred people at a country club but sure, call it a little get-together," Linden muttered.

"—to celebrate our fortieth wedding anniversary. Can you even imagine it? I couldn't see myself being forty years old when I got married but here we are, all these years later."

"You don't look a day over thirty-nine," I said.

"I knew you were special when I saw you but now I believe it too," Diana said with a hearty laugh. "So, we decided to seize the day and throw ourselves a bash before we become grandparents. Knock on wood that my daughter doesn't go into an early labor. The invitations have already gone out but, of course, all we want is to see these babies born healthy."

"And your party to go as planned," Linden added.

"It sounds wonderful," I said to her.

"It will be with you there," she replied. "You don't have to decide right now but having someone as special as you there"—she shot a meaningful grin at Linden—"would make my day. And Carlo's too. You'll meet him on Sunday but I can already tell you, he'll be thrilled."

He traced his thumbs along my hairline, behind my ears. I had to fight off a shiver. "I think Jasper might be able to make that work," he said. "What do you say, Jas?"

This wasn't real. I knew that. I was going along with this because Linden seemed to want that but none of it was real. He'd explain the nuances of this situation and I'd put on a good face come Sunday and again whenever this party took place but I wasn't here to stay.

And yet here I was, wondering how it was possible to want a man who insisted—and a mother figure who did too. I didn't know how I could live all these years believing I didn't want such a thing because it would rob me of all the self-reliance I'd built like fortress walls when it seemed as perfect as an overly tight embrace right now.

"I'll have to check my book though it really does sound wonderful. I'd love to celebrate with y'all."

"Y'all!" she hooted. "Oh my god, I love you already."

"Okay, all right, you've delivered your preserves and backed Jasper into a corner she's too polite to kick you out of. You've done your damage. Go harass someone else, would you?"

Diana pushed to her feet with an exaggerated sniff. It was sweet hilarity to watch these two ribbing each other. "I just left Magnolia, and Ash is at the office. Since your father is a golf devotee in his retirement, he won't be home until dark."

Linden circled a hand in her direction. "I see your game."

"No games," she replied. "Just very excited to meet Jasper. What a happy accident it was that I stopped in today."

"And now that you've caused this accident"—he gestured toward the door—"you have places to go, too many pumpkins to buy."

"Too many pumpkins?" She swung her purse over her shoulder. "I've never heard of that." Ignoring her son entirely, Diana bent down and wrapped me up in another soul-squeezing hug. "I am just so happy to finally meet you, Jasper. So happy."

She passed a thumb over the birthmark on my cheek and smiled at me with a type of joy I didn't actually understand. I bolted to my feet and glanced up at Linden, who must've interpreted my panic at being the source of his mother's cheek-stroking joy in some kind of urgent way because he looped an arm around her and steered her away, saying, "Jasper doesn't have all day, you know. Some of us have things to do that don't involve meddling or marmalade, or popping in unannounced."

"If you'd told me you had a special guest—"

"That's enough," he said, walking her to the door. "Save it for Sunday."

"Four o'clock," she called, waving to me over the ridge of Linden's shoulders. "Can't wait!"

I was still staring at the door when Linden returned to the kitchen, stepped into my space, and fisted his hands in the shirt I'd borrowed. "I should probably apologize for that ambush and tell you that you don't have to go to any of these things." He jerked me closer. "I should but I won't."

"Why not?"

He dipped his head to my neck, his beard rasping against my skin and drawing a slight squeak from me. "Because I want you there. I shouldn't. It's not fair to you because my mother will obviously get carried away. But I want you. There."

"I really don't want to ask what that means because I live quite contentedly without defining everything but what does that mean?"

From his spot against my neck and shoulder, he shook his head. "I don't know. I need a date for this party, is what it means. I have a family dinner coming up. I don't hate you, so—"

"You don't hate me," I said with a laugh.

He lifted his head, stared into my eyes. Down at my lips. "I don't hate you," he repeated. "I don't hate you at all, Peach."

So, this was new.

Until now, Linden had put on an ambivalent face where I was concerned. Even when he was kissing me and clearly turned on by me, it seemed as though he could just as easily not.

Yeah, he kissed me. Yeah, he backed me up against a tree or two and let me work out years of frustration. Yeah, he did something very terrible to my nipple the other day and something slightly obscene with my foot this morning.

And he didn't hate me.

"You just don't want to have to explain to your mother why I didn't come along," I countered.

Linden dropped the shirt and reached down, grabbing me by the ass and lifting me to the countertop. He liked doing that. Or, rather, he didn't hate it. "Because I want you there."

He leaned in and took my lips in a gentle kiss that seemed to go on forever, shutting down the world and responsibilities and bank balances and disappointments and all of it.

My hands flat on his barrel chest, I shifted my face to the side, asking, "What if someone recognizes me? I don't want to complicate—"

"Even if they do, there's nothing to complicate." He brought his forehead to my shoulder. "You're hell in heels. No one is going to come for you, knives out, at an anniversary party, especially not one attended by accountants and teachers. It's at a country club, for fuck's sake. The entire ethos of country clubs is making it as easy as possible for people to pretend everything is fine." He gave a quick shake of his head to my shoulder, ran his lips along my neck. "And if anyone has a problem with you, they'll have to go through me first. It's not going to be any other way, Jasper."

This insistence…I decided I could get used to it.

THIRTEEN
LINDEN

It wasn't my style to make snap decisions.

I didn't waffle or ruminate either but I preferred to take my damn time on the things that mattered.

The partnership with Magnolia was a good example.

Introducing Jasper to my family was another.

Lucky for me, my mother jumped in and took care of the latter for me. Awesome.

I probably would've invited Jasper along on Sunday if my mother hadn't beaten me to the chase. It wasn't like I wanted to keep Jasper away from my family. I didn't want them getting the wrong idea was all. I didn't want my mother gushing about how *special* Jasper was and how she had to attend the party, as if she could force this relationship into permanence if she pulled the right strings and pushed hard enough on the soft spots.

Permanence wasn't even in Jasper's vocabulary. She wasn't staying in a sleepy Boston suburb, first because she was only here to escape her present situation and second because she didn't want to stay here. This wasn't where she wanted to be. Even if recovering from her last job—and that marriage—she wasn't turning in her power heels for duck boots.

This was temporary and that was why I could live with taking her home with me on Sunday and to the party next month. When she left town and returned to her life, or some version of it, my mother would have to accept the absolute pointlessness of challenging me to find *someone special* on a prescribed timeline. She'd have to.

So, yeah. I told Jasper I wanted her with me. I meant it too. I liked Jasper and I knew my family would adore her. As far as the party went, well, that was for me. I wasn't positive Jasper would still be in town when that event rolled around but if she was, I got the bonus of hanging out with her all night.

Seemed like a good deal to me.

I wasn't getting attached. I was just looking out for her. Being a good neighbor, really. Or something along those lines. I liked her and—and, well, I didn't hate her. I wasn't irrationally angry about her fixing up Midge's house anymore, even if I did completely lose it when I saw her marching toward the half-dead rhododendron in the back-yard with an axe the other day. We only yelled at each other for ten minutes that time, which was progress.

We only yelled at each other for ten minutes because I grabbed the axe out of her hands, tossed it into my yard, and kissed her while she flailed those bony little fists at me, but it was still progress.

I wasn't getting attached. This wasn't attachment. It was something else. Something that made me want to physically shake sense into her at least once a day while also making me want to fuck her clear through my mattress at least five times an hour.

I still had to talk myself out of both in order to survive this invasion.

Her life was a bunch of puzzle pieces thrown up in the air and she wasn't staying. I was all about casual sex but there was nothing casual where it came to Jasper. Taking her to bed would mean something. If not to her, definitely to me. After she left, she'd always be the beautiful maybe-burglar who blew into my life with a cloud of bats at her back and a toxic banana bread. She'd always be the woman who told an eternity of secrets the first time she stepped into the heart of the woods. She'd always be the woman who made my heart stop when I saw fire trucks outside her house and the one who got woozy at the sight of blood. She was the one who'd catalyzed ordinary concern for my neighbor into the kind of worry that kept me up nights. And she was the only woman I'd ever met who could make a meal out of toasted bread.

I wasn't getting attached.

FOURTEEN
JASPER

LINDEN FOUND A REASON FOR ME TO STAY OVER EVERY NIGHT that week.

The overnight temperatures were dropping and he was worried about the heating system at Midge's house. (Very valid; I shared that worry.)

He didn't like the idea of me staying there with the porch demolished down to the joists. (Not sure I followed that one but okay.)

I drank two glasses of wine over dinner and he thought it was better for me to stay put. (Since the three-minute walk next door was so perilous.)

That sort of thing.

I argued with him every time because it was in my DNA, but there was no teeth to it. The fight was more a matter of custom at this point, something woven into the fabric of our neighbors-turned-whatever-this-was. Not that I had time to put into defining our *whatever*.

Sometimes, we kissed. Sometimes, I fell asleep on the sofa with my head in his lap. And sometimes, we fought hard over the right way to fold a bath towel and didn't want to talk to each other all day because of it.

It was fine.

We were fine.

Everything was fine.

Except for those moments when he'd look at me and I'd swear I saw a wolf behind those eyes. Like now, when he gazed at me with brutal intensity every time I handed him another dish to dry. Staring of that sort while someone was elbow deep in soapy water was excessive. It just didn't fit.

Except it did because this was Linden and everything about him was intense and excessive. That didn't mean I had to like it. "Those are some serious looks you're giving me. Are you still worried I don't know how to operate a garbage disposal?"

"I'm not worried that you don't know how to operate it," he replied. "I know for a fact that you don't know how to operate it and *that* worries me."

"Like I said earlier, I just won't use it." I handed him a bowl. "It's not that complicated. I can just pretend it doesn't exist."

"You think that will work?"

I reached into the sink to pull the drain. "I mean, yeah. I didn't know what that switch did until I flipped it earlier. It was purely accidental and I'll probably forget all about that switch."

"Until you go to turn on the light over the sink again and hit the wrong switch," he murmured.

"Oh my god," I groaned. "Would you just let it go?" I shook the water from my hands, giving him my most annoyed glare as I reached across him for a dish towel. "So there was a fork that had slipped into the opening and got whirled around a bit. It happens. We recovered it before anything tragic occurred so why don't we just put it behind us? It's not like I stuck my hand down there while it was on."

"Only because I stopped you from doing that," he cried.

I slung the damp towel over the front skirt of the sink. "Do you have any idea how obstinate you are?"

He leaned back against the countertop, his arms crossed over his chest. I was getting the sense that he knew how much I liked it when he crossed his arms like that. It was even better when he had his sleeves rolled up to his elbows. That dark dusting of hair on his thick forearms, the ropy muscle against the soft fabric of his plaid shirts. *Gahhhh.* It was amazing.

"I have a very good idea, yes." He shot me a smirk. "Do you know you're just as obstinate?"

"I am nothing of the sort."

"You are the most stubborn woman I've ever met."

"Wow. *Wow.* That's unspeakably kind of you to mention," I said. "I have to wonder, Linden, why you'd go to such trouble to keep me around when I'm obstinate and stubborn and dangerous with household appliances. Better yet, I'll stop wondering and return myself next door for the evening. I'm sure you could use a break from telling me how to do everything."

"You're not going over there."

"No? And who do you expect will stop me? It can't possibly be you since you're very busy being right all the time."

"How are you feeling?" he asked.

I narrowed my eyes at him. "What? Fine. What are you talking about?"

He pushed away from the counter and stepped closer,

trailed his knuckles along the buttons running down the front of my shirtdress. "I'm asking how you're feeling tonight."

I laughed as I shook my head because I couldn't understand why we were talking about this now. "For a stubborn, obstinate woman, I'm all right. Why do you want to know?"

His brows pitched up as he considered this. "I mean, it helps to know if you're tired or feeling down or just want to scream at me a little longer."

"So you can get out of the way?"

He jerked a shoulder. "Yeah, that. You know I like to see you mad but I'm not a total beast. I want to know if you're having a rough time."

"And why is that?"

He stared at my buttons for a second. "Is there anything else I should know? About how you're doing, I mean."

"How I'm doing," I echoed. "Are we talking about the garbage disposal again? Or being recently fired? Or newly divorced? Or my role as the star of last month's political shitshow? What is the concern in question?"

"Any of the above. What are you up for?"

"Why do you want to know?"

He reached out, thumbed open the top button. "Because I'm not going to throw you over my shoulder and toss you facedown on the bed if you don't want it."

"You're—oh." I watched as he opened another button. "Then you've decided the best way to resolve this matter of our shared stubbornness is putting me to bed, is that it?"

"I'm not putting you to bed." He hooked an arm around my waist, dragged me up against him. "I'm taking you to bed."

"And by that you're saying…" I peered up at him, hoping

to the heavens he'd finish the sentence for me, but after a beat it was clear that wasn't happening. No, I had to finish the sentence. "You're saying you're joining me in there."

"Fuck yes, I'm joining you."

"You're saying you're ready to finish what you started the other day."

"I've been ready all week. You were the one who needed to rest up. You weren't ready for me and you know it."

"That's highly debatable," I murmured.

"I don't fuck girls who haven't slept in a month," he replied.

I gave him a brassy smile. "Oh, is that what you have in mind? I wasn't sure where you were going with this."

He flipped open the next two buttons. "I'm going to rip this dress off like it's on fire and I'm going to taste every sweet inch of you. I'm going to fuck you until you can't take it anymore and then I'm going to fall asleep right beside you. And I think it's pretty cute how you make me spell it out for you when that was your job."

"I didn't need you to spell it out," I said with all the indignance one could muster with her dress open to her navel. "I just wanted to make sure we were on the same page."

"People have let you down before."

A considerable part of me wanted to argue with this sudden shift from our play-fighting to this very real, very unpleasant truth, to push him to explain that statement and why he felt it was appropriate to make it now. The other part of me was small and tender but it was starving, and it cried out at the recognition he offered. "Yeah."

"Right here, right now"—he lifted his palm to my cheek, slipped his fingers into my hair, tapped his thumb against my lips—"I won't be one of those people."

I shuddered. My whole body, it was one indelicate shudder. It wasn't necessary but I still said, "Okay."

"Do you know what that means, Jasper? Do you know how to trust someone to show up for you? Or do you play the part while knowing you're the only one who could ever give you what you want?"

"I know what it means," I said defiantly. "I just don't have much experience with anyone making good on those promises."

He rubbed his thumb over my lips again before tracing the shape of my birthmark. "I won't be one of those people."

Because I was a bratty little punk under all this polish, I shook off his thumb and gestured to the table. "Are you waiting for me to hop up there?"

"You fucking know I'm not," he growled, his hand sliding down to my neck. "I'm having a conversation with you here because I don't want any confusion in there."

I blinked away before saying, "Condoms."

"Of course."

"I'm not into pain or degradation."

He nodded. "Good, me neither."

"I'm serious. I don't mind a slap on the ass or two but if you think I'm going to count while you spank me, I will walk out of here naked."

"The last thing I want to do is spank you in any disciplinary way," he replied.

"What's the first thing?"

His brows bent up. "What?"

"You said the last thing you want to do is spank me. What's the first thing you want to do?"

He hummed for a second, then shook his head. He dragged his fingers up from my navel to my neck. "No, I don't think I'm going to answer that question. Not until you tell me what you want."

"I—" I almost said it. I almost spoke the words inside my head.

"If you can't say it, Peach, I'll—"

"Would you just wait a minute? My god. Let a girl speak, would you?"

I gave an exaggerated shake of my head as I fired a haughty glance at him. He knew it was bullshit but he seemed to know all my bullshit. Every last bit of it. I swallowed hard and dropped my gaze to his beard. There were flecks of silver in there but a dash of sun-kissed auburn too. I didn't know why that amused me but it did.

"I have all night and nowhere to be in the morning," he said, his knuckles gentle as they brushed along the line of my jaw.

"I-I just," I stammered, still struggling to grab hold of those words and share them without immediately regretting it. "I don't want to think."

Why did I say that? Just…*why*? Ordinary, healthy people didn't say things like that. They didn't ask to zone out during sex. They didn't expect someone else to do the work while lying back and letting it happen.

But that wasn't what I wanted. It wasn't about letting it happen. It was about letting *go*. It was not having to make one more decision. It was being safe and trusting that I'd get what I needed just as much as he would.

"Now I know you're ready," he said.

I glanced up at him with a glower, still feeling the sting of embarrassment in my face, my chest. "What does that mean?"

He studied my mouth for a long moment before saying,

"You wouldn't have said that earlier this week. That day in the woods? Never would've said it. You couldn't *stop* thinking." He met my eyes, a smirk pulling at the corner of his lips. "And just so you know, I'm not going to allow you to think."

———

I ALWAYS KNEW LINDEN WAS A WOLF AT HEART BUT NOW I KNEW he was a savage one at that.

We were barely inside the bedroom when Linden had me against the wall, my cheek pressed flat while he yanked my dress over my head. He didn't waste a single second rocking that hard shaft against my backside and murmuring, "No, baby, I'm not going to give you a minute to think."

"I feel like you're making a lot of big promises here," I said. "It would be disappointing if you didn't live up to them."

Linden dragged his fingers up my spine and with one flick of his hand, my bra was gone. I didn't even know how to get it off that quickly. "You won't be disappointed."

He kept one hand between my shoulder blades while he ran the other down to my waist and over my backside—and lower. With that broad palm and those thick fingers, he cupped my pussy in a manner I could only describe as crude. It had to be crude. No one with fingers like those could grab a pussy without being a tad bit crude about it.

Then, "This is mine."

"Bless you and that spirited male imperialism," I managed. Honestly, I could barely speak with him *squeezing my pussy* like that. As if anyone could speak.

He curled those fingers around the crotch of my panties

and yanked them down, sending them to the floor with less than a whisper. His hand tangled in my hair, he said, "Don't lie to me. You love it."

Since I did not actually want to lie and this was the best foreplay I'd had in forever, I stayed quiet while Linden nipped and kissed my neck and shoulders. That part was amazing but it was his scratchy-soft beard that had me clawing at the wall and arching my back to feel more of his shaft, anything, any friction I could get.

"You need to learn a bit of patience," he growled in my ear. "You'll get what you need when I'm good and ready to give it to you. Understand?"

What the hell *did he just say to me?*

"So, so imperious," I said, and those words weren't halfway off my tongue when he pushed two fingers inside me with more force than I'd ever experienced. I hadn't even been fucked this hard. I couldn't believe it. I couldn't even breathe because the pressure—my god, the pressure. But it was so good. It was good in that lip-biting, clothes-tearing, sheet-twisting kind of way.

A gasp stuttered out of me as he edged my feet apart and found that perfect spot right inside me. "There you go," he murmured. "There you are."

There was a minute when I did nothing more than breathe against the wall while Linden made me a hot, slippery, grinding version of myself that I'd never met before. I didn't let anyone pin me to a wall naked and say rude things while I rode their hand. I'd *never*.

I'd thought about it but I'd never.

There was the sound of a belt unlatching, a fly unzipping, fabric rustling, and I needed to see him. I *needed* it. There were at least two tattoos that required study and my hands itched to explore that husky body of his. My nipples too. It was completely deranged but I was dying to know the feel of his skin and the dark hair I was certain trailed down his chest against my breasts.

I started to shift, to pivot as much as anyone could while impaled on a pair of fingers, but Linden wasn't allowing it. "What did I just tell you? I'll give you what you need but you have to stop squirming."

"I'm not squirming. I'm—*ohhhh.*" He pushed his cock against my ass and I couldn't believe how hard and hot he was. It didn't seem real. "Please tell me we're not doing this against the wall. I can't see anything and I really don't like this idea."

"Where would you like me to do it?" he asked as his fingers speared inside me again and his thumb circled my clit. "Tell me what you want, Peach."

Those fingers were going to cause my entire body to implode. I was going to cave in. I was going to fall apart before I touched him and that seemed like a tragedy of terrible proportions. "I just want—oh my god, I want everything."

Linden kissed and bit his way up my shoulder. The soft laugh he breathed out sent a ripple of goose bumps down my chest, over my nipples. "You want to be more specific?"

"We could've stayed in the kitchen if you have a fondness for walls and standing. It's impolite to smush a lady up against a wall for more than a moment or two."

"Let me be honest with you now. I'm gonna be real impolite tonight," he rasped into my ear before he pulled away. The sudden absence of that big body—and those fingers— left me cold and clenching around nothing. "Come help me."

As I turned, I found Linden unbuttoning his shirt, his

jeans and boxers abandoned to the floor along with my dress. His cock bobbed under the tail of the plaid and I assumed that was the help he needed. I reached for him as he shrugged out of the plaid, pulled the t-shirt underneath over his head. He was huge. I didn't know a lot of dicks on a first-name basis but this one was huge. It was fitting—quite literally—as Linden was a tall, barrel-chested beast of a man and anything short of an impossibly thick shaft wouldn't make sense on him.

I was so happy for things that made really good sense.

"Like this?" I asked. I shot him a quick glance before running an appreciative gaze from his shoulders to his toes. The dark fuzz running down his chest and the thatch between his legs were just like his beard—soft and coarse at the same time.

A smirk pulled at his lips and he tilted his head to the side as I stroked him. "Exactly like that."

Light cut in from the living room, illuminating his lightly tanned skin and the tattoos on both biceps. There was the single mountaintop with the dragon and the portion of the sword, both of which I'd spotted before, but now I saw the sword was part of a larger piece where it crossed with an axe and an arrow. I ran my hand over that one. "What is this?"

"We can talk about the Three Hunters another time," he said, his hands sliding to my hips. "Same with Smaug and the Lonely Mountain. You asked me to stop smushing you so that's what I'm doing now."

He steered me across the room, backing me up against the bed until my legs couldn't go any farther, then he picked me up like I was the smallest little thing in the universe and set me on the mattress. Like this, with the room dark and only touch to lead the way, I felt like I could do anything. I could have anything. And just maybe, I could be everything.

I heard a drawer open and Linden tossed a shiny strip of condoms to the bed. "You decide how many I'm going to need."

I picked up the foil packets as he climbed over me, his shaft dragging up my thigh, along my belly like a warning. "Probably all of them."

Kneeling between my legs, he said, "You can't tease me like that."

"Who said I'm teasing?" I asked, drawing my legs up to wind around his waist.

I tried to urge him closer to me, to get more of that friction I needed, but he only smoothed his hands up my thighs like he was trying to calm a skittish horse. I really did not care to be the skittish horse in this scenario. I wasn't skittish. I knew what I wanted and I wanted it now. I just had to ask for it.

"If you're not teasing, I hope you plan to spend the entire weekend in this bed." He shifted one hand from my leg to stroke his cock as he watched me for a slow, heavy minute. The rhythmic slap of skin was the only sound between us. "Don't test me, Jasper. I will keep you here for the next sixty hours if you let me."

"Get that condom on. I'll decide how I spend the weekend when it's full."

He turned his gaze to the ceiling with a guttural groan that sounded something like *fuck me* and then made quick work of the condom.

"Tell me again. Tell me you're ready," he rasped, his fingers circling the base of his cock as he dragged it through my folds.

It came to me then, the filthy gust of confidence I always felt when I *needed it* more than I needed my pride or dignity. "If you don't fuck me right now, I'll walk out of here and find someone who will."

That was all it took. He shoved his hips forward, the headboard snapped against the wall as he pushed into me with a single powerful thrust that stole my breath. He was so much bigger than I'd estimated, I could barely think of anything save for the heat and pressure coiling through me. One thrust after another, he was tearing me apart and I wanted to do the exact same thing to him. I wanted to undo him in every way, wanted him as mindless as he made me.

"I can hear you thinking, Peach," he said. "Do I have to bite those pretty nipples of yours too? Is that what it will take?"

"Probably," I replied with the kind of bratty tone that required him to make good on that threat.

Lucky for me he did, and I got to rake my fingers over his scalp and through his dark hair while I writhed and wiggled against the merciless treatment his teeth gave me.

"You are *not* real," he murmured to the valley between my breasts.

"Neither are you." The harsh rhythm of the headboard knocking into the wall matched the pulse in my core, and every time he drove into me, my eyelids drifted shut because I couldn't feel that much and keep my eyes open at the same time. I couldn't. "Your cock is splitting me in two."

"Is that a good thing?"

"So good." I flattened my hand over my mouth to keep from letting out a rude, lusty groan.

I could be extremely rude and lusty in these situations. Not always but there had been times of remarkably rude and lusty behavior. There were no limits when I chased that first orgasm. It was like I doubted I'd get there unless I put every-thing on the table. I'd say anything, any depraved thing. I'd beg them to fuck my ass, to come on my tits, to let me sit on their face. Once I got there, I calmed down, gained some confidence. Some relief. It was like my body remembered how to do this and I didn't have to put so much energy into it even though the second one was harder to reach.

But I never reached the second because I remembered myself. I wasn't desperate anymore so I could think. I could replay those words in my head and then welcome in the awkwardness, the mortification. The shame.

There was never a second. Not with another person. When I was alone, I could hit the second, the third, the fourth. Sometimes more if the toys were playing right and the inspiration was strong.

So, I kept that hand over my mouth. Kept those crazy words in. Kept the shame and embarrassment at bay.

"You feel fucking amazing," he ground out. "I swear to god, you're better than any cock ring in the world."

He pumped in and then all the way out, and with one deft flick of his wrist, I was flipped onto my belly. He tucked my ass up against his thighs, the hair on his legs lightly abrading my backside as I went on rolling my hips toward anything hard and hot. I heard his hand connecting with my ass before I felt it, nothing more than a loose slap, nothing like the type of punishment spanking that made my skin crawl.

It was exactly what I needed.

His rough touch did something to me that was very, very right.

I turned my head to the side and sucked in a breath as I

watched him line up against my opening. I reached for the blanket beneath me, fisted my hands in the fabric. I needed something to hold on to. Something to shove into my mouth to muffle the overzealous things I was bound to say.

When he pushed inside me this time, I knew it was almost over. I couldn't stop the chorus of *more, now, my god, Linden, yes, yes, yes*. Even when I turned my face to the bed and closed my teeth around the blankets, I couldn't stop.

One hand on my hip and the other twisted around my hair, Linden fucked me without apology. Without sense. He shoved into me with that arrogant, possessive attitude of his, like he was fucking me for the same ancient reason anyone ever fucked—to claim and mark and keep. There was pleasure to be had, of course, but he moved in me like he was doing a job he was made for. Like he wouldn't stop until he'd fulfilled his obligations.

For once in my life, I really liked being the subject of obligation.

Since this position hit all the right spots for me, the wave of spasms through my body came in fast and had me panting out an unintelligible series of *fuck yes now*. There were shooting stars behind my eyes, and a glorious unraveling in my core, and despite Linden's relentless hold on my body, my knees went out from under me.

"Are you okay?" He didn't stop hammering into me. He went right on working every sated, tender ounce of me while I lay flat on the bed like a well-fucked pancake.

"I told you I was coming five different ways," I mumbled against the blanket. "Perhaps you heard that?"

With one arm, he scooped me up like a rag doll, settled my ass in his lap. "Nah, we're not done. We can do better than that one."

I glanced over my shoulder because surely I had misheard. "What?"

He smirked at me, asking, "Am I wrong to think you can get there more than once?"

Oh. Okay, then. "You're not wrong."

"Do you need a break or can you keep going?"

I met his eyes and the dark focus there. *Oh my god*. He *wanted* me rude and lusty. He wanted to work for the second, the third, all of them. My core gave a violent clench of delight. "I can keep going."

He entered me again and wrapped his arms around my torso, his beard brushing the back of my shoulder as he dragged his teeth along my neck. This wolf of mine. "That's right," he rumbled. "Show me what you need, baby. Show me how to get you there."

I didn't know what to do right now. Even if he wanted the rude and lusty version of me, I didn't know if I could do that. But now here we were, a hand splayed low over my belly and his cock owning me with every long, dragging thrust, and a simple request hanging in the air between us.

"Is your cock always this fat?"

Even saying that had the stirrings of a fresh orgasm building in my center. It was like a gateway opened to all the things I needed and now that I'd stepped through it, I could have them.

"Just for you, Jasper," he panted as he held me tight to his chest.

I brought my hand to my mound, parting the folds to trace the spot where his shaft moved in me and then up, up to the place that wanted more attention. "Pinch my nipples again. You're good at that."

He brought one hand up to my breast, quickly snagging

my nipple between his knuckles like he did that night when he had me up against the sink. It hurt in the most terrific way and I could barely hear my thoughts, let alone decide what to think. The only things that seemed right were working my clit harder and harder, screaming every time he let up a little on my nipple, and letting him pound me like this even though I knew I'd feel it everywhere tomorrow.

"You're getting close," he said, his lips on my neck.

"I don't need you explaining my vagina to me."

"Should I say that the next time you tell me my cock is fat?"

Heat started washing down my spine, circling my legs, unraveling in my center. "That was a compliment, not a status report."

His hold on my nipple turned aggressive, like he was trying to determine how far I'd let him go with this. Maybe I would've enforced a limit or stopped him if things were different but the warm, loose flutters inside me turned wild with that assertive touch of his. They went crazy as they expanded and spread out from my core into my limbs. I felt it in my face, my cheeks a little too hot and my lips tingling. It was overwhelming. It hurt in a desperate, needy way— that same old lustiness that made me say the filthiest things, it hurt like that. Like I'd die if I didn't catch hold of this sensation and send it somewhere because my body could not contain this, it simply could not.

I couldn't hear anything but my own rushing pulse and when I looked down to watch him abuse my nipple, I caught sight of his legs pumping between mine. I could see the stretch of muscles under the dark hair and the silvery lines of old scars. There was something about watching his body move as I felt the product of that effort while his hips slapped my ass, his cock dragged against every sensitive inch of me.

"You're not done yet," he said. "Don't check out on me now."

"I am not *checking out*," I said, my words barely more than a slur.

Linden closed his fingers around my wrist, pulling my hand away from my clit. "Hold on to me." He raised my arm, brought my hand to the back of his neck. "Let's see about taking care of you now."

I tried to protest. There was a lot of protest in me. I had things to say and I intended to say them. But also, when he covered my mound with two thick, blunt fingers and pinched the same way he was pinching my nipple, I lost track of those protests.

He continued pumping into me, a little more reckless now, a little more erratic. He let out a low growl as he slammed into me at an angle that did glorious things for everyone involved, and his teeth were on my neck. "I told you we could do better."

I could only murmur-groan in response. There was no way I could speak and make sense right now. I couldn't tell whether I was climbing toward a third orgasm or the second was spectacularly long and complex. I didn't actually care but it gave me something to think about as I tried to pull back the tension, the twisted-muscle clench that lived in my hips and belly, the one that only seemed to vanish when I imagined a big ball of rope methodically unknotting itself.

"I need—" I didn't know what I wanted to say. I just knew I needed *something*.

"Do you have a list about your orgasms?"

"*Wh-what?*"

"You make lists for everything," he panted. "I'm just wondering if you have one on how to make your cunt happy."

"Are you looking for some suggestions?"

He shook his head against my shoulder. "No, baby, I don't want the list. I want you to forget it ever existed. Rip it the fuck out."

All these sensations—his cock as he ground against me, his beard on my neck, his fingers holding my clit captive—they dragged me down as I reached for the edge of this orgasm. "Why?"

"Because that shit is over. Because I want the wild, screeching girl who can come on my cock twice without quitting. The one who doesn't think, doesn't plan a fucking thing. The one who wants it rowdy and messy and dirty. I want to be rowdy and messy and dirty *with* her."

"Oh my god," I whispered. "I want you to come all over me."

"*Yes*."

"I want you to eat my pussy after you come inside me."

"Mmm. That's it, precious girl. That's it."

"Would you? Really?" I asked, the doubt and shame prickling up my spine.

"As often as you wanted."

I didn't know if we were playing. I didn't really care. "*Fuck, fuck, fuck.* I want it."

He released his hold on my mound and that rush was enough to grab at my release but then *he slapped me*. He slapped my folds with barely enough force to consider it a true slap but my body did not care about such technicalities. No, my body was very busy learning how to have a catastrophic orgasm with the help of another person.

"That's right. That's what you need," he murmured.

In a distant sense, I knew he was talking and growling, and I felt him lash his arms around my torso and hold me tighter than was comfortable as he came, but I couldn't focus on anything but the unbelievable heat that seemed to radiate out from my pussy.

It was so much. *So much.* As if he knew I couldn't handle this, not all of it, Linden settled us against the pillows, his arms locked around me as I went on gasping and shaking. When I caught my breath, I realized he was still inside me, still twitching and pulsing.

"Whoa," I whispered. My head was soft and milky. I could fall asleep like this.

"Are you warm enough?"

He ran a palm down my arm and it was too much, just too much sensation. A shiver moved from my shoulders to my toes, and I clenched around him again, drawing groans from both of us. Then I shivered again. "I think so?"

"No, Jas, that's not what it looks like to be warm enough," he said, kicking the blankets out from underneath us and pulling them up.

Once the bedding was straightened out, he rolled away to handle the condom. When he returned, he ducked his head to my chest and teased my nipples with his beard. I sanded my fingers through his hair, sighing and squirming with every barely-there pass. Then he inched his way down my body until he was settled between my legs, the blankets bunched around his broad shoulders.

"Will you tell me about those tattoos now?" It seemed like I could ask this. Like I didn't have to bury my face in the pillows and pretend none of that had happened.

His lips skating along my inner thigh, he shook his head.

"You already know I'm a Tolkien fan. They're just stray bits from the stories."

I gestured to his right arm. I couldn't reach past his shoulder in this position. "What does that say?"

His gaze still locked on my leg, he recited, "'One Ring to rule them all, One Ring to find them. One Ring to bring them all, and in the darkness bind them.'"

"And this?" I tapped the other shoulder. "What are those?"

He shifted to the other leg and occupied himself with dragging his lips and beard up until I writhed and giggled. Then, "It represents the Three Hunters. Aragorn's sword, Gimli's axe, and Legolas's arrow."

"Is that a triplet thing?"

He shrugged. "Not really. But somewhat. Depends on your interpretation."

Yes, it was definitely a triplet thing.

He shouldered my legs apart as far as they'd go, ran his tongue along my seam. Another violent shiver moved through me. "What are you doing?"

"I keep promises," he replied simply. "And I'm keeping this one, as much as I can."

"You don't have to," I whispered.

"Here's what's going to happen now," he said, pushing up on an elbow. "I'm going to lick you until I get another one of those crazy screams out of you. Then I'm going to fuck you again and there's a pretty good chance I'll fall asleep after that because you are one hell of a handful, Peach."

I turned my head, glanced out the window at the night sky. "That's an interesting way of putting it."

"Don't do that." He reached up, pressed his fingers to my jaw, shifted me to face him again. "Let's get one thing straight, all right? If you even think about hiding from me now, I will hunt you down," he said. "I'll find you."

Everything they said about wolves? It was true.

They could see you better.

They could hear you better.

And they could eat you better.

FIFTEEN
LINDEN

FOR THE SECOND DAY IN A ROW, I WOKE UP WITH JASPER'S ASS tucked into my lap and my cock loving the sweet cradle of her cheeks. I could get used to this. I could get used to it real fast.

I shouldn't, of course. There were a ton of reasons why I shouldn't, though none of them came to mind when she reached back and took my shaft in hand. It was a sleepy kind of stroke, nothing hard or aggressive, just a slow skate up and down as I rubbed a thumb around her nipple.

If there was a reason this was wrong, I didn't want to concern myself with it. Not for a damn minute. Not when her whisper of a touch had sweat beading on my forehead and my hips jolting with that instinctual kick.

"Come here." A rough pluck to her nipple punctuated the order.

"Have we dispensed with pleasantries such as *good morning* and *hello* in favor of *come here* when it suits?"

My hand flat on the small of her back, I pulled until she

flipped over, pushed until she straddled me. "Good morning," I said with a swift buck of my hips.

"Nice to see you again." She stretched her arms high over her head which did the best things to her tits. The very best things.

As I admired the full flare of her curves, I rolled a condom down. Held myself by the base, an offering to my sweet, sleepy goddess. She was allowed to be tired. I'd reached for her at all hours of the night and most of the day yesterday. She was well used.

She shifted her hands to the headboard as she settled herself over me. We didn't have to say a word. We knew this now, we knew each other, and there was no need to discuss every move. We knew this.

When she sank down, I was reminded I fit inside her like I belonged there, and not in the old sense that a cock belonged in a cunt. I had it on good authority that a cock belonged in any number of willing places and this one wasn't simply willing, it had been made for me. It was mine.

Jasper moved over me with a steady pace, one designed especially for Sunday mornings. Every slide and stroke had me gripping her hips harder, holding her down longer. This was all I needed, this was it.

She leaned down, dragged her breasts over my chest, up to my jaw. She liked the way my beard chafed her skin and I liked the way her tits swung in my face as she fucked me. Even better when I managed to catch one of those nipples between my teeth.

"I'm"—she started, the word stretched out over a sigh —"I'm there. I'm right there."

It just didn't get any better than this. There was no way. "Yeah, you are, baby." I held her hips down as her muscles pulsed around me. Every orgasm of hers—every fucking one —felt like she was milking my soul right out of me. It was only a matter of time until she snatched it. "Get it. *Get it*, Jas."

The spasms rolled through her, pulling and sucking at my tip where it was buried deep inside her. Her body wanted me there, wanted to keep me there, and that did something to me. It fucked me up in a good, weird way. Made me think about keeping her in this bed all day, keeping her here always. It made me want to say that out loud, which was the truest sign I was fucked all the way up.

"I can't come again until you do," she panted, one hand working her clit while the other gripped the headboard. "Please. I need you to."

We were messy now, both of us hot and misted with sweat. I could hear the wet between her legs. Just like the lazy Sunday way it started, I wanted it this way too. I wanted it rough and unclean, and I wanted to feel her fingers around the base of my cock every time she worked herself the way she needed. Nothing about this was pretty. It wasn't beautiful, even when the most beautiful woman I'd ever met was bearing down on my shaft with such force I seriously wondered whether I might black out.

"I can't believe how hard you are," she whispered. "It's *rude*."

"You're rude," I growled back. "You shove those tits in my face one more time and I'll bite them."

She slammed down on me and when her breasts brushed up against my jaw again, I took hold of those beauties. They were mine now. I teased her with my beard because I knew she loved it and I teased myself with the feel of her light brown nipples on my lips because I loved it.

I felt myself teetering on the edge, just close enough to

fall over, but Jasper was enjoying herself, even if her brows were pinched in fierce concentration, and I wanted another few minutes.

I lost myself in nipping at the tender underside of her breasts and pinching those nipples between my fingers. She didn't like pain in the grand sense—she didn't want anyone belting her and I respected that—but she had no problem with bites and pinches and pulling hard enough to mark her with fingertip-sized bruises—and I was into that. I didn't want to belt anyone but I didn't know how to fuck without doing it rough. I didn't know how to do it without leaving marks.

And that was what I did to those gorgeous tits. I marked the fuck out of them and I lengthened and swelled every time she let out another breathy wail-sigh that told me she felt those bites in her cunt.

"Lin," she called out. "You're—" She lost her words on a sob. "Now, now, now. I need it now."

Reaching up, I closed my hand around her throat. My hold was loose but it did it for both of us. She ground against me, forcing my cock as deep as I could go, and purred as I filled the condom. I didn't know how she could feel it but she did. She felt it enough for her body to work me even harder. Everything was liquid heat, everything inside and outside too.

Jasper leaned in close and rubbed her cheek against my jaw. Her eyes drifted shut. I slipped my hand into her hair, held her close.

"What do you need, Peach?"

I figured she'd want me to lick her or pet her clit or take her into the shower and do this all over again. Something like that.

Instead, she rested her forehead against mine, saying, "I really want some toast. An extra toasty slice too. Nice and browned. Just butter and some of that clementine marmalade." She shrugged. "Probably two slices. Yeah, definitely two."

The only thing I knew was I wanted this every weekend. Every fucking one of them. And that was a really dangerous thing to want.

————

WE WEREN'T DUE IN NEW BEDFORD FOR DINNER WITH MY family until later in the afternoon so I talked Jasper into a post-breakfast walk in the woods. She wanted to make lists about her lists, or something of that sort, and I could not allow that while the conditions were bright and dry.

I couldn't allow us to stay in bed all day either. Regardless of what I'd vowed on Friday evening, sixty hours of sex wasn't going to fly. Aside from the fact I was not twenty-five anymore, I didn't want to use Jasper. Not even one bit more than was right—which was a line that never clearly materialized in the moment but glared obviously after the fact.

Enough people had used Jasper and they'd used her in ways that were wrong from the start. I wasn't going to be one of those people.

"Are we looking for anything today?" she asked. "A specific tree or something?"

"Nothing in particular," I said, watching as she picked her way around a cluster of rocks. "We might be able to find some chanterelles though. We've had a good amount of overnight rain in the past couple of weeks."

"And chanterelles are…?"

"Mushrooms," I replied, reaching for my phone. "Here. I'll find a photo so you can keep an eye out."

She leaned against my chest while I searched for a good image. Her hair was coiled in a low bun and smelled so lovely, just so lovely, and I could see down her shirt from this angle. Life was really good.

"Why are we looking for these mushrooms?"

"My mother likes them," I replied. "She doesn't have much patience for foraging but she's appreciative whenever I bring some home."

Jasper nodded as she studied the image on my screen. "So, you're trying to butter her up with fungus? Are you that worried about bringing me home to meet the family?"

I pocketed my phone, giving her a bland stare. "No. I'm not worried."

"But you'd like to get on your mother's good side. With the fungus."

"Believe me, Peach, bringing you home by itself lands me on the good side." I grabbed a fallen branch and tossed it out of the path. I wasn't sure how much I wanted to tell her—if anything—about my mother's anniversary party deadline. I didn't want Jasper thinking any part of this was a game to me. I really didn't want her to think I was manipulating her. "My mother is very interested in seeing me paired up."

"That is not new information." She glanced over at me, a cheeky grin stretched across her face. "She did not hide her enthusiasm the other day. There was definitely a minute when she looked me up and down and said to herself, 'Yep, those are some good birthing hips.'"

I barked out a laugh but didn't disagree because my mother would absolutely do that. "The chanterelles will give her something else to focus on for five and a half minutes.

That will help with the overall hovering and gushing. She might even hold off on asking you how many kids you'd like to have."

"Not for long," Jasper said with a laugh.

"Just ask her about Magnolia and the babies or Ash and Zelda's wedding," I said. "That will distract her."

"Okay, got it." She gave me the cutest wink in the world, one I was certain she didn't intend to be cute but came out that way nonetheless. Then, "So, family dinners are a pretty big deal for y'all, huh?"

This part of the trail was completely empty. That was normal around here. We were far from the primary trails, and even in the busiest of seasons, these woods rarely reached anything resembling busy.

"I can't decide if I'd call it a big deal or a normal mechanism of my family's functioning. The truth lies somewhere in between."

"Then you've made a tradition of it."

"I think we inherited the tradition, at least some parts of it. I think it goes back to my grandparents or even my great-grandparents."

"Yeah, that's a tradition." Jasper pointed at an oak tree ahead. "Is that your mushroom?"

"That's chicken of the woods. Not a chanterelle."

"Do we like that?"

I shook my head. "Not a ton, no."

"Okay, well, back to your multigenerational traditions, please. I want the full briefing before you send me in."

"It's not a multigenerational tradition, that much I know." I laughed because my parents were some of the least traditional people I knew. At least they'd started out that way. "Look, this might come as a shock but my parents were pretty countercultural before they had us. Anti-establishment, fight the power, down with the man."

"Is that why you and your siblings have botanical names?"

"Babe, you should hear our middle names. Magnolia got off easy with Lynn but Ash's middle name is Indigo."

"That's precious. Bless him and his bespoke-suited heart." Jasper stopped, turned to face me. "And what about you?"

"Wolf."

"What?"

"Yeah. I know. Wolf is a crazy name."

She gave me an owlish stare, her dark eyes round and her lips parted. "That can't be true."

I nodded. "Wild, isn't it?"

She turned her stare to the ground. "No, I mean—wait. I don't know how to explain this."

"Don't tell me your middle name is also Wolf. That would be weird."

"No, I don't have a middle name but you have a very wolfish way about you." She glanced up. "I've thought this for weeks. Since I met you."

"Tell me how you want me to take that, Jas."

"There's no particular way I want you to take it," she replied, her fingers on her temples because she found something about my response exasperating. "Just know that your parents got that one right and I won't be able to sympathize with you on their countercultural ways since it's worked out quite spectacularly for me."

I brought my hand to her shoulder, tugged her close. "I like the sound of that."

"I…I am just trying to process this new bit of reality. You should probably finish your story about dinners and traditions and everything while I have this existential moment."

"Well, my parents made a big deal about making the old ways fit into their lives and getting rid of anything they found unnecessary or overly formal. I've never paid much attention to the details but I know there's a holy war over the right time to eat on Sundays."

"There's a wrong time to eat?"

We continued down the trail, Jasper tucked under my arm and the sun shining down on us. "That's what I've gathered but I gotta be honest, I dipped out of those debates early on. All I know is my parents are on the side of regular evening mealtimes and my grandparents are on the side of post-church services, mid-afternoon mealtimes."

"You know what's funny? We used to do all this ethnographic research to prep the candidate in advance of campaign stops outside Georgia. Regional customs and moments of local culture, even the little things like how it's soda in St. Louis, pop in Omaha, and Coke in Little Rock, even if it's not actually Coke. We can't send a candidate to New England and have them order a milkshake, you know? It has to be a frappe unless you want to get dragged on social media over some local speak. But I don't think I've ever tuned into the demographic divide over mealtimes for Sunday family gatherings. I wonder if anyone has picked up on that."

"It might just be my family."

She sawed her teeth over her bottom lip as she thought about this. "Probably not. You'd be surprised how far seemingly small divides, especially the ones that track back to ethnicity and faith, spread."

"What about you? What are your strange old family traditions?"

Her shoulders went up in a shrug but they never fell. "Don't really have any."

"What do you mean? I thought the South was all about traditions."

"Mmhmm."

She shook out of my hold and moved ahead quickly, leaving me several steps behind. Since my quads were still overworked from all our time spent between the sheets, I didn't match her pace. It seemed like she needed the space, even if I didn't understand. She'd asked about this, hadn't she? Wouldn't she expect me to ask about her family in return?

"Hey. I found your fungus."

I looked up ahead and spotted Jasper beside an old oak. She circled the tree twice before dropping her knees to the ground. I figured it was another chicken of the woods clump because chanterelles didn't grow directly on wood.

"Are you sure about that?" I called.

She didn't respond while I caught up to her and it seemed like I'd earned that, either by questioning her foraging ability or prying into topics she wasn't prepared to discuss with me. When I came up on her, I asked, "What did you find?" Before I let her respond, I closed my hand around her elbow and yanked her up, away from the oak. "Those are *not* chanterelles."

"What are they?"

"Jack-o'-lanterns and jack-o'-lanterns are poisonous."

She stared down at the large spread of orange fungi. "Oh."

My heart was pounding. It didn't make any sense, not

really, since these weren't lethally poisonous. Unpleasantly poisonous, yeah, but that was it. She wouldn't even get sick from touching them. She'd have to eat them before things turned hairy. But I should've warned her not to touch anything. Should've told her what to avoid. What the actual fuck was wrong with me?

I relaxed my hold on her elbow, smoothed a hand up her arm and over her shoulders. "Here's a quick rule for you. Don't touch anything until you've confirmed its identity from two sources."

"Okay but"—she had an indignant set to her jaw, like she objected to me calling foul on her find—"these look exactly like the photos you showed me."

"They do look similar but they're different, babe. These are growing in clumps, see? And they're directly on the base of this oak. Chanterelles don't grow on wood and they tend to pop up without friends nearby." I bent down, grabbed a stick, and angled up one side of the orange caps, pointed to its underside. "See here? These little wrinkles that stop at the base of the stem? They're called gills. Chanterelles have fine ridges that cover the underside and stem."

"You know, I thought we were just wandering around and looking for little orangey things in the forest. I didn't realize this was going to be so complicated."

I looked up at her. I didn't realize it was going to be complicated either.

I pushed to my feet, looped my arm around her waist. "Do me a favor and don't touch anything. Okay?"

She shoved her hands in her pockets. "Under most circumstances, I'd argue with you about that kind of limitation but I'm going to let this one slide."

"Good plan," I said. "Let's turn back, okay? It's probably too late in the season for chanterelles anyway."

I didn't lie to Jasper when I said I wasn't concerned about introducing her to my family today. It wasn't as though I was bringing her home in some significant way. This wasn't like the time Magnolia brought her now-husband Rob home and that was it, the real deal, the *this is happening* announcement. This wasn't like the time Ash brought Zelda home and they nearly set the backyard on fire with all the sexual tension sparking between them.

This wasn't like any of that. This wasn't permanent and it wasn't complicated either. It didn't have to be. Even if I had a whole lot of fun with Jasper and I was getting pretty good at saving her from herself, this had an expiration date.

———

"Okay, let me give you some advice." I pulled in behind my brother's Porsche and killed the engine. "My mother is a collector. She picks up broken furniture off the side of the road and takes hand-me-downs from everyone. She'll try to collect you too."

Jasper laced her fingers together and dropped them to her creamy white skirt. It was one of those full skirts, the kind that fell just past her knees and seemed like it would flare out if she twirled. The wool fabric was slightly rough to the touch, but on the drive down here some pawing helped me discover it had a silky lining. I'd happily spend time on my knees if I could do it with my head under that skirt.

"Do I want to be collected?"

"Unless you want to help her organize a quilt raffle down at the church or get in on a meal train for someone's sister's cousin's best friend, probably not. My recommendation is to—"

"Linden."

"What's up?"

She fluffed her hair over her shoulders, letting it fall against her dark green sweater. The neck was high and there wasn't a stitch of skin showing but that sweater was devastating. It just…it killed me.

"I know how to handle just about everyone." She gave me a pointed look. "Just about."

I gestured to the house because we could not talk about how thoroughly she could handle me while parked in my parents' driveway. Could *not*. "Then don't let me slow you down, babe."

She tucked her hair over her ear and gave me one of her sinful smiles, the ones that made all her forced, fake smiles look like a low-quality inkjet printout of her, a loose replica but nowhere near the real thing.

"As if you could."

I reached for the door handle, saying, "Stay there. I'll come around."

But she already had her door open and climbed out before I could get halfway there, the enormous bouquet of flowers she'd insisted on bringing cradled in her arm along with a small basket loaded with something called pimento cheese, olives, and a variety of crackers. "I see we're still ignoring simple requests."

"Did you really expect that to change?"

I reached into the back for the beer and wine I'd brought along. My mother didn't stock either. She didn't need it with all the weed she consumed. "Not sure what I expected from you." I didn't give her a chance to volley back, saying, "Stay with me, would you? There are no fewer than forty pumpkins on the walkway and I don't want you tripping over any of them in those shoes."

"These shoes have managed through more than a couple of pumpkins," she replied with a motion toward her fancy heels. "You need not worry about me tripping over anything."

With my free hand, I reached for her waist. "You say this yet I'm still going to hold on to you."

"Go ahead." She beamed up at me. "But do it because you want to, not because you've contrived some sense of obligation."

I didn't argue with that. Not because I didn't want to but because there were a fuckton of pumpkins on the walk and the front steps, and one of us was liable to knock a gourd over if we didn't pay attention. I led her inside and down the main hallway toward the kitchen, knowing everyone would be congregated there.

My sister Magnolia was seated at the table with Ash's fiancée Zelda beside her as they pored over some documents. Magnolia's husband Rob was perched on a stool at the island, his phone in one hand and a vegetable peeler in the other. My mother was busy inspecting a selection of sweet potatoes and didn't notice us arrive.

"Hello there," Magnolia drawled. "Hi. I'm Magnolia and I'd get up but it would take me five minutes and I'd break out in a sweat so I'm going to do everyone a favor and stay put."

"Hi. I'm Jasper. Congratulations," she said, motioning to my sister's belly.

My mother whirled around. "Linden! You didn't tell me you were here!"

"We just walked in," I said.

"Oh, I'm so thrilled you came!" My mother elbowed me out of the way to wrap Jasper in a warm hug. She leaned back, her hands still clasped on Jasper's upper arms, saying, "This green, it's such a smart color on you. I love it, I just love it. And I have to say, I cannot get over how beautiful you are."

I wouldn't have noticed if I hadn't been watching closely but Jasper flinched at those words. Her jaw locked and her smile turned hollow, and it was like she blinked herself away in the moment. I didn't know why or what it was about my mother's enthusiastic delivery but it didn't work for my girl. Not in the least.

"Mom," I said, edging them apart. "Pace yourself, would you? We just got here. You have all night to suffocate Jasper."

"No worries," Jasper said. "I'm okay, Lin."

"Oh my god, she calls him Lin," Magnolia whisper-yelled. "It was totally worth the drive down here to watch this live."

"Does that include the two stops we had to make?" Rob asked.

"One of them was for a bathroom," she replied.

"What was the other for?" Zelda asked.

"I needed an ice cream sandwich," Magnolia said.

Zelda nodded. "Fair."

I handed off the drinks to Rob and draped my arm around Jasper's shoulder, steering her toward the table. "Jasper, this is Zelda. She's my brother's fiancée."

"This probably sounds crazy but I've heard so much about you," Zelda said as she shook Jasper's hand. "When Ash came home from meeting with Linden that day, he had all the stories in the world. I hope that's not too weird for you. Now that I say it, I feel like it's pretty weird and I'm making this awkward."

"Well, isn't that nice," Jasper replied. "I'd be surprised if he didn't have some stories after that very special turn of events. I mean, there were about a million bats flying out my front door. *That* was awkward."

She gave one of her fake laughs, the ones I hated so much, but Zelda didn't seem to realize it was fake. None of them seemed to realize because they were laughing. How did they not hear it? How did they not know?

"And this is Magnolia's husband Rob," I said, moving the introduction train along. "He does very boring things with money and handles my sister's ice cream sandwich requirements with a limited amount of complaint."

"That is extremely true," Rob said as he held out his hand to Jasper.

"Now, Jasper," my mother started, "we were just talking about Magnolia's shower—"

"I don't need another shower," Magnolia interrupted. "Rob and I've both had work showers and we've had a friend shower too. I don't need the church ladies and your teacher friends throwing me a shower. We don't need anything else."

"I'm the grandmother. I get to throw a shower if I want to," my mother insisted.

"Can you make it a college savings account shower?" Rob asked. "We have way too many blankets and tiny socks. College savings accounts, we don't have any of those."

"Good luck with that," Magnolia said to him. "Since the gang's all here and I will not be able to talk Grandmazilla out of anything, I think this would be a good time for us to discuss the hot topic of partnership." She gestured to me. "Ash is in Dad's office, if you're up for it."

I stifled a groan. This damn partnership. With a glance to Jasper, I said, "This won't take too long."

"Of course it won't," Mom said. "Your father should be back from the golf course any minute now and we're eating a tad earlier than usual because Zelda has a very early class tomorrow. You'll be finished with business soon enough to help me set the table for supper."

"Off you go," Jasper said.

I headed down the hall to my father's home office, Magnolia a few steps behind me. "We don't have to do this," she said, slightly breathless. "Not if you don't want to."

"Let's just get it over with," I replied. "I want to get back to Jasper."

"Zelda and Rob run a tight ship. They won't let things get out of hand," she said.

There was something deeply amusing about Jasper joining the ranks of Rob and Zelda. I couldn't explain it, I just knew I liked the sound of it. "I know that. I know she'll be fine."

We stepped into the office to find Ash standing beside Dad's desk, a file open in his hands. He glanced up, saying, "Are we ready?"

"Let's do this," Magnolia said.

I dropped into one of the armchairs in front of the desk. "Why does this feel like an ambush?"

"Because you and I didn't discuss this like we'd planned last month," Ash said. "Remember? Our meeting was interrupted by a series of unlikely events."

I nodded. "I do remember that."

Ash settled into the desk chair with an uneasy glance

around the room. "It's strange being on this side," he murmured to himself. "Anyway. The purpose of this meeting is to discuss potential partnership terms as well as the implications of this on projected profit over the next five years. Any questions?"

I didn't have specific questions though I knew I was uncertain about teaming up with Magnolia. It had nothing to do with her but my general unwillingness to commit to a big new thing that had the potential to disrupt my way of life. What if this meant I had to sit through meetings about finances and human resources? I'd hate that. I'd hate everything about it. And I didn't care what kind of paper we used to mail invoices or the design of our logo. I just didn't care about any of it and I knew I'd be agitated if I had to park my ass in an office and hear about it all the time.

This was why I tuned out my sister's questions about cost centers and ownership shares. It wasn't my language and I didn't want it to become my language.

"What about you, Lin?" Ash asked. "Any concerns about this schedule of terms?"

I didn't even know which schedule we were talking about. "I don't think so."

"That's probably because you haven't been listening," Magnolia said, the humor heavy in her words. "I mean, I'm sorry, dude, but you don't hide it especially well."

Ash leaned back, propped an elbow on the armrest. "What's holding you back here, Lin?"

I shook my head. "I don't know. I'm just not sure. It's a big move, you know? Maggie, you've been working with a whole staff for years, but it's just me. I don't work with anyone."

"And that's exactly why you should work with me," she

said. "You're assuming responsibility for equipment, insurance, everything—and if we teamed up, you'd wipe out nearly ninety percent of those costs. The economies of scale are too great to ignore."

"You sound like Ash," I muttered.

She laughed. "Between Ash and Rob, I have money men on either side of me. I can't help it."

"Here's what I see," Ash said, pointing his pen at me. "You are spread very thin right now. You are on the road every single day and you're going from the North Shore to the South Shore to the Cape. And then you manage all of your record-keeping and invoice reporting by hand. It's a lot of time not spent on your core competency of—"

"Oh my god." I shoved my fingers through my hair because what was this bullshit? "What are you trying to say? Can you tell me that?"

"I'm saying you're not able to use your time as effectively as you could," he said. "And we might have a solution for that."

"I'll go a step further," Magnolia said. "You're doing things you don't like just because it's worked well enough for the past few years. You're doing things you don't like just because you've been doing them a long time and change seems excessively complicated. Like, dude, I'm sure you're thinking of the dozens of things that could go wrong and all the ways it will be different from your current situation, which is not actually that bad."

"You're not wrong about that," I admitted.

"And you don't like working with the country clubs and golf courses because most of them only care about keeping their fairways pretty and they don't give a shit about much else," she continued. "How many times have you bitched up a blue streak to me about country clubs planting a dozen hosta or liriope around the base of oak trees? Or pruning the hell out of some dogwoods and wondering why they stopped flowering?"

I lifted my shoulders. I really hated when they choked the base of trees with plants because—apparently—trees weren't impressive enough on their own. I really hated it when they dug up perfectly good land and filled it with tightly packed flowers and bushes for the sake of creating *interest* only to turn it all over two months later. "Maybe a few times."

"But the retainer is nice, isn't it?" she continued. "That's nice, steady money."

Even if I did grumble about the country clubs, it wasn't that bad. I could handle it.

"I don't disagree with you," I said.

"The heart of this plan is giving you more time to do the things you're really, really good at and giving me access to your skills," she said. "That we get to reduce our costs and—most likely—increase our profits is a very nice added bonus." She reached over, squeezed my forearm. "I think it would be really cool to work with you. Even though I've had a staff, it's always felt like it's just me. It wouldn't feel like that with you."

"I'm not saying no," I said. "I just need time to think it over. That's all."

"Okay," Magnolia said, her hands on either side of her belly. "I need to stand up because I can't take a deep breath in this position and I'm also ready for food. Why don't we give Linden some time with the documents. It's not like I'm in any rush with this."

I helped her to her feet while Ash shuffled the papers

back in the file. "It would be nice to get this resolved before year-end," he said.

"That doesn't mean it's going to happen," Magnolia said. "Come on. We need to get back out there before Mom plans anything else."

SIXTEEN
JASPER

I didn't know if I was allowed to, but I loved Diana.

She was hysterical. Really, truly hysterical. She was all out of fucks but also a fireball, and I liked that combination. Hell, I wanted to *be* that combination.

"Hot plates, hot plates," she said as she carried two dishes to the dining room table.

I'd offered to help, obviously, but she banished me to the table with Zelda after we transferred some roasted vegetables to a serving plate and tucked the napkins through beaded rings. She'd made those herself, Diana informed us, offering a detailed origin story of the beads and how she crafted the rings. She could make us some, if we liked.

"We're not waiting on your father," Diana sang as she settled the dishes on trivets. "If he's late to supper, he'll eat leftovers."

"Isn't it almost dark out?" Magnolia asked. "How is he still golfing?"

"It doesn't have to make sense, dear," Diana replied.

"How about a drink?" Linden asked from the doorway, several bottles of wine and beer cradled in his arm.

"Yes, please," Rob said, holding up his glass. "Whatever you're pouring, give it to me."

"You make it seem like your life is dreadful and requires drowning in any available liquor," Magnolia said.

"That is not it at all, my love," he said. "More like I just spent half an hour talking *someone* out of hosting a gender reveal party."

"But everyone knows we're having boys," Magnolia said.

"I know." Rob nodded aggressively. "I know. She wants to do it anyway. At the very minimum, there will be a baby brunch."

"What *the hell* is a baby brunch?" Magnolia asked.

Rob stared at her. "Does it even matter?"

"Oh my *god*," Magnolia groaned. She elbowed Ash. "Can't you just get married and distract her?"

Ash shook his head at her belly. "You got yourself into this. Get yourself out."

Linden pulled the cork on a bottle of red wine and filled Rob's glass. "To your health, my friend."

"What do you have for beer?" Zelda asked.

"I grabbed that white ale you liked last time," Linden said, showing her the label on a growler. "Does that work for you?"

"Oh yeah." She held up the wineglass beside her plate. "Should I get a different kind of glass?"

"I'll get it," Ash said to her, dropping a kiss on the crown of her head as he stood. To Linden, he said, "I'll take a glass of red."

"Red for Ash, red for Dad," Linden said to himself, "ale for Zelda, Diet Pepsi for Mom, black cherry seltzer and a splash of ale on the side for Maggie because she's weird and needs to *smell* beer, stout for me. That's everyone. Good. All set."

"What about Jasper?" Magnolia asked, her brows pinched up like she was deeply offended on my behalf. "You didn't mention her."

He stepped away, grabbed a bottle off the sideboard table. "I've got Jasper covered." He dropped a hand to my shoulder and held out the bottle to me. "Is this what you want tonight? Or something else?"

It was *my* bottle. The same one I'd had the night he visited me on the back porch. The same one he'd pulled out of his refrigerator the night we ate stew and popovers, the night I'd assumed it was a great big coincidence.

"That's perfect," I managed. My cheeks were hot. So hot. They had to be glowing red right now. "Thank you."

"No problem, Peach."

"There you are," Diana said as an older man dressed in golf gear bustled in from the hall. "We almost sent out a search party." She gave me an aggrieved frown. "Jasper, this is Carlo. My very tardy husband."

"Sorry I'm late, sorry I'm late," he said as he settled into his chair at the head of the table.

"Where have you been?" Diana asked. "Your round was supposed to finish two hours ago."

"The group ahead of us was moving slowly. Everything got backed up." He lifted his hands and offered a sheepish shrug. "I'm glad you didn't wait for me."

"You know I don't wait around when the food is hot and ready," she replied. "Especially not when we have a guest. Carlo, say hello to Linden's *friend*, Jasper."

He glanced around the table as if he needed a minute to

find me in the sea of faces. As soon as he did, I felt something twist inside me. Something ominous.

"Good lord, you're the woman from the television. The one with the senator from Georgia."

I'd forgotten. For the past few days, I'd put Timbrooks and my hot-mic moment out of my mind. I'd forgotten long enough to be caught off guard and now I couldn't move. I couldn't even breathe.

"Dad," Linden warned.

There was a long, pulsing moment when everyone was completely silent. It was like the quiet between dropping a glass and when it hit the floor.

Then it shattered.

"I *knew* you looked familiar," Magnolia shouted.

"Wait a second. You're the one who said—about the senator?" Ash asked.

"How do you even know my brother? I don't understand how they know each other," Magnolia said to Rob. "Nothing makes sense right now."

"Watch yourself, Maggie," Linden said.

I was frozen stiff. Didn't move, didn't blink.

"What did I say?" she asked. "I said I don't understand anything and I just want someone to explain how you know this woman who is the modern day Joan of Arc, as far as some circles are concerned."

That seemed unlikely. Highly unlikely.

Ash wagged a finger at his sister. "Honestly, yes."

"Let's pass the rice, please," Diana said. "I don't cook rice so you can eat it cold."

I nearly laughed at that because I already loved this lady and her whole *no bullshit except for the bullshit I want* vibe. If I hadn't been completely frozen in panic, I would've passed the shit out of that rice for her.

Linden leaned in, his arm hooked over the back of my chair. "Are you okay?"

I nodded. That was the best I could do.

"I had no idea," Ash said with a slow shake of his head. "That day at the house, I had no idea."

"Are we talking about the candidate who dropped out of the presidential race? Like, a couple of weeks ago?" Zelda asked.

"Same one," Magnolia said to her. "Can we back up a second? What are you doing now, Jasper? What brings you to Massachusetts? And how do you know Lin?"

Rob lifted his wineglass. "It's a pleasure to meet you, ma'am."

Carlo leaned forward, resting his forearms on either side of his plate. Diana rolled her eyes at that but didn't comment. Then he said, "Thanks for knocking that blowhard out of the race. I couldn't stand him."

After a beat, I laughed—hard. "You're welcome. I think."

"Okay, I really need the full story," Magnolia said. "Everything. Tell me everything."

"There is *food* on the *table*," Diana said. "And I did not invite Jasper here for you to grill her with your questions, Magnolia Lynn. As you're all well aware, we do not conduct business talk during supper. That goes for"—she glanced to me, her eyes politely dazed like she wasn't sure how to describe the squall I'd brought to her home—"political matters too."

"But I really want to know," Magnolia argued. "So does Dad."

"That entitles you to nothing," Linden said. His tone was

absolutely lethal. I was actually surprised his family was still staring at us and not falling over, dead.

Suddenly, the freeze thawed enough to allow something inside me to click into place. I dug deep to find the smile I used to put others at ease, and the sweet, lilting tone that made everything I said sound gentle and complimentary. "I'm happy to offer some insight, aside from the pieces I've already shared publicly," I said with a self-deprecating laugh. "Though I couldn't bear to let this fabulous meal go cold."

"All I really need to know is how you and Linden are"—Rob gestured to us—"how this came to be."

"My goodness," Diana muttered as she pushed to her feet. She grabbed the rice and scooped some onto Ash's plate, then Zelda's. She went around the table, filling plates and murmuring about her family's sudden shortage of manners.

"I've decided to step away from Washington," I said. "Linden is my new next-door neighbor."

"Isn't that adorable?" Magnolia squealed. "It's *adorable*."

"That actually is pretty adorable," Zelda said.

"Do you know you have a legit fan club?" Rob asked. "My wife is obviously the chairwoman but you should know there are a lot of people who respect the hell out of you."

"Well, that's very generous," I said, even though I doubted every word of it.

"I'm the treasurer," Carlo added. "I don't know what you're doing now, missy, but you have my vote."

"Oh, my. No, no," I said. "Some people are candidates, some people are behind the candidates. I'm behind the candidate. Rather, I used to be, before I was relieved of my responsibilities."

"That was the shittiest thing I've ever seen on the internet," Rob said. "And there're a lot of shitty things on the internet."

"Robert," Diana chastised.

"Sorry, sorry," he murmured.

"You're better off without them. I have zero clue how you lived through all that chaos but I am certain you're in a better place now," Magnolia said. "You know what? We need to go dress shopping soon."

I hadn't used any of my warm-affable-outgoing skills in more than a month and found myself frowning at her when I didn't follow this jump in the conversation. "What's that?"

"Dress shopping," she repeated with a wave toward Zelda. "We need dresses for the grand anniversary gala my parents are throwing, and you are joining us. Weren't we just saying how we need to get together and find something to wear, Zel?"

Zelda bobbed her head. "We were comparing schedules last night."

"We'll have lunch too. It will be so much fun. Please say yes. Please?"

From the corner of my eye, I saw Linden draw in a deep breath. He shifted his hand to the back of my neck, gave me a slight squeeze. I wasn't sure whether that was permission or warning. Either way, I hadn't spent time with women in too long and dining out for lunch was a far-off memory. "I'd love to."

"Now, we're finished with all of this talk," Diana said firmly. "We will eat and stop interrogating Jasper."

"I don't mind," I said, which was what you were supposed to say when you minded very much but didn't want anyone else to feel uncomfortable.

"You might not, dear, but I make the rules at this table," Diana replied.

Very well, then.

Linden leaned in again, his hand still on my nape and his beard barely tickling the spot below my ear. "You're a snake charmer."

"Something like that," I whispered back.

"I can't decide if I'm impressed"—he dropped his hand high on my thigh—"or scared."

"Be scared. Very, very scared," I said with a quiet laugh.

"You don't have to do this dress thing. I can get you out of it."

"You must not have been very impressed if you think I need you getting me out of anything." I covered his hand with mine. "No need to worry. I'll be quite all right with your sister and Zelda."

"I don't doubt it," he murmured. "Just because you can doesn't mean you should though. There's nothing wrong with letting me handle things."

There was much wrong with letting him handle things but that wasn't an argument I'd win while whispering at his mother's table. I nodded, saying, "It's nice of you to think that."

"Right now, I'm thinking about getting us the fuck out of here. Want to fake a headache?"

I shook my head. "Not on your life."

He breathed a soft growl against my jaw. "You're such a tough cookie."

"Then it's a good thing you love eating cookies as much as you do."

His grip on my thigh tightened. "Mmm. It is."

"If we can't talk about Linden's cult celebrity girlfriend," Magnolia said, "we should at least talk about baseball."

"I can agree to that," Ash said.

With a slight groan, Linden shifted away from me. "Right. We'll be so much more civilized talking baseball than we were politics. Makes sense."

Magnolia brushed several pieces of rice into her hand from where they had dropped to her belly, saying, "The next game is at home. Thursday. First pitch at five o'clock."

"Honey. Sweetheart. Love. Do you really think this is a good time to go to *Fenway*?" Rob asked her.

"It's the playoffs, Rob. I'm *required* to go," she replied.

"You're not. You're not required at all." He glanced to Ash and Linden for support but found none. It was awkward as hell to watch a couple nice-fight but at least I wasn't the center of attention anymore. I could enjoy Diana's delicious fish and rice, and drink my wine, and enjoy the bear paw resting an inch from my panties. "Would that even be comfortable for you?"

"Probably not," she said.

"It's a lot of walking," he continued. "And those seats."

"But it's the playoffs. The three of us haven't missed a playoff game at home in twenty years. We're not starting now just because I'm pregnant."

"You're in your third trimester with very energetic twins," he said. "Pregnant is an understatement, my love."

"Magnolia, listen to your husband," Diana said.

She stared down the table at her mother. "I beg your pardon?"

"I'm just saying, your husband knows what's best for you."

"Shall I go rip the Equal Rights Amendment Now sticker

off your car? Or would you rather I wait until my husband gives me permission?" Magnolia asked. "What about the 'well-behaved women never make history' one? Should I grab that too?"

I took a sip of wine because I needed something to do with my mouth that wasn't laughing out loud. This family was hilarious. They were incredible. I didn't even know family could be like this. I didn't know people could belong to each other with so much love and humor and snark. I didn't know that was what family meant to some people.

I didn't know what I'd been missing.

Carlo blinked at his wife. "How many gummies have you had tonight?"

"Not nearly enough," Diana replied.

Rob blew out a breath and stared at Ash with *can you believe this?* eyes. Ash gave him the *I can't help you here, man* shrug. Linden smirked at both of them as he rubbed my inner thigh.

"So, Thursday it is," Magnolia said. "Does that work for everyone?"

Linden turned to me, asking, "Are you good with me going to a game on Thursday night? I'll be back late. Probably ten or eleven."

There was another beat of silence, similar to the first but without the same gravity. This one was curious and the proof of that lived in the six pairs of eyes trained on Linden right now.

"This is blowing my mind," Ash said under his breath.

"Same," Magnolia said.

"Ignore them," Linden said with an impatient shake of his head.

"Go to the game," I said. "I'll be fine. You don't need to worry about me."

"Yes, I do," he mouthed.

The meal continued in much the same way—the triplets snapping back and forth with each other, Diana and Carlo peppering in wildly amusing and slightly odd commentary, food appearing on my plate even when I insisted I'd eaten more than enough—and I couldn't shake the sense this was how it was supposed to be. This was what I'd been missing, the place and the people and the connection I'd longed to find in my life, and now it was here, all around me, and I didn't trust myself with it.

I didn't know how to wrap my arms around all of this—the burly bear of a man, the family that didn't make sense but that was what made sense about them, this quiet corner of New England—without reminding myself I couldn't keep any of it.

SEVENTEEN
LINDEN

I LEARNED THREE THINGS ABOUT JASPER TONIGHT.

One—she didn't like being called beautiful. I wanted to understand but I didn't want her shutting down on me like she did in the woods this morning. I'd figure it out eventually.

Two—I'd always known she was capable of crushing people but I had no idea she could do it without them knowing they were being crushed. She crushed my entire family this evening and it was the greatest thing I'd ever witnessed.

Three—it shocked her every time I remembered boring little things like the wine she preferred. This was the second time I'd watched that reaction whip through her and I was certain it was one of shock. I didn't see how something as simple as grabbing the bottle she favored was worthy of shock but I wasn't to make an issue of it. Not yet.

And one last thing—I was a bit more attached than I cared to admit. Only a bit. Not *very* attached, not *reorganizing my life to fit Jasper* attached. Not imagining a future. Nothing like that. No, I wasn't that attached.

I wasn't.

But I was beginning to think she'd crushed me too.

EIGHTEEN
JASPER

I HAD A COMPLICATED RELATIONSHIP WITH MY BODY.

Things were better now but I'd struggled to understand —and shield myself from—the ways people treated me as a result of this body.

When I was eight years old, I started attending church services with my extended family. They kept an eye on me when my mother couldn't so I was on my best behavior. Not a toe out of line, not even when the women who gathered to gossip over coffee and cookies pointed at me with their Styrofoam cups and called me "the beautiful one" with undisguised contempt woven into the words.

They never called me by my name but they stared, their eyes narrowed and their lips curled up as if they expected me to shape-shift into the kind of serpent who tempted Eve out of the Garden.

They announced with great authority that I was full of myself, I was a stuck-up brat. *Look at the attitude on her. Thinks she's something special.* They often said my family would have to watch out for me, that the trouble I'd cause would place a real burden on my aunts and uncles. I had no idea what any of that meant and it made me want to put my head down and hide, but I didn't dare stray from my aunt's side. I couldn't get in trouble. My mother couldn't handle that on top of everything else.

They took a great interest in my birthmark. Some of the more devout gossipers believed it was the devil's mark, that I'd been touched by evil, and evil was inside me. Those who didn't see the devil in everything insisted I had to get it removed. No one would want me with that mud stain on my face. Others proclaimed it was good for me. I needed a flaw to keep from getting a head about myself. Whatever that meant.

I never told my mother about it. She'd already explained there was no getting through to Aunt Leslie and that I just had to follow her rules, even if they didn't make sense. Her kids got the belt and unless I wanted that, I had to keep my mouth shut. There was nowhere else for me to go, not until the summers when I could stay with Midge. I had to be good, and quiet.

When I was twelve and my body was changing in sudden and unpleasant ways, they still pointed and stared. They said it would be any minute until the teenage boys got their hands on me, that they'd know what I was about, that I'd ruin families looking the way I did. I didn't understand that either but it *terrified* me. I was afraid all the time, looked over my shoulder constantly. I avoided my male cousins and their friends at all costs and refused to ride alone with any of my uncles.

When I was fifteen and in possession of what could only be referred to as tits—for they were not breasts, they were not boobs, they weren't even jugs, they were big, bouncing *tits* that seemed to develop overnight—those women replaced "the beautiful one" with "the slut," "the whore," "the trash."

I hated myself. I didn't want to be a slut, a problem, a girl who had something bad coming to her because she lived in a womanly body. I hated everything about myself and I wanted it all to go away. *I* wanted to go away.

So I learned to disappear.

I started wearing sweaters with blouses that buttoned up to the throat and full, A-line skirts that fell past my knees. At the time, retro was *not* cool and everyone thought I was going through some kind of *Bewitched*-meets-*Happy Days* phase but I didn't care. Endlessly rummaging through thrift shops and church bazaars gave me a project that didn't involve making myself small and ashamed, and my new style was distracting enough to take the attention away from my body.

At eighteen, I didn't know the expression *damned if you do, damned if you don't*. The gossipers still criticized and called me names and I didn't understand how my existence could be wrong all the time, regardless of how I showed up in this body. But I started sensing they were wrong, and after a decade of hardening myself to their cruelty, I taught myself to stop caring.

I figured out I could exist in this body without hiding it. I could be as much of a woman as I wanted and I'd take no shit about it. Tits, curves, birthmarks—they belonged to me, no one else. Skirts, dresses, pantsuits—it didn't matter. The only issue on the table was my competence, and on that, I delivered every time.

People still told me I was beautiful. I still felt the need to shrink and apologize.

I bristled when shopgirls made offhand comments like, "What can I help you find today, pretty lady?" or my boss said, "Our lovely Miss Jasper will take care of that" or my ex-husband introduced me as his gorgeous wife.

And then I felt awful for bristling because it was just a compliment! How silly was I to be injured by a few kind, simple words? Why couldn't I just accept the nice comment and move on with my life?

And then I remembered those gossipy women and the hateful, churlish things they said to me when I was a handful of years old. They were angry and insecure for reasons that had nothing to do with me, and that anger blinded them to the fact they were taking out their insecurity on a child.

I was better now. Time and distance eroded away the worst of it, even if I had occasion to freak out over a compliment. It was easier to be excessively competent than it was to be beautiful, even if beautiful carried more currency. It was safer and I'd weaponized that competence to protect myself.

I didn't hear the gossipers in my head anymore. Not usually. I knew they were full of toxic shit. Though I also knew they were probably gathered together after church every Sunday, clucking and cackling over my public downfall, which they'd predicted would come to me.

NINETEEN
LINDEN

MY BROTHER ELBOWED MY SIDE, SAYING, "I TOLD YOU SO."

Ignoring him, I finished typing a text message to Jasper. We had a very strict no-phones-at-the-game rule but that existed only because Ash would spend the first half answering emails. It didn't extend to the care and tending of the honey-haired belle I'd left at home with a reminder to be good and stay away from the tools.

Linden: Behaving yourself, Peach?

Jasper: Why start now?

"DO YOU SEE THIS?" ASH CALLED TO MAGNOLIA.

I should've known better than to sit between them. After that family dinner, I should've sat clear across Fenway Park rather than subject myself to this assault.

"Ash, I am a land whale. I cannot see anything," she replied. "If you want me to comment, you'll need to spoon-feed me the necessary info. And also nachos. I need you to feed me nachos too."

"*Lin* is *texting*," Ash said.

He couldn't have sounded more alarmed if he'd said *Lin is riding a rhino*.

It was Magnolia's turn to elbow me. "You never have your phone with you. This must be for real with the pretty politics girl."

"Could you two watch the game? For fuck's sake, it's the playoffs. You're gonna give birth any minute and—"

"Yeah, that's the plan. Born at Fenway," she joked. "No better birth story than that."

"Don't make me call your husband," Ash said. "Rob is not on board with that plan."

"Not his vagina, not his plan," she replied.

"Jesus Christ," I muttered.

Linden: What are you doing tonight?

Jasper: I'm not baking anything, if that's what you're asking.

Linden: That's a relief.

Jasper: I'm doing some research. Checking out jobs that might make sense for me.

Linden: Making some lists?

Jasper: You know it.

Linden: Any leads that sound promising?

Jasper: I don't know. There's some get-out-the-vote work that could be really interesting. It's not high profile, it's not glamorous, it's not going to make me rich.

Linden: …but?

Jasper: But it matters, you know? This stuff really matters. It makes a difference.

Linden: Tell me more about it later?

Jasper: All I do is babble out every single thought I've ever had to you so, yeah, I'll tell you more about it.

Linden: I'll hold you to that.

Jasper: You'll also hold me to a tree.

Linden: Any day.

"Maggie, he's still texting," Ash said. "When was the last time he even replied to one of your texts?"

I wasn't the best with phones. They were all too small for my hands and finicky. As much as I could get away with it, I ignored mine, often leaving it in the kitchen or in my truck. I'd removed all the notifications and alerts. I had to go looking for messages if I wanted them and I liked it that way. Jasper though…talking to her was a different story.

THE BELLE AND THE BEARD   259

"When I asked if you two wanted me to pick out a Mother's Day gift from all of us," Magnolia replied.

I glanced at her. "Did I ever pay you for that?"

She gave me one of those bright-eyed, stiff-lipped smiles. "Nope."

"Sorry."

"You can make up for it by telling us the true story of your very special friend Jasper," she said. "She's, like, famous. How did you—just, how? That's what I need to know. How did this happen?"

"She's not famous because she wants to be." I studied the field for a moment. "That was a bad situation for her. With that senator."

"I mean, that much is apparent," Ash said. "But you have to recognize the humor in it too. She decimated the guy's chances as a presidential candidate and she did it in three minutes. That's pro-level GOAT status."

"It was incredible," Magnolia said. "It was everything I'd ever wanted to hear about those crusty candidates. They try to come off all polite and principled but they're just dirty old men who sit around smoking in their underwear while their staff tells them everything they need to know."

"Yes, and the way she pulled the curtain back on the truth about candidates who are running but aren't in it with any intention of seeing it through?" Ash said. "I'd always suspected that but she just laid it out in the open." He shook his head like he still couldn't believe it. "What's she doing next? She could start a no-bullshit, underbelly of politics podcast or—"

"We're not doing this." I pushed to my feet and filed out of the row. "Nachos?" I asked, pointing to Magnolia. "Anything else?"

"Lin, sit down," Ash said.

"No, I need nachos," Magnolia wailed. "You can sit down once I have a snack. Oh, do you guys think you could get beers and let me be near them? I just want to smell beer. That will be enough."

Ash held out several bills. "Whatever they have on tap but you should know we like Jasper."

Magnolia nodded, her hands resting on her belly. "We do and we're genetically required to ask all kinds of nosy questions because you introduced her to us and—"

"Mom made that happen," I interrupted. It seemed like this was important to note. "She showed up at my place—"

"Oh, god," Ash murmured.

"And Jasper had just stepped out of the shower. So, Mom jumped to every possible conclusion—"

"Wait, are you not sleeping with her? Because that was definitely the vibe I picked up at the house last weekend." Magnolia shot Ash a meaningful glance. "Tell me I didn't imagine that."

My brother shrugged. "All I will say is I told you so."

"You're such a smug bastard," I said.

"Wait. What did you tell him?" Magnolia asked.

"The day Jasper arrived, and she had some difficulty getting into her aunt's house—"

"Ash thought she was a burglar," I added.

"We offered her some assistance," he continued, fully ignoring me. "And I told him to be nice to her."

"You said 'don't be an ass.'"

He bobbed his head. "I advised you to help her out and resist your natural tendency toward being an ass because—"

"Because you helped Zelda and now you're getting

married," Magnolia sang. "Awwww. Oh fuck, I'm crying. Linden, dammit, this is all your fault."

"You should get those nachos," Ash said with a pointed glance at our sister.

As I waited in line at the concession stand, I snagged my phone to check on Jasper again. I didn't need to check on her. I knew she was fine, and seeing as she'd hung up the baking mitts, there was little threat of the house burning down.

I just wanted to talk to her.

Linden: Ash and Magnolia are pretty much obsessed with you.

Jasper: I find that hard to believe.

Linden: They'd rather spend the night with you than me for all the questions they're asking.

Jasper: …what do they want to know?

Linden: How you got to be so awesome.

Jasper: Very funny.

Linden: I'm serious. They're co-presidents of your fan club.

Jasper: Not sure what to say about that.

Linden: Say that for all the shitty things that have happened recently, there are people who think you're amazing.

Linden: Before you ask, yes, I'm one of them.

Jasper: You're just saying that so I'll be naked when you get home.

Linden: I have zero objections to your being naked, preferably in my bed, but you know I don't say anything just for the hell of it.

Jasper: That's true.

Linden: You also know I don't need to compliment you to get your clothes off.

Jasper: Also true. Not sure what that says about me.

Linden: It says you follow directions on selected occasions.

Jasper: Again, I'm wondering what that says about me.

Linden: Only the best things.

Jasper: How long do these baseball games run?

Linden: This one should be over in an hour. Two at the most. Traffic adds another hour. Maybe less.

Jasper: Okay.

Linden: Should I expect to find you in my bed?

Jasper: Expect me on your wifi. Where I'm parked while I use it is a different story.

Linden: Good enough for me.

I RETURNED TO OUR ROW, DRINKS AND SNACKS BALANCED precariously on top of one another, and forced Ash to serve as Magnolia's nacho holder.

"It's good practice for you," I told him.

He snickered. "I have five years in the pocket before Zelda even looks up from her fieldwork and doctoral defense work. You'll be waiting on the pregnant wife before I will."

Reflex told me to disagree but longing told another story, one that blindsided the shit out of me. I could see it. I could see a ring on Jasper's finger as she pressed a hand to her belly, I could see us turning the den into a nursery, I could see us hiking through the woods with a baby strapped to my chest.

I had to thank the Red Sox for hitting one out of the park at that moment because my brother would've seen right through the vision detonating in my head. Not wanting to give him another reason to say "I told you so," I smothered it all with some well-earned celebration.

I'd let him be right about everything another time.

"Since we're not allowed to talk about Jasper, can we talk about this anniversary party?" Magnolia asked when we sat back down. "The one Mom and Dad planned for two weeks before I hit full term for twins?"

"What do you want to talk about?" Ash asked.

"Many things," she replied, "but first off, how about the fact those two hippies are throwing themselves a two-hundred-guest black-tie affair at a country club? Do they even recognize what they've done?"

"Not sure I'd go as far as that," Ash said. "It's a big party. Your wedding was a big party."

"My wedding was a glorious, blessed event," she replied with a sniff. "And, I will note, this is all your fault, Ash."

"That cannot be true," he said. "I did nothing."

She pushed to her feet and screamed at the umpire about his eyesight until the batter on base turned to stare at her, his mouth hanging open and his brows pinched high in shock. My sister always came to these games armed with some colorful commentary.

"Sit down, sit down," Ash said. "I promised your husband I wouldn't let you get too worked up."

"I don't know why Rob thinks *you're* going to prevent such a thing at a playoff game, especially one with that douche bagel of an ump."

"Me neither," he muttered.

"Anyway, can we just talk about them throwing a black-tie party? When we were kids, Mom wouldn't wear anything aside from hemp dyed with natural colors. Remember that? And she used to make bags from woven grass? Come on, you have to remember that."

"I remember the grass belts," Ash said. "Those were heinous."

"It was impossible to get them unbuckled in time. The number of near-accidents I had in kindergarten was outrageous," I said.

"And now we're having a fancy-pants party at a country club," Magnolia said. "It's almost like they've forgotten they were earthy-crunchy socialists once upon a time."

"Do you think that's just what happens as you grow up?" I asked. "Do you gradually reshape your ideals as time passes?"

Was that even possible? Was it a matter of bartering away your ideals or finding new ones that fit better? I didn't know but I had the sense people weren't supposed to be one stationary, static thing their entire lives. People were supposed to live a lot of lives in their time on this planet. They were supposed to reinvent themselves and reevaluate their beliefs. They were supposed to look back and shake their head at the things they did before they knew better. They were supposed to get all the second chances.

"Or is it more a matter of going into semiretirement and filling your days with golf?" Ash said. "I don't know about Mom but that's what happened to Dad."

"Mom fell down the rabbit hole with the first pair of Tory Burch sandals I bought her. It's a slow-growing addiction but it's a brutal one."

Ash and I glanced at her and then each other.

"I want you two to promise me you'll do the heavy lifting so I can sit in a corner with my feet up. You know, assuming I haven't popped by then."

"What do we need to lift?" I checked my phone one more time but didn't see anything new from Jasper. "Shouldn't the venue take care of all that?"

"I don't think she's referring to the furniture, man," Ash replied.

"I need you two mingling. I need the ladies in your life mingling. Shield me from having to engage in small talk with all of Mom and Dad's friends who will offer endless childbirth and parenting advice while this one"—she pointed to her right side—"separates my ribs, and this one"—she pointed to the left—"dances on my bladder. Do this for me and I'll take care of the anniversary gift from all of us."

"You're going to do that anyway," I said.

"Maybe." She shrugged. "I definitely won't forget to add your names if you promise to let me sit this one out."

Before I could say anything about my desire to protect Jasper from those two hundred guests and everything they'd heard about her on cable news, Ash said, "We've got it. Just keep those babies cooking until the day after the party, would you?"

"It doesn't work that way, Ash. I can't just squeeze my legs together and hold my breath."

"I mean, yeah, sure," he replied. "But you can still try, right?"

"You're going to be just adorable when Zelda's pregnant, aren't you? An adorable little nut that just needs to be bashed over the head a few times."

Ash glanced at me, asking under his breath, "Is she being serious? I don't know."

———

THE GAME RAN THE FULL TWO HOURS I'D ESTIMATED AND MY sister required me and Ash to accompany her to an ice cream shop that served up scoops in bubble waffle cones. She also required each of us to order cones for ourselves—but plucked those cones from us and claimed them as hers the minute we sat down. Thankfully, her husband arrived soon after Ash texted him our location and he took over Magnolia's ice cream needs.

Ash departed for Zelda and their Haymarket apartment and, for the first time in all the sporting event outings we'd shared as siblings over the years, I was eager to return home. I didn't want to steal a few more minutes with Ash and Magnolia, didn't want to laugh over ice cream or grab another beer while watching the game's highlights. I wanted to go home to Jasper, and that—that hit me as hard as the vision of her married to me.

It was late when I arrived home and Jasper was already tucked into bed, her hair gathered in the same nighttime bun she favored. There was something enchanting about that bun, the one she wore in private, liminal moments. Maybe it was that I knew about the bun and that was the enchanting part. I wasn't sure.

The best part—the absolute best, no substitute in the world—was finding her asleep in one of my flannel shirts. She had the cuffs rolled up and left the top few buttons open, and was there anything more perfect? I didn't think so.

I undressed and climbed into bed beside her, not bothering with any form of pajamas. No need. Jasper arched against me when I pulled her to me, a soft, sleepy murmur greeting me when I ran my hand up her thigh and found her ass beautifully bare.

"That's my girl," I rumbled, grabbing a cheek and giving it a thorough kneading. "Good and ready for me."

She replied with another murmur but there was no mistake about the way she wiggled her lower body into my lap. A condom came next and some strategic organization of pillows and legs as we settled into this side-by-side position. Then I pushed inside her, snaked a hand down the front of her shirt, groaned into her hair. We moved together in languorous thrusts and echoing sighs that skated the line between dreaming and waking.

There was no rush to find the end, not when we could float in this heavenly in-between.

I reached for Jasper's hand, the one busy squeezing my upper thigh, and shifted it between her legs. "Show me," I ordered, my fingers over hers. "Show me how you do it when you're alone."

"When I'm alone," she started, veeing our twined fingers over the place where I moved in her, "I lie back and let a toy suck my clit and another work my G-spot." She brought our fingers up to the hood hiding her pearl. "Don't see why I should have to do all the work when I can play with toys instead."

I closed my other hand around her breast, her nipple pinned between two fingers. "Will you show me that?"

A purr rolled through her that I felt in my bones. "Maybe. That might be interesting."

My hips jerked in a messy, erratic rhythm. "*Might be?*"

That gorgeous, piercing moan of hers filled the room and I knew we were close to the end, the in-between space behind us now.

"I doubt you can sit back and watch. You'll last two minutes before taking over. You'll want to show me the right way to do it."

That sent me shifting to my knees, both hands gripping her hips, turning her until she was flat on her back. "Isn't this better?"

She went on teasing her clit with luscious circles that made me want to fuck her and lick her and kiss her and bite her all at once. That made me want to *keep* her.

"It's different. It's totally different," she said, her head tilting back into the pillow.

"I guess I'll have to see that for myself." I pumped into her, fast and reckless now, like she was mine to break. That was the singular thought in my mind as her body clenched around me, sucked me in, held me prisoner.

"Does that make you jealous?"

"Of your toys? Not in the least. They're my coconspirators, Peach. Not my competitors."

"*Ohhhh*. I like the sound of that."

When I caught hold of my release, I caught another flash-forward, this time with Jasper in a wedding dress. As I filled the condom, I leaned into her, my lips pressed between her breasts to prevent myself from saying something premature. Something permanent.

As soon as I was able to walk steadily, I headed into the bathroom and straightened myself out.

This was the wrong time to run away with wild ideas about marriage and—*Jesus Christ*—babies. I'd told myself for years I didn't want any of it and I had to remember that some good times with Jasper wasn't meant to change anything. I preferred a solitary life. I didn't want anything else. Marriage and kids weren't the paths for me. Too complicated, too messy, too tenuous.

I believed that as devoutly as I believed in the religion of nature. And yet, when I gathered a sleeping Jasper into my arms and closed my eyes for the night, I thought about all the lives we were allowed to live with the time we had, and I whispered into her hair, "I wish you were mine to keep."

TWENTY
JASPER

I DROPPED TWO SLICES OF BREAD INTO THE TOASTER AND ASKED, "Do you happen to have a nail gun I could borrow?"

Linden belted out a tremendous belly laugh from behind the Sunday newspaper. As he set it down on the kitchen table, he gave me a fond smile that did terrible, terrible things to me. Just the worst. "Why do you think you need a nail gun?"

"I don't *think* I need one." I frowned down at the cherry tomatoes on the cutting board in front of me. "I *know* I need one. It's going to take me two years to finish the porch if I have to bang every single nail into place. A gun would make it much quicker."

"Also quicker to nail your hand to a board."

"I wouldn't do that."

"No one thinks they're going to shoot themselves with a nail gun. It's always an accident, Jasper." He shook out the newspaper, folded it in half and then in half again. "Why not work on something else?"

"I've done everything else. Generally speaking."

"What does that mean?"

I fussed with the burrata and basil for a minute. "It means I've cleaned out most of the house and done most of the work I can do on my own. You know, without a nail gun."

I didn't need to detail or justify my avoidance of Midge's bedroom. It did not need to be said this morning, not when it was a bright, sunny October day that had started out with the kind of *maybe we're asleep, maybe we're awake, maybe we're a little perverted* sex that legends were made of and I had this gorgeous pint of tomatoes to drizzle with balsamic glaze. I wasn't popping that bubble with my inability to step into Midge's room without crying.

"And you're sure you won't let my sister take care of it for you?"

I'd die. I'd drop dead. "That won't be necessary."

"She'd love to do it. She used to live in my aunt's house, actually. Up on the North Shore, in Beverly. Aunt Frannie. She moved to New Mexico a couple of years ago and handed the place off to Maggie because she was in between apartments—and other things. Once Frannie left, Magnolia renovated from top to bottom."

I grabbed the bread when it popped up. "Then she understands how much excitement comes with it."

"She understands how much of a pain in the ass it is."

"That too." Once I finished arranging the cheese and tomatoes, and topping it all with the balsamic glaze, I carried the plates to the table. "I hope this is okay. The burrata wasn't doing what I wanted it to but these tomatoes are really nice and—"

"It's more than okay, Jas." Linden hooked an arm around my waist and yanked me into his lap. He held me tight, his chin on my shoulder and his beard tickling my neck. "You don't have to cook breakfast every day. You think you do but you don't."

I did. I absolutely did. And I could've done so much more. I should've, really. I should be able to plow through Midge's room and finish the porch and get a job and fix my life. Breakfast was the least I could do.

"Not touching that one, are you?" he asked.

I shook my head.

"Didn't think so." He gave me a final squeeze before easing me off his lap and patting my ass. "Do you want some coffee?"

There wasn't much of the locally bottled cold brew Linden favored left and he usually went for two or three refills. I shook my head again. "No. I'm all set."

He stared at me for a beat. "You're sure? You haven't had any?"

I pushed his plate toward him. "I'm sure this toast will chill if you don't stop talking and start eating."

I shifted my gaze down, my focus glued to my plate as if the tomatoes would run away if I didn't keep a close eye on them. That was the problem with Linden. Not that tomatoes fled in his presence but that he noticed things. He noticed when I passed on coffee or sidestepped a question about my family or withered a bit at his offerings of assistance. He noticed and I couldn't gather myself up tightly enough to hide from his notice.

That was how I ended up staring at crumbs and running my palms up and down my thighs, the thighs once again clad in the matte black leggings I used to wear on the rarest of occasions. There was something disconcerting about being comfortable in clothes I'd once deemed inappropriate for my body and safe only for tasks like cleaning the house. I couldn't trust that comfort. Couldn't accept it.

And Linden noticed that too. He'd cover my hand with his when he caught me rubbing my legs or tugging the hem of my shirt lower. He'd invent reasons to dress me in his flannels or hoodies, and though he always looked at me like he wanted to take a bite, he never pushed an inch more than I could manage, even when I didn't know the exact location of that limit.

"Well, that was fucking amazing. Again," Linden said, his plate clean. "Here's what I need to know: Do you eat anything else for breakfast? Is it only toast?"

I lifted a shoulder as I chased a tomato through a drop of balsamic. "Nope. Just toast for me. But I should mention that toast isn't just for breakfast. I'm happy eating it all day."

"What about French toast?"

"Not my style. I'm not into sweets as much."

"Then"—he cocked his head to the side, his brows lowered—"does that mean you don't eat banana bread?"

"We're back on the banana bread bullshit?"

"I just want to know if *you know* what banana bread is supposed to taste like," he said. "Or pecan pie, for that matter."

This would've been a great moment to get up and busy myself with fixing a cup of coffee, but seeing as that wasn't an option I held up my hands and let them fall. "I've tried both, if that's what you're asking. I don't eat them often."

Linden leaned back, nodding slowly. "That explains it."

"If that's what you want to think, I won't stop you."

"What is it about toast?"

I shot him a bratty eyebrow. "I have to justify toast to you? Does that seem right?"

"If you ate toast like a regular person, no, I wouldn't say a thing about it. But you wake up in the morning and say, 'Mmmm, I can't wait to make toast.'"

He made me sound like a cartoon character and that chafed but not enough to stop me from laughing. "I've always loved toast. Even before I realized I could make it fancy, I loved it. There's just something that makes me so happy about a slice of warm, perfectly browned bread."

He gave me another slow nod, like he couldn't comprehend this, like he couldn't comprehend me. A chill chased through my shoulders and I had the urge to drop into a small, quiet place or lash out at him for criticizing this one innocent thing of mine—or both, yes, both, I'd lash out and then I'd leave and—

"I don't know how you do it. It wouldn't occur to me to make all these different things with toast."

It took me a second to gulp down the old fight-then-flight reflex that surfaced more often than I wanted. "It's fun," I said. "And it's inexpensive because you can stretch the ingredients. It's also better than cooking a whole big meal. Especially when it's just me."

"It's not just you."

I glanced at Linden before snatching his plate for washing. He liked to pepper comments like that one into conversation as if they were totally ordinary. As if my life wasn't a million pieces spread out before me and the instruction manual nowhere to be found. As if it wasn't just me and I wasn't making my way all by myself, not anymore.

"Then it's an extra slice of bread or two. No trouble." I pushed away from the table and filed the plates in the dishwasher. "It's not like replacing a porch with the same tools as the pilgrims used."

"Look at you, talking about pilgrims. If you stay here much longer, we won't even be able to find the South in you anymore." He came up behind me, brought his hands to my hips. "I bet I'll find it if I look real hard."

I dropped my chin to my chest and closed my eyes as Linden pushed my hair over one shoulder and dragged his lips along the nape of my neck. "Haven't lost it after all these years away from Georgia. Won't lose it now," I said as defiantly as anyone could in this position. "Even if I do find myself in Plymouth Rock country."

"I could say something about giving you all the *Plymouth Rock* you want"—he pressed into me, his shaft hard against my backside—"but I don't think you'd appreciate that comment as much as I'd enjoy making it."

A soft laugh shook my shoulders. "Lin, you *did* say it."

He kissed the nape of my neck then smoothed my hair back into place. He was careful though a bit clumsy about it, obviously unaccustomed to handling long hair. A ripple of tingles moved down my body and I was relieved he couldn't see my face because I knew my smile was delirious.

"Why don't you show me what you've done next door? I want to see everything you've accomplished."

"Is that the prerequisite for lending me a nail gun?"

"Baby, I don't have a nail gun. I have nine kinds of chainsaws and zero nail guns. I just want to see what you've been doing there the past six weeks."

Though my hair was back to rights, Linden continued running his fingers through the strands, tugging only enough to light up my scalp with the kind of warmth and softness that made me feel loose everywhere. "Then you're not trying to keep me away from power tools?"

"I am definitely trying to keep you away from power

tools. I'm also interested to see how the house is coming along."

"We could stay right here instead," I murmured.

He sighed into my neck. "I love your hair."

I blew out a breath, my eyes still closed and his shaft still heavy against my ass while those words soaked into me like the sun's rays in winter—strained, filtered, and inarguably true.

"It's always so soft," he continued. "I don't understand how anything could be this soft."

I nearly explained my shea butter conditioning mask but stopped myself in time.

"And you always smell so…lovely," he added.

Again, the shea butter mask. "Thank you."

He banded his arms around my torso and gave me a great squeeze, his face pressed to my neck. As he held me, a rumbly growl sounded from his throat, a noise that wasn't nearly as predatory as it was possessive. Like he was deeply satisfied.

I stepped out of his hold and away from the dishwasher. "What do you want to see first?"

———

It hadn't occurred to me that Linden would be critical of my work on Midge's house though when I led him through the front door, a blast of preemptive defensiveness flooded me.

"Obviously, I'm not an expert when it comes to any of this," I said.

"Wow, it looks so much better in here," he said, stepping

away to travel the length of the living room. "Such an improvement over the bat cave."

"Well, anything would be an improvement over the bat cave."

He kneeled down, ran his fingertips over the floor. "The hardwood needs a good refinishing but it's in decent shape. I wasn't sure if there was water damage."

I twisted my fingers in the hem of my shirt. "I don't think there's any. Not in here."

He stood and turned to face the wall, his brows pinched. "You painted this room, right?"

"Yeah, the walls were not pretty. I found a bunch of paint in the basement so I just used the colors Midge already had in the house." He continued staring at the wall with that pinched brow gaze until I snapped, "What's wrong? What's the problem?"

He gave a quick shake of his head and stepped toward me. "Nothing. Nothing's wrong. What else is there to see?"

I pointed out the freshly painted walls and ceilings in the hall, the spots where I'd pulled up the old carpeting, the rotted cabinets I'd ripped out from the kitchen. Linden murmured and nodded at the right moments, though I was still poised on the edge of a defensive cliff. I could fall off— or jump—at any moment.

When I led Linden into the little room I'd claimed as my own, he dropped both hands onto my shoulders with a rough groan.

"What? What's wrong?" I barked.

"Nothing is wrong, Jas. I just hate that I let you stay here alone—and that was before you did all this work."

I pointed to the wide windowsill where the cat slept, as

he often did when the morning sun shone in. "I'm never quite alone. This guy is always nearby."

Linden chuckled. "That's funny. I've never seen him as much as I have since you moved in."

"He's waiting for me to finish the house," I said. "Then he'll go back to his wild woodland life."

"That cat is as concerned about you and tools as I am." Turning to the opposite wall, he asked, "What kind of paint did you use?"

"I don't know. Regular paint. Paint from a can. *Paint* paint."

"Are you sure you used interior paint?"

"What do you mean, interior paint?"

"Okay. Let's go exploring." Linden steered me out of my room and toward the back of the house, moving through the kitchen and down into the basement. He stopped us in front of the long row of cans I'd organized on a shelf near the nonfunctioning washer and dryer. It was right across from the nonfunctioning water heater and the barely functioning electrical panel. Good times.

With one hand on my shoulder, he gestured to the label on one of the cans. "Exterior paint."

I wasn't on the defensive cliff anymore. I was in the self-sabotaging swamp again, the place where I could help myself but never did.

"What—what's the difference? Does it matter? Really? It doesn't. It doesn't, it can't. It looks fine. It looks like paint and it's fine so it doesn't matter. Right? *Right?* Did I screw the whole thing up? What does that mean? I can paint over it with the right type or—oh my god, please tell me I don't have to tear down the walls. Please, Lin, please tell me I don't have to replace the walls because I didn't notice it was exterior paint."

He closed both arms around my shoulders and chuckled into my hair. "Jas. Peach. It will be fine. But this is why I'm not putting a nail gun in your hands."

———

I FOLLOWED LINDEN OFF THE TRAIL, DEEPER INTO THE WOODS. After I'd started yelling "Why! Why? Why are you exterior?" at a paint can, Linden had ordered me into his truck.

With a long gaze at his denim-clad backside, I asked, "Why are you still single?"

His step faltered for a moment but then he called over his shoulder, "Is that what I am?"

"Unless there's something you need to tell me, yeah."

He gave a slight shake of his head. "If I'm single, what are you?"

Oh, no. No, no, no. We weren't going down the *what is this?* path. We were already lost in the woods, as far as I could tell, and there was no need to define what was most definitely a fling.

Since we weren't doing any of that, I replied, "I have been in a codependent relationship with my job since I was a teenager and laboring under the belief that a job would fulfill all my emotional and spiritual needs. That's what I am." I caught up to him, elbowed him in the side. "Back to you. Why are you single? Your fingernails are clean, you only hurl obscenities on selected occasions, and you don't appear to be involved in anything illegal. You're a catch, Lin."

"Is that all it takes? I never knew." He pulled out his notebook and flipped through the pages for a minute. "Seems like we should be talking about that codependent relationship."

I groaned. "Haven't we done enough of that?"

"I would agree if you didn't make it sound like a present-tense type of situation. Thought you quit that, Peach."

"One does not simply walk away from a career after fifteen-plus years in it. Even if they recently realized they hated parts of their job and maybe-probably engaged in big-time self-sabotage. One does not simply toss all that in the shredder."

He chuckled, still paging through his book. "Then what's your plan?"

"I wouldn't call it anything as sophisticated as a plan but I have been talking with a few folks about some consulting projects. Nothing solid. Optics are so important right now. No one wants to risk it at this point."

"And if that doesn't pan out? What then?"

"I could always write a tell-all book, which would then require me to become a commentator because you don't spill all the secrets and cross your fingers, hoping to get a chief of staff gig the next day. That kind of reincarnation takes ages."

"Would that make you happy? The commentator thing?"

"Probably not, which is why I'd sell Midge's house before I resorted to that."

He glanced up from the book. "And then what?"

I shrugged. "I don't know. This is a seat-of-the-pants season for me and it's more stressful than I can possibly quantify. That's why I need something else to obsess over, something less tragic and preventable. So, tell me why you're still single."

"You should've prefaced it with that," he replied, peering up at the tree.

I paced between the trees for a minute. "It seems like you prefer being alone."

"That's true," he said. "You know I'm a triplet. I grew up flanked by my brother and sister at all times. Never alone, never. When you're that close to people, you drop into your own world, and that's great because you always have a friend, always have a playmate. But it's also tough because you never learn how to think without another set of voices in your head or how to function outside that separate world. It's true what they say about multiples having a sixth sense with each other but I think it's mostly a result of spending every living minute together."

"I thought we were talking about how you liked being alone."

"We were." He shoved the notebook in his back pocket and pulled out a long belt-looking-thing. He looped it around the trunk and then secured it to his waist and—*holy shit*—climbed right up the tree.

"A little warning the next time you do that, okay? I need to prepare myself."

It was downright hypnotizing to watch the simultaneous flex of his thighs and shoulders, the way his backside tightened in those jeans, how he made this look like the most natural thing in the world.

"Move over to the left," he called as he unsheathed the knife attached to his belt. "Stay there. Don't move." A dead branch dropped to the forest floor. "One more coming."

I moved another step to the side and watched as Linden sent a second branch to the floor. He studied the treetop for a moment, shaking several other branches as he shimmied along the trunk.

I was reminded of meeting Linden, that first day when I'd arrived here from D.C., when he was out in the front yard. I never would've guessed that burly bear of a man could climb trees like a grizzly. I never would've guessed I'd invent reasons to spend time with him or look forward to our walks in the woods. I never would've guessed it would be my rude, mansplainy neighbor, the one who said not two hours ago that I couldn't be trusted with paint, to make me feel like I belonged here. Like I belonged with him.

"Coming down," he called.

He walked backward down the trunk, the belt sliding with him along the bark. It looked remarkably easy, the same way home renovation shows—which never talked about separate paint for interior and exterior—made everything seem remarkably easy. Which meant it was far more difficult than I could comprehend.

"So, you just do that?" I asked when he was back on the ground. "You just…climb the tree."

"I just climb the tree."

I motioned to the belt as he pulled it from around the tree. "Simple as that."

He nodded. "I can't explain it any other way."

I glanced at the tree and the spot where he'd removed the branches. It was really high up there. "You didn't even wear a helmet or anything."

He slapped the trunk. "This old girl? No need. Just a quick touch-up, no reason to pull out all the equipment."

I watched as he moved the branches to the side, out of the way of the barely-there path. "If you thought you could distract me by climbing a tree, you've forgotten that my job used to be puppet master of distractions. I don't get distracted. I do the distracting. It's obnoxious and one of the reasons people cringe when they see me but I get the job done regardless of how awful I am in the process."

"All the more reason for you to find a different line of work, Peach."

"What do you want me to do, Linden?" I cried, my frustration suddenly boiling over. "Should I wait tables? Answer phones? Maybe I should sell pharmaceuticals. I already know all there is about bullshitting so now I can really *help* people. How about that?"

"Why not? There's nothing wrong with any of those options."

"There's not, but—"

"But you don't know what your life is without your job. *I get it.* I know. I'm just saying, maybe you should take a minute to look around and realize *this* is your life without that awful, obnoxious, codependent job, and it's not too bad."

"No, it's not bad except I'm gaming out how long I can paint inside walls with outside paint and go for walks in the woods before I have to sell Midge's house. Aside from that and the everyday anxiety of it, everything is great."

He shook his head like he was at his wits' end with me. For a minute, he stared off into the woods. Eventually, he said, "Then sell the house. You can stay with me as long as you want."

"You don't actually want that. You're offering because you don't like me using tools and doing things by myself."

"Would you stop it? Just for a second, Jasper, stop pretending I'm the one holding you back from anything. Stop acting as though you're unbearable to be around, that you're intolerable and impossible. You're not. Stop saying that shit, would you? It offends me because I don't like anyone talking about you that way." He shook his head again, *now* past his wits' end. "I'm offering you a place to live while you're figuring this out."

"And why would you do that?"

"Because I...I don't hate you. That's why."

My belly swooped. It would've been better if he'd said he loved me. It wouldn't have hit me nearly as hard because not hating me meant a great many things, none of which I could handle. None of which belonged in a conversation where I continually reminded him he was single.

But then I went ahead and made it so much worse by saying, "I don't hate you either."

Linden stared at me, blinking hard. His hand tightened around the belt he'd used to lever himself up the tree. His other hand opened, closed in a fist, and then opened and closed again. "Now that we've cleared that up, maybe you could put some real energy into deciding what you want to do next. Not just work but what comes next in your life. And, I don't know, you might want to explore things that don't make you sound like you'd rather be stabbed by a hundred rusty steak knives."

"When did I sound like that?"

"When you were talking about the commentating gig. And again with the pharmaceutical sales."

I stared at the leaves on the ground around me. "I'd rather not do either of those things, even if I can."

Linden swung an arm over my shoulders and steered me down another nonexistent path. "Then don't, Jas. Sell the house if you have to, stay with me as long as you need, but don't keep doing things you hate."

I nodded, agreeing although I couldn't really agree to *moving in with him*. Even if I was sorta-kinda-maybe already there.

We were quiet as we walked, the weight of not hating each other lifting and falling down around us. Saying those words snapped the cord of tension we'd been twisting and winding for weeks—but it also broke all the vows of *only temporary, just for now, just a fling*.

Not hating a fling was serious business, or so I assumed, seeing as I didn't have many flings to my name and none in recent memory. But I knew I wasn't supposed to have not-hating feelings. Not when this place was only a detour for me.

This *was* a detour, right? This wasn't my destination.

I stopped, looked up at the bare branches, blinked hard at the sun. This wasn't where I was meant to be. It just wasn't.

"Okay there?" Linden asked.

"Yeah. Fine. Just thought I saw an owl."

"Not in the middle of the afternoon but maybe a hawk. A lot of those guys around here."

"Wait." I pressed a hand to his chest. "You never finished telling me why you're single, or why you've been single, and how that has anything to do with being a triplet."

He covered my hand with his. "I thought we'd moved on to more important topics."

"Like I said earlier, I spend enough time fixated on my problems. Let's talk about yours instead."

He laughed. "I don't have any problems."

"You're a thirty-six-year-old bachelor. Society would beg to differ." We started walking again, our hands clasped. "At least tell me about the triplet thing. I want to hear more about that."

"We grew up together, as you know, and we did everything together. We really did have our own tiny world—but then we finished high school and split up. It was a huge shock to the system. For the first time ever, I wasn't within an arm's reach of Ash and Magnolia."

"That must've been tough."

"It was weird," he replied. "It made me realize how much I prefer being alone and having things that belong only to me. They were still my best friends and I'd spend more time with them than anyone else, but not sharing everything with my siblings turned out to be very good for me. I don't mean that in a secretive way. It's like I learned to hear myself think for the first time and I couldn't go back to the way things used to be. Also, I think that split was good for them too. Ash stopped trying to herd us like cats, Magnolia stopped inventing things for us to do. We found things that interested us separately instead of everything being collaborative."

Out of absolutely nowhere, I said, "I don't have any siblings. A lot of cousins, but I wouldn't call any of them friends."

"Why not?"

"Lots of reasons." I didn't want to add to that. "You're all about solitude but you still dragged yourself next door and introduced yourself the minute I pulled into the driveway. Explain that."

"We've been over this."

"The attempted burglary, yes, but why did you keep inviting yourself over to the hot-mess house?"

"First of all, you invited yourself to *my* house after we met," he said. "But after that, I knew I'd be a suspect if you turned up dead. I had to keep tabs on you unless I wanted to be hauled in for questioning."

"Seriously," I chided.

"Seriously?" He scratched the back of his neck. "I couldn't sleep. Knowing you were all alone over there."

"But you like being alone. It's your thing."

He jerked his chin up as a deer, about twenty feet ahead, crossed our path. "This was different."

Since I couldn't cope with any more not-hating sentiments but I still wanted to press this bruise, I said, "Okay, you like being alone. How far does that reach? Have you sworn off relationships too?"

"It's been a couple of years since I've thought much about relationships. The casual thing works well enough for me."

"What happened a couple of years ago?"

"Nothing," he replied with too much conviction to ignore.

"Something."

He blew out an irritable breath. "I don't usually talk about this."

"I don't usually walk through the woods and I never wear pants and sneakers. Do you understand that? I'm a dress girl but I'm wearing leggings and ugly flat shoes because you told me to, and that requires you to return the favor by telling me all your gross, mushy secrets."

"I don't have gross or mushy secrets," he replied with a laugh.

"Then tell me about the thing you don't usually talk about."

Linden shot me a sidelong glance. "You talk *so much*. Do you know that? Like, nonstop."

"I do know that. Along with being exceptionally distracting when I want to be, I can talk the proverbial dog off the meat wagon. I can talk to walls and get them to respond to me. It's one of my many gifts and talents."

"Am I the dog or the wall?"

"Neither," I replied. "But you are the person who has heard all *my* gross, mushy secrets."

"Fair enough," he grumbled. "When I was in my twenties, there was someone. We were close through college and shared the same circle of friends so we were always hanging out once we were out of school too. Camping trips, snowboarding trips, beach trips. Always in the same group. I had feelings for him, some big feelings. Bigger than I'd had before then, and I'd dated more than my share of people during college."

I smothered a laugh at his bashful grin.

"There were a few times when we got close to—I don't know—*something*. But then he started seeing someone or I started seeing someone and it didn't happen."

He stopped, kneeled down to inspect some flowers alongside the path. I wasn't positive though it seemed like the flowers were not part of his overall inspection of these woods but an opportunity to stop speaking.

That was fair. I'd stared at a lot of flowers and rocks in these woods to avoid talking about my issues too.

"I spent a ton of time thinking about those feelings. Obsessing, really. I was always working up the nerve to tell him. It went on for years, even after we hooked up on a camping trip. I had a clear shot at asking for more and I didn't take it. Sometimes I think back on that and wonder what the fuck was wrong with me."

"I literally ask myself that every single day," I replied. "The other day, I relived an intern orientation meeting I led twelve or thirteen years ago. I don't understand how anyone put up with me. I was the absolute worst."

Linden squeezed my hip, saying, "It wasn't as bad as you remember. Promise. And neither were you."

"Back to your obsessing. I need to hear the rest of this. It's really helping to recalibrate the scales in terms of which of us is the disaster. I've been the hard favorite for much too long."

"There isn't a rest of the story. I didn't say anything. He moved to Idaho and I didn't tell him."

"Just because he moved doesn't mean you can't—"

"I know," he interrupted. "*I know*. After he left town, I decided I was ready to reach out because distance didn't matter. Why would it, you know? I'd made it through all these years of keeping those feelings to myself, I could make it through some distance too. But there was an accident."

"Oh, no."

"Yeah." Linden bobbed his head, his gaze fixed on the ground. "He was on life support for months. His family was convinced he'd pull out of it. He was young, he was healthy. All those things. And there was always a story about some other young, healthy guy coming out of a coma. Seemed like it was possible. Like we weren't hanging on to empty hope." He sighed, stayed silent a moment. Then, "They let him go about six months after the accident. They told everyone when they were doing it, in case people wanted to say goodbye before they took him off life support."

"Oh my god. Linden. I'm so sorry."

"I could've gone to the hospital. The whole group from school went out to Idaho. I should've, actually. But it just felt like I'd have to tell him I'd had all these feelings and that seemed like opening one door while closing another. At the time, it didn't seem right. It didn't seem fair—to me, to him, I don't know."

All I could say, again, was, "I'm so sorry."

He continued as if I hadn't spoken. "Altogether, it was five, six years of my life spent getting close and losing him over and over, each time worse than the one before. After he died"—he stopped, pushed his fingers through his hair—"I just didn't want to go through that ever again. I didn't want to invest all that energy into *hoping* and *wanting*. I didn't want to watch while someone slips out of my fingers and I didn't want to wish I'd figured out my shit sooner."

I took his hand in mine, squeezed. We walked without speaking. He stopped every so often to make notes in his book, other times to push fallen branches out of the trail.

After about ten minutes of heavy silence, I asked, "How long ago was this?"

Linden glanced to the side, almost as if he was surprised to find me there. "Right before I turned twenty-seven, so, nine years ago."

"That's more than a couple of years, you know."

"Yep."

"And the casual thing has been working for you since then?"

Again— "Yep."

He sounded as confident about that as I did about my career prospects, and that was why I let him get away without pushing on that response. He didn't have all the answers and neither did I.

TWENTY-ONE
JASPER

"You're sure you won't let me drive you?"

I glanced at Linden in the bathroom mirror before returning to my makeup. "Positive."

"I have visions of you calling me from Providence or Springfield because you missed an exit or something."

He dragged his gaze over my denim shirtdress, his eyes narrowed in a manner that suggested he either loved it or hated it. Even if he hated it, I wasn't changing. This dress was my casual weekend girls' lunch go-to. Denim was never appropriate at the Capitol so I didn't have much of it, and while this dress looked like a boring blue sack on the hanger, the right belt made it magical on me. In my last life, I very much resented that I couldn't wear it to work.

"That probably won't happen. Your sister gave me very explicit directions and told me exactly where to park too. I'll be fine."

"What about a car service? Uber or something like that."

I twisted open the mascara. "Your concern is unnecessary."

"My concern is founded upon you getting lost in a small town on multiple occasions."

"I've survived the traffic circles. I will be quite fine on my own, thank you."

"Rotaries." He peered at me as I fluttered my lashes against the wand. "How old is that car of yours?"

"I bought it used when I finished college but it runs like new."

"Do you even know what new runs like?"

I capped the mascara and went for the eyebrow pencil next. "It runs like it did when it was new to me, which is good enough. I've never had any trouble."

"Why would you buy a used station wagon when you were just out of college?"

"Because they were fresh out of cute little BMWs and white Jettas at my price point, okay?"

He crossed his thick forearms over his chest. "I still don't like the idea of you driving into the city. I'll take you."

"Really not necessary."

I dropped the pencil into my makeup bag and reached for my perfume. I ran the rollerball behind my ears and down the line of my decolletage. Linden watched closely, momentarily distracted from this little disagreement of ours. In truth, I had some hesitation about driving into Boston for lunch-and-shopping event but I wasn't admitting that to him.

"Okay. That's it," he said, stepping forward. He flipped my skirt up over my waist and pushed my panties down to my knees as I fumbled to close the perfume pen. He pressed his hand to my back, between my shoulder blades, forcing me to bend forward. "Hands on the sink. I've had enough of this."

"Enough of what?"

The hiss of his zipper sounded and then I felt the heavy heat of his shaft as he dropped it on the curve of my ass. "Enough watching you. Enough of this dress. Enough arguing with you. Just…enough."

Watching Linden snatch a condom from the cabinet and quickly sheathing himself had my blood whomping in my veins and my core aching. At the same time— "I just spent ten minutes on my face."

"It's not your face I plan on fucking."

He ran his hand between my legs in a rough, demanding pass before fisting his cock and pushing inside me. Any words I might've had gusted out of me as my hands scrabbled to grip the edges of the vanity countertop.

"I told you to hold on," he growled, his hips thrusting in a slow, relentless rhythm.

"I-I'm—trying," I stammered.

With one hand on my waist, he twisted my hair around his palm. "Try harder."

"Do not ruin my hair," I warned.

"I couldn't if I tried," he rumbled. "Even when you're wrecked, you're perfect to me. You're always perfect the way you are."

I couldn't explain why those words hit me so hard but they knocked everything out of me. All I could do was watch Linden in the mirror, watch the wrinkle of concentration between his brows and the stiff set of his jaw as he drove into me.

"Get there, Peach. I'm not waiting for you."

He'd wait. He'd definitely wait. But it was fun to pretend he wouldn't. It was fun to hand over that power and let him demand something of me that we both knew he'd provide.

"Almost," I managed. I couldn't say anything else. I could barely breathe. He was always thick but in this position, he was impossibly, ridiculously thick. I was certain he was tearing me apart.

I felt him everywhere. That fullness, that pressure—it sent prickles racing across my shoulders, over my scalp, through my cheeks. I felt tiny electric vibrations down to the tips of my fingers and along the backs of my thighs. My entire body was wired to go off and all it really took to get me here was some coarse, selfish thrusting and a growled demand. I couldn't decide if that was a credit to me or Linden.

He shifted the hand stationed on my waist to my backside, saying, "I love your ass like this. It makes the sweetest heart shape."

He dug his fingers into my skin, holding me hard enough to sting, to leave marks. Honestly, it was rude how comfortable he was using my body in whichever way he wanted. Completely rude.

"I mean it. I'm not waiting for you. If you think I won't finish and then send you off to lunch all angry and needy and empty, you're wrong." He slammed into me, pinning my body tight to the vanity and holding me there as I writhed and wiggled to find some friction. "I'll do it, Jas. I'll leave you miserable."

"And what will that prove?"

He met my gaze in the mirror, his feral to my frantic. "I'm not proving anything. You are."

His hold on my hair tightened as he found an aggressive new pace. I knocked the hand soap from the countertop, the toothbrushes too. He twisted my nipples through the dress, pinched my clit, bit my shoulders, teased my asshole. There was no limit to the ways he used me. No limit to this rough, imperious treatment.

"Come on, Jasper. Stop making me wait for you."

I'd never thought of myself as the kind of person who required words or emotions to get off, not when I had a perfectly reliable clit to handle the job for me, but once again I was wrong because those words set me on fire. There was nothing special about them, not really, but they found a space inside me that desperately needed them and I was done. Just done.

"There you are," he murmured, his hold on my ass no less vicious than before the orgasm moved through me. "Just like that."

I dropped my head between my outstretched arms as Linden chased his release with fast, punishing thrusts that I felt too deeply to keep my eyes open. He made a gorgeous, growly sound as he came and slowly unclenched his fingers from my backside. What was left of it.

Still pulsing inside me, he reached up and smoothed my hair into place. His touch was absurdly gentle in comparison to the nearly cruel pounding he'd just given me. It was like he could dismantle me but then gather all my pieces and reassemble me with the greatest care. I didn't think that was possible. I didn't think anyone could exist within such great extremes without largely residing in one or the other.

"That's it," he murmured.

I blinked up at his reflection. "What?"

"I'm driving you to lunch."

The only response I could manage was "Okay."

———

"I'M SO HAPPY WE COULD MAKE THIS HAPPEN," MAGNOLIA SAID as she clinked her glass against mine and Zelda's. "No one told me the third trimester would be so busy. Let that be a lesson to you two."

Zelda and I exchanged a glance that said *we're not seeing a third trimester any time soon.*

"I'll note that," Zelda said with a laugh. "I hope I remember in five or six years when I'm ready to think about getting pregnant."

Magnolia waved a hand in the other woman's direction. "Don't worry. I'll remind you."

I laughed down at my menu. I didn't want to think about babies, not in any personal way. I could handle the abstract notion of babies, even the localized idea of them in the sense that Linden would soon be an uncle, but not when it came any closer.

It couldn't come any closer.

"That's entirely enough about me," Magnolia said. "All anyone ever wants to talk about is me and the contents of my uterus, which is entertaining at first but gets old. I want to talk about the beautiful ladies in my brothers' lives. Do you know how long I've waited for a lunch like this? Dude, I was starting to think it was never going to happen."

Zelda busied herself with unfolding the cloth napkin in front of her and spreading it over her lap. She had a shiny ring of sapphires and diamonds on her left hand. Ash wasn't the one who'd held up Magnolia's fantasy lunch plans. This was about Linden and his long history of casual relationships—and me, the woman who crashed into his life and hadn't cleared out yet.

I had the overwhelming urge to explain to these women that I didn't know where I'd land next and I probably wouldn't be a fixture of their Santillian girls' lunches and I didn't see how I'd be the one to make it happen for Linden.

Magnolia wasn't having a second of it. "I know what you're thinking," she said, "and I get it."

I was thinking my ass hurt, I probably had a bruise across my bikini line from the bathroom counter, and I didn't belong in Magnolia's regular rotation of lunch companions.

She gave me a kind smile. "Things are new. I get it but I'm still happy you're in Linden's life." With a tip of her head to the side, she added, "Right now."

That part was for my benefit though it was obvious she hoped for much more. I wasn't sure I could do the same. I wasn't sure I could look more than a few days or weeks ahead.

"Just don't make her try on any wedding dresses today," Zelda said.

"For the record, that was my mother. Not me." Magnolia glanced to me. "We were there for my final fitting. There were dresses everywhere. It's not like I planned to put Zelda in a dressing room but it worked out well. She doesn't have to find a dress now. Cross that off the wedding planning list."

Zelda made a checkmark in the air. "One less thing to worry about."

The waiter sidled up to the table to take our orders. While the other women requested Caesar salads without anchovies and an order of fries for the table, I planned my pivot. Linden and I could not be the subject of this lunch and we couldn't make it all about me either. God, no.

When the waiter stepped away, I shifted toward Zelda. "You have the dress. Do y'all have a date?"

She bobbed her head as she reached for the bread basket.

"No, I'm a super huge problem child when it comes to setting a date. My field work schedule—I'm in grad school, by the way—is up in the air for a few more months. I have a good idea what the next year or two will look like but I can't commit to anything until it's finalized."

"Ash is going to carry you off to Lake Tahoe some weekend and elope," Magnolia said. "Unless he's already done it."

"I can promise you he has not carried me off to Tahoe yet," Zelda replied. "Mentioned it, yes. Hasn't done it."

Magnolia glanced to me. "He'll do it. His patience wouldn't fill a shot glass."

Zelda shook her head in a patient, conciliatory kind of way that seemed to suggest Magnolia knew an awful lot about her brother—but not everything. "I'm not sure I'd say that," she said, her attention again fixed on the bread. "He wants the big party of a wedding."

"You could have a big engagement party," Magnolia said. "Then go elope."

"He wants a big party for a wedding," Zelda replied gently.

"What do you want?" I asked.

She gave me a quick shrug. "I don't have too many priorities. I just want to end up married." She reached over, patted my forearm. "The party and the whole big event, they don't occur to me as things I'd want because I've never had parties just for me. That's why I defer to Ash. He thinks we deserve a special day to celebrate with our friends and family, and I have to remind myself he's right. He's right and we *should* wait until we can set a date because it wouldn't be the same without the celebration."

I found myself staring at her, slightly dazed, as I worked

through those words. Then, without any consideration what-soever, I admitted, "I haven't had many parties either."

"Then you understand," Zelda said, her hand still fixed on my forearm. "You know how odd it is to plan something big and grand just for yourself."

"I'm not sure I could."

She smiled, saying, "That's where Ash comes in. If I tell myself it's for him—and he reminds me it's for *us*—I can get past the awkwardness of doing something that tends to feel deeply selfish."

"It's easier to help other people be selfish," I murmured.

She gave a sage nod. "It is but that doesn't make it right."

It was my turn to reply with the knowing nod. "It's hardly ever right."

She glanced away for a second, as if she was considering her next comment. "I know we barely know each other and you're experiencing many shifts in your life"—I snorted out a laugh at that—"so I hope it's not inappropriate for me to say I'm happy you're here. I'm happy you've come into Linden's life but ours too." She gestured across the table to Magnolia. "I hope we get to have many more days like this one."

"What she said," Magnolia added. "I hope we get more of this too. I already know that once these babies are born, I'm going to need some moments away from all the boys in my life, even if I am wildly obsessed with them."

"Yes, that. Even if you're wildly obsessed with someone, you need time away from them too. The past year has taught me that it's important to have friends outside of relation-ships, outside of grad school," Zelda said. "I love my grad school crew, they're great, we can talk for hours. But my life has many facets and the people I spend time with should be reflective of that. I can't throw myself all in one direction and still expect to feel whole."

I leaned a bit closer to her. "Could you say that again?"

"I just realized that I need to account for the dimensions in my life," she said. "When I started grad school last fall, I met all these wonderful people. Really, the best people. Though they're all about that one thing, and our relationships, even the best ones, are all about that one thing. I love that I have a community because I didn't know many people when school started and they helped me feel like I belonged somewhere—"

"And me. I helped," Magnolia said.

"That's what I'm getting at," Zelda said with a motion toward her future sister-in-law. "I had an amazing connection to Magnolia and Ash's family, who made me feel so welcome and loved. And then there were Magnolia's friends, who were like an extra special bonus of connection. I mean, Erin Walsh and Alex Emmerling are some of my favorite people in this entire city. I can't believe I get to know them."

"You'll meet them," Magnolia said to me. "You'll love Shannon Halsted and Lauren Halsted-Walsh. Andy Asani too."

I didn't know who any of these people were but I nodded, saying, "I can't wait."

"I had all these glorious people," Zelda continued, "and I had my school connections, who made me feel like part of the academic community. I'd missed that for years. But I know I can't let school or any one thing become my entire existence. School will end and I'll be forced to start over again because we all know that relationships formed around that one thing rarely last beyond those structures. I have a camp friend from forever ago but that's the exception, you know?"

I grabbed for my water goblet and took a long gulp because I knew all too well. "Yes. I do understand that."

"And it's always so awful when you realize people from work or school have moved on without you. That's why I know I have to stop stowing all my community eggs in one basket." She took a bite of her bread. "And, like I said, I'm happy you're here."

Because my life was a series of unforced errors, I said, "I hope I can stay."

"Why wouldn't you stay?" Magnolia asked.

The waiter was kind enough to arrive with our meals and save me from responding for a minute. When he left, I was met with two pairs of curious eyes, both ignoring their food in favor of my response. With a soft sigh, I said, "I'm still sorting out my next steps with work. It's all a bit…wonky at the moment."

While Zelda accepted this response with a sympathetic murmur, Magnolia pressed on. "But you want to stay here," she said.

I picked at my Cobb salad, pushing the croutons to one side and the tomatoes to another. "I hope I can," I repeated.

That was the truest thing I could say. Nothing was definite. Nothing was settled. It didn't matter how much I was beginning to enjoy the little life I'd cobbled together with my burly lumberbear and my DIY projects. It didn't matter that, sometimes, I wondered how I'd ever return to a world where my phone was an extension of my body and I woke up at five every morning only to discover I was already three hours behind on the day. I wondered how I'd go back to run-walking in heels as a matter of course and working weeks at a time without a full day off. And I wondered how I'd give up lazy evenings on Linden's sofa where he explained how, when filming *The Lord of the Rings: The Two Towers*, the textually male Riders of Rohan had to be played by women because they couldn't find enough men with adequate horseback riding skills.

"We're going to cheer you on," Zelda said. "Regardless of where the wind blows you."

"Yes. What she said." Magnolia wagged her fork at Zelda. "But you're still coming to the anniversary party, right?"

"I'm sure I will," I said, hoping that put the topic to rest without forcing me into a blood oath.

"We're shopping for dresses today. You have to come to the party," Magnolia insisted.

"Sweetie, Jasper is doing her best. She's going to be there if she can, okay?" Zelda turned her attention from Magnolia and grinned at me. "Don't worry about Mag. She gets a little chippy when she's hungry."

"I'd blame it on the twins but I've always been this way. The twins just make it socially acceptable." She reached into the basket of fries as she eyed us from across the table. "I was wrong. I got it all wrong."

"No, stop it. You're always allowed to be hangry," Zelda said.

"Not about that." Magnolia swung a glance between us. "I was wrong about my brothers and who they needed. I mixed it up. I guess that's a good reminder that I have no business in matchmaking."

"What do you mean?" I asked.

She dropped a hand to her belly as she took a sip of water. After a pause, she said, "I had a vivid idea in my head of the people my brothers would end up with—"

I dropped my fork into my salad bowl. "Oh, we haven't—I mean, we aren't—I'm still—"

"I know," Magnolia said carefully, "I do. I know that and I understand. And I know it doesn't change the fact I was wrong about them. I had the right ideas"—she pointed one hand toward Zelda, another toward me, and then crossed her arms at her wrists—"for the wrong brothers."

I didn't know what that meant and I wasn't content with the apparent finality of it but Zelda rescued the moment, saying, "Enough about the men. We don't need them to make us interesting."

"We do not," I agreed with far more zeal than necessary.

"Not at all," Magnolia agreed. Then, "*Oof.* They don't appreciate those comments." She rubbed a hand along the side of her belly, her eyes glowing. "You have to feel this. Come on, both of you. I swear, they're break-dancing. Or wrestling. Oh my god, they're going to wrestle all the time, aren't they?" She patted the bench. "Humor me, please. You have to feel this. It's like a legit stampede."

Zelda and I shared a glance before joining Magnolia on the banquette side of the table. She grabbed our hands and pressed them flat to her bump.

"Just wait," she murmured.

A moment passed, and another, and then I felt very silly sitting here, waiting for something to happen inside Linden's sister's body. Just as I decided to politely pull away, a swift kick connected with my palm. "Oh—oh my," I stammered.

"That was an elbow," Magnolia said. "He's always throwing those elbows around. I think he's the instigator."

"Holy bananas," Zelda yelped. "How are you, I don't know, living through this? It's like big, bony popcorn popping but it's inside you."

"It only hurts when they get curled up under my ribs. Or wherever they are that feels like they're under my ribs and having a competition to see which of them can crack one first. Or when they're stomping my bladder. I barely got any sleep last week because they were having such a good time."

"That sounds dreadful," Zelda cooed. "I want to have a baby. Not right now, obviously, but someday. I want a little someone who likes to rumble around and throw elbows."

As another jab connected with my palm, I thought to myself for the very first time, *Me too*.

———

I WASN'T KEEPING SCORE BUT I WAS CERTAIN I'D MEASURED THIS porch at least forty times and still couldn't come up with the same numbers twice. As was the theme for this moment in my life, I didn't know what I was doing wrong or the right way to fix the issue but that didn't stop me from trying like hell.

Since the most recent measurement made no sense whatsoever and I refused to cut the wood until I had these figures correct, I set down my notebook and tape measure, and walked away.

Midge's yard was just like Linden's in that it extended back to the edge of the forest but he didn't have a dozen-odd wooden planter beds in various sizes, shapes, and states of disrepair. When I'd visited Midge in the summers, she'd put me to work weeding the vegetable garden. She'd grow everything back here. Zucchini, beans of all sorts, ten different types of tomatoes.

There was always one plant that didn't work out. One year it was the cucumbers. They'd send out tendrils and coil around the support lattice, they'd flower, they'd sprout a spiky little cuke, and then…nothing. We had spiky little cukes, far too immature to harvest, and nothing else. The whole crop turned out that way.

Now, the beds were tucked under a blanket of fallen leaves. Some were warped and weathered, so much that a heavy rainstorm was all they needed to collapse at the seams.

I hadn't given the garden much consideration because the growing season had mostly ended for the year when I moved in. It would be fun to bring the garden back to its original glory come spring. I didn't remember the specifics of Midge's planting strategy—and she always had a strategy—but I knew I could come up with something. It would be a good project and one that wouldn't require quite so much precise measurement as the porch.

There were at least six months between now and the spring growing season. I'd have to *be here* in six months to rebuild this garden, which was ridiculous. I wouldn't be here come April. I couldn't be. If I was still here in April, still picking up random projects and making a mess of them, something had gone terribly wrong.

I stopped, turned to face the house and the sad skeleton of the porch. What if I *was* here in April? What if I had a garden? What if I was right here, growing sweet little tomatoes and huge zucchini that required constant comparison to penises? What if I did all the things Linden suggested and just let myself stop worrying about what came next? What if I stayed with Linden and it wasn't temporary?

Walking backward, I took a few steps into the deepest corner of the garden. From this distance, I could see slumps in the roof and irregular tilts in the gutters. It all needed to be replaced if I had any intention of staying.

Did I want that? Did I know how to do that? How to stay and stop worrying about the next thing? Not knowing had never stopped me before.

I could stay here and we could do this. It was an option, one that scared the hell out of me for fifty different reasons, but it was more an option now than it had ever been. I could plant a garden, get an entry-level job canvassing for a candidate or the party, live with Linden. Those were real things and I could have them.

I took another step backward—and nearly fell on my ass when my shoes connected with soft, slippery, uneven earth. Once I righted myself, I blinked down at the ground, seeing but not understanding the apples beneath my feet. With a glance around, I spotted many more decaying apples nearby.

"Why the hell are there apples all over the yard?" I asked out loud.

The familiar old black cat leapt from one of the raised beds and picked his way through the apples before darting off into the woods.

"You're so helpful," I called after him.

I made my way back toward the house and grabbed the supplies I'd abandoned before crossing into Linden's place. He was catching up on paperwork this afternoon and I knew he'd welcome a break from that to investigate my apple problem.

When I entered from the deck, I had the pleasure of watching as the scowl he'd aimed at the documents in front of him melted into a familiar smile. I couldn't explain why that quick moment of blown-open honesty warmed me more than any words or kisses ever could but I felt that heat in my cheeks, my hands, the back of my neck.

"That didn't take long," he said, holding a hand out to me.

I knew he intended to draw me into his lap but I didn't have time for that. "There are apples. All over the backyard. And they're, like, rotting."

He bobbed his head as he beckoned me closer, unsatisfied with my position on the opposite side of the table. "From the trees, I'd imagine."

"Which trees?"

"The apple trees."

I peered at him. "Where are there apple trees nearby?"

Linden dropped his outstretched hand as he laughed. "They're in your yard, Peach."

"Where?"

"In the back," he said, pushing to his feet. "Four, maybe five of them? They're fairly young. Less than ten years old, I think." He rounded the table and hooked his fingers inside the waistband of my leggings, yanking me up against him. "Sometimes you are too far away from me."

"What do I do about the apples?"

"Not letting that go, are you?"

"I just discovered I have an orchard, Linden. I can't let that go. What do I do about all the apples? Isn't it a problem to leave them there?"

He kissed the top of my head and patted my backside. "Sit down. The apples can wait a minute."

He pulled out a chair and shoved me into it as sweetly as anyone could. I grinned in spite of myself. I didn't mind a good shove when it was Linden doing the shoving. I wouldn't mind him pushing and pulling me around for the next six months. Or longer.

I heard him rustling in the cabinets and then the fridge as I said, "How is it that I didn't notice I had apple trees until now?"

"I don't know what to tell you other than you are extremely gifted with many complex things, and less gifted with a few basic things."

"Are you trying to say I'm some kind of savant who can't change a light bulb?"

"I'm saying you're some kind of savant who can't exit a rotary."

"I *can*, it just takes me a few tries."

"I know, babe. I know. It's what makes you special—and completely unreliable with the most random things." I heard him shaking the milk carton over my shoulder. "Wait a second. You didn't have any coffee this morning."

"Hmm?"

"The coffee. You were in the shower when I filled up before leaving for my appointment in Weymouth. You didn't drink any today."

I glanced up at him. "Oh. Yeah. I must've forgotten. I got distracted with emails."

Linden set the milk down as he leveled me with a stern stare. "You haven't touched the clementine marmalade all week."

I shrugged. "Haven't been in the mood."

"Is that it? Really, Jasper? You're forgetting to pour yourself a cup of coffee in the morning, not interested in the last bit of marmalade?"

I shot him the same disinterested look I used on anyone

who skated too close to the truth for my comfort. "I can't imagine why any of this is an issue."

Linden growled something I couldn't make out and returned to the task of fixing his coffee. It seemed like we were finished with the topic of me leaving the last of the cold brew and Diana's homemade marmalade for him, and that was a relief. The only thing worse than worrying about taking too much was having a discussion based on someone noticing I worried about taking too much. Hell, that was almost as bad as someone noticing *and talking about* my constant need to arrive early.

Linden set a mug down in front of me, another one beside the stack of papers he'd been working on when I came in. I wasn't sure when he'd picked up more of the locally roasted, small batch, slow-steeped coffee he preferred, seeing as there'd been only one serving left earlier today.

He ran a hand over my shoulders before circling the table and dropping into his seat. "Let's get a few things straight, Jasper."

I eyed him, a brow arched up in an automatic show of defiance. I couldn't help it. Most of the time, I didn't even notice I did it. But I didn't take well to anyone else doing the straightening. I was the sheriff in these parts.

"There will be no more of you leaving the last few spoonfuls of marmalade, the last cup of coffee, none of it. You don't think I see you insisting on showering after me?"

"On the rare occasions in which you permit me to shower independently? That evidence seems insufficient to me."

He rested his forearms on the table, his shirtsleeves rolled up to his elbows, and leaned in. "I don't usually go for it when you use that dagger-sharp, killer boss lady voice on me but it's working right now. It's working."

I couldn't stop the smile from tugging at the corners of my lips. "Perhaps it would serve you well to discard this nonsense topic in favor of one more mutually agreeable."

"You're so fucking cute."

I replied with a playful shrug and took a sip of the coffee he'd fixed for me.

"You're cute but I'm not letting you shrug your way out of this," he said. "I don't want to see you leaving the last of anything for me, you understand?"

I studied him for a second. His beard looked thicker than usual today, as if he'd let days pass between trims. I liked it. I liked him slightly overgrown, slightly wild. It suited him.

As uncomfortable as I found this conversation, a small, fragile piece of me also liked when he took charge. When he *insisted*. I didn't want to like it, I didn't want to feel seen and protected because he noticed me leaving the coffee—and the hot water—for him. I didn't want to be needy in this way. And that was why I pressed my hands to my eyes and let my shoulders fall, saying, "But I can't. Okay? I can't."

"That's tough shit, Jas, because you're going to have to. I'm not putting up with these pointless restrictions of yours anymore."

"You're letting me stay here. The least I can do is make sure you have a hot shower in the morning."

He reached across the table, pulled one hand away from my face. "Why do you think I can't handle a lukewarm shower? Or a cold one, for that matter."

"I know you can handle it," I replied. "But you'd be in there, grumbling and growling about how you could've had hot water if I hadn't used it all."

"Ignoring for a moment that I have a tankless water heater that can accommodate two long, hot showers without a problem, I don't give a single fuck if you use all the water. If you drink all the coffee, eat all the marmalade. I don't give an actual fuck. But I do give a fuck about you forbidding yourself from living here the way you should."

"But I don't want to be a problem or take up too much of your space. I know how protective you are and how you don't like anyone encroaching on you and—"

"Yeah, you're right. I have to be pretty damn sure about letting anyone in."

I couldn't determine whether we were having a small conversation about coffee and showers or a big conversation about the relationship that had sprouted in the space between my personal disasters and his preference for all things casual and detached. I didn't know what this was so I nodded like I understood and hoped that was the right answer.

"I don't hate you, you know," he continued. "I don't hate you one bit and I don't want you limiting your marmalade intake because of me. You're going to eat all the marmalade you want and you're not going to apologize for it, you hear me?"

"But it's the last jar of the clementine! And you like the clementine more than any of the others!"

"The only time I want you saving marmalade for me is when you want me licking it off your tits. Got it?" he asked, his voice raised.

"I will never ask you to do that because I hate my skin feeling sticky," I shouted back.

"That's good to know because I don't like mixing food

and sex, and your tits don't need anything to make them more appealing to me."

"Okay, then why are we yelling?"

Linden rolled his eyes. "Because you think it's a crime to take up space even though I want you to take it. I want you to take as much of me as you want."

There were so many layers of discomfort for me in this conversation. I never wanted to admit to keeping myself small or tiptoeing around people. I never wanted to acknowledge that the confidence that entered a room ahead of me was paper thin and dependent upon situations where my role and power were clear. I never wanted to be weak, helpless, voiceless.

I took a sip of the coffee at the center of this debate. "Can we discuss my apple problems now?"

Linden stared at me with a broad grin that seemed slightly manic. "You're impossible."

"I've heard that a few times."

"Yeah? Ever in the context of someone trying to give you everything while you refuse to take hardly anything?"

"Perhaps not," I mused, taking on a lighter, more playful tone than this moment required. When Linden rolled his eyes again, I added, "I heard what you said. I understand. I appreciate it all—"

"Oh, Jesus, Jasper. Don't start appreciating me again. I know what follows your appreciation and it was hard enough the first time. I don't think I can handle another round of your baking."

"I won't bake ever again if we can drop this and talk about my apples."

Linden laced his fingers in mine. "Just as soon as you say you don't hate me."

A heavy moment passed as we stared at each other. Then, when the pressure of keeping those words inside—the ones that weren't the ones but just about close enough for it to matter—was too great to bear, I said, "I don't hate you. Not even a little."

"I know, Peach. I just like hearing you say it." He squeezed my hand, nodded, and continued, "You don't need to worry about the apples. I'll take care of them."

I didn't like the sound of that. "What does that involve? I'm sure I can handle it."

"As with *most* things, I have no doubt you can handle it. I'm saying you don't have to."

He smirked at me over the rim of his mug and I was absolutely certain I did not hate this man. Oh, I really, *really* did not hate him.

"Where do you get this coffee from? I've looked up the shop but every time I try to go there, I can't find it. The place seems to exist in another dimension."

He ran a hand over his beard, saying, "This is why I'm going to pick the last of your apples for you. From the trees you didn't notice until now."

"I can do that."

"It's going to require a ladder so no, babe, you're not."

Regardless of how much I enjoyed the tension that grew inside me when Linden insisted, I glared at him. "What about the apples that have already fallen? What should I do about those?"

"Either leave them where they are and let the deer munch on them or clear them out. Another option is we dig a compost heap and let them decompose on the edge of the woods. The woodchucks will burrow into it but they're harmless."

"There are woodchucks out there?"

Linden stood, rounded the table, and jerked my chair back. He bent, wrapping his arms around me and pressing his face to my neck. "Just so you know, I love it when you're impossible."

TWENTY-TWO
LINDEN

"WHAT ARE YOU SUPPOSED TO BE?"

I turned away from filling the candy bowl and found Jasper crossing between our yards. I gestured to my black and red flannel shirt and red suspenders. "Isn't it obvious? I'm a lumberjack."

Her shoulders slumped as she sighed. "How is that a costume? You wore that shirt last week."

"I just said you needed a costume. I never said it had to be a complicated one." I eyed her black and white dress and cherry red heels. "Tell me about this."

"Since I thought I had to really dive in, as you'd suggested on several occasions, I went for the Cruella de Vil vibe." She ran a hand over the spiked red headband. "People always ask me if I'm trying to look like Cruella or Moira Rose when I wear this dress. That's why I hardly ever wear it. It's not like I need any reminders, you know, but I thought it would work. If I'd known I could've gotten away with something else—"

"Nope, nope. You're fine. Don't question it."

I turned back to the candy bowl because two things were happening to me right now. One, Jasper looked hot as hell. She was winning the shit out of the sexy Halloween costume thing and she wasn't even trying. I wanted to drag her inside and do terrible things to her while she wore nothing but those heels.

And two, I hated the self-deprecating comments she made. *Hated them.* I didn't know how this woman could be both a bone-crushing kraken queen who had more power in her little finger than most people could conjure in a lifetime, and the source of her own poison. It didn't make any sense to me though it did make me irrationally furious. I wanted to slap the shit out of the people who put that garbage in her head.

"You're going to need a coat," I said over my shoulder. "It's getting down into the low forties tonight."

There was a pause that stretched long enough to tell me I should've found a way to say something nice. She was trying and it was Halloween. I didn't have to focus on the negative simply because it knocked me upside the head.

"Yeah. I'll be right back," she said.

I dumped another bag of candy into the bowl. "For fuck's sake," I muttered to myself.

Abandoning the candy, I headed inside to grab the items I'd prepared for tonight. Trick-or-treating ran two hours past sunset, and while we didn't get too many kids coming this far down the street, I liked to have all my bases covered.

When I returned to the driveway, Jasper was there in a long, creamy white coat and black gloves trimmed with faux fur. If it didn't feel so wrong and harmful to me, I would've told her she made one fine Cruella.

Instead, I said, "Those shoes, Peach."

She popped one leg. "What about them?"

I glanced at the street, checking for early trick-or-treaters. Empty. "Can I get them over my shoulders? Or digging into my ass? Because...damn, babe, you make them look good."

"Why, thank you." She glanced at the bowl. "How does this work? What do we do?"

"We hand out candy, Jasper. It's Halloween."

"Oh, I know that," she replied. "But it's clear you have a strategy in place. You have a system. You might even have trade secrets. I don't know. I'm new to all this."

I handed her the box I'd brought out from the kitchen. "Stay right here." I headed into the garage, grabbed the beach chairs stored there, and returned to the driveway. "Here's the trade secret. We fill the bowl, set up the chairs, and kick back with a cocktail." I pulled the insulated drink bottles from the box. "My first Halloween in this house, I'd forgotten all about trick-or-treaters but Midge covered for me. She also had the beverages covered. White Russians."

"Somehow that doesn't surprise me."

I laughed. "She didn't let me forget about the candy after that."

"Why do I suspect she didn't let you forget the drinks either?"

"That lady kept a strict cocktail schedule. Nothing got in the way." I held out my hands. "That's the system. That's the strategy."

"And the secrets." She clutched the insulated bottle to her chest. "Let's do it."

We stationed ourselves at the end of the drive, candy propped on the overturned box and blankets draped over our laps because it was fucking freezing now that the sun was past the horizon.

"I got an email from Preston this morning," she said, her gaze fixed on her blanket.

Since I had no patience for the ex-husband, no patience whatsoever, I heaved out an irritated breath. "What does that fucking guy need now?"

Still occupied with straightening the blanket, she replied, "That fucking guy used to be my best friend in D.C."

"Best friends treat each other better than he treated you. So do husbands. It's a damn good thing he's on the other side of the ocean." When she shrugged like that wasn't the cold, hard truth, I asked, "What did he have to say for himself?"

"He forwarded a job he thought I might want to explore."

I waited for her to elaborate but she didn't. "Do you?"

"I'm not sure. It's interesting but it's different." I motioned for her to continue. "He knows some people who put together an organization that identifies regions with the highest levels of voter suppression and engages in extensive community activism to move the needle. What's fascinating to me is they've taken a fully non-partisan approach—or, as nonpartisan as possible, considering the intentions behind suppression efforts—and they've found some positive results." She lifted a shoulder. "Preston said they want to double the number of regions in which they work this year and he thought it might be a good fit for me."

"Am I right to think this sounds very different from your last gig?"

"Yeah, for sure. Completely different. The goal of this organization is increasing access for all voters. They don't take a stand on candidates or issues aside from those specifi- cally tied to voter suppression." She tucked a wisp of hair over her ear. "I mean, it sounds great but, if I went that direction, it would be an enormous change."

"Would that be so bad?"

"I don't know what it would be other than a massive shift from working on a senator's Capitol staff to being fully removed from the Beltway. That could be nice, considering D.C. is not real life and has no connection to the needs and priorities of real people."

She was a bit breathless as she spoke, as if she couldn't get the words out quickly enough. There was a lilt to her voice, the same one I'd heard when she talked about toast and her problems with the local highway system. "You sound excited."

"I might be? Maybe? I'm not sure."

"You're allowed to be excited," I said.

"I'm aware of that, Linden."

I had to smile at the snap in her tone. God, I loved it when she was brutal. "You can see yourself doing this."

"Again, maybe. It could be good or it could be the most boring, dead-end thing in the world. All I know for sure is it won't lead to me being anyone's chief of staff and I probably won't work on another major campaign if I wander down the nonpartisan rabbit hole but—" she held up her hands —"I'm not headed in that direction anymore, am I? It's been two months. There have been other scandals. My hot-mic moment isn't a relevant news story anymore. I'm not getting any calls because no one wants to call me."

"You've gotten plenty of calls. You've rejected them all."

"Yeah but that was different," she replied. "It was media and political privateering."

"You're allowed to be excited," I repeated. "And you don't have to view this as a last resort."

"That remains to be seen." She glanced up the street. "What's the deal with this town and Halloween? There was the Spooky Stroll at the elementary school last weekend and the jack-o'-lantern gallery in the town center, plus the two thousand pumpkins or so on the lawn outside the town hall. And all of that is on top of the actual event. That's a lot, right?"

Okay. Moving right along and away from Jasper and her next steps.

"Even though Salem gets all the attention, this whole region is witchy and haunted as hell. Gotta lean into it."

"Fair enough."

After a family dressed as the feelings from *Inside Out* headed back up the street, Jasper turned to me with a strange smile. "I bet you and your siblings had some precious group costumes when you were kids."

"My mother always tried to make that happen but there was only one time when we were old enough to know what was going on and still allowed it." I took a sip from my bottle. I didn't care much for Kahlua or vodka but tradition was tradition, and I honored that shit. "For reasons I still don't understand, she made vegetable costumes for us. Magnolia was a green cabbage, Ash was a beet, and I was a purple onion."

"Bless her earthy-crunchy heart," Jasper said, laughing. "That is just preciously bizarre."

"What about you? Any wild costumes?"

The brightness in her smile dimmed by a million watts and she turned her gaze to the street. "There's only one Halloween I remember as a kid. It was when we were living in Japan."

"You…lived in Japan."

"I was born there." She didn't look at me as she said this. "My father was stationed at Misawa and we lived there, on Honshu, until I was five. He was in the Air Force." She twisted the cap on her bottle—open, closed, open, closed. "Halloween in Japan isn't anything like it is here. Or it wasn't when I was there thirty years ago. The base still had some fun with it though and we did a family costume that everyone loved. I've tried to remember what it was but I keep coming up empty. I just know it was great and that was a good year for us."

Several things were true at once. Jasper had never spoken at any length about her family before. She sounded deeply sad, almost mournful. And the finality in her voice made it clear that this one happy Halloween was an endpoint of sorts.

I didn't know what to say. Part of me wished a horde of kids would come bombing down the street and break this melancholy with their shrieks and excitement. The other part of me knew Jasper had shared a lot of personal things with me over the last two months but not a word on her family which meant this was a fine opportunity for me to listen if she wanted to share.

"That's one of the only times I remember being with him," she continued. "That Halloween on base."

I reached over, took her gloved hand in mine.

"We moved to Louisiana after he was discharged, and then to his family's land in Georgia. They'd been selling off pieces of the old plantation for decades but there was still enough for us to live on one side and never see the relatives living on the other. It was good for a little while. Until it wasn't."

I gave her hand a squeeze but I wanted to scoop her out

of that chair and gather her up in my arms because the next portion of this story was going to be rough. Whatever it was, was going to hurt and I couldn't just *sit here* while she shared that hurt. I could have her wrapped up like a burrito and perched on my lap in one minute. I'd do it too—the second she gave me the signal.

Not that Jasper was one for broadcasting all her signals but I had a good idea after two months of close study. Enough to know she didn't want me swooping in just yet.

"He ended his life that summer. I didn't understand but there was no time to deal with it because my father's family blamed my mom for his death and said all kinds of horrendous things about suicide. They made her pay them the full amount of his pension for us to continue living in the little one-room cabin that had neither kitchen nor heating. Of course, that request was bananas and she shouldn't have agreed to it but no one makes good choices when their world has fallen apart. They just don't. That's how we ended up living in that cabin with no money and nowhere to go, and I don't remember celebrating Halloween again after that."

Okay, I didn't care if she gave me the signal or not, I needed to hug this girl until the broken pieces fit back together again. I threw off my blanket and shifted toward her but Jasper held up a hand.

"No. Please, don't. Thank you. I'm fine right here. By myself."

It was almost the same thing she'd said to me when I told her she couldn't stay in Midge's cottage. She'd told me she'd seen worse. Fuck, I hadn't believed her. How could anyone believe there was worse than a house previously occupied by bats?

I hated this. All of it.

"Did it get better?" I asked.

She bobbed her head as she resumed opening and closing her bottle. "Yeah. Things always get better if you wait long enough. Eventually, my mom found work with an international airline. She'd learned Japanese while we were overseas and…yeah. That helped. But it meant I had to stay with my father's family—god, I get so angry when I think about them—and they were the worst. Old-fashioned in a horse-and-buggy sort of way but only when it suited them, you know? They loved diesel trucks and big TVs but were conveniently suspicious of pop music and anything with bright colors."

"Bright…colors," I repeated.

"Not really but at the same time, yeah. Totally. Anything neon was out of the question for them. The basic primary colors were the only ones anyone needed. Everything else was some kind of devilry. Obviously, it had nothing to do with actual colors but what color represented. They didn't want to hear about new things or variations. Differences were a waste of their time. Same with mental health. They just didn't buy into it. There was no such thing as depression or PTSD. Those were new inventions and if they were new, that meant they didn't exist before. If they didn't exist before, they couldn't be real, you know?"

"I think I follow you," I said.

"They liked their fire and brimstone, their traditional gender roles. It took me forever to figure it out but eventually I realized they blamed my mom for the suicide because she didn't pledge allegiance to the typical housewife routine. She also owned more than a few hot pink items of clothing and pushed my father to get treatment for his depression, all of which added up to her being the problem, not the disease."

"I am so sorry."

She shook her head in a way that said *it's fucked-up, right?* But then she said, "It's fine." It wasn't fine. "I ended up living with my aunts and uncles, and their kids, in the main house when my mother started regularly flying on international flights. It was a giant old plantation house but it was in the worst shape. Everything was falling apart. It hadn't been maintained or updated but they were fierce about that place. Like their heritage was baked right into the walls and I guess it was, when you really think about it. But it's not Georgia or the South. That sort of thing is baked in everywhere. It's here just as much as it is on the pecan plantation where I grew up."

I didn't know what to say to that. I didn't know what to say about any of this but I definitely wanted to break something. At the minimum, chop the shit out of some wood. And I wanted my mother to fawn over Jasper some more. I wanted her to have the oppressively loving family experience she'd lost as a kid.

"My mom was gone four nights out of the week, and staying alone in the cabin was only a slight improvement over staying with people who wanted to groom me to serve the needs of men."

"Jasper—" I didn't know what I was going to say next but I couldn't say nothing. I wanted to haul off and find the people who put her through that—while she was grieving the loss of her father—and teach them a lesson or two. What the actual fuck was wrong with people? What the actual fuck.

"It's fine. It is." She patted my hand like I was the one in need of comfort. "They were terrible people but they never hurt me. Not in any way that left marks." She shot a rueful grin at her bottle. "They were never more than an errant thought or one too many belts of moonshine away from it but I learned quick enough to stay quiet and stay out of the way. They didn't like listening to me anyway. My uncles did this thing where they ignored everything I said. Every single word. It made me so mad but there was nothing I could do. After high school, I left."

That was why she'd come here instead of going home to Georgia. Why she was alone. Why she had no one to lean on during this time. Why she didn't need anyone's help, ever, thank you kindly.

But— "How were you related to Midge?"

Jasper opened her bottle and took a deep drink. With a laugh, she said, "I'm not, not in any blood-relation sense, but she was still my aunt. My mom's family moved around a lot when she was a kid—it was the army for her—and she had Midge for a teacher the one year she lived in this area."

"Your mother was one of Midge's high school students," I said slowly. "Wow. I can't believe that."

"Mmhmm. Eleventh grade United States history. They stayed in touch when my mother's family moved. Midge told my mom she liked getting letters from all over the world."

"She really loved her mail," I murmured.

"Oh, I know. I remember." Jasper giggled. "When we lived in Japan, we'd send her letters and packages with all kinds of local stuff. My mother would write little notes translating everything and explaining it. Midge would send us packages from the States. It was always such a special day when a box from Aunt Midge arrived."

"And you visited her in the summers?"

"Mmhmm." She busied herself settling the blanket around her legs again. "My mother knew the Cleary house was the least healthy place on the planet, especially when I wasn't in school all day, so she started flying me up here as soon as school let out." She glanced at the street, forced one of those fake smiles into place. "Where are all the kiddos? I thought you said we'd be mobbed."

I lifted a shoulder. "It's different every year."

"We are going to have a ton of leftover candy at this rate."

She pawed at the contents of the bowl like she didn't just crack open a case of major childhood traumas and pour them out into the street. Again, I didn't know what to say but silence wasn't an option, any more than staying in this chair while she mused about candy surpluses was an option.

"All right." I stood and edged the bowl away with the side of my boot. "That's enough. Come here."

I held my hands out to Jasper but she only blinked at me. "Where is it I'm going?"

I gestured to my chest. "Right here."

She gave me a cool up-and-down study. "And why am I doing that?"

"Because I want to hold you, and if you'd stop acting like you don't need anyone for just a minute, you might decide you want to be held."

She folded the blanket and fiddled with her drink. "I don't *want* to need anyone or anything. That isn't a place I like being."

"I know." I took the bottle from her hands, set it down. "But I'm standing here, needing you. Do you really want to say no?" I snapped my suspenders. "To a lumberjack?"

"Are you trying to seduce me into thinking I should need you? Or anyone else?"

I hooked my thumbs under the suspenders again. "Is it working?"

With a husky laugh, Jasper pushed to her feet and stepped into my arms. "Okay. Fine. You got me. *For now*."

Wasn't that the truth.

TWENTY-THREE
JASPER

I PACED FROM THE END OF LINDEN'S LIVING AREA TO THE FRONT door and back again because I had to *do* something, I had to move. The last time I tried to stop for a minute, I charred a very nice piece of bread and had to mourn that waste as I tossed it in the trash.

Lunch was unnecessary. It was too late now anyway. There was no sense in eating at four in the afternoon, not unless I wanted to be off-kilter the rest of the day.

I laughed out loud at that idea. It was not possible to feel more off-kilter than I did now. Not humanly possible.

I knew I was overreacting. I was sure of it. But I just couldn't stop. I'd tried distracting myself *several* times. I tried steaming the dress I planned on wearing to Linden's parents' anniversary party next weekend but ended up spilling water all over myself. I tried making a salad to go with dinner but destroyed a tomato in the process. The distractions weren't working.

As I reached the wall of windows at the back of the house, I heard Linden's truck pull into the driveway. A moment later, there was a metallic slam and a moment after that, the front door swung open.

I was still pacing—I really could not stop—when Linden spotted me. His expression shifted from pleasure to curiosity to concern inside a matter of seconds.

"Where's the fire?" he asked, a small box tucked under his arm and a ball cap on his head.

"No fire. I just left the toast in too long."

"Okay." He nodded but gave the kitchen a careful study before glancing back to me. "What's wrong?"

"Nothing's wrong," I said automatically.

"Then why are you wearing a hole through my floors?"

I dragged my fingers under the crewneck of my sweater. "It's nothing, really."

"Stand still and say that to me."

I shot him an amused glance before shoving my hands in my pockets. Thank god for skirts with real pockets. "I decided to start on Midge's room today. It seemed like it was time."

He set the box on the countertop, dropped his hat beside it. "Don't tell me you burned that down."

"There was no fire, okay?"

"It smells like there was a fire."

"I burned the toast. A lot," I added. "But no flaming fires."

He shrugged out of his coat and dropped into a chair at the kitchen table. "All right. No fires. What happened in Midge's room?"

I started pacing again. "I figured I'd begin with something small, you know? It's really emotional for me and I don't feel like I can part with any of her things yet but I figured I could make a small dent in her closet since I noticed she had a bunch of old shoeboxes in there. I don't know why she kept them but I decided to open them because I figured she might've stored old bank statements in there or, I don't know, more coupons for stores that don't exist anymore."

He nodded as he flipped open the buttons at his cuffs and it was inconsiderate of him to roll up his sleeves while I recounted today's trauma. Seriously inconsiderate. I loved those forearms. The muscles, the hair, the veins. It was so strange to love veins but I *loved* his veins. And when he crossed his arms over his chest with his sleeves rolled up? My god. There was no saving my panties from that.

"And…what did you find in those boxes?"

I pressed my hands to my eyes and turned to face the windows because Linden's forearms could not exist in the same world as today's discovery. "Adult products."

"What? I didn't catch that, babe."

"Adult products," I yelled, my back still turned to him.

"What does that mean?"

Since he wasn't making this inference on his own, I said, "I thought it was a box of old broken chains. Like, bracelets or necklaces or something. I dumped it out because it seemed like that would be important. Come to find out, it was a comprehensive and varied collection of nipple clamps."

In the window's reflection, I saw him push to his feet. "What the fuck did you just say?"

A slightly manic laugh stuttered out of me. "You heard right. A whole box of nipple clamps."

Linden laced his fingers around the back of his neck. "Oh my fucking god."

Nodding, I banded my arms around my torso. "And I figured it was okay, you know, she was a vibrant woman.

She was allowed to have an equally vibrant sex life. Who am I to judge any of that? Not my place. Not my business."

"Good for you," he murmured.

"But then I opened the box with the double-ended dildo which didn't take me nearly as long to identify because *I have the same one*."

"Holy fuck." He rubbed his eyes, asking, "So, what did you do with all that?"

"I shut the closet door, shut the bedroom door, and walked my ass out of there. I have to throw them away, right? What else can I do? They're not recyclable. It's not like I can donate them to needy kinky people."

"Holy fuck," he muttered.

I turned, saying, "Yeah, I know."

"Hey, Peach?" He gestured toward me, an odd frown on his lips. "Some other time, we'll talk more about that dildo, right? The one *you* have, that is."

"Sorry but I'm not sure I can ever look at it again without thinking about finding one in an old shoebox." I shook that memory out of my head. "And just so you know, they can be very tricky to use well. It's a lot of coordination. You'll feel it in your abs for a week."

"Looking forward to it." With a nod, he walked over to the refrigerator, saying, "Get your coat."

I glanced out the windows. "Isn't it a little late for a walk in the woods? The sun's almost set."

"We're not walking." He held up a bottle of wine—*my bottle*—and plucked a glass from the cabinet. "We're going out back. We'll start a little bonfire and then I'm going to do my best to get you drunk. You deserve it, babe. After this conversation, I do too."

"Seems like a reasonable solution."

He knocked his knuckles against the box he'd brought in. "One of my stops today was at a dairy farm. They sent me off with a cheese plate."

I reached for my coat, held it to my chest as I studied him. "Do you usually get paid in cheese?"

He popped the cork on the wine. "When I ask if they'd put together something for me, yeah, I do."

"And how often is that?" I didn't know why I was pushing on this. I didn't know what it was I hoped he'd say.

He set the open wine bottle beside the cheese and grabbed a beer from the fridge before putting his coat back on. "Only when I have someone at home who lives for toast, wine, and cheese."

"The Old World Parisian way of life has always appealed to me," I joked as I shoved my arms into my coat.

I followed him outside to where the sun was low in the sky and the November air was cold enough for me to see my breath. Linden led the way off the deck and toward a small stone fire circle in the center of the yard, a pair of white Adirondack chairs stationed on either side.

"Sit down," he ordered as he dragged the other chair closer.

"You know, I would've done that without your instructions."

"Maybe." He set the beverages and cheese plate on a narrow table and stalked off toward the side yard. A moment later, he returned with a bundle of wood tucked under his arm. He pointed at me, saying, "Drink that wine."

"Didn't need that order either," I replied.

Linden only shook his head as he arranged the wood in the stone circle. It didn't take him long to get the fire going and then he settled into the seat beside me. He busied himself with removing the plastic wrap from the cheese plate and popping open his beer while I obediently sipped the wine.

Since I couldn't keep it in any longer, I asked, "You just keep sauvignon blanc on hand?"

He returned the plate to the table between us. "Why is it so difficult for you to accept that I have it for you?"

I stared at the fire, watching it crackle and climb. "It's not."

"Clearly, it is."

"You really don't have to do that, you know." I sighed. "You don't need to—"

"Has it occurred to you that I want to keep your fruity wine in my house? That I have a case of it in the basement because I want to have your favorite things here? Or that I want to ask dairy farmers if they'll take out their tree work in trade because you're mad for cheese? Has it occurred to you even once that I do these things *for* you? And that I like doing these things for you?"

I went on staring at the fire while Linden stared at me. On the other side of the yard, I saw the black cat blink at us a few times before darting into the woods. Such a funny guy, always popping up at the most random moments.

Eventually, I said, "I don't know how to trust that sort of gesture."

"This is how." He held out the plate to me. "Eat something. You'll feel better."

I picked up a wedge of creamy white cheese with a black-speckled rind and a cracker studded with rosemary and raisins. "Thank you."

He nodded, taking a pull of his beer. Then, he held up the

bottle, saying, "To Midge. A woman loved by many and freakier than anyone would've guessed."

"Bless her," I said, tapping my glass to his bottle. "Even if I'd rather pretend I knew none of it."

"At least you've solved the mystery of the closet shoeboxes."

"Lin, I opened *two*. There are at least twenty."

He grabbed a piece of cheddar and a grape from the plate, saying, "Yeah, maybe don't look in the rest of them."

"Maybe I'll just put off going into her room a bit longer. It was hard before the dildos entered the picture."

"If I've said that once, I've said it a hundred times," he muttered.

I laughed then, loud and bawdy and deep enough for it to rattle my bones a bit. It was good to laugh, to soften into the heat of the fire and the warmth of the wine. It was good to be here and it was good to be with Linden. I didn't want anything to change. Not yet.

––––––

THERE WAS A TIME WHEN I'D SERIOUSLY CONSIDERED ATTENDING law school. Everyone in D.C. was a lawyer so why shouldn't I add some letters to the back end of my name too?

I'd decided against it because law school was really damn expensive and the notion of leaving my job and dropping out of the day-to-day work of politics seemed impossible to me, even if I would come out of it with the right to throw around expressions like "As an attorney, I can tell you…" and "I can only give you my opinion, not legal advice."

If I'd only known leaving the job and day-to-day politics

for law school would be less complicated than termination via tweet. If only.

Now, as I wandered a circuit around the house while Midge's attorney droned on in my earbuds about filing tax returns and signing off on another set of documents, I thought about law school again.

Was it too late for me? Did it make sense to adopt a three-year-long project just because I didn't want to rely on this guy to explain things to me? Was that a valid reason to spend upwards of two hundred thousand dollars on an education? Would that give me the time I needed to sort out my life? Probably not but was there really a price I could put on not needing anyone for anything?

Then again, it would be much less expensive to learn the right way to fix up this house. Fewer exams too.

As I looped through the kitchen, I heard a great *thwack*. I glanced around for the source of the sound, peered at my phone to see if there was a wacky new notification there, darted halfway down the basement stairs and then back up when I found things mostly in order.

Then I heard it again.

It was outside. Definitely outside.

I murmured in agreement as the attorney said something about property taxes and escrow accounts and I hurried out the side door, down the steps I'd rebuilt. I was still proud of them, even if one did have a troubling wobble.

Walking along the side of the house, I headed toward the street until I realized the noise wasn't out there. I doubled back toward the very much in-progress porch and held a hand over my brows to block out some of the afternoon sun. It was hot today, unseasonably hot for November. This sweater was an enormous mistake.

As I heard that *thwack* again, I made my way along the remaining perimeter of the porch, my eyes narrowed while the attorney said something about title insurance. I didn't need to pay attention to that. It was fine.

Then I spotted Linden.

More specifically, I spotted the axe as it slashed through the air and *then* I spotted the man holding it. Another *thwack* went up and I watched two wedges of wood tumble off the stump in front of him and drop to the ground.

He stood with his back toward me and his feet planted a shoulder's-width apart as he lifted the axe again. A line of sweat dampened the back of his t-shirt. The tattoos on his biceps peeked out from under his sleeves and gleamed in the bright autumn light.

Then he swung and I felt that *thwack* inside me. I didn't know whether it was the thrill of covertly watching him or witnessing the insane ripple of muscle as he struck the wood but I didn't care because it was the sexiest thing I'd ever seen.

He tossed the split wood onto the neat stack he'd constructed near the edge of his deck. It was handy, I realized, to have all that firewood lined up for the winter. He planned it this way, of course. That was how Linden operated. Careful and precise and…fuck me, those shoulders were glorious. It was no surprise to me that my guy was next-level hot but this—*this*—was a lesson in lumberbears.

He bent down to heave an absurdly large slab of tree onto the stump. It was *absurdly* large, at least three feet tall and four or five wide. There was no way in hell he'd be able to cut that with an axe.

That was exactly what he did.

I stayed here, leaning against the porch with one hand

shielding my eyes from the sun, the other flat on my chest, a lawyer yammering in my ear about state pension accounts and accrued benefits, and I watched Linden smash that round of wood. It took several swings of his axe but it wasn't long before that absurdly large slab was divided into a dozen wedges and added to the pile.

And I'd never been more aroused in my entire life. I was panting a bit, though I blamed it on the weather. *That* was the source of my heaving bosom. I had my legs crossed at the ankle, my thighs tight together. My skin was outrageously sensitive. I found myself tipping my head to the side and exposing my neck without thinking about it. A million filthy fantasies flashed through my mind. My pussy had a pulse.

"Okay, sir, yes, that's very good. Very good information. I'm going to have to call you back about all this. Good day and goodbye." I was halfway across the yard when I called out, "Hey."

He turned, ran his wrist across his forehead. With a grin, he asked, "All finished?"

"Yeah," I said, plucking the earbuds out and shoving them in my pocket along with the phone. I reached out, grabbed him by the front of his shirt. "I hope you don't mind but I need to drag you inside and take your clothes off you right now."

He smirked. "Is that so?"

I drew in closer. "You have no idea how much I want you."

His gaze dropped to my chest and I could *feel* him staring at my nipples. They were shamelessly pebbled against the wool of my sweater and begging for attention. "I think I know." He glanced up, still smirking. "Is that how it is, Peach? Chopping wood works for you?"

"We can analyze it later," I said. "After you've"—I motioned to the stump, even though it made no sense —"*after*."

Linden stepped back and I had to release my hold on his shirt but that wasn't a problem because he peeled it off his skin and over his head, and used it to mop the sweat from his chest.

I was *this* close to coming. *This close.*

"Get in there," he said with a flick of his wrist toward the house. "If I have to take that skirt off you myself, I'll rip it. You've been warned."

Ohhhhhh. I really did love it when he insisted.

I darted inside, beside myself with want and need. It should've been simple, really, just follow Linden's directions. Get in here and get naked. So simple. But I lost myself when I played back the words I'd spoken. The way I watched him and demanded use of his body. It didn't matter that he was game for it. No, he didn't figure into this shame spiral at all.

Still, I pulled my sweater over my head and straightened my hair once it was free. It was a relief to undress with this heat—and everything I'd stirred up while watching Linden. I slipped off my shoes, a cute pair of mid-heeled oxfords in the cutest shade of cognac, and took my phone and earbuds from my pocket. I had to put them back in their case and that meant *finding* the case. I'd lost one set of earbuds on a flight to Milwaukee and another to the spin cycle once, and I couldn't do that now, could not allow such a silly waste.

Linden found me rooting around in my tote bag, the one I used to ferry clothes back and forth from here to Midge's house. I wasn't prepared to hang my things in his closet or even have the discussion about claiming space in his bedroom. No, it wasn't necessary.

"What the hell are you doing?" he asked, the sun at his back and his chest still damp with sweat.

My breath caught. This man could be so incredibly rude with his arms and his shirtlessness. "Putting away my earbuds."

"Is that what I told you to do?"

"It's not but if I don't put them away immediately after taking them out, I lose them or drown them in the washing machine." I snapped the case shut. "And I needed to, you know, breathe for a second."

His gaze locked on me, he toed off his boots. "You're still dressed."

I glanced down at my skirt. The pinstriped wool brushed the bottoms of my knees and suddenly felt like a stifling blanket. "As I told you, I needed a second to breathe."

He unlatched his belt, drew down his fly. Left his jeans hanging open. My nipples ached behind the lace of my bra. "You've had a second, Peach."

Linden strolled past me into the bathroom as I struggled against the outrageous mix of desire and insecurity. I felt so much of both, and that conflict kept me stuck there, my fingers still closed around the earbud case.

He was quick to return and settled himself on the sofa, right in the middle with his legs spread wide. He beckoned to me, saying, "I want you over here."

Enough of my brain fell in line at his rough command to allow me to walk over there but my cheeks were hot. My chest too. I went to him, climbed into his lap, brought my hands to his shoulders. "I want to rip your clothes off," I said softly. "But I also feel strange about that. Like I shouldn't say it. Shouldn't want it."

"Why shouldn't you?"

"I don't really know," I admitted. I'd never spoken words like these before. "But sometimes I feel that way and it's overwhelming."

He reached under my skirt, both hands on my ass cheeks, and tore my panties in half. I gasped at the burn and pull of the fabric and the depravity of that move. "Tell me when it's overwhelming, okay? Tell me. I'll get you out of your head until it goes away."

With both hands, Linden gathered my skirt, twisting it until it was tight and rucked up around my waist. He dropped his gaze between my legs, staring at me with the kind of cool, unaffected focus that should *not* have turned me on. I didn't know why it did, why this inspection left my skin feeling too hot, too tight, but I couldn't escape it.

And I didn't want to.

"There's a condom in my pocket. Handle that," he ordered.

I was shaking now, every part of me flooded with this confluence of right and wrong. But that wasn't the whole of it because this *wasn't* wrong. There was nothing wrong with wanting a strapping lumberbear to fuck me into next Friday and there was nothing wrong with asking for it in rude, lusty terms. The part of my brain that set off these shame spirals, it was lying to me. It was lying about beauty and dignity and the space I was allowed to claim as my own. It was lying about everything—and I didn't know why I'd never noticed that before. I was allowed to have this. *I was allowed*.

His hips bucked when I edged his jeans down to his

knees and rolled the condom over his length. He had the sort of erection that was so hard, his shaft pointed straight at the ceiling. I enjoyed them all but this type was special.

"If you don't sit that cunt down on my cock right now, I'll find that little clit-sucking vibrator of yours and torment you for the next six hours."

I groaned out loud because the one and only time we'd played with my toys, there were catastrophic orgasms for all. Linden slept for eleven hours. I couldn't sit, stand, or walk without feeling it for three days.

"Always so imperious," I murmured.

My knees braced on either side of him and my hand on his shoulder to keep me steady, I guided him into my opening. He ran his knuckles up my back, twisted his hand around the band of my bra, holding me in place and then forcing me down as he surged up. I looked down at my obscenely pebbled nipples, the skirt around my waist, the thick cock pounding up into me. I'd never felt as strong and desirable and *adored* as I did when he was inside me. I'd never felt adored like this before.

Was that the word for this? Adored? Was this it?

Or was this what it meant to feel beautiful?

I didn't know. Beauty was always wrong to me but this was too right. I closed my eyes and allowed myself to disappear into the pleasure of the shaft pounding between my legs and the rasp of his beard on my chest, my neck. I matched his rhythm, rocking my body against his to grab every bit of friction I could, and I stopped thinking. I stopped wondering whether Linden fucked the way he worshipped and if it was possible to be beautiful while also being depraved and if this was what it felt like to fall in love.

TWENTY-FOUR
LINDEN

I FROWNED AT MY REFLECTION IN THE MIRROR, ADJUSTING MY bow tie again. God, I hated these things. Ties in general but the ones that accompanied tuxedoes were such a pain in the ass. My parents just *had* to make this anniversary party black tie. As if the event would somehow increase in value because everyone was straitjacketed in fancy clothes.

I called through the bathroom door to Jasper, "You're sure you don't want to spend the night in Dartmouth? Ash and Zelda got a room and Magnolia and Rob are going back to my parents' house."

"We don't need to do that," came her muffled response.

I wandered through the kitchen to keep myself busy, straightening a few stray pieces of mail, placing a runaway lemon back in the fruit basket, pushing in the chairs. Jasper's notebook sat open on the table, her tidy writing calling to me from the page. On the bottom half, she'd jotted a grocery list of *avocado, bread for toasting, bread for Lin's sandwiches, hand soap, cinnamon.*

I didn't know why that made me smile but it did. A big,

sloppy smile that felt hysterical. It was completely hysterical to read this little list and feel an enormous ball of heat in my chest, like the sun now lived inside me, and it was even more hysterical when I heard myself think, *You love her*.

The bathroom door opened then, while I was fool-grinning at her notebook and burning up from the sun I'd swallowed and thinking outrageous thoughts, and Jasper stepped out looking like that same sun trapped behind my ribs.

"You," she breathed, giving me a thorough once-over. "You clean up quite nicely."

I didn't know when I started moving but I stopped in front of her, still blinded and sloppy and maybe very much in love with her. I trailed my knuckles over the fabric covering her collarbones. "What color is this?"

"It's a very pale yellow," she said as she watched my hand. "In certain lights, it almost looks white. In others, it's buttery yellow. Chiffon is like that, it plays with the light."

"Is that what this is? Chiffon?" It seemed to swirl and billow around her, from her shoulders to her wrists and around her ankles. "It looks good on you."

She made the most adorably indifferent face in the world, saying, "This old thing?"

I traced my knuckles down her arm and back up again. I couldn't stop touching her, though I was also terrified to grab her and hold her the way I wanted because it seemed as though this dress was liable to disintegrate in my hands. There were times for ripping clothes and there were times for waiting until after the big party to do that.

"Did you get this with Magnolia and Zelda? That day when you went shopping?"

She shook her head and the wisps of hair that had

slipped over her ears brushed her cheeks. I tucked them back into place, as careful as I could not to ruin the intricate bun at the back of her neck.

"I've had this," she said. "I actually found it at a second-hand shop in D.C. a couple of years ago. I bought it as wishful thinking that I'd wear it to the next inauguration ball."

"Get real. A fortieth anniversary party at a country club on the South Coast of Massachusetts beats an inauguration ball any day," I teased.

"It might." She ran a finger down the front of my shirt, saying, "I like this look on you. Not more than your everyday look but I like it. Where do you even hide your Swiss Army knife?"

I patted my side pocket. "Right here."

"Ah. Very good. Never know when we'll need the aid of the Swiss Army."

"Isn't that the truth," I murmured. "And you're sure you don't want to spend the night down there?"

A thoughtful wrinkle in her brow, she glanced up at me. "You said it's only an hour from here?"

"Yeah, about that."

"No, I'd rather come home at the end of the night. I like it here. And I have a few calls in the morning, on the early side. Preston has a list of people he wants to put me in contact with but he wants to prime me on all of them first which is great, really, it is, but I'd be fine with just the list."

I stared at Jasper for a moment, waiting for her to realize she'd called this home. I didn't even care about the ex-husband who couldn't decide between hounding and abandonment. I'd care about that later but right now, I needed her to acknowledge she wasn't staying at my place or Midge's place, she was *at home*.

"If that's what you want," I said. "To come back home after the party."

She rubbed her thumb over the shiny buttons running down the front of my shirt. They weren't called buttons but that didn't matter. The sun was inside my chest and my grin was too big, much too big, and it was slightly, potentially, completely possible that I loved her. Nothing else mattered. "Yeah, that sounds good. We don't have time to pack up for the night anyway."

"Peach. How many times have I told you that pajamas are unnecessary?"

"They might not be but I'm not interested in walking out of a hotel in the morning wearing a dress from the night before," she said. "I'm finished with the scandal life, you know."

I nodded because I didn't know what else to do. "Then we'll come home."

———

I SPENT THE NEXT HOUR LISTENING AND MURMURING AT ALL THE right moments while Jasper told a seven-part story about the people she worked with on the senator's first reelection campaign. She'd spoken to one of them recently and caught up on old times.

Contrary to Jasper's belief that all her allies had deleted her number, there were plenty of people who reached out to her with frequency. It wasn't that she was dismissive of those people but it was that she expected people to walk away from her. The ones who didn't were the anomalies, not the rule.

I didn't follow her story, not all the way, but I noticed how Jasper talked about her work with the senator. It wasn't tinged with bitterness or resentment, or even the wistful fondness I'd picked up on certain occasions. It was remarkably past tense, much in the way people talked about the good old days of high school or college. It was over for her.

And that meant she could stay. Not simply because Midge's cottage was uninhabitable and my house was *home* but because she didn't have to return to that world. She didn't have to leave. She could stay here and we could—god, I didn't even know what came after that. Anything could come next, anything.

"It was like a family," she said, her words warm with nostalgia. "Some people have theater production families, some people—like Zelda—have summer camp families. I had campaign families."

Had.

"That's really cool," I said as I turned down the country club's driveway. A tight line of excessively pruned hydrangeas gleamed woody and leafless in the headlights and I was reminded of my sister and the partnership she wanted to form with me. Not tonight though. We'd get to that another time.

"Speaking of which." Jasper flipped down the visor and studied her reflection in the tiny mirror. "What are the chances we'll have a repeat of that awkward moment at your parents' house?"

"Which one?"

"You know what I'm talking about," she chided. "When I was *that woman from the television*."

I swung into a parking spot, saying, "Zero chances. I've handled it."

"What does that mean? You've *handled it*? What did you handle?"

I studied Jasper out of the corner of my eye. She didn't need to know about the phone call my father received from me the morning after that gathering or the extremely clear boundaries I cemented into place. She definitely didn't need to know I railed at him for at least fifteen minutes about calling her *that woman* and how I didn't bring guests to the family table for them to meet a firing squad.

"I asked my father to use some discretion," I said. "And make sure his friends do too."

"You didn't have to do that."

"Maybe not. I did it anyway."

She glanced over at me and it was clear she wanted to push back. But then she said, "Thank you."

"Anytime." I pointed at her door. "Now, listen. You don't wait for me to open your door but you're doing it tonight."

"And why would I entertain such a thing?"

"Because you're all dressed up and I'm not going to let you step in a puddle or catch your skirt on the door. Argue all you want but I'll lock you in here if I have to."

She snapped the visor back into place. After a pause that made me wonder whether she'd fling herself out of the truck right now, just to piss me off, she said, "All right. I'll let you help me. *This* time."

"This time," I echoed.

"Mmhmm."

I climbed out and came around, more than a little surprised to find her in the passenger seat rather than smirking at me from the blacktop. I opened the door and settled one arm around her waist, the other behind her knees, and scooped her out of the truck.

"I will never get used to this," she said, a giggle bursting over her pale pink lips. "I just can't."

"That's okay," I murmured to her neck. "Just get used to it for right now."

I set her down, holding on a moment longer than necessary. She smelled as lovely as always but the familiarity of that scent caught me off guard. How long had it been since that scent was new to me? And how long since it had become an everyday part of my life?

"Oh, it's chilly here," she said, hugging her arms close to her body.

"Yeah, let's get you inside." I grabbed my tuxedo jacket from the truck and steered Jasper toward the main entrance. "If you want to leave early, just give me the signal."

"What's the signal?"

"Trust me. I'll know. Your face reads like a book."

She glanced up at me when I tucked her hand into the crook of my elbow and led her up the steps. "I guess I've lost my poker face. It used to be legendary."

"You still have it. I can just see past it."

She started to respond but we found ourselves sandwiched between Rob and Magnolia and Ash and Zelda.

"Ah, I see we're operating on triplet time tonight," Rob said. "Could the three of you circle up and decide on a departure time? I've been awake for two days."

Magnolia shot him a broad smile, saying, "Play stupid games, win stupid prizes."

Rob said to us, "I had to go to London."

"For a day," Magnolia said with a laugh. "Not even a day. Four hours. A meeting."

He bobbed his head. "Yeah. That's true. But I closed the deal which means I shouldn't have any other deals to worry about this year and the babies can come any time they want."

"Not any time," she replied.

"You know what I mean," he said. "And now that's handled, I'm going to fall asleep on your shoulder during dinner, wife."

"It's a good thing you're pretty, Russo," she said to him.

"Don't we look gorgeous," Zelda sang as she hooked elbows with Magnolia and Jasper. She eyed Jasper's dress with appreciation. "You were right about not needing any of the dresses we made you try on. This is just breathtaking."

"It really is," Magnolia agreed.

"Thank you," Jasper said.

Ash glanced at the great stone hearth complete with a roaring fire and club chairs stationed in front of it. "Do you think we could skip out on the part where we remind all of Mom and Dad's friends where we live, what we do, and whether we've kept in contact with their kids and just hang out here instead? Or—"

"There you are," my mother called, huffing and clucking as she marched over.

"Probably not," Ash muttered.

"Why are you standing around out here like a bunch of loiterers?" She waved us away from the entry and led us down a thickly carpeted hall. "There we go, yes, you too, Robert. Have some tequila, it will wake you up."

"I don't think that's accurate," my sister said.

"It won't hurt to try," Mom replied. "Enough with the scowling, Linden, and Ash, stop making that face. People will think you have an ulcer."

"I might," he murmured.

"You don't," Mom said with a definitive shake of her head. "Zelda, dear, you are just glowing. Is there anything you'd like to tell me? A very special anniversary gift perhaps?"

"*Mom*. What the fuck?" Ash snapped.

Zelda glanced at him as she ran a hand down her belly. "I look pregnant?"

He rubbed his temples. "No, love, you don't."

"I think it's just the new shimmery highlighting stick," Zelda said to Mom, gesturing to her cheekbones. "That's all. I promise."

"Well, I can't have all my dreams come true, can I?" Mom mused. "Oh, and Jasper. Aren't you a treasure tonight. My word." She hit me with an approving grin. "One of the best anniversary gifts of all."

At the reappearance of my mother's terrible Southern accent, I said, "Enough of that."

"All right, all right." She looked us over with a grim smile as if the six of us barely passed muster. She did this when we were small, before sending us off to school in the mornings. "Magnolia, dear, you also look beautiful but you'd look so much better if you smiled. Try that, would you? Just remember, carrying triplets is more difficult than twins." She glanced around our group, saying, "In you go. Mingle. Have fun."

My mother darted inside the ballroom, her sequined dress shining after her.

Magnolia said, "It's so wonderful when she's lost her mind. Like, it's entertaining in a mildly toxic way."

Ash shook his head. "Why is she so chippy?"

"Because throwing big events is so stressful," Jasper said.

"It's so much coordination and there are always last minute problems. Even when we hired event planners, I still ended up managing something and eating nothing. You have to force yourself to stop working and let things happen." She sent a quick glance around the group. "I don't know, I'm just saying it's really difficult. Whenever I was steering the ship, I know I was terrible to the people working with me. Your mom probably expected the country club's event coordinator to handle everything and didn't hire an additional coordinator to make sure it all got done to her liking."

There was a collective moment of sheepishness before Magnolia said, "I'll stop grousing about being ninety-four months pregnant with these precious little mountain trolls and schmooze with the grown-ups if someone keeps my husband awake and away from the tequila."

"But that sounded like such a winning idea," Rob said.

"Never a good idea," Zelda said as she steered Magnolia and Jasper into the ballroom. "Never ever."

"No tequila, no complaining," Ash murmured. "Got it."

"Nothing we can't handle." I clapped Ash and Rob on the backs. "Isn't that right, children?"

———

I HATED SMALL TALK—*OBVIOUSLY*—THOUGH I USUALLY muddled through these types of parties by letting my sister do all the talking or pretending to be extremely interested in the random things other people had to say.

That was before Jasper.

I still hated small talk but now I had the kraken queen of bullshitting with the best of them on my arm and there was no overstating how much I loved watching Jasper work a crowd. And the girl did not stop. She plowed right through the cocktail hour, kept my siblings laughing their asses off through dinner, and now she was charming the hell out of everyone we encountered during the dessert and dancing portion of this evening.

Where I would've grunted my way through a painful conversation with our childhood neighbors and then escorted myself to the bar for a long talk with Johnnie Walker Blue, Jasper had these people telling a hilarious story about getting lost and running out of gas on their way to Canada during the oil crisis in the 1970s. There was a bit about wandering onto private property and getting picked up by the Royal Canadian Mounted Police somewhere past the Vermont border.

"And then they took the men into a separate room," Mrs. Freitas said, her gaze bewildered.

"What happened then?" Jasper asked Mr. Freitas, a shorter man with a shiny bald head.

"I won't say," he replied with a deep chuckle. "I've never talked about it and I won't start now."

"Secrets taken to the grave," Jasper said with a grin that was nothing short of contagious.

"I did not know what was going to happen," Mrs. Freitas continued. "I had no clue. I just kept asking to call my embargo—which is the wrong word, I know that now but I was nineteen and not smart and thought I was saying *embassy*—and they kept telling me I couldn't do anything about the oil embargo."

"I've never driven through Vermont with anything less than a half tank since," Mr. Freitas added.

"I bet you don't," Jasper drawled.

She patted his forearm and he knew the same thing I did —this woman was *the best*. The very best.

"That was a night to remember, believe me." With a pointed nod toward Jasper, Mr. Freitas said, "That's a spitfire you've got there."

I laughed because it was the damn truth. "I'd have to say you're right about that."

"I love seeing all you young kids paired off," he continued. "Makes me happy, you see?"

I nodded. I had no idea where this was going but I nodded. "Sure."

"We heard the good news," Mrs. Freitas jumped in. "We just wanted to give you both our best."

"The good news," Jasper repeated.

Mrs. Freitas leaned in, dropped her voice to a stage whisper. "It's so sweet of you to announce your engagement after the party. You know, to give your parents a night all to themselves. This is so special for them."

"Our engagement," Jasper said.

I blinked. Glanced at Jasper. Blinked some more. They had to be thinking of Ash and Zelda. Had to be. Because… no. That had to be it.

Mr. Freitas reached into the breast pocket of his tuxedo jacket. "We have a little something for you. Just a date night on us. Vincenzo's. It's our favorite spot. Their tiramisu is enough reason to drive to the city."

He handed me an envelope as Mrs. Freitas said, "It's so important to continue dating each other. You have to keep the romance alive and you can't do that eating pot roast off your everyday-ware plates."

"Mmhmm. You're right about that," Jasper said. "Thank you so much for thinking of us. You're too kind."

"We're just so happy for you." To Jasper, Mrs. Freitas said, "It's like I always say. Even if a man doesn't think he's ready, he gets ready when he meets *the one*. When he knows, he doesn't play around."

Get out of my head, lady.

"Mmhmm. That's such a generous sentiment," Jasper said.

"If only our Janelle would find a nice boy, we'd have a wedding to throw," Mrs. Freitas added.

"Give her time and you will," Jasper said with a wink. "Soon enough!"

"Oh, are the Barkwoods over there? Near the bar? We should say hello to them before they leave," Mr. Freitas said, tipping his chin in that direction. "They always leave early."

"Congratulations again," Mrs. Freitas said, giving Jasper a quick squeeze.

We watched as they walked away, neither of us speaking for a moment. Then, Jasper said, "I hear we're engaged. Well, that's just so nice."

I was waiting for her to freak out. When it didn't hit, I said, "I don't know where that came from but I'm impressed with the way you rolled with it."

"If you think that's impressive, you should give me harder challenges. That was as simple as getting your aunt to stop complaining about how much this shindig must have cost your parents and start complaining about her congressman."

"She's going to take all of your advice," I said. "I'll bet you anything she shows up at his local office first thing Monday and doesn't leave until she airs all her grievances."

"Good. That's the point of electing officials. They're duty

bound to listen to concerns from constituents and then do their best to remedy or at least advocate for those situations. They have state-based and D.C. staff for precisely those purposes. If you're not hollering at your reps every now and then, you're letting them earn a paycheck without sweating for it."

I glanced inside the envelope. "We got a hundred dollar gift card out of it."

"And here I was, thinking I'd be the source of awkward conversations tonight. I should've known it would be safer to create a diversion." She leaned into me, her arm snaking under my jacket and around my waist. "I probably should've mentioned this sooner but I need my next marriage proposal to be excessive. Over the top. So big I can't blink, miss it, and hear about it from the people who used to live next door to you."

"Yeah, me too," I murmured.

We stared at each other for a heavy minute. This was a mistake. A moment of playing pretend. It wasn't real. We weren't engaged, we weren't getting married. We didn't even know what next month would bring. But—but it wasn't wrong. Fuck, it wasn't wrong in the slightest and Jasper knew it. She knew it as well as I did.

"Do you think they confused us with Ash and Zelda?" she asked.

"I don't usually get confused for Ash."

"They only got engaged a few months ago, right?"

"Yeah, end of the summer." I tucked the envelope in my pocket. "We're keeping the gift card."

"We're totally keeping the gift card," she said.

"That's my girl," I said, leading her across the room. "Come on. We've done enough chatting. I want you all to myself and it seems like the only way I'm getting that is on the dance floor."

"I wouldn't have pegged you for a dancer."

"Babe, you haven't pegged me at all."

"Not yet," she said with a wicked laugh. "Forget the dance floor. I'm sure there's a locker room or two around here. A lady golfer lounge or something like that. Maybe an extra cloak room or a deserted office."

I loved this girl. I did, I *loved* her. "Now you're talking."

We slipped out the side door and down the hallway past the entry and the huge stone fireplace there. It was quiet out here, the party barely a murmur in the distance, and it seemed certain we'd find a place to be alone.

Until we ran into Ash and Zelda.

"What are you doing down here?" I asked.

"What are *we* doing here?" he asked, his arm tight around Zelda's waist. "I could ask you the same question."

"But I asked you first."

"Boys," Zelda said firmly.

With an exaggerated sigh and an equally unnecessary eyeroll, Ash leaned toward me, angling himself away from Zelda. "There's a room back there."

"I figured as much," I said, my voice low.

"Make sure you lock the door," he murmured. "Uncle Bart got lost on his way to the bathroom and…well, thankfully he has no idea what's going on at any moment ever but make sure you lock it."

"What are you, seventeen? Of course I'll lock the fucking door." Matching his eyeroll, I said, "You better get back out there. People are starting to think I'm you and congratulating us on the engagement."

"So? Only a matter of time, isn't it?"

"Get your girl a scarf or something. You left beard rash all over her neck." He glanced back at Zelda as I muttered, "Amateur."

He patted my lapels, saying, "Lock the door. All right?"

We parted, Ash and Zelda heading back to the ballroom as Jasper and I located the door in need of locking. I paid no attention to the room, didn't even look around before popping the lock and shoving Jasper back against the solid panel.

"We have to make this quick," she whispered against my lips. "Anyone could walk in at any moment."

She said this though it didn't stop her from palming my cock over my trousers or edging me closer to her with a leg hooked around my hip.

I groaned into her neck when her rhythm intensified. I pressed my teeth to her skin, not enough to mark but just enough to taste her, to feel the thrum of her pulse beneath her skin. "Then you should hurry, Peach."

"What should I do?" she asked, her hips bucking against mine. "If I have to be quick, what should I do to you?"

"Anything you want." *I* wanted to tear that dress right off her. If we weren't obligated to rejoin this party at some point, I would. "Anything, Jas."

Her head thunked back against the door as her body arched toward mine. "You're going to get me all wrinkled," she said, her words breathy. "We can't have that."

"Don't see why not," I said, licking a line up her neck. "We can get away with it. We're madly in love and getting married. Of course I'd drag you into the nearest corner to ravish you."

The amount of risk involved in saying those words out loud...*fuck*. It could all go up in flames right now.

"It seems that we are," she said, laughing. "But I think I'd rather be the one doing the ravishing tonight."

Jasper slid down the door, working my zipper as she went, and before I could grumble about her slipping out of my hold, she was on her knees with my cock in her mouth. No teasing, no prelude. Just my cock on her tongue and her lips tight around me. I couldn't see, couldn't think. The only sounds were my own gasps and the pulse pounding in my head. I braced my forearms on the door because I couldn't fuck up her hair, even if I wanted to pull it *so fucking bad*. Without thought, my hips surged forward and an angry, near-vicious growl rattled up from the depths of my chest.

I'd wanted to hold back a bit. I'd wanted her to set the pace. That was what I'd intended. I didn't succeed. Not when my body was twisting with need like no other, just boiling. I didn't care whether this lasted two minutes or two hours. It was mind-blowing and perfect, and most importantly, *I loved her*.

"Peach," I rasped, my hand settling on her shoulder. It was the only part of her I could touch. "Jasper, I'm—oh, fuck, I'm—ah, *fuuuuck*."

She hummed around me and that was the ballgame. That was it. She dug her nails into my thighs, my ass, and every last inch of me vibrated. My hips snapped against her face in fast, almost frantic thrusts. Her tongue worked the underside of my shaft in the most amazing way. There was pale pink lipstick all over me and, for reasons I didn't understand at all, that pushed me over the edge.

A snarling roar came loose from inside as I rode out the bone-shaking spasms and I kept that hand steady on her, my fingers rubbing small circles into her shoulder while she swallowed me down. A shudder moved through me as I continued jerking and pulsing on her tongue. It seemed endless, as if orgasms achieved in moments like these were that much longer.

When it was over, Jasper took my shaft in hand, still thick and heavy and throbbing for more, and dusted light kisses over my skin before tucking me back into my pants. I cupped her chin, tipped her face up, and stroked my thumb over her lips. *I loved her.*

For a moment, we stayed right there, Jasper in a pool of barely-yellow sunlight and me looming over her. I wanted to tell her—to tell her everything—but there were no words for this moment. And they didn't belong here, not really. This wasn't the place for those confessions. Not the right time.

"Here's what's going to happen now," I said, my thumb still tracing her lips. They were pink and swollen, and I bet they tasted like me. "I'm going to help you to your feet and I'm going to give you a minute to fix your face before we go back out there. Then, we're saying our goodbyes. Don't you dare think about chatting anyone up. If you do, you're the one who will suffer. It's an hour between here and home and I like watching you squirm so I won't be the one to make you feel better until you're stripped bare and flat on our bed. Understand, Peach?"

A rebellious breath burst from her lips and she arched her brows up. "Maybe I'll be the one to make myself feel better."

I held out my hand. There was a second where it seemed like she wasn't interested in taking it but she did. She also ran her tits along my chest as she stood so we were even. "You can try but you won't get what you need."

"Mmhmm." She raked a glance over me, saying, "Seems like we should be on our way then."

TWENTY-FIVE
JASPER

THIS BATHROOM GAVE NEW MEANING TO VINTAGE. IT WAS THE sort of throwback that was *almost* old enough to be in fashion again but in an antique, historical way. Unlike the rest of Midge's house, this room wasn't falling apart or the site of any unfortunate bat nesting. It was just *really* old.

Sitting on the lip of the tub, I ran a hand down the mint green tiles that covered the walls and the border of shiny black tiles capped off the art deco look. The problem was, all of this minty splendor seemed to be in decent condition. It wasn't moldy or cracked or even faded. It was just…old. That, and I knew nothing about fixing up bathrooms, which left me with nothing to do in here.

If I didn't have a week or two of work in the bathroom, I had to put my energy into Midge's room instead. There was nothing else for me to do. It was the bathroom or the only other room I'd avoided. I didn't make the rules.

"All right. I guess I'm ripping out some tile," I said to the empty space.

Before I could lift my trusty crowbar to the mint chip, my

phone vibrated across the floor, a number I didn't recognize flashing on the screen.

I knew better than to answer calls from unknown numbers but— "Hello?"

"Hey! Is this Jasper-Anne Cleary?"

Immediately, I went on high alert. I should not have answered. It was a bad idea to take calls from *anyone*. I didn't need to fumble my way through a "no comment" with another reporter.

"Yes," I said, though it came out like a question.

"Okay, great, cool. This is Dino Thatcher-Wheelwright with the NCVC."

He paused and I had to believe that pause was meant for me to respond with something like "Oh, the NCVC, of course, how's Marsha doing these days? She still with you guys or what?" but I had no idea. It could be the North Carolina Veterans' Coalition or the Nevada Commission on Visitor Commerce or—

"Northern California Voters Count," he said, chuckling just enough to forgive me for not knowing. "I bet you see your share of acronyms, huh?"

"Show me someone in this business who hasn't." My words sounded rusty, like I hadn't spoken out loud in days.

"The reason for my call, Jasper-Anne"—I didn't invite him to call me Jasper because I needed to know what he wanted before I could do anything else—"is we're hoping you want to come on out to California and help us get a few new members of Congress elected."

"I want—what? What did you say?"

"I hear ya, this is a big change of pace. NorCal is a totally different world, and that's just in regard to the rest of California, never mind the East Coast politics game."

I found myself saying, "Mmhmm."

"And we know you're a big-time player in that game while we're small potatoes but we also know you've had your fill of business as usual in Washington."

Again— "Mmhmm."

"I'll be straight with you," he continued. "We don't have the humanpower to get it done by ourselves. We're damn good at turning out voters and we've had some early success fielding a bench of candidates to run in state and local races, but we don't have the smarts to get them elected. That's where you come in."

By now, I was in the mint green tub, my knees to my chest and my head on the wall and my hand cramping because my grip on the phone could be categorized as one of those crazy adrenaline feats of strength. "Mmhmm."

"The team is pumped about getting to know you. We would love it if we could get a day or two with you, on site, to see if this is the path you want to tumble down next."

It took me a moment to realize it was my turn to speak. "On site," I repeated. "You're looking for me to visit you in California?"

"I know it's short notice but we could fly you out tomorrow. If you can't swing that, we can make it work later in the week."

"Tomorrow." My entire conversational strategy centered around repeating him—and it seemed to be working.

"Yeah, obviously it's suuuuuuper short notice but we figured you didn't have too much going on right now."

That hurt. A little. Just enough to get me out of this echo stupor. "Dino, I appreciate the call. Great to hear about what you're doing and I'm all for initiatives like this one. Before I can commit to flying to California, I need to engage in some due diligence and see if my schedule has any flexibility."

"Got it, got it. Here's what I can do for you. I'll shoot you some of our documents and a snapshot of the team's availability this week and early next. If you feel like our paths might align, I'll have our ops manager reach out to coordinate the travel arrangements. We're running a lean show here so I can't promise anything like you're used to but—"

I snorted. "Don't worry about that part, Dino. Every campaign operates on a shoestring. Even the ones that look like they have it made."

"It's those insider secrets we need," he said with a laugh. "That and enough dirty tricks to send a few incumbents packing."

There were too many emotions exploding inside me to properly process Dino's parting remarks. There was some denial in there, to be sure, but I let excitement and relief and pride—*I was back!*—crowd out the unsavory bits.

I was out of the bathtub and sprinting across the backyard in an instant, the raw November wind cutting through my clothes in a too-late reminder I'd left Midge's house without my coat. But it didn't matter. I was nearly home and I'd warm up while I looked into the NCVC, the organization that wanted me to transform Northern California's political scene.

It sounded simple enough but that region was a mosaic of people and competing interests, and it was nothing like Southern California. The opportunity to get in there and make something happen was immense. And it would be all mine.

When I reached my laptop on the kitchen table, my hands were shaking so hard from the rush of it all, I couldn't type. I just sat there, my entire body caught in an endless shiver, and let the tears fill my eyes.

I'd kept going. I'd put my head down and let it all blow over. Just like always, I'd survived. I'd made it through. I'd survived.

TWENTY-SIX
LINDEN

I RETURNED HOME TO FIND JASPER CRYING IN THE KITCHEN. Elbows on the closed lid of her laptop, head in her hands, hiccup-gasp crying.

Seeing as this wasn't the first time I'd come upon Jasper crying, I could've learned something from the past rather than repeating those mistakes. Instead, I dropped a wooden crate of assorted cranberry products gifted to me from a client on the countertop and asked, "What happened?"

Jasper started, of course, popping out of her seat and flattening a hand to her chest. She blotted her cheeks on her sleeve and sucked in a steadying breath. "You scared the hell out of me. What are you slamming and yelling for?"

"I came home and you're sitting here crying, Peach. I don't like seeing that. Who did this to you? If it's that ex of yours bothering you again, he can direct his inquiries to me. I'll handle Preston from this point forward, okay?"

She tore a wad of paper towel from the roll. "It's not Preston but your vehemence is extra special today."

I set my hands on her waist and waited as she thoroughly blew her nose. "Should I keep guessing?"

Leaning back against the cabinets, she said, "I got a job offer."

"You—what? When?"

She waved with the balled-up paper towels. "This afternoon. I got a call from a candidate farm and—"

"In English, Jasper. English."

Again with the paper towel, she said, "An organization that prioritizes races and develops a roster of candidates to take out incumbents or go after historically uncontested or uncompetitive seats. They raise money to grow candidates."

"And…" I couldn't finish that sentence.

"And they want me to fly out to California to meet with their team. They want me to run the farm."

As was always the case with Jasper, several things were true at once. She sounded happy but she was shaking, there was a proud, slightly haughty gleam in her eye but she'd been sobbing a minute ago, and she hated this stuff but clearly believed the offer was a step forward after taking a million steps back.

And she wanted me to share her enthusiasm even when this job was an airplane flight away.

"Where exactly is this job? This farm?"

"Northern California. The office is based in Sacramento but the work would include everything north of San Francisco." The way she said this told me it hadn't occurred to her that was the opposite side of the country. If she knew, she didn't care. "Come *on*. Say something. You can't just stand there, staring at me. My day went from almost demolishing a bathroom—"

"You almost did what?"

"—to a political action committee wanting me to run their operation. It's been a *day*, Lin."

"I'm happy for you," I managed. "But, Jasper, babe, Peach, I didn't think you wanted to do that anymore."

A beat passed before she deflated, her shoulders dropping, her gaze falling to the floor. Even the hand clutching the paper towels drooped to her side.

"I have to *do* something."

"No, you don't. There's no reason you have to do anything. You've said it yourself. You can swing a couple more months before you make any decisions."

"Just because I can doesn't mean I should," she replied.

"Maybe it does, Jas."

"I can't—I can't sit here all day, painting and repainting walls and organizing old junk. Okay? I can't do this. But I can go to California and raise some viable candidates. So what if I hate it? *So what?* Everyone hates their job. It's not special to me. It's everyone. And I'm good at it! I am good at this, even if I hate it. It's the best I've got. Okay?"

I shook my head and that was not the right response, not by a mile, but I wasn't going to watch her lie to herself. "Then stop repainting walls. Do something else. Do whatever the fuck you want but only because you want to do it."

"Maybe I want to run a candidate farm. Have you considered that? Maybe I want to shake up Northern California. It's a lot less progressive than people expect."

I crossed my arms over my chest. "Is that right?"

"Very much. I can't ignore the opportunity to do something important."

"It's interesting how you can't ignore this but you can ignore your own needs and interests indefinitely."

An irritable sound rattled in her throat. "Why can't you just be happy for me?"

"Why can't you stop punishing yourself?"

The look on her face—I thought I'd seen every shade of Jasper's fury but I was wrong. Irrevocably wrong. "You have no clue what you're talking about."

"No? Really? You're sure about that?" Her only response was a glare that reminded me of the day we met—and how my first impression was that she could destroy humans without breaking a sweat. "You worked for Timbrooks to spite your backward family. You stayed married to a guy after he left the country. You forced yourself to stay in Midge's cottage despite the squalor over there, and you've chosen to be a victim the past few months rather than the hero everyone who's fed up with the bullshit political games thinks you are."

"Once again, you know everything about me."

"Once again," I countered, "I know what I see. For fuck's sake, Jasper, you dressed as Cruella de Vil for Halloween because you think you are some awful devil woman."

"Would you just get over the Cruella thing? My god. I knew I should've said I was Moira Rose but I figured kids wouldn't understand the *Schitt's Creek* reference."

She tossed the paper towel to the table and closed her fingers around the back of a chair. Her hair was a wreck, as if she'd been shoving her fingers through it, and her eyes were swollen. She looked like she'd lived through something significant the same way people in hundred-year-old photographs did. Haunted, wary—and un-fucking-stoppable. She was still standing and she wasn't going to let me forget it.

"I'm sorry. Forget I said anything about Halloween. But

ask yourself, really ask, whether you want to move to California and let another job swallow your life whole."

She shook her head impatiently. "I can't just stay here forever."

"Why not?"

"Why not?" she repeated, the words climbing into a screech. "Because what am I then, Linden? Living in your house and wandering through the woods with you while I figure myself out—what is that?"

"It's exactly what you need."

"How can you say that? I mean, did you really think I could abandon my entire professional life just because I didn't love every moment of my work? Because that was never going to happen. I was always returning to that world, one way or another."

I rocked back on my heels as her words hit home. "So, that's it? This is where it ends?"

There was a moment where the stubborn set of her jaw slipped and she looked far less certain about her plans, though it was only a moment. Vanished before it truly existed. Then, "This would be easier if you were happy for me."

A lot of things would make this easier but that wasn't one of them.

"It only matters that you're happy," I replied. "You never wanted me to be part of this equation. My opinion shouldn't matter to you." Since another minute of this conversation was going to succeed in tearing my limbs from my body, I took a giant step back and snatched up my keys. "I'm gonna take off. Stay here tonight or don't. It's up to you. I won't be here either way."

"Linden, don't—"

"Nope, it's good." I held up a hand to stop her because I couldn't. I couldn't live through any more of this. I couldn't stay, not with her in my house and *all these things* I wanted to say to her, to beg of her. And I couldn't survive the night with her next door. I couldn't do any of this. I couldn't put myself through this only to watch her drive away. "Listen, I hope you get everything you want out in California. Your blood is probably too thin for a New England winter anyway. But you know where I am if you change your mind." I backed out of the kitchen, reached behind me for the knob. "Good luck out there."

I didn't wait for a response before slamming the door.

TWENTY-SEVEN
JASPER

I WAS ON THE FIRST FLIGHT OUT OF BOSTON THE NEXT MORNING and I spent every minute of the five and a half hours in the air telling myself Linden was wrong about everything.

He had to be wrong.

I wasn't punishing myself for anything. That was ludicrous. It didn't even make sense.

I kept telling myself that because if I stopped fuming for even half a second, I was going to fall apart and I couldn't have that before I met Dino and his associates.

Besides, I wasn't the kind of woman who fell apart. Not when it mattered and *this* mattered. Yeah, my research last night—which I did after stomping around Midge's house for a good hour—revealed the NCVC had a lot less cash on hand than I would've liked and their operations seemed to push the definition of shoestring, but the early years with Timbrooks were like that too. And start-up organizations were fun! They were fun. Everyone worked hard and had fun.

It would be great. I'd missed working with an eager new

team where everyone was obsessed with the possibilities ahead rather than choking on jaded bile. It would be hard though, and a ton of work. Long days, long weeks. But it would be great.

There was a lot to love about fresh starts. I'd have to learn everything about the region and figure it out on the fly but I'd done all that before. And I loved a challenge. Who wanted the same old same old? Not this girl.

I didn't know anyone in California, not anyone I'd consider a friend rather than a contact, but that was fine. I could make new friends. That was part of the adventure. New places, new people, new experiences. I'd find a community for myself. It would be fine.

Out of nowhere, I flashed back to Sunday dinner with Linden's family. They were such a strong unit, their lives woven together in more ways than I'd ever be able to parse. They were a community all of their own but they didn't exclude anyone. They sucked you in with tight embraces and marmalade and inside jokes. They were wonderful.

Too bad Linden hadn't asked me to stay.

He hadn't even hinted at that. Of all the things Linden said to me yesterday, not a single one of them involved passing up this opportunity because it meant moving to the other side of the country and the end of our relationship as we knew it.

He hadn't even mentioned us and that told me everything I needed to know. It was fine. It didn't matter. I didn't need him or his lumberbear vibes. I didn't need anything at all.

It wasn't like I expected him to fight for me or anything like that. God, no. How ridiculous. As if he'd have a grand speech about how much he wanted me in his life. Of course not. That didn't happen to real people. It just didn't happen. We'd had a fling and now it was over. I expected nothing from him. Moving right along.

Even if he had asked me to stay, it wasn't like I would. *Please.* I couldn't. I couldn't dawdle around a quiet Boston suburb while a moody beast of a man encouraged me to find my passion in life, all else be damned. That didn't happen to real people either. Real people pulled themselves together, worked their asses off, and knew no one was going to help them.

This stop was never meant to be permanent. Nothing was permanent and I'd do well to keep that in mind.

———

DINO AND HIS COLLEAGUES MET ME AT A RESTAURANT THAT served everything in mason jars or on rustic bread boards. The menu was scrawled on a great chalkboard covering the top half of one wall and the patrons sat at mismatched picnic tables. The music was loud yet mellow.

It was real nice. It was charming, when I gave it a minute. I didn't even mind the awkward bench straddle I had to do with one hand plastering the front of my skirt down, the other on the back because, for the first time in months, I knew how to work this situation.

Nonetheless, I couldn't stop myself from wondering what Linden would think about this place. Would he hate the just-so-ishness of it? Would he love the vibe but hate wedging himself into a damn picnic table? Would he stare at me from across the table, a slow smirk filling his face as he said, "You look good, Peach. You look real good."

I shook myself back into the conversation, murmuring

and nodding as Dino, Chester, Slater, and Saylor recounted an effort to get younger voters to the polls in the last election cycle. They *loved* their work, that much was plain to see, and it reminded me of my early days with Timbrooks.

I'd loved that little campaign family and it *was* a family. There was always a mom and a dad, little brothers, middle sisters, weird uncles, crazy aunts, cousins for whom we couldn't trace the bloodline, stepsiblings who came to us through concession speeches and endorsements. It wasn't a strict gender paradigm, of course. There were female dads, male middle sisters, nonbinary cousins.

Much like my own identity, it was about minds and hearts, not parts.

For me, I was always the bossy big sister, the one who got shit done and made sure everyone else got theirs done too.

I'd always angled for the dad role though I was never the mom.

The moms were essential to campaign life—someone had to manage the advance team and get in the weeds with the inch-tall details about matching or contrasting balloon strings and hotel room assignments—but they were never the stars. No one received recognition for the work of having the flags staged appropriately behind the podium at a press conference or moving the senator briskly through a rope line. You couldn't hold everyone together and be a star shining bright enough to stand out at the same time.

Saylor wasn't the mom of this operation. She had more of the youngest child essence, the one who stood out because she was new and that meant all her stories started with "Since this was my first election cycle..." and "At my previous gig..." Of course, that meant Dino, Chester, and

Slater had to follow those moments with recaps of events before she joined the team.

Tons of big brother energy.

They all wanted to be the dad but that required them to stop having experiences where someone slept in someone else's bathtub after a raucous party attended by other coworkers.

The problem wasn't the party or even the bathtub. It was that Dino couldn't be Slater's boss *and* drink enough with his direct reports to find an apartment tub suitable for a night's sleep. He could but that never worked out too well for anyone and I didn't get the impression he'd come to that realization on his own.

The big sister would have to sit him down and explain the stakes of carrying on like a frat boy in the evenings while attempting to sway public opinion toward equity and access during the day. That was how it was for the big sisters.

Not that I minded. I was good at this sort of thing. Eerily good, actually. I could engage in the types of difficult conversations that left most people hyperventilating as easily as I could place my coffee order. Ultimately, it didn't matter to me whether I was liked. I didn't have to be liked. I had to be effective and capable.

Being liked was the priority of the moms—but only when everyone was fed—and the middle children—because no one ever noticed them. That was the same reason neither of those groups lasted long in this kind of work. They let the churn of campaigns and then the outrage-and-fundraise cycles exhaust and demoralize them. They didn't get the love and attention they needed to flourish.

I didn't need love or attention. I didn't need anyone coddling me with reminders about how much they wanted me on their staff. I didn't need anything. Didn't need anyone. Didn't need a family or a Sunday supper tradition. Didn't need a pair of semi-sisters to laugh a weekend lunch away with or an extra mom to drag me into a community. Didn't need a cozy cottage in the forest or people to call my own.

I was a goddamn professional and I didn't need anyone but myself.

"Okay, real talk," Slater said, dropping his elbows to the table. "I have to ask, Jasper, how did you pull it off?"

Since I was busy bulleting out the convo I'd have with Dino in six to nine months and the redirection I'd give Saylor in a year or two—because those would be the hurdles ahead for me, nothing else—I missed the lead-in to this question. I blinked at him for a long moment, smiling just a touch to keep it pleasant. "What did I pull off?"

He snicker-laughed and shot an *are y'all with me on this?* glance to his colleagues. "Taking down Timbrooks."

I started to object but Chester chimed in with, "That was the ultimate drag and you played it so cool. Like it was an accident."

They hooted with laughter and clinked their mason jars together because they believed I'd planned this disaster. They believed I'd orchestrated this to knock Timbrooks out of the presidential race.

They believed I could manipulate at that mastermind level, that I'd even sacrifice myself to the cause. I wasn't sure I wanted to examine what that said about me.

"I think about taking down out-of-touch, two-faced elected officials *all the time* but I'd never considered the suicide bomber route," Slater added. "It's so fucking genius."

I flinched and froze the way I did every time someone spoke of suicide in a glib way but the group didn't notice.

They were busy agreeing with each other over my tactical brilliance.

"It's genius but it's also a little dangerous," Saylor said with a laugh. "I mean"—she lifted a shoulder, gave an uncomfortable smile—"it could've really backfired on you, right?"

It did, Saylor. It did.

When I didn't respond immediately, she added, "I'm just saying it could've looked like a personal implosion—and some of the networks did run with that angle, if I recall correctly—rather than an intentional character assassination, and that could've really screwed things up for you."

You don't know how right you are, Saylor.

"Who did you work with on this?" Chester asked. "Not to say you couldn't pull it off yourself—we've admired your work for the past few years and I have to say, it is A-plus— but that kind of coordination requires more than a lone gunman."

"Or gunwoman," Saylor said with the kind of stretched canvas smile that told me she made those remarks often and they tended to fall on deaf ears.

I focused on this because reading between the gender politics lines was less painful than the implication I'd conspired to kneecap my boss on cable news. Not only that, I'd conspired and I'd kneecapped and these people *admired* those choices. They wanted me because I was nightmarish and manipulative and willing to play dirtier than anyone else. Anything else I brought to the table was a bonus so long as I brought the lead pipe I'd used to take out Timbrooks.

A deep voice in my head asked, *How long have you hated your job?*

And that was the first time I had a specific answer to his question. I'd hated it since the work stopped being about the possibility of positive change and making good trouble— about the idealism of it all—and started being about tricks and games and manufactured scandals. When the people turned into an afterthought. When the senator's votes turned into commodities available for sale. When I placed winning above all else.

I smiled but it felt wrong. Forced, like I was wearing those horrible wax lips people gave out at Halloween. Those were terrible Halloween treats. I didn't know why anyone did that to children but I shook all of this away, saying, "A strategist never reveals her secrets."

"Not for free," Dino chirped, and the group erupted in laughter.

Again, that deep voice said to me, *It's not a badge of honor, you know.*

Yeah. I understood that now. I *finally* understood.

After another round of glass-clinking, Slater said, "And that's why you're here now. As I hope Dino explained, we want to get you on board and put some of those secrets to work remaking the local scene."

Saylor nodded while subtly gesturing to the nearby tables. "We shouldn't talk about this here but Slater's right. The only way we'll unseat some of the problems in this region is by getting messy."

They went around the table, echoing this sentiment with various metaphors in case I was somehow confused—gloves off, mudslinging, take no prisoners, hills to die on, and such. They wanted to declare war on some of the elected officials in this part of the state and they didn't mind slashing and burning everything in their path to claim victory.

In one sense, I had to give them credit for calling me. My work history was exactly what they needed to accomplish their goals. In another sense, I was working hard at not sliding off the bench and wishing myself away from this conversation because *oh my god*, I hated this breed of politics.

I hated this and yet it was the only thing I knew how to do. It didn't matter whether I was skilled in policy or voter enfranchisement or even fundraising, every operation's big bugaboo. It didn't matter because I could make an on-air accident look like a strategic fire set from inside the house.

As they talked, I kept my wax-lipped smile in place and nodded at the correct moments, and I stopped feeling sorry for my former self. I stopped aching for all the things I'd lost in the last few months and I allowed cold, sinking numbness to fill that space. I listened though I felt like I was observing this conversation from the bottom of a deep pool, the shadows of figures at the surface moving over me, moving on without me.

I was here, such a great distance from the surface, and I was alone and empty because I told myself this was better. This was what I wanted.

TWENTY-EIGHT
LINDEN

THERE WERE A FEW ROUTES I COULD DRIVE WITHOUT THINKING. It was some form of muscle memory where I knew where I was going and could get there on autopilot, without much recollection of the trip. It always bothered my brother when I said anything to that effect since he found driving with anything short of undivided attention to be the height of recklessness.

I didn't set my autopilot to his Boston apartment because he asked too many damn questions and he always expected concrete answers to those questions, though I did point myself in the direction of New Bedford. The only place it made sense to go was home to my parents.

Before I did that, I stopped at a sports bar where I nursed one and a half beers and a burger I didn't taste. A football game claimed the majority of the patrons' interest and energy, and on most occasions, that much noise would've bothered me. I didn't care about it now. I just wanted to drop into all that noise and distraction, and forget that I'd given

Jasper everything I thought she'd needed but none of it mattered because she was leaving.

It was stupid of me to get attached. It was stupid to think we could be—well, that we could be anything. It was stupid of me to try. There was never any chance of this arrangement lasting. And it was an arrangement, by no means a real relationship. We'd only known each other a handful of months and we didn't even like each other very much.

I don't hate you.

Fuck. Just…fuck.

But Jasper had been stuck here. Trapped, really. Now she had a way out and only a fool would pass that up. Jasper was a lot of contradictory things but she was no fool.

When the game was over and the burger felt like concrete in my stomach, I drove to my parents' house. I'd constructed a half-truth about an early appointment in Dartmouth and wanting to avoid morning traffic on 495, and my mother had texted back an emoji-heavy response that promised fresh sheets in my childhood bedroom.

I made a point of arriving there too late for anything more than a quick *hello, good to see you, good night,* and promptly closed myself in the room I used to share with Ash. It was a guest room now, stripped of its boyish blues and browns, and refined in a way it'd never been when we were kids.

I spent the night alternating between staring at the ceiling, checking my phone, and sleeping in fitful, disappointing bursts. There was a pinch in my chest every time I opened the messaging app and found nothing new from Jasper. I was capable of texting her, though that seemed like the wrong course of action. She was clear about what she wanted and I had no business standing in her way.

I couldn't offer her much, but more than that, she'd have to give up everything she thought she wanted to stay here with me. And I knew it made me the exact mansplainer dickhead she accused me of being by suggesting she didn't actually want any of the things she went after, but it was the truth.

She didn't want that job out in California, she wanted the redemption it represented.

She didn't want to work on another campaign—or whatever the hell it was—she wanted to be sought-after.

She didn't want to devote her entire existence to another politician, she wanted a place and a family and—

Well, that didn't matter.

None of it mattered.

That morning, I was up and out before my parents. My appointment in nearby Dartmouth wasn't until the afternoon but I kept myself busy checking on trees at two South Coast area golf courses until then. I went a little overboard with my note-taking (completely illegible nonsense) and scaled a few more trees than the conditions called for (none of them needed a moment's attention) but I couldn't obsess over Jasper and her decisions while twenty feet off the ground and holding on with one hand and a toehold.

I obsessed enough with both feet on the ground.

———

WHEN IT CAME TO TREES I'D NEVER EXAMINED BEFORE, I LIKED to sit with them for a time. It helped me understand how they'd grown and the ways in which the wind moved through them. Usually, I had no trouble focusing on this task. Being among trees was the most natural thing in the

world to me and it didn't require any deep level of aware-
ness but today, dammit, today I could not see anything but
Jasper.

Every time we went into the woods together flashed
before me like a memory book. Every time I backed her up
against a tree. Every time she looked at me with those round,
vulnerable eyes and told the truth about things that scared
her. Every time I swore she'd figure it all out.

And she did. She figured it out. She figured herself right
out of my life.

I managed to get through the consultation despite my
complete inability to function, and got the hell out of Dartmouth. I returned to my parents' house because Jasper might
be at home or she might be gone, and neither option was
acceptable. If push came to shove, I could avoid my house
for a full month.

I stopped short when I entered the kitchen and found my
sister seated at the table, her feet propped on the opposite
chair, her laptop and notebook spread out in front of her.
"What are you doing here?" I asked.

"What are you?" she shot back.

I hooked a thumb over my shoulder. "I had work in
Dartmouth."

She placed both hands on her belly. "Rob had a last
minute thing in New York and since I require full-time
supervision, Mom picked me up this morning." With a
shrug, she added, "She ran out to the grocery store because I
told her I need organic baby carrots."

"Are you that much of a pain in the ass or did you need a
break?"

"Yes."

We shared a laugh and that was probably the first time

I'd managed more than a scowl in twenty-four hours. It felt...strange.

I dropped into the chair beside her feet. "How are you not losing your mind with everyone hovering over you?"

"Oh, I've already lost it. I lost it back when the ultrasound tech said 'and we have a second heartbeat here.' It's been a downward spiral of wild and wacky times since then."

"And you're just going along with it? With Mom taking custody of you because your husband is away for the night?"

She gestured to her belly. "Do I want someone babysitting me? No. Of course not, Lin. But I have five more days until it's time to evict these boys and I have a serious suspicion they'll beat that timeline. I need someone around if for no other reason than to get me carrots when I feel like them. I'm not working this week because—"

"Excuse me." I tapped the lid of her laptop. "What does this look like to you?"

She rolled her eyes. "Okay, yes, it's *work* but I'm not in the office and all of my calls are being forwarded. I even put my email on out-of-office too."

"That's so brave of you."

Another eyeroll. "I need Mom hovering right now. I'm not interested in driving myself to the hospital any more than I'm interested in a home birth." She shifted in her seat, gave a wince, and held up a hand as if warning off the concern I was about to express. "It's all good. Just my bones feeling like they're all in the wrong places."

"That sounds terrible."

"It really is but I have high hopes they'll go back where they belong after the twins are born." She nodded emphatically and I couldn't help but smile in response. "Since I have you here, I just want to say it's okay if you don't want to work with me. No, please let me finish before you tell me your thoughts on this. Lin, I'm giving you permission to say no and step away. It's okay. I'm not interested in this partnership if you aren't. Why would I want to force you into something like this? I wouldn't. I don't. That wouldn't be fair to either of us. So, if you want to put this behind us and never speak of it again, just say it because I want to move that item off my project board before I go into labor."

I almost did. I almost told Magnolia I didn't want to do this because partnerships and working relationships with legal backbones were not my style. More than either of those issues, I didn't care for commitments.

But that wasn't true, not in any authentic sense. I wanted the *right* commitments, the ones that belonged to me because I made them and cherished them.

"I would like to move forward with your proposal," I said, the words sounding as unsteady as I felt.

She blinked. "Wait. Dude. Are you serious? Or are you saying you want to move forward with my proposal to never speak of this again?"

I bobbed my head as a rusty grin stretched across my face. "I want to work with you. It just took me some time to think it through."

She blew out a breath as she rubbed her belly. "Was not expecting that."

"Me neither."

With a laugh, Magnolia said, "You do realize, it's going to take you a *decade* to ask Jasper to marry you."

Whatever relief I felt from finally making that decision died at the mention of Jasper.

And marrying her.

Fuck. Just…*fuuuuuuck.*

"Oh." Magnolia frowned and it was clear she knew what happened. Maybe not the texture and dimension but enough of the shape to understand. Sometimes it helped to have a triplet who could read your mind. "I'm sorry, Lin. I didn't know."

"No one does," I said with the acrid energy of someone who'd replayed a conversation so many times the words no longer sounded real or made sense. "Happened the other night."

"Do you want to tell me what happened? I won't say anything. I'll just sit here and munch on antacids."

"Not really." I said this and I meant it but then I continued, "She got a job offer. Or an interview offer. I don't know. Whatever it is, they want her to move to California and take over a big project."

"That must be exciting for her."

"What happened to you sitting there silently and munching on your antacids?"

"Sorry. Sorry, dude, sorry. Please continue."

"Well, she was pretty excited about the whole thing." My sister cupped a hand over her mouth to suppress a laugh as she gave me *told you so* eyes. "I would've been excited too if she didn't hate that work. Maggie, you have no idea how much she truly detested her old job but believe me—"

"What about it? Because she came off so confident and energetic when she was here for Sunday supper. Didn't seem to detest anything."

"You don't know how to sit and listen, do you?"

"No, apparently I don't," she said with a laugh.

"Look, I don't know exactly which part she hated but I know she did. I also know this job won't be any different for her. I can tell. Plus, it's in California of all the damned places."

"Okay, first, how do you know this job will be the same? How do you know it won't relieve that one pain point that made things insufferable in the past?"

"I don't," I admitted, "but—"

"No, you can't argue that. Small changes can make all the difference in the world. You don't know that she needs a completely different career—"

"I do," I said under my breath.

"—and you don't know this situation won't be a dramatic improvement for her."

"Maybe not but I still think she's making a big mistake by—"

"By what?" Magnolia interrupted. "By interviewing? By considering the terms? By checking it out and getting a feel for the role? No, that's not a mistake. That's a smart girl keeping her options open."

"It's still in California," I replied.

"Which requires her to leave," Magnolia said. "Did you ask her to stay?"

I shook my head.

"Why not?"

I didn't answer for a minute. Then, "If she wants to go, I won't hold her back."

"Even if she's going to a job she will hate and moving to California of all the damned places."

I shrugged. "It's her choice."

"But you tried to talk her out of the job, no? Did I misunderstand?"

"I shared my concerns."

"Right, so, you told her it was a disaster in the making

but did you tell her *you* wanted her to stay? That you cared about her and you wanted her in your life on a daily, in-person basis?"

It felt like I was stepping on a land mine when I replied, "No."

"Let me ask you again: Why not? And you can't say anything about holding her back because you negated all that by trying to sink the job from the start."

"Because—because I don't know. All right? I don't know. And I meant it about holding her back. I don't want her staying here for me."

Magnolia shook a few tablets from the antacid bottle. "Why not?"

"Because that's not a good enough reason to make anyone stay."

"Isn't it though?"

I stared at her, confused. "How can you even say that? I can't ask her to give up everything just because I want her with me."

"Didn't she give up everything before she met you?"

Given up or taken away, the difference was all in perspective and perspective was the only thing that mattered. "I can't ask her to stay for me," I repeated.

"I can tell you believe that but I don't think it's true. I think she needs to hear that you want her to stay. You can't leave it up to inference." Magnolia shifted and winced again. "You are a lot of great things but expressive and communicative are not among them. Tell her that you want her here *and* you also want to make it work with her career."

I shook my head because it wasn't that simple, it was never that simple, but my mother bustled in through the back door before I could respond. It was a good thing. I didn't want to talk about this anymore.

"Let me take those," I said to Mom, relieving her of the heavy grocery totes. "What is in here? A twenty-pound turkey?"

"A fifteen-pound chicken," she replied. "Your sister asked for my lemon roasted chicken with orzo and—"

"And she needs fifteen pounds of it?" I asked with a laugh.

"For the record, I did *not* ask for lemon roasted chicken with orzo. I mentioned that I'd been in the mood for orzo but I only liked it with Mom's chicken."

I gave Magnolia a smirk. "Close enough, don't you think?"

"Linden, put those cartons of milk in the fridge for me while I check your sister's blood pressure."

"Your sister's blood pressure is fine and doesn't need hourly monitoring, thank you greatly," Magnolia said. "But her foot is asleep and she could use a hand getting up so she can visit the bathroom for the second time in an hour."

Mom rushed over to help Magnolia gain her feet while I filed away the groceries. They went back and forth about how my sister was feeling, who my mother ran into at the market, what we'd do about Thanksgiving dinner, seeing as the babies would arrive by then and they, of course, changed everything.

That seemed so strange to me. I didn't know what it would be like for everything to change. As far as my life went, there wasn't much variation. Trees and forests, my family, ball games. Sex when I felt like it, adventure when I was bored. That was enough for me. It was all I needed. All I wanted.

I didn't want the most stubborn, independent woman in the world. No. Not at all.

Except I did, I wanted her very much and I wanted her to abandon her fake smiles and the affected voice and all the things that drained the range and raw beauty out of her.

I wanted her to change everything for me because of course she would, and someday, I wanted my mother to hover over her and roast a chicken simply because she mentioned it. I wanted to burn with fury because she created another hazard for herself without realizing any of it. I wanted to be driven to distraction by her inability to manage simple things like rotaries and wall paint and her simultaneous ability to pull off the impossible with little effort. I wanted to wonder what we'd do about the holidays because everything had changed, everything.

But I hadn't asked her to stay—didn't even think I could —and I was too busy scowling to go home and see about salvaging this wreck before it was too late.

I was allowed my scowl, dammit. I was allowed some bitterness, some resentment. She crashed into my world, all crowbars and chaos and that peach-sweet charm, and I was damn well entitled to snarl over the fact she picked up the mess she made of me and left.

This was her fault. She was responsible for this, for my scowling. I didn't ask for any of it. The last thing I needed was a woman who didn't notice her own apple trees. For fuck's sake. And my god, the crockpot. The fucking crockpot.

A hard, painful laugh twisted in my chest as I put the last of the groceries away. I shut the refrigerator and let my forehead fall against the cool surface. "I'm so full of shit."

"What was that?" my mother chirped. "Am I setting a place for you at the table tonight? There's plenty."

"No, I have to get back," I said, and I knew that was the right answer. Maybe not right but it was the answer. I had to get home and do something. I didn't know what but I knew it was essential.

"You're sure? It's no trouble." She paused, lifted her brows. "I haven't seen much of you lately."

"These are the consequences, Mom. You tell me to find someone special, you have to expect I'll spend time with her."

She reached for a dish towel. "It's a price I'll happily pay, my darling son."

"Anything else I can do for you while you have me here?"

"Mom!" Magnolia shouted from down the hall. "I think my water broke."

"Are you sure you didn't have a little accident? That happened to me more than once," she called back, suddenly wandering in circles around the kitchen.

She opened the oven, closed it. Opened the freezer, closed it. I watched, not sure what I was supposed to do in this situation.

"Mom! I would know if I had a *little accident*, don't you think?"

"I said the same thing," my mother replied, now opening the cupboards and drawers. "They sent me home from the hospital twice and told me to stop thinking my water broke every time I sneezed too hard."

"What are you looking for?" I asked.

She waved my question away. "Oh, nothing, honey, nothing. Just my phone. And my keys. Yes, I'm sure I left them around here. I should call your father. But he's at the golf course and you know he never takes his phone out with him. So, I'll have to call the course. And Rob! Good grief, he's in New York City. I don't even know who to call there. I have a friend, Eleanor Greene, who lives in New York City. But I haven't spoken to her in ages. She's such a complainer. Everything is a problem with her. That's why I don't call." Her keys and phone were on the small table beside the back door as always. "And my pocketbook, I'm looking for my pocketbook. I'm sure it's around here."

I blinked at her for a second. "Okay. You keep looking. I'll just check on Maggie." Around the corner, I found the door to the under-the-stairs powder room open and my sister tossing hand towels on the floor. "Everything all right?"

She pressed her foot to one of the towels and moved it around the floor. "Everything will be fine," she replied with forced calm. "Mom's flipping out, isn't she?"

I glanced back in the direction of the rattling pots and pans. My mother operated on three speeds: steamroller, scatterbrained, or stoned. There were no other options—I'd looked—but there were mix-and-match combos. She could be stoned *and* steamrolling, as was often the case, or stoned *and* scatterbrained. I didn't think she was stoned right now but she was running at max scatterbrained. "Not more than I'd expect."

"I knew I should've stayed with Zelda today," she murmured. "She was in class until four and I didn't want to bother her with exams coming up but at least I'd know she wouldn't lose her shit when it was go-time." She glanced up from her pile of tiny towels. "Everything will be fine."

I heard more clanging from the kitchen and a slammed door, which had me smothering a laugh while I rubbed my temples. My sister was having babies, my mother was panicking, and Jasper needed me to fight for her.

I asked for none of this.

Not one bit.

And yet— "Do you think you can make it into my truck? Is it too high for you to climb in?"

Magnolia pressed a hand to her lower back. "If you give me a hand, I'm sure it will be all right."

"And you can tell me where you need to go?"

She nodded. "Yeah. For sure. But you don't—"

"You really think I'd leave you here with Mom while she roots through the frying pans for her phone? Not a chance. We're feeding her some weed gummies and getting you to the hospital before anything else happens."

"What about Jasper? You need to talk to her."

I brought an arm around Magnolia's shoulders and led her out of the bathroom. "I'll talk to her later. Or tomorrow. I know she'll understand this."

We entered the kitchen to find Mom with her arm elbow deep in a bag of flour.

"We are not baking right now, Grandma," Magnolia said. "It's baby time. My husband is a four-hour train ride away and I had five more days to prepare and I didn't get the lemon chicken and orzo like I really wanted but it is baby time. Remove yourself from the flour."

"I thought I might've dropped my phone," she replied. "The last time I had it, I was thinking about baking some chocolate chip cookies but I don't think it's in here."

"Probably not," I said. Scatterbrained. So scatterbrained.

"Please do me a favor and get your special candies so you can calm the fuck down. I am going to give birth to two babies in the next few hours, preferably with my husband by my side, and I need you to turn all of this"—Magnolia waved both hands at my mother—"way down."

"Right, yes, okay." My mother dusted her arm off as she walked in another circle around the kitchen until she stopped at a cookie jar in the shape of a fat monk and plucked a small zip-top bag with a dozen purple jellies from inside. "Time to go, then!"

I grabbed the bag Magnolia pointed out near the door plus my mother's keys and phone, which were exactly where she'd left them after coming in from the market not long ago. "Yep. Time to go."

TWENTY-NINE
JASPER

I STARED DOWN AT MY PHONE FOR A LONG MOMENT BEFORE tapping the icon beside my mother's number. Since leaving the NCVC offices—a former electronics store in a semi-abandoned strip mall—this evening, I'd fought off the nagging urge to call my mom. I never felt this way. I couldn't remember a single moment in the past twenty years when I'd *needed* my mother but I knew, for reasons that made no sense, I needed her right now.

I stared out at the tarmac and the workers in reflective gear that flashed back at me as the call rang. I hated taking red-eye flights. I hated half sleeping and half waking in a different time zone, and then pretending I was a functional human. I *hated* it but I hated my overwhelmingly beige hotel room more. I didn't want to stay in Sacramento another night.

"Hello? Jasper?"

"Mom," I said, tears immediately burning my eyes for no good reason. "I hope it's not too late to call."

"No, it's only a bit after ten and anyway, it's never too late," she said. "Are you flying in or out tonight?"

My mother knew airport noises the way I knew congressional districts. Another two minutes of her listening to the noises behind me and she'd be able to name the airport right down to the terminal and concourse. "Out. Heading back to Boston. I'm in Sacramento. There was an interview."

That felt like an appropriate description of the events. *There was an interview.* I was not interviewed. I was systematically backed into corners with questions that reached a little too far into confidential territories and repeatedly chided into sharing specific details about my work on previous campaigns. But hey, I blabbed about my former boss's bathroom habits on cable news. As far as they were concerned, nothing was sacred with me.

"Oh! I wish you'd told me! I could've flown down and taken you out to dinner."

Only my mother would think a flight from Seattle to Sacramento was a reasonable commute for dinner. "No, it's okay. I was tied up most of the day."

"Another time, then," she said, and it was obvious she didn't know what to do with me now.

She'd never really known but she'd tried and I gave her credit for that. She'd tried so hard even when everything was stacked against her. Even when her options were impossible. She'd tried and she did the best she could with the loss and devastation life handed her.

"I'm trying my best," I said, a wave of tears threatening to streak down my cheeks. God, I didn't want to cry in the middle of this airport. I just wanted to hold it together a bit longer. Just a bit. "I'm trying to do the right thing but nothing is working."

"It's going to work, honey. I'm sure of it. You've always tried so very hard, even when you were too young for anyone to expect that of you." She paused but I didn't respond because all the tears would fall and I'd sob and I didn't want that. I didn't want to be the person who cried on the phone in the middle of the airport. I didn't want to be the person who fell apart all the fucking time. "Why don't you come up to Seattle tonight? I'll make a call and change your itinerary, and we can have a day together."

I shook my head when I heard her typing. "Do you remember Halloween? That last one we spent on base?"

The typing stopped but there was a moment before she spoke. "I'll never forget it."

I let out a watery laugh. "See, that's my problem. I can't remember it. All I know is we had a good day."

She hummed in agreement. "It was a great day. All the families on base worked together to organize activities for the kids. Your father was in strong spirits too. You're right. It was one of the good days."

"Did we have a family costume? Something like that? I keep thinking we did but I don't recall what it was."

She laughed, saying, "We tried. I'll tell you, we tried but you wanted no part of it. Every year, I came up with a new costume and everything would be set but when it came time to dress up, you pitched a fit."

"That sounds nothing like me."

"Toddler Jasper was just as determined and stubborn as grown-up Jasper," she said. "That's how your father and I ended up dressed as Fred and Wilma Flintstone and you wore that sweet little black cat costume from Auntie Midge. The one you wore three years in a row."

An announcement sounded for my flight. "I don't remember any of that."

"You were a baby. You wouldn't. But you loved that costume. It didn't matter what season it was, you wanted to be that cat. You asked me to draw whiskers on your face all the time. A pink nose too." She laughed softly. "You loved the costume like crazy, even if it did ruin my plans year after year."

I shook my head. I didn't know what to do with any of this. "Mom, I have to go."

"I can get you on a flight," she said. "You can always come here, Jasper. I know I don't say that enough and my shifts never align with your work but there is always space in my life for you. Always."

I reached down for the handle of my carry-on bag. "I know, Mom."

"I want you to visit me, Jasper. Maybe not tonight but sometime soon. I'm certain I can find photos from that Halloween for you."

"I'm not sure what my—" I stopped myself before using my almighty schedule as a shield for the millionth time. I didn't have a schedule anymore. I didn't have anything but a gaping hole in my chest where my heart should've been because he didn't ask me to stay, and the ever-present sense I was missing out on something important that everyone else seemed to find without trouble. "I am not sure where I'm going. In my life. At all. I don't know what I'm doing."

Another announcement for my flight rang out but there were plenty of people lined up to board. I had a few more minutes.

After a beat, she said, "I needed to give myself permission to start over. I didn't think I was allowed to do that. I didn't think I could when I was a mother and in my mid-thirties but I realized I had to do it to save myself and save you too. I had to convince myself that starting over didn't mean I'd forgotten your father or that I didn't still love him dearly. It didn't mean the life we'd lived wasn't worth treasuring. It meant it was time for me to go in a new direction and I couldn't persecute myself over that choice. I couldn't hate myself for walking away from things that hurt me."

I didn't know what I was supposed to say. I sniffled. "Mmhmm."

"It's okay to change your life, Jasper. It's okay for it to be messy and it's okay to wonder if you've ruined it all."

"What if I actually *have* ruined it all?"

"That's just not possible, honey. It's not. You have so much ahead of you. Learn from the past but leave it there while you build a life that brings you joy and peace."

"I don't know how to do that," I snapped, angry for no good reason.

She laughed, gentle and rueful, and said, "Figure out what doesn't make you happy. Start there. Make a list. You've always loved your lists. Then, get rid of all that shit. Or as much as you can without going to prison for tax evasion. You'll figure out soon enough what you want."

"What if I mess that up too? What if I never get it right?"

"Then you live a life filled with new experiences. There's no limit on the number of acts in your play. You get as many as you want. You just have to keep getting on stage."

The final boarding call for my flight gave me a minute to dry my tears and take a breath before responding.

"If you're going to Boston tonight, you need to get on that flight," she said.

"I am," I replied, shuffling toward the gate. "I'm going."

"Call me in the morning. I have two shifts next week but I can visit the week after that, if you want. Or you can come here. I'll fly you out. There's always a place for you here."

"I know, Mom. Thank you."

"You're going to make the choices that are right for you, Jasper. I believe that."

I stepped into the short line of passengers waiting to board. "Why do you believe that? How do you know?"

"Because I know what it sounds like when you're in the middle of a storm and you can't see the hand in front of your face. And I know you're in that storm now. It's different than mine but it's still a god-awful storm. I know it and I know you, and I know you'll make it through."

I drew in a long, shuddering breath and decided I didn't care if I walked onto this plane with tears all over my face. I just didn't care. I was sad and lonely, and lost in a world where I used to know my place, my spot. My feet hurt and I knew I wasn't going to sleep tonight, and I wanted to call Linden and ask him why he didn't ask me to stay but I wouldn't. I *couldn't*.

"I love you, Mom."

"Love you too, honey. Call me tomorrow?"

"I will." I handed the gate agent my boarding pass and proceeded down the jetway. "Thanks for listening."

"Thanks for talking," she said pointedly.

I sighed. "I know I've been bad about—"

"Let's stop beating ourselves up tonight, okay? You've been doing what you needed to do and you don't owe me an explanation. Go easy on yourself. You deserve it."

"Good night, Mom."

"Good night, Jasper."

When I made my way to my seat, I grabbed a notebook

from my bag along with the flannel shirt I'd nabbed from Linden the other day because I was mad at him and wanted him to think of me every time he went looking for it. I draped the shirt over my shoulders like a shawl and flipped to a fresh page in my book.

I stared at it, pen poised over the paper, for a ridiculously long time. Long enough that I had to stow it in the seat-back pocket during takeoff and wait until the plane leveled off to return it to my lap. I stared at it through the beverage service and through half a bag of Cheez-Its, and then I wrote: *The Person I Want to Be Now.*

THIRTY
LINDEN

THERE WAS SOMETHING ABOUT THE SUN ON CRISP NOVEMBER mornings. It cut through the clouds at harsh angles and pierced the thick fog in a way that made those lazy billows glow. Mornings like these made me feel quiet yet very much alive.

Maybe it had nothing to do with November or glowy fog but everything to do with a long night spent celebrating the safe arrival of my new nephews. Add in the stress of driving my sister to the hospital in rush hour while she whisper-screamed at her husband to get the hell home as rapidly as he could manage and the past eighteen hours were some of the craziest of my life.

It didn't end at getting her to the hospital—and then collecting Rob from the airport because an hour-long flight bested a nearly four-hour train ride in this situation. It was then, after Rob and Magnolia were reunited but before the babies arrived, that my sister remembered we'd forgotten her Boston terrier back at my parents' house. Since my father was within twenty minutes of the city—he'd been golfing with his phone off and last to hear the news—I volunteered to drive back to New Bedford, fetch the dog called Rob Gronkowski, and ferry him back to Boston where he'd spend the next few days with Ash and Zelda before meeting his little brothers.

That was Magnolia's expression, not mine.

Once Zelda and I had the pup situated, we got word the babies had arrived and all involved were healthy. The hospital kicked everyone out—including my mother, who'd pulled herself out of the scatterbrained spiral just in time—and my father decided this called for a celebratory dinner. That led to a great deal of confusion since my parents were at the hospital, Ash was at the office, and Zelda and I were at their apartment.

I'd call it a clusterfuck but the entire day had been a clusterfuck of proportions I'd never imagined.

Eventually, we circled up at a steakhouse my parents favored. There was champagne, probably more than made sense for the occasion but that didn't slow anyone down. There was steak, a perfectly reasonable amount for any occasion. And there were stories. So many stories. The day Ash, Magnolia, and I were born. The day our parents took us home. The day we wouldn't stop crying, not a single one of us, and the day Ash and I crawled under the living room sofa and stayed dead silent while our mother went nuts trying to find us.

It was a night well spent but there wasn't a single minute where Jasper's absence didn't stab at my sides. Where I didn't have to choke down the desire to turn to her, reach for her, whisper something private into her honeyed hair.

I wanted to share this with her. I wanted to fill her champagne flute again and again and tell stories with her. I wanted to pass out in Ash's guest room with her in my arms. I didn't want to do this or anything else alone. I wanted her here and I knew that made me a greedy bastard but I couldn't help it. I'd tried. I'd tried since sending her on her way to California but I couldn't do it anymore.

The only thing I wanted to do—aside from chasing away this throbby champagne headache—was feel sorry for myself. It was a selfish answer to a selfish problem but I didn't care. I'd shower and dress, chug some coffee and feed myself anything but toast, and slog through my day with all the self-pity I wanted.

It seemed only fair, considering Jasper was long gone. I hadn't heard from her in—well, I wasn't sure how long it had been since the days were a blur of babies and dogs and strange dreams but it was long enough to know she'd moved on. I was sure of it.

Except—

I came to a hard stop in the middle of my street, right where the dogleg bend opened up to reveal the pair of cottages at the end of the cul-de-sac and Jasper's old station wagon parked at a drunken angle in the driveway.

I stared at it for a long moment, blinking to make sure I wasn't hallucinating from the hangover, the adrenaline, the terrible nights of sleep I'd managed since letting her go. I blinked again and no, no, I was not hallucinating. Yet I didn't trust any of this. There were plenty of reasons for her to be here. It meant nothing. It couldn't.

I told myself this but I parked in my driveway and marched straight into her yard, not stopping for anything.

The front door stood open and I glanced inside. She'd abandoned her shoes and carry-on bag in the entryway. I decided that meant nothing. Same with the vague thumping

I heard coming from the direction of the back bedroom. She could be packing the last of her things or knocking down a wall, or anything in between. That was how Jasper operated.

Part of me didn't want to find out. I didn't have the stomach to walk away from her again.

I followed the sounds of the low thuds until I found myself in the doorway to her little bedroom. It was such a sliver of a space, though I couldn't focus on that, not when Jasper was busy throwing shoes into an open-top box with bananas printed on the sides. At first glance, it seemed like she was packing, but this wasn't packing. It was demolition.

"Hey. The door was open," I said.

She turned, two different shoes in each hand. "I don't want these anymore," she said, her dark eyes brimming with as much determination as I'd ever seen them.

I shoved my hands in my pockets. It was all I could do to keep myself from reaching for her. "Okay."

She chucked the shoes into the box. "I don't want any of them. I don't want to need high heels to feel powerful."

"Fuck the shoes. You're already powerful."

"I don't want to do this anymore." She stared at the box of shoes and the clothes she'd piled on the bed. "I don't want to be a nightmare. I don't want to be known for that." She blinked up at me, her eyes shiny with unshed tears. I fisted my hands in my pockets. "I don't want to go to California. I don't want the job. I don't want any job like that one. I don't want to win at any cost and I don't want to sell my dirty tricks. I don't know when I stopped being that person but I don't want to go back."

"You don't have to." I had a million questions but there was only one I really needed her to answer right now. "What do you want?"

Jasper thumbed away her tears and turned toward the bed where she rifled through the clothes heaped there. From somewhere near the bottom, she produced a notebook. If I knew anything about Jasper, I knew that book was full of lists.

She flipped through the pages, saying, "I spent all night on that."

"Is that how long the front door has been open?"

She shook her head. "I landed in Boston at six this morning." She stopped at the right page and glimpsed at me before reading, "I want to have friends who are unrelated to my job. I want to surround myself with people who care about me and don't measure my value by the access or information I can grant them. I want a job that means something to me but not one that means everything. I want to wear clothes I find comfortable, not those that function as armor or intimidation. I want to get some hobbies and I don't care if I'm very bad at them." She glanced up from the book. "While I am very bad at baking and home renovation, I don't think either of them qualify as hobbies I want to continue."

"That's understandable." I bobbed my head as a smile pulled up one corner of my mouth. "Anything else?"

She nodded, saying, "I want a community of my own, a place that's mine because I choose it, not because I'm stuck with it. I want to let myself rely on people, even when that's scary. I want a home that people want to visit because it's so happy and welcoming. I want to belong somewhere and to someone. I want to start a family and have a baby or two, and I don't want to wait until everything is perfectly right to do it. I've waited so long and I don't think I can wait anymore. Actually, no. I can't wait. I know that."

I stepped into the room, edged the banana box of shoes aside as I went. "You're not going to California."

She gave a slow shake of her head. "Another day, I'll explain all the ways in which you were right about the job and how wrong it was for me."

"If we're tabling that discussion for another day, does that mean you're staying here? That you're choosing this place?"

Jasper studied her notebook for a moment, her fingers drumming against the back cover. "You didn't ask me to stay, Linden."

"Because I couldn't ask you to do that for me. If you didn't go out there and see about that job for yourself, you would've regretted it. You would've wondered whether it was what you need and—fuck, Jas, I had to do it. I had to let you go, even if it killed me."

She tossed the notebook to the bed. "You can't make those decisions for me. You can't decide you're going to withhold information from me and hope for the best. It's not fair to anyone. And what if I went out there and decided to take the job, even if I hated it? What would happen then, Lin? What would you do?"

"I'd live with it."

"And that way we'd both get to be miserable? Just because you didn't want to say the wrong thing to me? Is that really the solution you went with?"

I folded my arms over my chest. "I didn't say it was a good solution, just that it was better than trapping you here."

"It wouldn't be a trap if you were up-front with me. Do you have any clue how much I needed to hear you ask me to stay?"

"Obviously not. Okay? I didn't know. I thought I was protecting you."

She blew out a breath, rolled her eyes to the ceiling. "If you stopped acting like you have to protect everyone from the things you want, you could be honest instead."

"You want honest?" I took another step toward her. Any closer and we'd be right up on each other. "Okay, babe. I'll give you honest. I am in love with you. All right? I fucking love you and it physically hurt when you left and I really hope—"

She reached out, twisted her hands in my shirt, and yanked me to her chest, sealing her lips over mine before I could get another word in. It took a stunned second for me to process this before I could react, before I could respond.

"Jasper," I whispered against her lips.

"I love you too," she said. "I love you and I want to be with you, even if I have no idea what comes next."

I closed my arms around her torso, held her tight to me. "You just told me what comes next."

She inched her hands up my chest and over my shoulders until she could rake her fingers through my beard. "Only if you want the same things."

I was ready to scoop her up and get the hell out of here. Take her home, take her to bed. The dark smudges under her eyes told me she'd slept about as well as I had these past few days and I needed to fix that.

"I'll tell you what happens now," I said, pivoting her in my arms and steering her toward the door. "I'm taking you home. That's what it is, Jas, it's home to you. What you decide to do with this place is entirely secondary and that choice is not going to occupy space in your mind anymore. Keep it, sell it—doesn't matter because we live next door and you don't need to worry about finances."

"I don't like the idea of relying on someone in that way,"

she said. "My entire life has been a series of rebellions against that sort of thing."

"Believe me, I've noticed and I understand. But I don't worry about money and I won't, especially now that I've agreed to partner with Magnolia and—"

"You did? What? When did that happen?"

"A few days ago—no, wait—it was yesterday. Jesus, this week has been a fucking blur." When we reached the entry-way, I picked up her bag and motioned to her shoes. "Yesterday afternoon, right before she went into labor."

Jasper pressed her palms to her cheeks. "Oh my god! The babies—they're here?"

"They arrived last night. The first weighed in at five pounds even, the second at a little over four and a half. Magnolia is doing well but don't ask her about names because they haven't decided yet."

"Oh my god," she whispered, her hands still on her cheeks. "That's wonderful. It's just wonderful. And you're going to do it, you're going through with the partnership. I'm so happy you came to a decision and—oh, wait just a minute."

She hadn't put her shoes on yet and that was driving me crazy so I dropped the bag, kneeled down, and did it for her. "No, I won't wait even a minute. We're going home. We can visit the babies later."

"No, that's not what I meant. I was trying to say I don't want to be a kept woman, regardless of your new business arrangement."

"That's tough shit because it's how it's going to be. Maybe then you'll be able to figure out what to do with your life when you don't have to worry about survival."

She gave me an arched eyebrow and a pouty mouth. As

if I could resist any bit of that. Not today, not ever. So, I grabbed her ass and kissed her hard.

"What was that for?" she asked.

I shook my head while I closed the door behind us. "I don't need a reason."

"I see we're being extra imperious today."

I hooked my arm around her waist and led her down the walkway. That same old cat shot out from near the rose-bushes and mewed at us as we walked by. "I'm not finished telling you how this is going to go."

With a full, husky laugh, Jasper said, "I can't wait to hear the rest of this."

"You are going to belong to me and I am going to belong to you," I said, the words thick as they caught in my throat. "You're going to rely on me even when it's really fucking uncomfortable for you. Even when you want to prove you can do anything and everything by yourself, you're going to lean on me because that's what we do. Got it?"

"And what about you? Are you going to be honest and up front about the things you want even when it's really fucking uncomfortable for you?"

"Yeah," I said, setting her things down to pull the house keys from my pocket when we reached the front door. "I am."

As I pushed the door open, she said, "That's not going to be easy."

"You think any of this is going to be easy? It's not, Jas. It's not. It's going to be hard every day and we're going to have to work at it but there is no one in the world I'd rather fight with over crockpots and rotaries—"

"Traffic circles."

"—and all the other random bullshit we argue about than

you. No one in the fucking world. When you're ready, I'm going to marry you the way you deserve to be married and—"

"What does that even mean?" she asked with a huffy little laugh that meant she didn't enjoy this topic.

"It means you're getting a ring that will definitely have some Elvish writing on the inside and an over the top proposal that I promise won't involve a single Hobbit. We're going to eat a ton of cake samples and agonize over stupid shit like seating arrangements. My mother is going to throw you a big-ass bridal shower and she's going to live for the single purpose of making our day everything you've ever wanted. My sister will adopt you into her circle of no-bull-shit, boss-lady friends and they'll throw you a filthy bache-lorette party that will test all of my tolerance of such things. And when our day comes around, I'm going to wake up beside you and love you so hard that you walk down that aisle on shaky legs. I'm gonna love you like that on the good days and the bad days and all the ones in between. And I'm never, ever moving to Northern Ireland without you."

"That wasn't funny." She said this as she laughed—*hard.* "About Northern Ireland."

"Yeah, well, I wasn't joking when I said I was marrying you the way you deserved and you did not deserve that shit."

Still stopped in front of the open door, she said, "Let's not talk about Preston anymore. Although I will probably have to call him to get me an interview with that community activism organization. I think I want to learn more about that."

"I'll allow that." I gestured to the doorway. "What do you say, Jas? Are we doing this?"

She raked her teeth over her bottom lip. "Anything else? Or is that the whole high-handed plan?"

Because I couldn't take it anymore, I really could not, I set her bag inside and then scooped her into my arms. "High-handed, is it?"

"What the hell are you doing?"

"I'm moving things along," I replied as I headed for the bedroom. "It's too damn cold to stand on the front porch when there's a perfectly good bed waiting for us in here."

"Sometimes you are extremely ridiculous."

"And you're impossible. I still love you."

I felt her staring at me as I marched into the bedroom. I felt her gaze, warm but still a bit wary. Why wouldn't she be? Everyone else in her life let her down. They left, some more overtly than others, but they all left. I wasn't going to be one of them.

The clothes came off in a rush, both of us helping the other until we realized we were making it much more complicated, and finished the job on our own. The blankets and sheets came down as we climbed underneath, turning to face each other, to wrap ourselves in each other.

"I'm going to marry you the right way," I echoed, one hand on her outer thigh, the other coasting down her back. "I'm going to give you as many babies as you want, all the family you can handle. I meant it when I said you're going to belong to me, Peach, but you're also going to belong here. You already do. Understand?"

She reached between us, took my shaft in hand. It was very unfair, considering she intended for us to carry on a serious conversation while stroking me. "Is that what you want? A wedding and babies and everything? What happened to being alone? What happened to protecting your quiet, your space?"

Since that single minute of her palm sliding over my aching cock was too much, I climbed over her, caging her beneath me, and pried her thighs open. "You happened."

A laugh moved through her, up her chest and across her shoulders as it softened the anxious set of her jaw. "That doesn't seem like enough."

"And that's why I make the high-handed plans," I replied. "Because you're busy thinking you didn't crack open my world the day you came at me with a crowbar."

"That is *not* what took place and you know it."

I notched myself at her opening, my bare cockhead burning against the wet of her. "Is this what you want?" She stared down the length of her torso to where I held myself steady. When she didn't respond for a moment, I dragged my cock up, circling her clit. "You did, you know. You cracked everything open. I haven't been the same since."

"Is that a good thing?"

"It's the best thing."

She nodded, shifted her knees up to my hips, and said, "I haven't been the same either. I don't want to be the same. But I know I want you." I pushed inside her and watched as she arched back, parted her lips, breathed out a quiet sigh. "I don't hate you."

Her hips rolled, soon finding a rhythm, and I was sliding into her, a little deeper with each pass. "I never hated you." I pulled back before slamming in again. "Never once."

"Are you sure about that?" she asked, angling her hips to find the position she wanted.

"You know I am."

She hummed as my cock slipped out and over her clit. My brain wanted me to thrust into her and fuck her until neither of us could move but some other part reminded me to go slow, to savor this. She arched up and we stayed there, kissing, thrusting, whispering all the things we couldn't stop saying.

I love you. I've loved you for so long. I don't want to be without you.

We moved together, *slow slow slow*, and the only thing in the world for me was this woman.

"Lin. I need more," she groaned, clenching around me.

I shifted my hands to her waist and found a faster rhythm as I held her, my fingers driving hard into the soft of her skin. The early pulses of her orgasm triggered my muscle memory, the one that reminded my hips how to fuck in that quick, urgent way and made my cockhead unbelievably sensitive, and untwisted the tension of separation and distance and loss. The one that knew this woman was for me and I was for her, and nothing else mattered than the connection we shared right here, right now. I felt it in my balls, and then that sensation spiraled up and down my spine, right on the edge of explosion. Another thrust ripped a groan from me, and I matched it with a quick pinch to her clit.

"I want to feel you come for me now," I said against her ear. "Let go for me."

I pinched her again and her groan turned into a gusting wail. She was unbelievably hot and wet, and when her muscles fluttered around me, I folded her into my arms as I emptied myself into her. We rolled together, still panting and sighing, and I couldn't help but kiss every inch of skin I could reach. Those kisses told her how much I wanted her, how much I loved her, how she was mine.

And she was mine, in as great a way as any single person could possess another.

She glanced over her shoulder at me. "Twins and triplets run in your family, don't they?"

I grinned. "It passes on the mother's side."

She shifted until her back was flat against the mattress, her head pillowed on my arm. "I probably should've asked that before"—she gestured between us—"any of this."

"Would it matter?"

She gave me a wink that tightened my chest with how adorable it was, saying, "No. It wouldn't. I don't think there's anything that could change this."

I eased my arm out from under her and made my way to the bottom of the bed. "And you're all right with that?"

"I'm more right than anything else." Her lips quirking, she asked, "What are you doing down there? What are you doing now?"

I settled between her legs, my shoulders forcing her thighs open wide. "Giving you everything you've ever wanted."

EPILOGUE
JASPER

The next autumn

I used to think getting fired was the worst thing that had ever happened to me. That losing my job—the only thing at which I'd ever been good and the source of all my pride and confidence—had crushed me in the most absolute sense.

And it did, it completely crushed me. It stripped me right down to the barest of my bones. It took away everything I believed to be right and true about myself.

It forced me to figure out what I *wanted* to be true about myself.

It made for a tough year but it was a really important one too.

I started working at a local organization focused on expanding voter registration, knowledge, and engagement. Community activism was a good fit for me, a *really* good fit, but all I'd ever known was diving head and shoulders into work and I couldn't do that anymore. I didn't *want* to do it anymore. I needed Linden to help me enforce limits like leaving the office at a certain time, switching off my phone when I was at home, committing to work-free weekends whenever possible. Obviously, this required more than a gentle reminder from my lumberbear and there were more than a few situations where I found myself tackled at the front door and relieved of my phone and laptop. A few other situations where my phone just disappeared for the weekend. Another when Linden called me from outside the office and gave me a three-minute warning to pack up for the day unless I wanted him to march in and toss me over his shoulder.

The past year was tough. It was good—wonderful, really —but it was tough.

We hired a crew to complete the work at Midge's cottage. It wasn't like I could refinish the hardwood floors myself or replace the roof or update the electrical system. And goddamn, that porch. That porch. It made sense to hand that over to the professionals, especially since my mom and Martin visited in the spring and we rented it out shortly after.

I asked my mother-in-law to help me clean out Midge's room since she'd only met the woman in passing and wouldn't burst into flame if she came across a stray dildo. True to form, Diana had the place packed up and straightened out in an afternoon, and she didn't say a single word about sex toys.

Oh, yeah. My *mother-in-law*. I didn't bother with any *future* business and it wasn't like Diana would allow such a thing anyway. Linden made good on that over the top proposal promise with a New Year's Eve party at a restaurant in Boston. Instead of everyone yelling "Happy New Year" at midnight, they fell silent while he pulled out a ring. After I sobbed all the tears in my body and managed a jerky nod that yes, *yes*, I'd totally marry him, the confetti flew and the "Happy New Years" rang out and that year started off right.

I found best friends—sisters, really—in Magnolia and Zelda though those relationships didn't come easily to me. I still found myself waiting to text them if they hadn't texted me yet in a given day. I didn't know how to ask for their help without immediately acknowledging their assistance in excessive ways. It wasn't until Zelda sat me down over the summer and explained that I could not send her dozens of cookies every time she joined me for a wedding dress fitting or offered her opinion on flowers or bands. She insisted she wouldn't help if she didn't have the time or interest, and she didn't need more than my words of gratitude. Especially since Ash devoured all the cookies before Zelda even got her hands on them.

Linden and Magnolia's partnership launched without a hitch. Instead of regular office meetings, they decided to sit down together at Magnolia's South End brownstone every Friday afternoon at three. Ash often joined too. Those gatherings quickly expanded to include a family dinner and we rotated between our homes. It was my favorite part of the week. I loved hosting everyone at our house or visiting Ash and Zelda or Magnolia, Rob, and the twins in Boston. I loved these newborn traditions of ours. I loved having a home and people to fill it with.

And now, a full year since losing my job and all the

things I thought I knew about myself, I glanced in the mirror in my hotel room to check my hair one more time before a limo delivered me and my bridesmaids to the orchard where I'd walk down the aisle to marry Linden. My hair was in the same wavy style as always but though I didn't think of it as my something old. The handkerchief sewn into the lining of my gown, right over my heart, was something old.

I'd borrowed the single strand of pearls around my neck from my mother. She'd worn them on her wedding day.

The perfectly peach flats peeking out from under my creamy white gown were new—a gift from my best ladies, Zelda and Magnolia.

The bite mark on the underside of my breast was something blue.

As I stared at my reflection, I caught sight of Linden watching me from the doorway. He eyed the lace running down to my wrists, over my back. It felt appropriately vintage to me, nearly Grace Kelly in its vibe.

"Didn't think I'd forget, did you?" he asked.

I shook my head. Linden didn't forget. He didn't break promises. He didn't let me down. Like he'd said all those months ago, he wasn't going to be one of those people. I'd assumed that was nothing more than pillow talk. The kind of things people said when they were drowning in sexual tension.

I knew better now. I knew he'd meant it.

"Never doubted you for a second," I said.

He stepped closer, his hands held wide as they ghosted over my dress. "How long do we have?"

In the reflection, I spied the digital clock beside the bed. "Five minutes. Maybe one or two more if Magnolia can stall."

He shucked off his suit coat, tossed it to the bed. Flipped

his tie over his shoulder. Rolled up his cuffs. "Gonna have to be quick," he said, dropping to his knees behind me. He carefully lifted the skirt to my waist, skimmed his hand up my thigh and dragged my panties down. "Hold on, Peach. I'm gonna make this good for you."

He placed a hand below my navel, an anchor to keep me from pitching over when I lost my footing. I would, of course. I'd fall apart for him now the same as I always did.

His lips traveled up my bottom, his soft-coarse beard the very best tease, and I groaned out loud when he elbowed my stance open and ducked his head between my legs.

He parted my folds with his tongue, licking just enough to force a desperate moan from my lips. My heels came out of my shoes as I leaned up on my tiptoes. He speared his tongue inside me and I arched into it, into the devastating heat of it. His growl rumbled through me. "Oh, fuck, yes. Yes. Eat that pussy."

"That's right, little wife," he said. "This is all mine."

I stared at my reflection in the mirror, finding myself with hazed-over eyes and slack-jawed lips as he tugged my most tender places between his teeth, sucking and nipping, and fucking me with two fingers. There was no way I'd walk down the aisle on steady legs and that was exactly the plan.

"I can taste myself on you, from this morning," he whispered.

"I love that." This position didn't let me see him—not much, anyway—but I loved that too. It was a perverse spin on wedding day superstitions. Though I didn't have to see him to know he was hard and throbbing right now. "Get your cock out. Make yourself come for me."

"Not until you do," he said.

"I asked you," I started, my tone as clipped as ever, "to get your cock out. It would be a terrible thing to disappoint me on my wedding day."

I heard his belt rattle and the rustle of clothing. I felt his groan when he had himself in hand. I didn't have to see him to know he was treating himself to a slow rub down his length, a twist at the crown, and then a rough jerk back to the base. I knew he'd let out a hummed growl any minute now as he sped up, let his hand fly faster over his cock as he found the rhythm he needed.

Linden sucked hard at my clit as he stroked himself, his fingers still working my pussy, and the mixed chorus of our groans and cries seemed to gather around the fine lace of my dress, the crisp cut of his suit. We were getting married within the *hour*.

"I love you so much," I gasped. "I want you to come on my ass."

I didn't know what it was about those statements that made them so profoundly right but my orgasm came at me fast, a jagged, thorny throb that spiraled through me and left everything from my belly button on down shaky and unsteady.

Linden growled out something as he pushed to his feet, replacing the hand around his cock with the one he'd had buried in my pussy a moment ago. He held my dress in place as he pressed me down, his big palm on the center of my back. "I fucking love you," he rasped.

I watched in the mirror as his arm flexed, his hand shuttling over his cock. The sound of slapping flesh and the brush of his knuckles between my ass cheeks left me aching and clenching and clinging to the last aftershocks of my orgasm.

Again— "I fucking *love* you."

And the hot lash of his release hit my skin.

This new chapter of my life, it wasn't nearly as tough as the ones that came before. It wasn't lonely or sad or defensive. It was dirty and messy, rude and lusty, and safe and loved. It was everything I'd ever wanted.

EPILOGUE
LINDEN

Three years later

We named them Sawyer Reuel and Savannah Eowyn.

It surprised me when Jasper suggested names that called to mind her home state but home wasn't something she needed to avoid anymore. The middle names were straight out of *The Lord of the Rings* and I was very pleased about that win.

Maybe it shouldn't have but the discovery we were having twins came as a shock. It knocked Jasper right over. She wanted everything to be perfect for them, everything to be *just* so, and that meant the first five months of her pregnancy were mayhem.

We put an addition on the house because she insisted we needed more bedrooms, more bathrooms, more space. More of everything. She had to paint and decorate and prepare— and then change it all and do it again. We took the classes, read the books, learned everything there was to know while my mother clucked about not worrying because these things came naturally. I had to gently ask her to stop filling my wife's head with any of that *you'll know what to do* nonsense. That wasn't Jasper's operating system.

The other two and half months of Jasper's pregnancy were also mayhem because the doctors put her on bed rest. If there was ever a time when she had to ask for help and lean on other people, it was then. She managed as well as anyone could manage nearly three months of confinement. Magnolia developed a schedule so that my siblings and their partners, plus our friends, were constantly dropping in to visit with Jasper while I was working. Some of them got really good at making fancy toast during that time. My brother-in-law was still a convert. My mother kept trying to make sandwiches but we forgave her that because she was there for us every minute of those months.

The twins spent two weeks in neonatal care until they reached fighting weight and we brought them home. I was glad we'd read all those books and taken all those classes but my mother was right about knowing what to do. I didn't tell her that but she was right. I understood what to do when I held them. It was the same way I understood what to do when I held Jasper.

They were almost one year old now and Magnolia's boys, Elijah and Ethan, were three. No kids for Ash and Zelda yet but they were busy looking for a home outside the city now that they were finally married. Jasper was lobbying hard for them to move in next door, into Midge's cottage. I didn't think it would happen but I couldn't deny it would be nice to have them there.

It would give that impossibly old black cat someone new to stalk.

We had nine crockpots in our pantry and two styles of toaster oven on our kitchen countertop, and six different baby carriers for walking in the woods. That was our life now and I loved it more than I could explain.

Magnolia and I worked together every day and this partnership was one of her best ideas and my best decisions. Commitment and responsibility weren't nearly as awful as I'd imagined. Jasper was the executive director of a community activism organization because world domination was only a matter of time when it came to my wife. She also hosted book (wine) club meetings every month, grew a mean kitchen garden, and had a standing pedicure date with her friends.

I loved the complex simplicity of it. The order and the routine but also the chaos. Babies were fucking *chaos* and they knew it. I even loved the noise, the ever-present noise of people and crying and *what the fuck was that?* and living. Living was loud—and so was love—and I treasured it all more than I could explain.

"There you go, you little Hobbitses," I said, setting Sawyer and Savvi back in their crib. We had two cribs. We had two of everything. Still, they only slept when they were together. "You have full bellies and clean diapers. You can sleep for another few hours." Savvi babbled at me indignantly. "Then, you can play quietly but it's too early for us to wake Momma."

Sensing the cause was hopeless, Sawyer flopped back to the mattress and shoved his thumb in his mouth. He always gave in first. His sister was a different story. After a pause, Savvi brought her blanket to her chest and wobbled over to her side.

I watched them as I backed out of the room. They'd

babble to each other for a few minutes but they'd nod off after that. The trick was making sure they believed it was sleepytime. If they thought their Momma was awake, rattling around the kitchen and fixing toast, they'd throw all of hell and damnation at me until I picked them up and allowed them to toddle free.

I climbed back into bed beside Jasper. Her hair was half in its usual bun, half out, and her plaid shirt had slipped down her shoulder. It was *my* shirt but it was hers. Anything that was mine was hers.

"Did they settle down after their bottles?"

"Mostly," I replied, tucking her ass into my lap. "They'll be all right in there for an hour or two if they don't. They can talk to each other."

Jasper reached for the video monitor on her bedside table. The screen showed the twins were lying on their sides, facing each other. Sawyer still had his thumb in his mouth but that didn't stop him from babbling to Savvi. She had the blanket under her head and yammered back at her brother with a quick kick of her little legs.

"They're the cutest things in the world," she whispered.

"I know." When she continued watching, I took the monitor from her hand and returned it to the table. "They'll still be cute in an hour."

"If you're trying to tell me you won't be grumbly and growly for me in an hour, I'm going to have to disagree with you there, husband. You're grumbly and growly all the time."

"You're right about that, Peach. I am." I kissed that exposed shoulder all the way to the base of her throat. "Always."

―――――

Thank you for reading! I hope you loved Linden and Jasper! If you'd like to read a baby brunch bonus chapter featuring Jasper, Linden, Magnolia, Rob, Ash, Zelda, some Walsh family friends, and (of course) Grandmazilla, sign up at https://geni.us/BATBBC

―――――

*Join Kate Canterbary's Office Memos mailing list (*https://geni.us/officememos*) for occasional news and updates, as well as new release alerts, exclusive extended epilogues and bonus scenes, and cake. There's always cake.*

*Visit Kate's private reader group (*https://www.facebook.com/groups/TheWalshery/*) to chat about books, get early peeks at new books, and hang out with over booklovers!*

*If newsletters aren't your jam, follow Kate on BookBub (*https://geni.us/KCBB*) for preorder and new release alerts.*

ALSO BY KATE CANTERBARY

The Magnolia Chronicles — Magnolia
Boss in the Bedsheets — Ash and Zelda
The Belle and the Beard — Linden and Jasper-Anne

Talbott's Cove

Fresh Catch — Owen and Cole
Hard Pressed — Jackson and Annette
Far Cry — Brooke and JJ
Rough Sketch — Gus and Neera

Benchmarks Series

Professional Development — Drew and Tara
Orientation — Jory and Max

Brothers In Arms

Missing In Action — Wes and Tom
Coastal Elite — Jordan and April

Get exclusive sneak previews of upcoming releases through Kate's newsletter and private reader group, The Canterbary Tales, on Facebook.

ABOUT KATE

USA Today Bestseller Kate Canterbary writes smart, steamy contemporary romances loaded with heat, heart, and happy ever afters. Kate lives on the New England coast with her husband and daughter.

You can find Kate at www.katecanterbary.com

facebook.com/kcanterbary

twitter.com/kcanterbary

instagram.com/katecanterbary

amazon.com/Kate-Canterbary

bookbub.com/authors/kate-canterbary

goodreads.com/Kate_Canterbary

pinterest.com/katecanterbary

tiktok.com/@katecanterbary

ACKNOWLEDGMENTS

The Belle and the Beard is my twenty-first published novel.

I can only speak for my own creative process and the labor of love that is telling the stories of the people in my head, though I'm comfortable saying it doesn't get easier. The stories, the journeys, they couples—they're all different. No two are ever written the same way.

And I'm extremely grateful to the people who put up with me as I discover the new ways I'll create each day. I'm thankful to loved ones and dear friends who allow me to continue figuring this out.